To Margie Jordan
in appreciation for
her love and friendship

Author's Note

Throughout this work of fiction set in 1805, the ancient wilderness path stretching between Nashville, Tennessee and Natchez in the territory of Mississippi is referred to as the Natchez Trace. Prior to the 1820's, when the thoroughfare actually became known as the Natchez Trace, it was used widely by the boatmen from Tennessee and Kentucky on their return trips from New Orleans through Natchez—as well as by post riders, preachers, traders, settlers, and highwaymen—and was known officially as the road from Nashville in the state of Tennessee to the Grindstone Ford of the Bayou Pierre in the Mississippi Territory.

Unofficially, the well-traveled path bore several names. The Choctaw Indians lived in the area holding the lower half of the Trace, while the Chickasaws occupied the upper section. Depending on one's location, the route could be referred to as the Path to the Choctaw Nation or as the Chickasaw Trace. Some tried to label it the Path of Peace and then the Columbian Highway, but such lofty titles disappeared. Because of the dastardly deeds from gangs of highwaymen and cutthroats, the Devil's Backbone became a known title.

Few settlers lived along the 450 miles of the Trace, and travelers often asked to be taken into their homes at nightfall for safety. The first inns, or stands as they were called, probably resulted from settlers wishing to augment their income by offering shelter and food to wayfarers. Except for the postal riders who switched to fresh horses along the way and made the journey from one end to the other in ten days, travelers could expect to travel no more than twenty-five miles each day. Several stands, trading posts, and ferries were run by white men married to Indians.

A leisurely trip on the Natchez Trace Parkway, with stops at points of historical significance, provided much background information and enthusiasm for this historical romance. Two printed sources offering special enlightenment are *The Natchez Trace* by James A. Crutchfield[1] and *The Devil's Backbone* by Jonathan Daniels.[2]

An attempt has been made to present believable fictional characters who could have played out their roles along or near the Natchez Trace in 1805, two years after the acquisition of the vast area called the Louisiana Purchase. Here was a place and time of new growth, excitement, and romance, almost a prelude to the full development of what was then called the West. In this novel, some places are taken from history, but the majority are figments of this author's imagination. The main characters and events are fictional, and even when historical persons and incidents appear, they are presented fictitiously.

Myra Rowe

[1]Nashville, Tennessee: Rutledge Hill Press, Inc., 1985.
[2]Gretna, Louisiana: Pelican Publishing Company, Inc., 1985.

The Highwayman of the Natchez Trace
by Myra Rowe

While the ghosts yet come a'riding, riding the night winds
    with whimpers,
And the rains still come a'falling, etching the old trail of
    mem'ries,
Let us go a'fancying, drifting back to an age of adventure,
When out of the brooding darkness, a highwayman came
    riding, riding the Natchez Trace.

The Trace was a trough of shadow, beneath a canopy of
    trees,
While the steed of the daring highwayman clip-clopped
    away at the miles.

Blue of eye, the rogue vowed he came searching, seeking
    revenge and treasure;
But winsome face and golden eyes came luring, evolving
    into his prize.
A love song throbbed in the young man's heart, banishing
    forever the need for revenge.
A daughter of the Trace rode beside him, eyes dancing a
    promise in the moonlight.

A celestial body hovered before them, sprinkling stardust
    to light their path.
Their laughter floated up like ground fog, as they rode
    westward after their dreams.

Some whispered they were naught but phantoms, chasing
    moonbeams as they galloped along.
Moss-edged and leaning, twin tombstones deny: Here lies
    a legend of the Natchez Trace—the Highwayman
    and His Treasure.

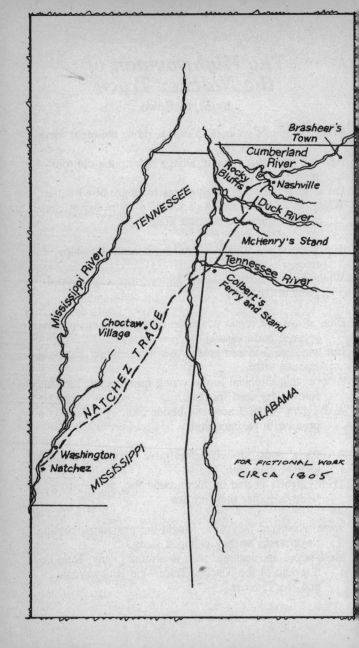

Chapter One

"Somebody's coming!"

At her young brother's high-pitched announcement, Treasure Ryan glanced up from her task inside the blacksmith's shed. Slowing the action of the currycomb on her horse's rump, she looked across at the boy and his friend, then cocked her head to listen for herself on that brisk April day in 1805.

"Danny, why don't you and Walking Bear go back outside and act normal?" Treasure asked, turning to toss the currycomb onto the nearby workbench with a loud clatter. "We don't need to be scared, just cautious. I'll get Papa's rifle."

Whoever was heading toward the small farm near the Duck River in Tennessee was riding at an unhurried pace, Treasure reflected with a frisson of fear. Maybe, she told herself, a hopeful gleam in her eyes, it was the old peddler Hank Marcellus, already starting south on one of his yearly treks up and down the Natchez Trace.

Treasure well knew that since the soldiers had widened the central Trace leading into Fort Nashborough a few years back, not many traveling between the Tennessee settlements on the Cumberland River and Natchez down in the Mississippi Territory took the older, narrower fork. Once an Indian trail, the worn path passing near the Ryan farm snaked northward before dipping down into what some of the newer settlers called Nashville. Having been born and reared in the Ryan cabin beside the Duck River, Treasure sometimes found it hard to think of the town six hours to the east as anything but Fort Nashborough.

Listening more intently and detecting the nearing sounds of only one horse, the young woman shook her head in disappointment. It couldn't be Hank. He would be leading his packhorse with the tarp stretched high over his wares.

Maybe it was somebody from Rocky Bluffs, farther up the Trace—like the evil-eyed Amos Greeson.

At that unsettling thought, Treasure muttered to the horse standing beside her, her husky voice lowering another notch in intimacy, "By jingo, Vagabond! Amos knows Danny and I haven't had time enough to make any money to pay on that debt." She backed the gelding to the outer edge of the shed while venting her frustrations aloud. "Ever since Papa died Amos has been pushing us harder and harder. If he makes another offer to marry me and take Danny in, too, I think I'll haul off and slap his silly face."

Moving quickly, as she was wont to do in most cases, she patted the horse's chestnut nose, then looped the reins over a peg on one of the supporting posts of the low-roofed shed. She confessed silently that she preferred the visitor be Amos rather than a total stranger. Not that the widowed storekeeper was ever welcome, but the last time strangers had come to the Ryan place some three months ago . . .

Her face settling into lines too grim for one only seventeen, Treasure smoothed the leather smithy's apron covering almost all of her threadbare black skirt and one of her father's old shirts. She noticed that the twelve-year-old boys still stood wide-eyed inside the shed. Wishing to dispel the look of fear lurking in her brother's eyes, she urged, in what she hoped was a calm voice, "Get on outside, both of you—unless you think you'd better go on back to your village, Walking Bear."

"I stay," the Chickasaw boy said. "Promised to help

get horse shod, and you promised piece of syrup pie." He darted a look toward the meager pile of graying coals in the crude forge, then to the dilapidated bellows lying close by. "I can work bellows when you say."

"So can I," Danny boasted, turning to fix dark eyes on the Indian youth who had been his playmate since early childhood. "I'm the one who taught you how, remember?"

"Boys!" Treasure scolded the two who stood almost as high as she. Her tone was the same one she used when reprimands were called for during the sessions of teaching them to read and cipher: loving but firm.

After they grinned sheepishly and ambled outside to lean against the broad trunk of a soaring red cedar and resume their whittling, she shucked off her work gloves and poked at stray locks falling from beneath the old coonskin hat she wore to fend off nippy mountain breezes. She didn't stop until she figured that she had all of the honey colored curls tucked out of sight. As an afterthought, she wiped a forefinger across the lip of the coal bucket and smudged her cheeks. Over the past couple of years she had learned that the few men coming to her father's blacksmith shed paid her scant attention if she hid as much of herself as possible and appeared unkempt.

Tall, with a broad shouldered frame appearing almost boyish in its ill-fitting covering, Treasure reached with graceful, practiced ease for the rifle propped near the anvil and checked it. When she was satisfied, she swung her gaze to the small brass objects hanging from a nail up high on the nearest post and shuddered. Devil's claws.

Treasure's heart bucked as she looked at the evil looking instruments fashioned by obviously clever but fiendish hands to slip over a man's fingers and enable him to take off the side of another's face with one swipe. With a deep, shuddering breath she glanced down at the ivory handled knife she had begun wearing in a holster fastened around her slim hips.

Blackie Ryan might not have been the greatest farmer or blacksmith—or gambler—Treasure mused with an objectivity about her father that she had learned to muster only recently, but he had been an expert at making good blades and teaching his two children how to use them. When she heard the sounds of the approaching horse getting louder on the path up the rocky incline to the Ryan cabin, she felt herself grow tense. Had her brown eyes taken on that wary, calculating look Blackie had often said belonged to a Tennessee wildcat? she wondered.

At times like this, Treasure pushed aside the memory of her long dead mother's disapproval of her only daughter acting sometimes more like a boy than a girl. As Blackie would have said, she reassured herself, survival seemed far more important than what people might think. And vengeance. She couldn't forget vengeance.

Rifle steadied against her shoulder, the young woman aimed it at the man coming into view over the rise and called in her unusually low-pitched voice, "Stop right there and state your name and business."

David Fortner Copeland, reining up his handsome gray horse, squinted from beneath his hat brim through the bright sunlight toward the figure inside the shadowy shed. His own rifle rested loosely in the crook of his right arm with his hand close to the trigger, but the barrel pointed to the rock strewn ground.

"My horse threw a shoe since I left Rocky Bluffs, and he needs attention," he said.

Immediately suspicious, Treasure asked, "Why have you come to this place? Have you been here before?"

"No, but somebody told me the farmer living here raised horses and was also a farrier."

"Somebody lied, mister. There's no smithy here, or extra horses either." Who would have told him that? she puzzled. Everybody at Rocky Bluffs knew Blackie was buried almost three months ago on the hill alongside Danny's and her mother. Nearly every one of the twenty-odd citizens had come to the dismal affair, plus the few farmers living closer around. "Get on back to the Trace." Treasure gestured dismissal with the rifle barrel, noticing from the corner of her eye that the boys had paused in their whittling to peep around the cedar at the stranger.

"Isn't that a smith's shed you're standing in?" Fortner asked, his deep voice revealing annoyance. "My horse is already getting stone bruises on that hoof." As if to prove his point, he urged the animal forward up the incline into full view. He stopped again when he saw the rifle once more aimed straight at him.

Treasure's heart swelled at the sight of the limping horse's front leg apparently causing much pain. As did nearly all blacksmiths in the sparsely settled areas in the wilderness, Blackie Ryan had become quite skilled at doctoring ailments of horses, especially of their hooves. His eager daughter had soaked up that knowledge, no more from her having followed him around at every opportunity than from her possessing a deep love for animals. Without a shoe replacement, the handsome gray with the black mane, tail, and legs, if ridden on the rocky Trace, would likely be crippled before nightfall.

"Where are you from?" she asked.

"Upper Cumberland River."

"What's your business way down here?"

"Traveling through on my way to Natchez."

Natchez. Treasure almost sighed with longing upon hearing the name of the place where her mother had grown up and lived before eloping with her father, a place where people obviously lived a far better life than those in the hills of western Tennessee.

She wrenched her thoughts to the moment. The stranger seemed less threatening with each exchange. Not once had he altered the downward angle of his rifle barrel. The sight of a neatly coiled whip tied near his saddle bothered her, though. It was a relief to note that the gray didn't appear to have been abused, but what did he use the weapon for? From her distance of some two hundred feet, she couldn't make out his features due to the shading hat brim, but she could tell he was clean shaven and that he seemed younger than thirty.

"Put up your rifle and come closer," Treasure called, relieved to see him hesitate only a few moments before sliding his weapon into a saddle holster without protest.

No longer interested in what the man looked like, she watched the animal favor the front left leg with each step it made toward her and felt more confident that she had made the right decision. The imprints made in the dust by the three shod feet had no identifying marks.

"Then there *is* a farrier here," Fortner said after dismounting and tilting back his hat. He glanced around the place with a cautious look, taking in the smith's shed tacked onto the front of the disreputable barn and the shiny coated chestnut tied off to one side, exchanging nervous little nickers with his own horse.

"Step out of the way. I'll take a look at that hoof."

His tall, lean frame as straight as a ramrod, Fortner ignored the gun toting figure moving to the other side of his horse and turned toward the two boys beneath the cedar. "Well, now, which one of you shoes horses?" he asked, a grin hitching up the corners of his generous mouth as he approached with a surefooted gait.

"Neither one," Danny replied, relaxing his hold on his knife and the piece of wood he had been carving. He couldn't have said why he no longer felt afraid after he heard the stranger's teasing bass voice and saw the grin, but he didn't. "My sister is about as good as you ever saw, if somebody helps her hold up the horse's feet."

Fortner Copeland jerked his head around at the boy's words to stare across at the bent figure coaxing Brutus into lifting his shoeless front hoof for inspection. "Sister?" he asked in a low, doubting voice. "That's . . . that's a woman? I never heard of a woman shoeing a horse."

Only then did Fortner's gaze take in the bottom of a black skirt hanging below the filthy smithy's apron and brushing the tops of narrow work shoes. He craned his neck, as if to find another hint that the one in the coonskin hat talking in husky tones to his horse was a young woman.

"What's your name, mister?" Treasure called. Palming the reins with the hand holding her gun, she cupped the other for the black nose to nuzzle and looked over at the trio in the deep shade of the cedar. The man was taller than she had first thought, she realized when she saw that the boys, though twelve years old, appeared dwarfed.

"Fortner."

"Fortner what?"

"Most just call me Fortner, ma'am." Looking around as if expecting someone else to appear from within the cabin he had passed, or else from the barn behind the shed, he asked, "What's yours?"

"I don't have anything to hide," she replied testily, watching him saunter toward her in what she deemed a cocky manner. Why had he refused to give her more than one name? "I'm Treasure Lindsay Ryan. That's my brother, Sean Daniel Ryan, and his friend, Walking Bear, the son of Chief Gray Owl."

Treasure decided the stranger must not be from anywhere nearby, for he didn't let on he knew that Gray Owl was a Chickasaw chief to be reckoned with. The closer the man came, the more she got the impression that he was a study in friendly, comfortable browns. Brown boots and tight fitting breeches, brown leather jacket with dark brown hair brushing its collar, and brown hat.

"Pleased to meet you, Miss Ryan." He removed his hat and smiled, first at Treasure, then at the youngsters. "And you, too, boys." His smile and his gaze switched right back to her.

Treasure had no choice but to strike out her first impression. Whoever this Fortner was, he was not a study in comfortable browns, not with those startling eyes of pale blue flashing from within frames of black lashes, and not with that dazzling smile capable of doing the work of a demon to disarm and beguile the unwary.

Like a bell warning of danger, bits of the frightening sermon she'd heard the rabid evangelist Lorenzo Dow preach last summer in the campground upriver jangled stridently in Treasure's mind. Was it true that the devil moved in varied disguises to win people over to ways of wickedness? Had those claws hanging inside during the past several weeks been formed to fit the stranger's fingers? Her glance darted to the fringed tip of the whip coiled on the young man's saddle before returning to his tanned face. Did she imagine it, or did his piercing pale eyes take on a sudden warmth as they traveled across her features? Figuring it was a trick of the strong light from the sun almost directly overhead now, she squelched an unexpected impulse to return his smile and kept a straight face.

"I hope you've got money to pay for shoeing your horse, Mr. Fortner," Treasure told him as she wheeled about and led the animal into the shed. Once inside, she sneaked sideways looks to see if he was showing undue interest in the place. His attention seemed centered on her.

"Yes, ma'am, I have." After they agreed upon the price, he asked in a deep, doubting voice, "Are you really a farrier?"

Sensing that he might be grinning, she retorted over her shoulder, "Looks like I'm the closest to one you'll find in these parts. I have coals heating up because I was about to shoe my own horse. Does yours fight being shod? If he does, then you'll have to hold him still, or I can't get the job done. I count on cooperation."

"Brutus is a gentleman. He won't give you any trouble," he assured her. "Most farriers tell me that he's got as much horse sense as our President Jefferson."

Ignoring the attempt at humor, Treasure propped the rifle near the anvil and called to the gawking boys, "Come on in here and help me, will you?"

No matter what she thought of its owner, Treasure placed priority on helping the horse and went about getting things ready, her mind on matters other than what her hands were doing from habit. Brutus? What kind of name was that for a horse with such a seemingly mild nature? she wondered while pulling on her gloves. Her father once said that he never had heard of Shakespeare until her mother began having Treasure read aloud from the books a longtime friend had sent from Natchez.

Could it be that this Fortner was learned and knew about the wily Brutus, Treasure's thoughts ran on, or had he merely heard the name somewhere? Now that she thought upon it, his way of speaking did sound different from most of those in her part of the Tennessee hills, just as her mother's always had . . . and as everyone said Danny's and hers did.

Soon Walking Bear was pumping the noisy bellows, the wheezing rushes of air turning the coals from gray to red. Danny dragged over the low, wide-topped sawhorse that Treasure used to help her support horses' upended feet during shoeing, then assisted her in propping up Brutus' front left leg after she bent it inward. Her mind on the job at hand, she selected several from the small supply of varied preformed shoes and held them up one at a time to the upended, unshod hoof.

"Do you mark all your shoes this way?" Fortner asked, picking up one from the workbench and running a finger over the deeply indented "R" at the toe. "The 'R' stands for Ryan, I take it."

"Yes," she replied, watching his face covertly while impressions tumbled through her mind and became full-fledged thoughts.

Now that the hat no longer hid his features, Treasure could tell that the man calling himself Fortner was down-right good looking, maybe even handsome by some standards. A straight nose in his unscarred, slim face told her he was no brawler, or at least not one who lost very often. There was an air of quiet strength about him that she admired, like maybe it stayed in reserve till needed.

The few young men Treasure had been around seemed in a hurry to flaunt their prowess in whatever field they thought they had mastered, yet the only sign Fortner gave that he might be a tad proud was in the cocksure way he walked and held his broad shoulders so upright. And hardly any of the young men she knew—no, none at all, she corrected—would have stood still for a woman to nail a shoe on his horse's foot, no matter that she claimed she knew how.

Purposefully, Treasure volunteered more information, her assessing gaze still fixed upon the stranger's features. "The mark on the shoes was my papa's idea. It shows up in the horseprint as long as it stays on the foot, even in the shoes that are used more than once. Maybe you've seen that print somewhere.''

"Don't believe I have."

After Treasure detected no visible sign that he lied, she returned to the job at hand. Once she found a shoe with a fair fit, she buried the curved piece of iron in the hot coals and went back to the horse.

"You're a gentleman, Brutus, just like Mr. Fortner said," Treasure remarked in her warm voice, sending a gloved hand to stroke the nose turning her way. "I never saw a horse balance any better on three legs. I'll try not to be long."

Like the well-trained assistant that he could be when it suited him, Danny handed her the long file and stood nearby while she leaned over and flung a leg over the propped black one, the action lifting up her full skirt to the middle of her calves. Cautiously she backed up until her rear touched the hindside of Brutus' bent leg, then filed and shaped the broken edges of horn on the upside-down hoof. The rhythmic, rasping sounds of the metal chewing against the horn matched up with those coming at intervals from Walking Bear's handling of the bellows.

Treasure removed her gloves after the filing and pressed gingerly with long fingers in search of deep stone bruises on the sensitive tissue of the sole, her husky voice reassuring the handsome horse with easy phrases. Though no spot seemed to pain the animal, she applied a generous coating of ointment that she and Blackie had made the previous fall from ground bluestone and castor oil.

While she worked, Treasure was aware that Fortner stood behind her near his horse's head, holding the reins and observing her every movement with those disturbing blue eyes. True, she had been engrossed in her task, but not once had she caught him looking about as if searching for something. Though tempted, she had not allowed herself to glance up at the devil's claws hanging on the post, and she silently commanded Danny to follow her lead.

Amused at the man's apparently skeptical interest in her performance, Treasure went through the necessary trial and error period of a farrier. Removing the white-hot horseshoe from the forge with long-handled tongs, she rested it across the pointed end of the anvil while hammering it into the individual curve she recalled from fitting it to Brutus' foot. After plunging it into the trough of water to cool, she held it up to the hoof to see how closely she had come to duplicating its shape. After the first reheating and subsequent hammering, she reached her goal.

"You amaze me, Miss Ryan," Fortner said after Treasure had nailed on the shoe with swift, accurate blows from her hammer and brought the hoof forward to rest upon a lower sawhorse. He watched while she used giant clippers to snip off the points of the nails poking through to the front wall near the edges of the hoof. "I've seldom seen a horse shoed any faster or better. You must have had a fine teacher."

"Treasure's really smart, isn't she?" Danny asked, smiling upon hearing praise for his adored sister. "She's about the finest cook, too, isn't she, Walking Bear?"

The Indian boy flashed one of his rare smiles and nodded.

"Thanks, but I couldn't have managed without help from Walking Bear and my brother . . . and the horse." By then she had filed the tips of the snipped nails to acceptable smoothness. Smiling at Danny as she motioned him to take away the sawhorse, Treasure stepped back, let go of the delicately shaped black leg, and straightened up after she saw the hoof settle naturally against the dirt floor. When it took on its proportionate share of the horse's weight without flinching, she nodded with satisfaction. "And yes, I learned from a fine teacher—my papa, Blackie Ryan."

Not looking in Fortner's direction, for she could sense his pale eyes were still studying her, Treasure removed her gloves and gave Brutus' proffered nose a final pat. Only then did she realize that the exertion had no doubt brought a tingling warmth to her face. In fact, she felt unaccountably warm all over. She jerked off the furry hat and tossed it onto the anvil near the propped rifle, forgetting all about her original plan to keep the loaded weapon beside her until the stranger left. She strode to the edge of the shed to stand in the refreshing spring breeze.

Aware of the brilliant cobalt sky outlining the ridges close by, Treasure lifted her face to the welcome rush of coolness and pressed her fingers to her scalp before combing them through the hair now tumbling down her back in a riot of honey colored curls. The clean smells of early spring rode the gentle breezes. She was glad she had remembered to smear soot on her face, for she had no wish to make the stranger think she was trying to flaunt herself as a woman. She had merely become too warm, she assured herself while gazing toward the river and seeing that yesterday's yellowish globs of color on the numerous dogwood trees were beginning to unfold into creamy blossoms.

As he had watched the amazing young woman perform the work of a skilled farrier inside the shed, David Fortner Copeland had allowed his mind unlimited freedom in collecting thoughts about Treasure and how he happened to find himself at the Ryan place that April morning in 1805. It was rare for him to be agitated easily. He had done his best not to admit that from her first unfriendly words she had stirred up something inside him. Maybe it was just that he had never before seen one so young appear so boldly defensive, almost like a wild animal protecting its young.

It was George Henry, the oldest and the meanest of the Thorpe Brothers' gang, who had mentioned in Fortner's presence last fall that, in case an emergency came up, a onetime notorious gambler called Blackie operated a black-smith shed and a horse ranch off the old Trace near the Duck River. Fortner couldn't recall the outlaw mentioning that the man had children, only that Blackie owed him. Getting his horse cared for held priority with Fortner or he would have turned back to his travels immediately upon not finding Blackie about.

As soon as Brutus threw the shoe earlier that morning, Fortner had regretted his decision not to take the main Trace. He had figured that he had time to spare, though, before meeting Bear-John at McHenry's Stand farther down the Trace and had followed the seldom used loop from Nashville since first light, knowing that before mid-afternoon it would lead into the well-traveled, central path of the Natchez Trace.

Now that he had made his last trip to the Copeland farm on the upper Cumberland River and had the money from its sale stashed in his saddlebags, Fortner told himself that he had no interest in anything but what he might find along the Natchez Trace. Events happening over the past two years had convinced the young man that his earlier dreams of tilling his own soil and rearing a family were not to be. He had come to accept that men were not always what they seemed and beautiful young women never were. For some time now he had thought of himself as no more than an adventurer with each day's existence his only goal—unless one counted his gut need for revenge against a certain outlaw known to him as Whitey.

Fortner slapped a lid on such bothersome thoughts and returned his ruminations to the moment. Not that he didn't understand the need for settlers to be cautious about strangers, he reminded himself during the shoeing, but the grimy-faced Treasure that he had mistaken for a young man seemed so cocky and brash that he had been tempted to prove that her rifle and her knife did not necessarily make her equal to a man. After they went inside the shed and he deduced that no other adults were around, he was even more surprised at her uppity actions and tried to figure out if they came from bravery or innocence or plain ignorance. Something about the tall, boyish looking young woman pulled at him in a way he didn't understand. He elected to pursue his customary habit of waiting to see what happened.

Giving the shed a cursory inspection upon first entering,

Fortner had sighted the devil's claws hanging upon the post. He pretended he hadn't seen them because the unfriendly farrier seemed suspicious about every move he made, and he had no wish for her to change her mind about replacing the lost shoe. The dull brass claws with their evil points seemed familiar.

Later, when Treasure and the boys were too involved to pay him any attention, Fortner took a longer look at what he judged to be the weapons of a coward and pursed his lips in thought. Damned if he didn't believe the claws identical to the set that George Henry Thorpe carried and frequently displayed in warning whenever he felt threatened. More than once last fall Fortner had heard the leader of the infamous gang of highwaymen preying on those traveling the Natchez Trace brag that a metalworker up in Kentucky had made them expressly for his fingers.

A double-barreled question rose in Fortner's mind: Did the lethal weapons belong to George Henry, and if so, what were they doing here in a smithy's shed gathering soot and dust? Following closely behind came others: Was there truth in the rumor that one of the Thorpes had been killed recently—and had it been George Henry? Where was Blackie Ryan?

Things had gone well with the shoeing, Fortner reflected when Treasure set Brutus' hoof down and he saw with relief that it no longer pained his saddlehorse. Though he had not yet figured out exactly what prompted her to act so brash and sure of herself, he had discarded the possibility that it was ignorance. More likely, he reasoned, she was a dirty-faced tomboy mimicking her father in an attempt to cover up the fact that she was not likely to attract a suitor—though his partial view of her long limbs while she unself-consciously straddled Brutus' legs had been rewarding.

Fortner's deduction having to do with tomboys fell as quickly as had the red squirrel peeking at him from around a soaring beechwood trunk barely an hour ago. Treasure's quick feminine movements—the careless shucking of her coonskin hat that released the golden curls and then the moving on light feet to face the breeze—cut as cleanly as had his shot at the squirrel. Bang! She removed the holster holding the knife, then the enveloping leather apron. Whoosh! Thud! His careful reasoning lay dead at his feet. The one that he watched had no reason to conceal anything.

"We're all through straightening up now, Treasure," Danny called. He smiled across at Fortner, wondering what had the man looking as if maybe he had just fallen from a mountaintop. He walked toward his sister. "Could we ask Mr. Fortner to noon with us? Walking Bear and I caught more than enough catfish this morning to feed us all."

Now that the smithy's apron hung from a peg, Treasure was refastening her belt and holster over her skirt. She glanced over her shoulder and glared at her young brother, thinking to squelch him.

Danny surprised her by asking, "Couldn't we, please?"

Fortner forced himself to stop staring at the golden-haired young woman and led Brutus outside the shed before trusting himself to speak. "I wouldn't want to be a burden, Daniel, but I thank you for the thought." He was hoping Treasure might relent, but he was disappointed. Reaching into his pocket for coins, he brought out some and examined them there in the sunshine. "I need to pay you for the shoeing, Miss Treasure."

Unaware that her given name had fallen from his mouth, Fortner walked toward her, palm upward, holding the money. "As you probably know, I'm a long way from shelter now that the lost shoe has slowed me down. I won't likely reach McHenry's Stand before dark, so I'd expect to pay somebody for a night's food and lodging for Brutus and me. If you could take us in, I'd be grateful to be allowed to stay in your barn. I don't favor sleeping in the cold beside the Trace. Guess I'm at your mercy... or whatever."

Treasure turned then, the flash of the gold catching her eyes. His hand seemed full of coins, and her mouth all but watered. Danny and she needed money desperately if they were going to pursue their dead mother's dream of getting her children to her family in Natchez to insure a better future for them. What was the harm in opening their place as a stand for the one day and night?

Her thoughts racing, she reckoned that the stranger did appear well-bred and harmless, in spite of the unsettling way he had of glueing pale-eyed gazes all over her. She reminded herself that she still had a soot-streaked face and that the ill-fitting skirt and shirt concealed her feminine form, so there was no chance the man viewed her as a possible conquest. Besides, she probably smelled like a horse after the intimate contact with the sweaty Brutus. The man apparently had not been here before, and he seemed not to have noticed the devil's claws at all, so . . .

"All right, Mr. Fortner," Treasure heard herself saying in a voice huskier than normal. She cleared her throat, for something seemed stuck in it. "We'll take you and your horse in until tomorrow morning."

"I'll lead Brutus into the horse lot and untie Vagabond so they can drink from the trough," Danny said with a big grin at his sister. "Walking Bear can bring the fish from where we stashed them in the river while you set the grease on."

Left alone then with Fortner outside the shed, Treasure searched for a suitable place to look. Suddenly she felt hemmed in by an invisible force and, every bit as confusing, felt helpless to dispel it. She slapped at curls being blown across her face by a pesky breeze and held them back, her eyes chasing across the unusually bright horizon before settling on a nearby redbud tree with pink bumps swelling along its graceful branches. Had she made a mistake in allowing the stranger to stay? Was the price too high for what she had in mind to gain for Danny? Her heart fluttered in a nameless kind of new fear.

Fortner let his gaze follow Treasure's, but it swiveled back to note with wonder the way her eyes, which he had believed plain brown, had become a pale, golden amber in the bright sunshine. Her eyelashes, dark brown and long, curled up in a tangled sweep of silk, as if there were too many to lay in normal fashion. Her up-tilted nose, the only part of her slender face not smeared with soot, appeared as sassy as her full lips . . . and seemed as much a reflection of her personality, he mused with a half grin. In spite of willing himself not to notice the way her uplifted arm brought a well-formed breast to push against the loose shirt, he added the latest charming sight to the earlier ones counted and wondered if he might not be looking at the most naturally beautiful young woman he had ever seen. Dirty face, perfume from a sweaty horse and all.

From the corner of her eye, Treasure glimpsed the glitter of the gold still held loosely in Fortner's palm. Relieved to discover something to say and break the mesmerizing moment of silence, she asked, "How much will you pay?"

Fortner sucked in a breath. Damn! She was no different from that other young woman he once had found so pleasing to the eye, the one who had not kept her promise to wait for him to return and claim her. He recalled how she had informed him almost casually in her tiny voice that a woman had to grab what seemed the best offer at the time. Right then he decided that Treasure was not one whit different and that, in spite of the longing he suspected he had read in those tawny eyes moments earlier, dreams were not what she sought.

No doubt, Fortner mused, a young woman didn't have to be frail and daintily curved to view the world through selfish, greedy eyes. He told himself that his only surprise and disappointment came from having dared believe, for a few unguarded moments, that Treasure Lindsay Ryan might be unlike other young women.

Exhaling the air from his lungs, he said slowly, almost sadly, "All you see, lady. Every last coin."

Grabbing her hand then, Fortner opened it and dumped the coins in her palm, turning them loose as though they were tainted. Shaken from his unwelcome conclusions more than he cared to acknowledge, he spun about on a booted heel and strode to the shed to retrieve his hat.

Once in the shade of the low-roofed shed, Fortner glanced back and saw Treasure walking slowly in the sunshine toward the cabin, her eyes seemingly fixed on the gold gleaming in her outstretched hand. All his eyes could fix upon was the gold of her hair.

Chapter Two

The midday meal of fried catfish and potatoes turned into a time of storytelling. When Fortner mentioned that Daniel Boone had visited his family's farm several years back, before the famous frontiersman moved on westward to Missouri, Danny and Walking Bear had perked up, eager to hear all.

"Was Daniel Boone really brave and was he really adopted by a Shawnee chief?" asked Danny, his dark eyes wide with awe.

"So it would seem," Fortner told both the talkative Danny and his reticent Indian friend. He chuckled then, caught up in memory. "Guess he would have had to be brave to hang around our place for a week, what with us four boys hanging on his every word and getting him to help us with our trapping and shooting."

"Three brothers?" Danny asked. "That must have been some fun! Your papa must have been proud to have four sons." He shot an apologetic glance at Treasure. "Of course girls are nice, too."

Both Treasure and Fortner laughed, and even Walking Bear managed a rare smile. For some reason, Fortner found the deep sound of her laughter especially soothing. Did she do everything so naturally and spontaneously? Despite his being on the lookout for it, he could detect no artifice about her.

Between bites, Fortner noticed that Treasure had tied her long fall of hair at the back of her neck with a strip of cloth. The thought that only a silk riband should nestle amidst such beauty came to mind, startling him. Despite the confining cloth, a few curls sprang loose in a feathery, golden frame around her nicely sculpted features—oval face with strong chin and high cheekbones smoothing like creamy satin into faint hollows, a perfect setting for her gracefully shaped nose and generous mouth. Seeing the way her pretty teeth flashed whitely in her washed face made him think again that Treasure Lindsay Ryan was a rare beauty. And a damned good cook, he added with appreciation for the crusty catfish, crisp potatoes, and fried cornbread.

As soon as Fortner had entered the cabin and seen its deplorable lack of luxury of any kind, he almost forgave Treasure for what he viewed as her feminine weakness for desiring gold to buy material things. He couldn't help but wonder how it was that Blackie Ryan, whom she so obviously adored, had failed to provide even ordinary comforts for his family. A closer look about made him wonder if the place might not have been ransacked recently, for he could see several sets of marks on the battered puncheon floor indicating that furniture had once stood there. Or had previous furnishings been sold to buy necessities? The idea came as an afterthought when he recalled the threadbare states of the Ryan children's clothing.

Responding to the air of eagerness on the faces of the three sitting with him at the table, Fortner dug further back into his twenty-five years, back to memories so old that he could bear bringing them forth there in the Ryan cabin.

"My parents were in a party that Boone led in 1775 over the trace he'd helped build through the Cumberland Mountains," Fortner began, brushing back a lock of hair no longer content to be tamed by water. "They settled on the upper Cumberland River in Tennessee, only it was called Transylvania then, before it became a state." His pale eyes clouding, he went on in a remembering voice, "By the time Daniel came to see us—I was about sixteen, not a lot older than you, Danny—a tree had fallen on my papa and killed him. It was good for us to have someone teaching us how to become better shots, so we could fend for our mama and ourselves.''

The deep, manly voice rising and falling as it related a few rousing anecdotes about Daniel Boone sounded good there in the main room of the cabin, Treasure thought for the second or third time since the meal began and Fortner became so congenial. To her way of thinking, the brown-haired man with the arresting blue eyes was a natural born storyteller . . . as Blackie had been in his better days, before her mother had died. She didn't understand the cause of Fortner's abrupt change of mood earlier when she had asked about payment, but she was glad that he seemed to have put aside whatever bothered him. People who gave in to their moods didn't rate very high with her.

As for herself, Treasure had puzzled over her sense of being helplessly caught up in some kind of spell out there in the sunshine, but had put it aside as a likely case of the ''spring dropsies,'' those unorthodox maladies that some hill folk claimed rode the spring breezes and bedeviled the minds of dreamers. Surely if that was the case it would not return, for she hardly classified herself as a dreamer. Not when she knew the cold, brutal facts of life as she did.

Still listening to Fortner's soothing masculine voice, Treasure followed the fascinating movements of his generous mouth and dancing blue eyes and let her subconscious run on in that way it chose to do more and more lately. Too many serious, unsettling conversations had taken place at the small table that Danny and she had put together after everything was destroyed, she reflected. It was time—no, past time—for laughter and light talk to spill out once more into the cabin, along with the aromas of game and simple food caught and prepared by determined, loving hands.

How strange that a young man passing by on the Trace should be the first to lighten the hearts of the two so burdened, Treasure thought. Well-intentioned neighbors had tried periodically, but failed.

''Did any of your brothers become what you told us you are—an adventurer?'' Danny asked when it seemed Fortner had come to the end of his stories and was polishing off the last crumb of catfish. Treasure must really be feeling good that the man seemed to like her cooking so much, he thought, for she had that happy smile on her face he had missed seeing for such a long spell. The way her eyes crinkled at the corners was always a good sign that she wasn't smiling just to be nice, as she did when old Amos Greeson called every Sunday. "Who runs the farm now?"

Clearing his throat and then taking a swig of water from his tin cup, Fortner replied in a tight voice devoid of that carefree, bass lilt Treasure had so enjoyed hearing, "My mama and brothers are all dead now, and I sold the farm recently." His long fingers left the cup and balled up against his palm.

"I'm sorry," Treasure said warmly, her words followed by similar ones from both of the boys. "It sounds as if you had a wonderful time growing up, though, and I well know that counts for a lot."

His gaze measuring the husky voiced young woman with the honey colored curls edging her pretty face, Fortner slowly unclenched the fist resting on the table and nodded his agreement. Except for the chirrups of robins outside the open door, a silence claimed the simple cabin for a moment.

All at once, a quick smile wreathing his face and dancing in his eyes, Fortner mentioned his destination, Natchez, and the boys perked up again. More tales spun out. This time, Treasure took a more active part in the lively conversation.

"No," Fortner replied when she asked a question during a lull, "I don't recall meeting any Lindsays in Natchez the few times I was there over the past two years, but I've heard about Lindwood, the family plantation." When her face fell, he remembered her stating her complete name earlier and asked, "Does your middle name Lindsay come from that family?"

"Yes," Treasure replied. "My mother was Marie Lindsay, and she meant to call me Lindsay, but Papa insisted on the one he chose." For a second she could almost hear

Blackie's musical voice proclaiming over the years that his daughter was, indeed, a treasure and could never have been called anything else.

"I've gathered your mother has been dead a good while, but where is your papa?" He watched brother and sister exchange uneasy looks. "Is he gone, too?"

"Yes," Treasure answered quietly in her low-pitched voice, meeting Fortner's compassionate gaze. "We buried him nearly three months ago beside our mama on the hill, close to the garden patch. They had two babies born dead, and they're there, too." With her lips held firmly to prevent their trembling, she darted a commanding look at Danny and, in an attempt to stall off further questioning, added, "Papa died sudden-like."

"My sympathy to you both."

Under Fortner's solemn scrutiny from across the small table, she hid her eyes behind her thick lashes and rose to fetch the pie she had made earlier that morning before the breakfast fire in the iron stove burned out.

The golden crusted pastry with its sweet filling of syrup flavored custard brought smiles and words of praise from the three males while they cleaned their tin plates. Treasure giggled and nigh blushed when Fortner, taking Danny's half whispered advice as to how to win her favor, crossed his heart and swore solemnly that he would kiss the knees of a grasshopper if she would give him a second serving.

Taking in a traveler from the Trace wasn't a bad way to earn money, Treasure decided after Fortner and the openly worshiping boys left for a tour about the farm. She washed up after the noonday meal without her usual haste, letting her mind sift through some of her nagging problems. As often as she had thought upon it, Treasure yet doubted there was any way she could convince Amos Greeson to do more than keep the deed to the farm when the time came for Danny and her to start down the Trace to be united with her mother's family . . . and meet the man she would marry.

Once she finished her cleaning chores, Treasure stirred up the fire in the old cookstove and added a stick of wood.

Into a little water in her one big cooking pot, she put the nicely dressed squirrel Fortner had brought her when he came to eat, slapping on the lid to insure its tenderness while simmering. When she had demurred and felt embarrassed that he had paid generously for the meal and yet was offering to supply its main ingredient, he explained that he had killed it only a few hours ago because he had a yen for squirrel stew. As she had nothing planned for the evening meal and he sounded sincere, she welcomed his contribution.

Treasure's thoughts ran on as she fetched some of the last of the potatoes and onions from the root cellar hollowed out beneath the back of the cabin. After lifting her face to the fragrant spring sunshine and sniffing appreciatively, she drew up a bucket of water and washed the vegetables out beside the well, then dropped onto the bench beside the back door and began peeling them with the knife from her holster. It seemed to her that the debt owed Amos was not large enough to cover the true value of the place, she mused there in the bone warming sunshine. Fenced and cross-fenced as it was for raising horses, and with its own spring branch across the back acres, the farm probably would bring a good price if she could find a buyer.

With a tightening of her mouth, she recalled that Amos Greeson had the reputation of squeezing each coin twice before turning it loose, so she expected no favors from him, any more than she expected to find someone interested in buying the place for cash. She sometimes savored the feeling she would gain if she could pay back the sum Blackie had borrowed over the years, plus the interest the storekeeper charged, and prove the name Ryan could stand for honesty and dependability.

Treasure was dicing the vegetables when memories demanded her attention, memories she had squelched as long as she could. She recognized it was not a good time for examining the past, but her mind raced back without permission to the events of that last time she had talked with her father.

* * *

"But why, Papa?" Treasure asked, tears forming at the startling news that Amos Greeson was threatening to take over the farm and the horses before summer unless a good payment was made on the debt owed him. With a sigh she recalled how, ever since her mother's death from an ailing heart five years before, Blackie had seemed to drink heavier and to stay away longer in search of the elusive Big Pot. Black eyes sparkling, he would tell his adoring but doubting daughter that he knew, because of his Irish luck, that the Big Pot must be waiting for him. Always it was "Next time, sweetheart. Next time."

"I'll tell you why Amos is impatient. He has no faith in me, just as your mother never did," was Blackie's drunken excuse, one offered so frequently that both his daughter and son could have mouthed it for him in his faintly Irish accent. Having come over to Boston with a distant cousin when only a thirteen-year-old orphan, he had told his children often how hard he had worked to rid himself of the telling mark of his poor background in Ireland.

"If you'd only leave the jug alone and spend more time smithing, Papa, mayhap we could pay Amos some without having to sell off our horses when they're colts and not worth much. Now that we're down to only two brood mares, time is against us. I can do more work in the shop this year if you'll be here to tell me what to do."

Even at the age of seventeen, Treasure recognized her words as the very ones a man like Blackie abhorred. No matter that he had tried to become a blacksmith, a farmer, and a horse breeder, her father was at heart a gambler. Treasure would have figured it out by herself even without her mother having told her so again and again, she reflected. Now that the years were creeping up on Blackie and his beloved Marie was dead, that weakness seemed determined to join with his passion for whiskey and master the big man. To make matters worse, his daughter knew too well, Blackie Ryan believed in Lady Luck far more than he believed in himself.

She didn't draw out the scene in his bedroom, for it

would have done no good. Besides, Blackie's once hand-some face was taking on that brooding, puffy look that told her he would soon be snoring. Rising from the footstool, she left the room.

The next morning when Walking Bear rode over the ridge and banged on the door, snores still rattled at intervals from Blackie's bedroom.

"Is it Star?" Treasure asked, ushering the solemn-faced Indian boy inside after scolding Tiger for barking at one he was accustomed to seeing. She had remembered that his horse was due to foal in January. The boy's features looked pinched from more than the cold. "Is she ready to foal?"

Blackie had insisted that the boy's young mare be bred its first time to Shamrock, his fine-blooded stallion. Trea-sure realized that, aside from her personal love of the horse, saving both the foal and its dam was of utmost importance. Chief Gray Owl seemed pleased at the possibility of beginning a better bloodline for his tribe's horses. Often she had heard Blackie and others talk about the need for strengthening bonds between the settlers and the Chickasaw. They seemed more content with the recent treaties and the monies received for their land than the tribes of Creek to the east, but instances of violence still cropped up frequently.

Walking Bear nodded, walking to the fireplace and holding out his hands to the fire. "Star needs help. Father sent me to fetch Blackie. Medicine man sits with sick children. Big hunting party still far in mountains."

Troubled at the thoughts of all that can go wrong during foaling, Treasure replied, "I can understand why you need help. Papa isn't feeling well and won't be able to come until later in the day, but Danny and I can return with you right now."

"Father won't like woman coming," Walking Bear told her, even as Danny and she conferred and made ready to leave. "Besides, snow is in the air."

"I understand, but you well know that I've assisted Papa with foalings and that I can tell someone else what to do, even if I'm unable to handle it myself. Snow won't bother me.''

Walking Bear shook his head doubtfully at Danny, but he made no further attempt to change her mind.

Hastily, for she knew that a hard two hours' ride over the mountain ridges rising across the back of the Ryan farm lay ahead, Treasure scribbled ''Walking Bear's Star'' on the flyleaf of a book lying upon the table. She knew her father's habit of stumbling to the kitchen to ply himself with the coffee that she always kept on the back of the stove for him. If left to awaken on his own, she reasoned, Blackie would come nearer to having a clear head and steady hands and prove more helpful with the foaling.

Within a short time she had bundled up and was racing away on Vagabond, behind Danny and Walking Bear on their mounts, relieved to see that the big dog seemed content to obey her and stay behind with his sleeping master.

What Danny and she had found in the smith's shed when they returned the next morning would likely haunt her all her life, Treasure reflected with a shudder while going inside to dump the vegetables in the pot with the squirrel meat. Her joy from having left a healthy male foal nuzzling its dam back in the Chickasaw village had disintegrated instantly.

One side of his face and neck ripped open cruelly, Blackie had lain sprawled grotesquely on the scuffed ground near the anvil, his life's blood spilled around him in a congealed, blackened pool. She recalled how she had at first thought a wild animal had attacked him. A gaping gunshot wound in her father's chest showed that human hands had committed the foul deed. Obviously Blackie had tried to defend himself, for his knife lay clutched in one bloody hand. When her foot brushed against an object on the dirt floor, she looked down at a man's crumpled hat, the likes of which she had never seen before. As if he had tried to protect his master, Tiger lay in a bloody heap not far away.

Somehow Treasure had managed to convince the distraught Danny to get a hold on himself and ride up the Trace to Rocky Bluffs for help. What she did during those awful hours of waiting she couldn't recall, even when she tried, which wasn't often.

After she stirred the vegetables and returned the lid to the pot, Treasure fetched more sticks of wood and tended the fire. Thinking that she was done with reliving that trying period three months earlier, she slammed the door to the firebox and went outside. But the grim happenings returned to her mind with agonizing certainty.

Amos Greeson, the storekeeper at Rocky Bluffs, led the group that returned with Danny that bleak January afternoon. With them were Frank Sutter, the smithy at Rocky Bluffs, and Henry Varley, a farmer living halfway between the Ryan farm and the small settlement up the Trace. Buster Tadlock, the sheriff, would be along later, someone announced.

After the sober-faced men insisted that Treasure and Danny go inside the cabin and wait for them there, they did what had to be done.

Inside the cabin, Treasure tried to answer Danny's questions, but it was impossible when she had so many of her own. She had built a fire at some time during his absence, and now its warmth was the only thing that seemed at all real.

"No, Danny," she said, dropping to her knees beside his huddled figure on the hearth. "I have no idea why anyone would come here and tear up our house and . . ." She couldn't go on.

Looking around at the broken furniture, mutilated books, and smashed objects, Danny said, "It looks as if they might have been searching for something and got mad when they found out we didn't have anything worth stealing." His eyes raced then to the halved log serving as mantel above the fireplace, and he stood up. In a child's tear-filled voice, he said, "They even took my Jew's harp."

Treasure stood then and put her arms around him,

marking how he was nearly as tall as she, even at twelve. "Never you mind, Danny, I'll get you another." Her hand cradled the boy's head of black curls, so like their father's.

Together they walked into the three smaller rooms opening off the main one serving as kitchen and living room, for Treasure had gone no farther than the front room earlier; or if she had, she didn't recall doing so. They saw the drawers of their mother's chest lying broken on the floor, their contents strewn about carelessly. With a little smothered cry, Treasure searched for the tiny satin covered box holding her mother's gold locket, the only piece of jewelry she had brought from Lindwood when she had eloped with the then dashing gambler, Blackie Ryan. It was gone, as were the two lovely woolen shawls Marie had crocheted during the long Tennessee winters after she became an invalid.

Nothing else had been taken, but nothing else had any monetary value, Treasure reasoned with a tightening of something akin to hate around her wounded young heart. Any money belonging to the Ryans, and she doubted there had been any, would have been in Blackie's pockets, handy for the next game of cards or dice. The beds sat stripped to their crude slats, with mattresses and linens tumbled upon the floor. Marie's sewing rocker lay in smithereens, another act of what Treasure deemed pure malice.

Returning then to the front room, Treasure tried to ignore the sawing and hammering coming from the shed. She looked around the room more carefully. Neither Danny nor she let on that they knew a casket was being built for their father's body. Where was Blackie's rifle? she wondered. He had always left it hanging on the deer horns fastened above the mantel for her to use until Danny reached his teens and learned to shoot.

"We found this knife and rifle out in the shed," Sheriff Buster Tadlock told Treasure when the men stomped their boots noisily on the porch right before dark and came inside, hats in hands. "Did they belong to Blackie?"

Treasure and Danny exchanged surprised glances, for

they hadn't realized the sheriff had finally arrived. It was common knowledge that the high-spirited Blackie and the saturnine sheriff had always clashed. Relieved that the knife had been cleaned, they replied almost in the same breath, "Yes."

"I'm a'figurin' that some of Blackie's gamblin' and drinkin' friends came to get their horses shod. Then they had a high heel time out there gamblin' afore gettin' drunk and startin' a ruckus. Somebody shore knew how to fight dirty. The ground's all tore up inside the shed, like maybe there was a bunch here. Amos and I figure from the tracks out front that there might have been as many as four, 'cause there wuz a heap of horse tracks afore the snow started a while ago."

Danny blurted, "Papa never would have taken his gun out to the shed with him if he hadn't been suspecting trouble. Whoever came weren't his friends, Sheriff."

"Well, now," Amos Greeson said, gaining the men's full attention by virtue of being the owner of Rocky Bluff's general store. "They could have been strangers just needing a horse shod. We all know Blackie's reputation for starting up games of chance with most anybody."

Unusually tall and thin, and noticeably humped in the shoulders, Amos sneaked a look at Treasure, his prominent Adam's apple jerking up and down. Not that it helped his looks any, but he raked back loose, gray-streaked locks of hair and held his shoulders straighter.

Just then Henry Varley came in, his eyes narrowed. "The horses are gone, ever' last one of 'em."

Treasure's hand flew to her mouth, but her moan of anguish escaped anyway. She hadn't noticed before that the neighbor wasn't with the other men when they came inside. He was the only one who knew much about the stock on Blackie's place. True, Henry had not seemed overly friendly to Blackie, but his wife and children always put forth an effort to be neighborly, especially since Marie Ryan's death five years before.

"Then some of the tracks out front came from our own horses," Treasure concluded. "We have no idea how many men were here." Tears sprang to her eyes. "And I agree with Danny. These people weren't Papa's friends, else his gun would still be over the fireplace." She watched then as Amos lifted the rifle back to its resting place above the mantel.

"Do either one of you kids recognize this here hat?" Sheriff Tadlock asked, holding out a black felt hat with a fat red feather stuck in its snakeskin band.

Treasure recognized the hat as the one she had seen in the shed and recoiled from touching. She still had no wish to be near it and moved closer to Danny.

In his backwoods drawl, the sheriff went on, "We found it out there. I never seed one with a feather docked like that, did you?"

When both Treasure and Danny shook their heads in denial, the four men exchanged disappointed looks. Everyone knew that nearly all men in the area wore hats and were often as well known by those items as by their features.

"And what about these?" the sheriff added. He drew a pair of ivory dice from his pocket and held them out. "Would you say these belonged to Blackie? Found 'em in the dirt not far from—" His round face screwing up in apology for his near blunder, he went on, "Can you tell if they're your pa's?"

This time Treasure and Danny said, "Yes." As when the knife was offered, neither reached to take the dice.

Frank Sutter, the blacksmith in Rocky Bluffs who had helped Blackie hone his skills at smithing when he first came to the area with his bride, had been prowling through the bedrooms during the conversation, his gray head shaking from time to time, his lips tightening on the stem of his corncob pipe.

"I'm staying here tonight with these kids," Frank announced when he rejoined everybody gathered around the fireplace in the front room. He knelt and stuck a twig from a pile of nearby kindling into the blazing fire, bringing the flaming end up to light the tobacco in his pipe. Once he got the pipe drawing and smoke was drifting around his weathered face, he said with a stern-eyed look, "Looks like somebody kicked in the stove, but I can fix it. They ain't even got a chair left to sit on. I'll help 'em get things straight."

In the end everybody, including the numbed Treasure and Danny, agreed that the best thing was for them to accompany Henry Varley to his farm and stay there with his family until the funeral the following afternoon. To Treasure's everlasting gratitude, the kindly Frank Sutter had spent the night at the farm and watched over the long wooden box stored in the corn crib. He had also repaired the cookstove and the four straight chairs.

Soon the snow became too deep for easy travel, and only a few neighbors braved the drifts at intervals to bring food from their womenfolk and to check on the Ryan children's welfare. Everybody knew that Blackie had often left them to fend for themselves during his absences, so it didn't appear odd that they stayed alone in the cabin.

Amos Greeson came calling the first Sunday after Blackie's burial, an action that eased into custom. Not until the fourth Sunday afternoon did he mention what the three in the cabin already knew—he held the mortgage to the Ryan farm.

Dressed in his best black suit, the widower stood tall and gawky before the fireplace that windy, overcast afternoon, sipping at a cup of coffee that Treasure had made at his suggestion . . . and from the package he had brought along. He had asked Danny to get his horse from the barn as the wintry light was fast fading and he planned on returning, as usual, to his large, comfortable house in Rocky Bluffs before dark.

"Treasure," Amos began, his Adam's apple jumping up above his black cravat, then sliding down. "Sheriff Tadlock has given up trying to find out who came and did the dastardly deed here last month." When she merely looked at him from where she sat stiffly on one of the mended straight chairs, he cleared his throat and went on. "I don't know if you're aware that Blackie turned over the deed to this place in exchange for loans over the past years, but—''

"Yes," Treasure interrupted, meeting his beady eyes without hesitation. "I know all about it. Danny and I intend to pay on the debt as soon as spring comes and we can do some smithing. Henry Varley told me he'll spread the word to others. They'll be bringing over their horses to be shod and any tools needing repairs when the weather breaks.''

"That sounds well and good, but we both know it'll be a spell before you can earn much." He fixed a piercing look upon the lovely face lifted to his and shuffled his feet. A flush washed his sallow face. "I'm thinking it might be best if you marry me, and then you and Danny will have a home.''

Treasure burned with anger and indignation, both at Amos' seemingly offhand proposal and at his announcement that the sheriff had washed his hands of looking for whoever killed Blackie. How she longed to scream her refusal, to tell the man old enough to be her father that she would never consent to such an obscene proposal.

Calling upon instinct to guide her, she replied in her husky way, "Thank you kindly, Amos, but I need more time before I make a final decision about the future.''

Amos narrowed his eyes and pursed his thin lips, as if holding back something unpleasant trying to pop out. Sending his Adam's apple on an up-and-down journey beforehand, he said in a businesslike tone, "We'll speak of this again in the spring. In the meantime, give it some thought. My house has been without a decent woman in it for six years now, and you'd be a welcome sight to my four young'uns. Having an old Indian squaw caring for them ain't exactly like having a white stepmother. You'd fit in right well at my place." Noisily Amos slurped the final drops of his coffee and stalked over to slam the cup on the table.

The next week, during a warm spell, Treasure and Danny went to the blacksmith shed to give it a good cleaning. While down on his knees before the storage shelves, pulling out straw that had served a scampering field mouse as its winter nest, Danny saw something shiny on the ground underneath the lowest shelf.

"Devil's claws," Treasure told her brother in ominous tones when he raked out three brass objects and held them out for her to see. Goosebumps trailing up her spine, she said, "I've heard Papa tell tales about some terrible fights among gamblers where men slipped pointed metal caps on their middle fingers and clawed at each other's faces." She sucked in a painful breath. "Those things are bound to be what some lowdown skunk used on Papa and Tiger. They must have gotten kicked under the shelf during . . . during the scuffle."

She fought down a hot sickness knotting her stomach and rising back in her throat and took the claws from the suddenly white-faced boy and examined them. Going over to the bucket of water they had been using for cleaning, she washed them, trying not to think about how it was Blackie's blood she was removing. "There seems to be some kind of mark inside them, but I can't make out what it is."

Danny, his face still blanched, took one of the shiny objects that looked much like an elongated thimble with a curved, pointed claw at the narrowed end instead of a rounded tip. Holding it up in better light, he examined it and then the others. "I see what looks like a 'T' inside each one."

"I never heard of anyone in these parts using a mark like that. I'll bet they didn't come cheap, what with their being made out of brass and being all polished up like that. Wonder if they belong to the man who left the hat?"

Her full mouth set in a grim line, Treasure took back the claws and strung them on a strip of leather. There was no point in telling Sheriff Tadlock about her find, for he had obviously given up trying to find the owner of the rakish hat. She had no wish to see again the look on the sheriff's face that seemed to say that seeking the murderer of a known boozer and gambler was a waste of his valuable time.

With purposeful steps she walked to one of the shed's supporting posts. "I'll hang them here on the post, Danny, and if anyone comes and claims them or knows who they belong to, we'll find out who killed Papa."

But no stranger had come until Fortner arrived that very morning, Treasure reflected after going inside to check on the fire and the squirrel stew. In a way she didn't bother trying to understand, she was relieved that he had seemed blind to the devil's claws hanging in the shed. She didn't know exactly what an adventurer did to earn his living, but she had decided that whoever this Fortner was, he was not among the strangers who had descended upon the Ryan farm and killed her father and his dog, stolen the horses and ransacked the cabin.

The thought of her killing a man, even to avenge Blackie's death, pressed sorely upon Treasure's young conscience, but she had told herself over and over that when the time came to face the murderer—her need for revenge was so consuming that she never doubted that one day she would meet him—she would find the necessary strength to do what had to be done.

The musing young woman stirred the bubbling stew while adding coarse grains of salt from the small leather bag kept near the cookstove. Then she sniffed at the rising odors to determine the correctness of the seasoning. With a shrug, she pulled the last dried red pepper from the string hanging from the ceiling and crumbled it before sprinkling it into the simmering stew. As she set the hollowed wooden flour tray on the table and prepared to make dumplings, she put aside somber thoughts of grief and revenge and called up more pleasant ones.

Over the past grueling weeks, Treasure had come up with a plan to get Danny—and herself—to Natchez. She recalled how even before their mother's death five years earlier, Danny had shown that he was no ordinarily bright scholar, as she herself was. He was unusually intelligent, and he deserved the chance to study at a real school, even a college. As the doting sister saw it, the boy had the makings of a leader, maybe like Andrew Jackson, the highly respected lawyer and judge from Fort Nashborough for whom she had heard much praise. After all, if the talk was true, Judge Jackson had come from humble beginnings and had also lost his parents when very young.

Last year, when one of the infrequent but comforting letters from Marie's childhood friend, Mrs. Olivia Crabtree, arrived—Aunt Olivia, she corrected, adhering to the unseen woman's request—telling about the recent founding of Washington Academy near Natchez, Treasure had begun taking seriously Marie's oft spoken dreams for her children. Perhaps, now that Blackie was gone, Danny and her getting to Natchez and meeting their mother's family and friends were truly the only ways to insure their future.

A pleasant smile on her face, Treasure poured water from the kettle into the little well she had made in a mound of flour in the tray and stirred lightly. Gently, as Marie had taught her as soon as she was tall enough to reach over the cookstove, Treasure dropped spoonfuls of the sticky dough into the bubbling broth, waiting until each glob floated to the top before continuing. Returning the lid to the cook pot with a clang after adding all the dumplings, Treasure thought about how she was not particularly looking forward to meeting Aunt Olivia's son, Thornton, and viewing him as a future husband, as the woman's letters always hinted at strongly.

Could Marie have been so right about what was needed for Danny's happiness and yet just as wrong about Treasure's needs? she wondered. Vividly she remembered her mother's almost wild-eyed rantings about her dream of seeing her pretty daughter married to her best friend's son. Thornton Crabtree was sure to be genteel and a perfect husband, Marie would say in her light, feminine voice. Her smile always widened when she added the next part for her adoring daughter's ears—he was the heir to Merrivale, the plantation next to Lindwood. The names of both plantations would drift out in the same reverent tones that Marie used when referring to Heaven.

A young woman had one chance at happiness, Marie

often told Treasure during that last year of her life, and it rested in making a good marriage, one to a man who could care for her properly and give her and her children security. Her mother's sad-voiced warnings about how a woman who let her heart rule instead of her head was blazing a sure path to heartbreak sank into the growing girl's heart like well planted seeds.

With a deep sigh, Treasure wondered what could lie ahead for her in the hills of Tennessee except marriage to the reputedly tightfisted Amos Greeson? And how could such a union benefit Danny... or her?

Thinking then upon the way Amos had recently begun eyeing her breasts with looks that she suspected were lustful, Treasure shuddered.

Chapter Three

"You and Danny have a fine place here, Treasure," Fortner said that evening after the three of them had eaten the savory squirrel stew with dumplings. They were sitting out on the porch watching a fiery sunset fade behind the ridges in the distance.

Treasure saw Fortner lean the straight chair back on its hind legs and prop up his feet against the post in the same way that Blackie had favored. He didn't look at all like her black-haired, black-eyed father—didn't sound like him either—but there was something about the way Fortner acted that reminded her of him from time to time. Could it be the same air of cocksureness that he could make up his own rules and come up with all the right answers to life? she mused. Then, with her usual honesty, she asked silently, and was he just as wrong as Blackie had been?

"We thank you," she answered out loud, shivering a bit from the twilight's sudden chill and crossing her arms across her chest in an attempt to warm herself.

"Maybe you should go inside, now that it's getting dark and nippy out here," Fortner said, aware of her movement in the chair down the porch from his own.

"I'll fetch your coat. This is the first evening warm enough to sit outside this long, and I can tell you're liking it," Danny volunteered from where he sat on the single step, leaning back against the same post holding Fortner's propped feet. Before she could reply, he jumped up and hurried inside on coltish legs.

"You must be proud of your little brother. He's a lively one, but he seems headed in the right direction."

"I am proud of Danny. He's a smart boy and deserves to be in a good school somewhere so as to study higher up."

"What about Davidson Academy in Nashville?"

"I've heard there's a new school opening in Mississippi Territory at Washington, down near Natchez."

"That's right," he said with a thoughtful nod. "The Trace goes right beside the site where it's being built. Washington Academy it's called. Maybe someday Danny can go there."

"I hope so."

"What would you do if he left, search for a rich husband?" he teased. He flashed a grin over at her, expecting her to demur and make blushing denials.

"Probably," Treasure snapped, surprised at the instant flood of anger washing over her and putting her on the defensive. "But I'd not have to do any searching, because one has already spoken."

Did he think that a marriage to a fine young gentleman from down near Natchez was unbelievable for a poor hill woman? Treasure huffed to herself. True, the tendered proposal came from Thornton Crabtree's mother, not the young man himself, but she resented Fortner's remark so much that she didn't feel guilty over telling him a white lie. She hugged her arms closer about her ribs and leaned back straighter against her chair. The horizon, where a few stars were beginning to glow, served as a far safer place to look.

"Good for you, Miss Ryan. My best wishes to you both."

Fortner had heard the wounded tones in Treasure's low-pitched voice. He caught his breath when he saw the increased thrust of her shapely breasts as she tightened her hold underneath them and leaned back, her eyes fixed on the darkening landscape. Why did the thought of her marrying someone rich and powerful upset him, even for that brief second? Mayhaps she *was* a dreamer, as he had first thought upon seeing the golden specks in her far gazing eyes, and she had formed a fantasy about some well-to-do man. Had he not already learned that he had no inkling as to the workings of a woman's mind or heart?

Why, he scolded himself, should he care what the cocky young woman did, or if she told the truth, which he strongly doubted? Not only had he paid generously for the services received, but also he had complimented her extravagantly on her talents at shoeing his horse and at preparing delicious food.

Treasure Ryan was nothing to him but a naturally beautiful young woman with the greedy heart of her kind, Fortner reminded himself as he patted the cigar in his shirt pocket. And he did not even hold that against her, he thought with self-proclaimed magnanimity, for it was an infernal curse upon those of her ilk. He would never see her again after he rode for McHenry's Stand in the morning.

"I think I'll go see if there are enough coals left in the cookstove to light a piece of kindling," Fortner said as he rose and went inside. "I feel like smoking a cigar."

When Fortner returned to his chair and fired his cigar with the flaming sliver of pine, he glimpsed her gleaming golden eyes fixed upon him speculatively. With a flash of long forgotten deviltry, he wondered what Treasure would do if he kissed her. His grin at the obvious answer almost caused the cigar to slip from his mouth. What the hell! He had been slapped before.

Treasure watched Fortner's profile in the flare of the

flame being held to the end of his cigar and wondered what had him so amused. Was he laughing at her partially true declaration that some wealthy young man wanted to marry her? Sniffing at the masculine smell of tobacco smoke drifting her way after each of Fortner's draws, she thought again of how most people would call the self-proclaimed adventurer handsome. More honest than she had allowed herself to be that morning upon first seeing him, she counted herself among them. Fortner was, indeed, handsome.

His clean shaven face showed up tanned even in the small flares of light, she reflected, pleased that for the first time she could study him without his knowing it. The one eye that she could see was no more than a slash of silver, even more mysterious than when the pale blue dominated. His straight, manly nose formed a fine profile, matching up as it did with the slightly rounded forehead and the strong chin jutting outward from beneath the full lips clamped around the cigar. She had already noticed that unless he had recently plastered it down with water or hidden it underneath his felt hat, his thick hair had a habit of springing up in glossy brown waves on his forehead and across his ears. The longer back length seemed content to stay within the bounds of the leather thong holding it together at his nape.

Without warning, Treasure felt giddy and guessed the cigar smoke might be causing it. She entertained the crazy wish that Thornton Crabtree of Merrivale might turn out to be half as handsome as the young man sitting on the porch with her in the fading twilight. And wouldn't it be nice if he happened to have blue eyes?

Danny's voice intruded then, followed by the nearing shuffle of his bare feet upon the puncheon floor. "Here's your coat, Treasure. Is it all right if I go on to bed? Walking Bear and I showed Fortner how to climb into the hayloft."

Treasure leaned forward and shrugged into the welcome warmth of her raccoon-lined coat, bothered a bit at the thought of remaining on the porch alone with Fortner. "Sure. Go on to bed. I'll be in shortly."

Danny and Fortner said their good nights. Another silence claimed the two on the porch when the boy went on in and closed the door to his bedroom. Now that all vestiges of pink had disappeared from the westward ridges, darkness was falling like a soft curtain.

Fortner puffed on his cigar lazily. Treasure stared out into the night, attuned as always to all that went on around the only home that she had ever known in her seventeen years. She heard the bullfrogs beginning to "be-deep" from the river down below the rise. A few early insects were humming and circling around the lantern on the table inside. From somewhere far up on a ridge, a fox barked, the eerie sound floating upon the night breeze along with the sweet smells of sun-warmed earth and its plants beginning to swell in celebration of spring.

"Good night, Fortner," Treasure said, standing. He had seemed as caught up in the spell of the spring night as she, she realized when he jerked his head toward her, as if he, too, might have been deep in private musings. "Will your blanket be enough cover out there in the barn?"

"Sure. Likely with the hay to burrow up in, I'll not even need it." Standing and tossing his partially smoked cigar out on the ground, he stretched his long, lean body, then flexed his shoulder muscles until they felt relaxed. He walked, seemingly without purpose, over to where Treasure stood just outside the open front door. His gaze drinking in her loveliness and his deep voice warm with sincerity, he said, "I thank you and Danny for taking in Brutus and me. Good night, Treasure."

As swiftly but as surely as a spring breeze darts around a corner without warning, Fortner's arms encircled the unsuspecting Treasure's slender body. No beginner at stealing kisses, he ducked his head to hers before she could do more than guess his intentions.

The delicious softness of Treasure's mouth—half opened in surprise—filled his being with far more excitement than he had counted on. Fortner felt as though he might be sipping nectar, so sweet and innocent was the taste of her. Adding to the sudden racing of his pulse was the provocative feel of her protesting body curving against the planes of his. Mentally he begged her to stop trying to escape; and she must have heard and obeyed, for all at once her full lips were answering his in the most delightful way. Her arms slid upward by inches until they found resting places, first upon his shoulders and then around the back of his neck. An unexpected warmth spread from where her fingers touched his skin underneath his hair. He knew it was crazy, but he suspected that his heart might have skipped a beat in its wild rhythm. The dance of her silken curls across his arms felt as natural as the way the tall young woman fit into his embrace and yielded her honeyed mouth to his.

Treasure had not expected such a rash move. No man had ever before attempted to kiss her, and she hadn't realized it could happen so fast. When her heart roared in her ears with frenzied beats and her lips felt as if they might be on fire, she struggled for freedom to breathe. Somehow, though, the way Fortner's mouth moved so delightfully against hers and the way his arms held her so tightly against his firmly muscled length began feeling more right than wrong. She gave in to an urge more compelling than the earlier one to escape. Besides, she assured herself, she wasn't having any more trouble breathing than Fortner seemed to be having. A part of her felt freer and more alive than before his arms had imprisoned her, as if it had awaited such a surprising movement to release it.

She gave herself up to the sudden desire to hug Fortner closer and sent her arms up eagerly, up to those broad shoulders, then to his corded neck. Her fingers got lost in his crisp hair; she had not realized that his skin and hair would feel so warm and vibrant . . . so intriguing. His mouth tasted of cigar and spring and pure masculine essence, though Treasure never had considered until that instant that such an essence existed or that it could be so heady. The pure notes of a night warbler out in the red cedar seemed all mixed up with a kind of magic that Fortner—a man she had only met that morning, a confessed adventurer who hadn't even told her his full name, she realized with panic—was working on her.

Magic? Treasure questioned. *She* didn't believe in magic! *She* dealt with reality. Taking advantage of an apparent relaxing of the arms holding her, she broke off the kiss and stepped back from his embrace, once more outwardly in control of herself.

"Good night," Treasure said in a voice even huskier and throatier than normal. She had not believed that her breath wouldn't return as rapidly as it had run away. For lack of air in her lungs, she squashed the plan to lash out at him. It seemed that her heart might be planning to leap from her body at any second. Once when she had stumbled and fallen backward from a rocky ledge, she had felt much as she did right then.

Treasure's hand weakly brushed back a lock of hair falling across her flushed face. Wondering why Fortner stood staring down at her with pale eyes gone silvery and why he offered no apology for having forced himself upon her, Treasure summoned the strength to wheel about and dart inside. With trembling hands she slammed the door and slid the bolt into place. Not until she at last heard his boots make retreating sounds on the porch did she move from where she leaned, spent and shaken, against the door.

All night the troubled young woman tossed and wriggled around on her bed in search of peaceful sleep. Screaming for recognition was the hateful thought that she must have lost her mind to have allowed the stranger to kiss her. Then, her face burning, she would recall what truly happened and add, *and why did I kiss him back?*

Walking Bear appeared early the next morning before Fortner came from the barn. If Danny and his friend noticed that Treasure's greeting was unusually warm, they didn't let on.

"Came to help get Vagabond shod after he got passed by yesterday," the Indian boy explained, walking silently in his moccasins to the corner beside the cookstove. The leather bag that he had brought settled to the wooden floor with a soft thud.

"Thank you," Treasure said, eyeing the bag that she knew contained coarse cornmeal pounded out laboriously by the Chickasaw women with stone tools in deep, cleverly crafted stone urns. "Tell your family I appreciate all the cornmeal they've sent us. You and Danny go wash up for corncakes and syrup. They'll be ready soon." She cast an eye out the opened front door, for the windows had naught but scraped skins for coverings. Trying to show no more than concern for a paying guest, she asked, "Did you see Mr. Fortner about when you came by the barn?"

"He was saddling Brutus," Walking Bear answered over his shoulder while following Danny out back to the well.

The boys had returned to the cabin when Fortner rapped at the open front door, his hair damp and his face reddened from the cold well water. The boys welcomed him and insisted that he take his place at the table. Both Treasure and Fortner seemed relieved that she was too busy turning over the browning cakes to do more than send him a glance over her shoulder and acknowledge his mumbled greeting with a similar one. She could feel his gaze upon her back.

Fortner rose and brought his cup for coffee. The fragrance of his shaving soap seemed set on reminding her of last night's kiss. Treasure refused to glance higher than the muscular arm reaching out to tip the gray enamel pot and pour some of the fragrant brew into his cup. Wordlessly she handed him the lifting pad to keep him from burning his hand, feeling flustered when her fingers grazed his and seemed to catch fire. Her cheeks burned so hotly then that she wondered if he might not be taking a full look at her. She didn't dare glance to see, not even when he handed the pad back to her. This time she made sure there was no touching. What was wrong with her?

Thanks to the slow process of cooking enough corncakes to satisfy the obviously starving boys, Treasure stayed busy between the cookstove and the table. It seemed to her that Fortner had far less appetite than at yesterday's two meals, but she realized that she was too rattled to be sure.

Not very hungry herself, she at last sat and tasted the corncakes, too aware that the others had finished eating by then and had nothing to do but watch her while they talked. Especially the one with blue eyes.

"Halloo!" came a man's voice from outside, joined by the hoarse bay of a coon hound.

Only then did the foursome realize that someone was coming up the rise from the river. Treasure tensed, reaching to poke a loose curl back underneath the black kerchief covering her head and tied at the back of her neck. Fortner saw her eyes take on a wary look and race to the rifle resting above the fireplace, then drop to the powder horn and coonskin hat lying on the mantel.

"That's Mr. Varley and old Rastus," Danny announced and promptly dashed for the door, Walking Bear following at a more sedate pace. "He said he was going to bring some of his horses over to be shod as soon as warmer weather came."

Grateful for the kindly neighbor's timely appearance, Treasure rushed to greet Henry Varley and his two towheaded boys, both in their early teens out on the porch. She saw that Rastus, the coon dog, had slowed beneath the redbud tree and was jumping up on Danny and licking his face. And that Brutus, fully saddled, was tethered beneath the big cedar down in front of the blacksmith shed.

"I shore will take that cup of coffee, young lady," Henry replied amicably when she offered, his eyes full of open interest as they raked over the young man rising from the table near the cookstove. "I saw the gray outside but didn't recognize it as a horse from around here."

After Treasure introduced the two men, she left them to size up each other before she served coffee. She stepped to the door for a moment or two and watched Danny and Walking Bear horsing around outside with the two high-spirited Varley boys and their dog. She needn't have worried about the men finding something to talk about, she mused while pouring them coffee, for they sat at the table and seemed to be hitting it off well—after Henry had found out why Fortner was there and all.

Once the talk dwindled, Fortner drained his coffee cup and stood, knowing that the time to leave was at hand. When the neighbor appeared, he had admitted to himself that saying good-bye would be far less strained before an audience. Both Treasure and Henry followed him outside where the four boys stood talking.

Fortner Copeland was far from new at the kissing game. He had lost no sleep over his startling reaction to kissing the beautiful blonde. He had given it more than a passing thought, he acknowledged while relaxed talk rose up around him in front of the Ryan cabin. After all, he reflected, he had initiated the kiss as a kind of playful test to see what the fiesty Treasure might do. That she had melted against him and stirred up passions he barely recognized as his own had staggered him and left him standing like a lightning-struck fool on the porch after she went inside and slammed the door. Well, that was last night, he consoled himself, and things always appeared different in the cold light of day.

Treasure was speaking with one of the Varley boys, and Fortner sneaked a measuring look at her in the early morning light. He was no longer sure that his rationalizing was true, for she didn't seem any less beautiful than she had last night on the dimly lighted porch, despite the fact that only the back part of her honey colored hair was showing from beneath the ugly black kerchief.

Something about the young hill woman—and he had a gut feeling that it had nothing at all to do with the way she looked—tugged at a hidden part of Fortner Copeland that he didn't care to pull out and examine. Hell! He didn't have time for such thoughts. It was time for Brutus and him to make tracks. Now that he knew the Natchez Trace held what he sought, he needed no diversions . . . especially the feminine kind with golden eyes and thoughts of marriage in mind.

"Thanks again for your kindness, Treasure and Danny," Fortner said when all walked with him to his horse and wished him Godspeed. Maybe if the Varleys hadn't been there he would have done more than nod politely. Not having to meet Treasure's tawny gaze for more than a brief instant suited his sudden need to get away. Somehow he felt itchy.

Holding up a hand to shield her eyes from the sun rising over the ridges, Treasure, along with the others standing outside the Ryan cabin, watched Fortner mount and ride away on the high stepping gray with black mane, tail, and legs. If the others spoke, she did not hear; her ears were too filled with the dwindling squeaks of saddle leather and the patter of horseshoes striking soundly on the rocky path. The inverted bowl of blue sky seemed to deny that a world existed beyond the circle of her vision, and she had the wild notion that the solitary horseman might see there was nothing to pursue outside the small sphere and return. She chided herself for the ridiculous thought and blinked hard, dispelling the inner vision of him galloping back into her world.

How like an adventurer, Treasure thought when he turned just before dipping from view down the rise and waved his hat jauntily, not to know that even though he moved on as if nothing had changed, his brief presence had left those behind different somehow. She knew with certainty that she would never forget the man calling himself Fortner.

To Treasure, so newly awakened to the mysteries of her body, the soul-shattering kiss from the handsome man with the pale blue eyes seemed as important a part of her maturing into a young woman as had the appearance of her menses and the growth of her breasts. She glanced at the buds on the redbud limbs nearby, surprised at how much they had grown overnight. All at once, she felt a mysterious yet sad kinship with the pink swells. Like them, she realized with a sinking feeling, she could never again be the same as she had been yesterday.

Chapter Four

On the Sunday following Fortner's departure, Hank Marcellus rode up to the Ryan farm. Greeted happily by Treasure and Danny, the stout peddler dismounted with groans about his aching joints. He smiled when the boy insisted on taking the high stepping Duke and the mild mannered Daisy, the pack horse hauling his wares, to the barn.

"Such bad news is hard to bear," Hank said after Treasure and Danny finished telling him about Blackie's death. In his soft, whispery voice, its tone not much lower than Treasure's, he went on, "I don't have to tell you two that I've known you since before your ma died. You've become almost like family." Reaching into a back pocket, he pulled forth a big red handkerchief and blew his nose, his protruding belly shaking a little with each honk.

As always, the peddler traveling up and down the Natchez Trace each year had brought special little gifts to the young Ryans. As they sat on the porch visiting, he fished in his pockets and brought out this year's treats.

Danny asked right off if he could trade the new pocketknife for a Jew's harp. When the old man learned that the other one he had given the boy several years back had been taken that dreadful day in January, he insisted that he could spare one without Danny swapping the pocketknife—if the boy would promise to play a tune for him. Smiling because someone was showing kindness to Danny, Treasure hugged the man's big but pudgy shoulders in double gratitude after she discovered her gifts were a little round mirror and some lengths of riband in several colors.

His pocked, discolored face turning a deeper shade of purplish red, Hank sniffed and sent a broad but uncalloused hand to tug at the neckline of the reddish wig he always wore. As usual, Treasure noted with amusement, the adjustment did little to make the bushy wig seem a natural part of his head. She recalled that, when Hank first came calling on the Ryans, Danny had been so young that he had asked why the peddler's hair looked so funny. Hank had given one of his rare cackling laughs and teased, "Danny boy, I'd just as soon tell you as spit on an anthill. A wig don't catch no Indian's eye. And besides, bald looks even uglier."

When Amos Greeson rode up later that afternoon, he found the trio out in the blacksmith shed and joined them there. Having brought along a ham from his overstocked smokehouse behind his store, the one with the heaviest coating of mold and thus the least likely to sell before hot weather made it spoil, he planned to stay and eat the evening meal with the Ryans.

Visions of the lovely young blonde in his bed were hampering Amos' sex life with the plump Indian squaw who had run his house ever since his wife had died six years earlier. He would have been mortified had he known that the Indian woman talked freely about her life in the Greeson home. Any of the twenty-odd adults in Rocky Bluffs who listened to gossip knew as much about Amos' unspectacular sex life as he did.

No one dared tell Amos such things, though, or anything else he did not want to hear. The townsfolk remembered how, when Amos first came to Rocky Bluffs to establish the only store, a carpenter had questioned payment for his labor while building the store and had witnessed an awesome display of unrestrained ill temper. Not only had Amos stomped and waved his long arms about while upbraiding the man scathingly for suggesting he had underpaid him, the carpenter had reported, but also Amos had refused to extend credit to him or lend him money, no matter what the circumstances. Others whispered about that and about still more instances of the well-to-do storekeeper's volatile temper. They tread softly in his presence.

On that April afternoon, Amos had in mind pushing the sultry-voiced Treasure into accepting his proposal by showing her that he was no old man incapable of fulfilling the role of husband. Just the thought of shucking off her ill-fitting clothing and seeing what he suspected lay hidden underneath swelled more than his heart. What penniless young woman could resist a wealthy man who plainly found her kissable and perfect for his name . . . and his bed? Amos had come loaded with more than moldy ham.

The storekeeper was mad as hell when he saw the old peddler, for he knew that Hank usually stayed overnight at the Ryan farm before heading on down the Trace. Every once in a while over the years, Hank had stopped at Amos' general store in Rocky Bluffs to restock small items he had already sold on his trek down from his winter quarters near Nashville, so the two men knew each other . . . about as well as either cared to know the other.

"Amos, I appreciate your bringing the ham," Treasure said after he greeted everyone and then made the grand gesture of laying the package on the anvil and telling her what he had in mind. She saw no reason to explain that they had wandered out to the smithy shed and had become involved in serious conversation. "Your plan to stay and eat is fine. Hank has already agreed to eat supper with us and sleep in the barn."

Inwardly Treasure was fuming at the way Amos seemed to be stepping up his courtship when she had told him that she would let him know when she had an answer to his proposal. Now that she had tried out her idea on Hank about Danny and her riding along with him on his way to Natchez, she felt that she might as well make final plans before the day ended. Hank hadn't been exactly enthusiastic about allowing them to accompany him, but neither had he flatly opposed the idea. When she had pointed out that she could do the cooking and that Danny could take care of his horses, the old man had warmed to the idea considerably and had done everything but say the final yes.

If Amos hadn't arrived when he had, she concluded after taking the ham to the cabin and asking Danny to split some stove wood, they likely would have worked out all the details by now. Bringing her hands to rest upon the ever present holster around her slender hips, Treasure let out a sigh. The loveliness of the warm April afternoon seemed diminished, as if a cloud had suddenly marred the faultless sky.

Hacked that Danny hadn't offered to care for his horse before going to help Treasure get a fire started, Amos left Hank inside the shed and led his mount around to the lot and took off the saddle. Moving in that quiet, long-legged way of his, he rounded the corner of the barn just as Hank lifted down something from the far post in the shed and stuck it in his pocket.

"What are you taking?" Amos demanded. After all, everything on the Ryan farm belonged to him. He had a deed and a signed note from Blackie that said so. A faint red haze colored his vision.

Hank jerked his head in Amos' direction and frowned. He had thought to deny having taken anything, but the beady-eyed storekeeper was almost upon him by then, and he looked threatening. "What is it to you?"

"You might not know it, but I hold title to everything on this place." He tried to square his shoulders so as to tower over the old man who stood a few inches short of six feet.

Deciding to make light of the matter, Hank laughed in his raspy way and said, "Yeah, I believe Treasure said something about that being the case."

"Show me what you took."

Hank brought out the devil's claws then, dangling them by the looped leather thong. "I was thinking they might bring a goodly sum down in Natchez."

"Then you admit you were stealing them?"

"No, I was going to talk with Treasure and offer to take them off her hands." Hank looked down at the brass objects and asked in a wondering voice, "Don't reckon you know how they came to be hanging here, do you?"

"As a matter of fact, I do." A note of importance crept into Amos' voice. "Treasure and the boy found them. They were cleaning out here after Blackie was killed by a gunshot and a going-over by some kind of weapon—but I guess they've told you all about that."

The old man nodded, frowning and staring at the claws thoughtfully. One hand fidgeted with his weathered chin. "Go on. What did the sheriff say?"

"You seem mighty interested in those claws."

"Maybe I'm just curious," Hank replied.

"By the time the claws were found, the sheriff had already given up trying to find who was here that day Blackie was killed. Treasure decided to hang them in the shed. Somebody might come back to get 'em or maybe tell her who they belonged to so she could find out who killed her pa. I call every Sunday, so they told me about what they'd found. Leave them alone, or I'll be forced to report your interest to Sheriff Tadlock." His eyes boldly assessing the rounded figure before him, Amos said in a sneering tone, "Don't reckon you were the scoundrel who tangled with Blackie and won."

Apparently not caring that Amos had ridiculed his status as a red-blooded man, Hank turned enough to slip the claws back into his pocket unseen before straightening his wig. "I'm not a violent man. I doubt anyone would think that . . . even you."

Danny called to the men from the porch then. They walked toward the cabin, apparently putting aside for the moment their near quarrel. Amos was too intent upon scheming as to how he might have some time alone with Treasure to give another thought to the devil's claws.

"Since there's a moon already up, we could walk down by the river," Amos said to Treasure when they left the cabin after supper.

Treasure slid a disapproving look at the tall figure ambling alongside and wished again that Hank, standing in the doorway behind them, hadn't been so obliging about her accepting Amos' surprising invitation to take a stroll with him. Danny was already yawning and announcing that he was going to bed, for by the time she had fried the ham and cooked up the very last of their potatoes the hour had grown late. The boy had almost nodded over his food, she recalled.

"I'm not sure there's enough light," Treasure replied. "There are some dangerous ledges down there."

Treasure had decided that she might as well take advantage of being alone with him to tell Amos that tomorrow Danny and she were leaving to travel down the Trace with the peddler. When she had whispered again about her plans to Hank before supper, he had nodded agreement without hesitation. What better place to tell Amos her plans than down by the river? The nights were still too cold for snakes to be crawling about, and she knew every inch of the bank by heart, moonlight or not.

"Have you been giving my proposal much thought?" Amos asked after they had walked down the rise and could hear the water rushing along its rocky bed. He could see her hair gleaming in the moonlight and could barely keep his hands from reaching out and touching it. All afternoon the haze of red that often plagued him when he was agitated had kept marring his vision at intervals. No matter how Amos viewed Treasure, though, she appeared beautiful and desirable. His heart was thudding; his groin was heating up painfully.

"Yes, Amos, I've given your proposal thought. I've needed time to think things over."

Gruffly he said, "You've had plenty of time."

They had reached the place in the path where some outcroppings began angling upward sharply, almost like broad, man-made stairs. When Treasure would have sidestepped them and followed the worn path directly down to the water, Amos grabbed her by the arm and led her upward.

"Where are we going?" Treasure asked, not liking that he had jerked her arm so rudely or that branches of bushes and low-limbed trees were snatching at her hair and clothing. She knew that each step upward carried them farther into what seemed a darkening tunnel of overlapping branches. Back before Danny was born, she and her parents had camped atop the outcroppings when the Duck River, in a onetime display of muddy force, had flooded their cabin and barn. She had disliked the high perch ever since. "I've never seen you act like this, Amos. This path won't take us to the river."

"I have something to show you." Could that be admiration for his daring that was making her voice higher pitched? Amos wondered.

Amos was ducking his head and missing most of the punishing limbs, but they slapped back at the lagging Treasure as soon as they left his tall body. No matter that she tried freeing her arm, he kept his painful hold upon it. The fleeting thought that she had received no such high-handed treatment from Fortner, a total stranger, fueled her temper even higher. Surely a man who had known her all her life owed her as much, if not more, consideration and courtesy than the handsome adventurer had shown.

Should she yell for Hank and hope he might hear her back at the cabin? Treasure wondered. Could it be that Amos was overly enthusiastic about some imagined surprise he had in mind and forgetting to act courteous? She decided to try reasoning with him.

"Amos, you're likely mixed up due to the darkness. All we'll see from up here is a partial view of the river straight below. I'm ready to go back."

"But I'm not." Amos was short of breath. The red cloud was returning, whirling slowly in circles behind his eyes. "Do you think I'm too old to reach the top?"

"No, I just want to go back."

"Not yet. You owe me the chance to show you whatever I choose." When he heard her gasp in what sounded like anger, he turned his head and peered down at her. "You're not mad just because you're not making up all the rules, are you?"

Treasure had never before heard Amos speak in such a sarcastic way, and she puzzled over his aberrant behavior. Had she not thanked him properly for all the food he had brought Danny and her since Blackie's death? And she had cooked ham for him just an hour or so ago. What did he mean about her making up all the rules? She had chosen to tell him in private that she wasn't going to marry him because she didn't want him to think her uncaring or crude. The last thing she wanted was to hurt the man's feelings or make him angry at her. After all, she well knew that by law he could have turned Danny and her out in the cold long before now.

"Look, Amos," Treasure began, her body slamming into his when he stopped abruptly. "I've seen the view from up here all I care to see it." She couldn't back very far away from him in the poor light, for they had reached the flat top of the pile of boulders. Some forty feet below them lay the Duck River, shallow with a rock-lined bed. "I'm sorry if you think I appear ungrateful, but you see—"

Amos looked down at her uplifted face and heard messages in her trembling voice that weren't there. His body diffusing with unreasoning desire and somehow blending with the whirling red cloud behind his eyes, he grabbed Treasure close and planted his mouth on hers. That she struggled only fed the fire building within both his mind and body.

Treasure gagged from the cruel assault on her mouth. No thrilling sweetness, as with Fortner's, accompanied this kiss, and she struck at the tall man savagely.

"Amos," she demanded when she at last freed her mouth, "stop this! Danny and I are leaving tomorrow with Hank to go to my mother's people in Natchez—"

Treasure never finished her story, for Amos growled obscenities low in his throat while fastening his hands around her neck and forcing her frightened face upward.

"Tell me you're making that up." His long fingers tightened at the back of her neck, and his thumbs pressed upon her windpipe. His voice rose to a shrill, piercing tone. "You belong to me. Everything here belongs to me!"

Shocked that the usually mild mannered Amos was acting so demented, Treasure tried to scream for Hank. No sound louder than the moan of a dove could edge past the small space allowed by his punishing thumbs at the base of her throat. Amos seemed oblivious to her pummeling fists. She stared at his face, whimpering at the crazed look of his eyes in the partial darkness and trying not to listen to the loud, impassioned talk about what he intended to do to her body after he ripped away her clothing. She realized that if his fingers continued to press so hard, he was going to choke her.

Already the terrified young woman was suffering waves of blackness, but her tormentor seemed unaware of her gasps and her frantic attempts to fight him off. He was too tall for her hands to reach his face or she would have already scratched out his eyes, Treasure told herself when Amos seemed not to care that she slashed his hands and arms with her fingernails. His height allowed him an advantage, too, when it came to her kicking him, and she was able to land only a few ineffectual blows on his booted shins.

Treasure realized that she could no longer hope Amos might come to his senses before it was too late. Fearful that she might have already allowed too much strength to be sapped, she dropped her right hand and jerked her knife from the holster. Her thoughts only slightly coherent, she slashed repeatedly at those choking arms and hands, rewarded somewhere deep inside at the sight of blood, yet punished even further by an increasing of the pressure on her windpipe. The eerie sounds that Amos was making sounded less than human. Reaching as far as she could in hopes of striking his chest with her knife, she blacked out completely.

"My God, Hank!" Treasure murmured, unable to do more than get out a rasping whisper. The pain in her throat was almost unbearable. "How did you know where to find me? How long have I been out?" She knew that she lay upon cold, hard rock. Her throat hurt as if it had been trampled by a team of runaway horses. In fact, she felt that her entire body might have been in their path, now that she was trying to bestir herself. "What happened?"

Treasure desperately wanted to hear an account from the kindly old man kneeling beside her. The events that her own mind was showing her were too ludicrous to be real. The only thing she knew for certain was that she was still clothed and that Amos apparently had not carried out his frightful threats.

From the corner of her eye she glimpsed the still body lying close by and shivered. It was too dark to tell if Amos was breathing. She sat up, almost screaming until the thought of Danny asleep back in the cabin brought her to a partial sanity. She had no wish to alarm him. "What happened, Hank?"

"I gather you had to kill Amos to keep him from having his way with you," Hank replied, his own voice almost as ragged and unrecognizable as Treasure's.

"No! Oh, tell me he's still breathing," she beseeched, lunging toward the inert form in the shadows. The old man's restraining arms prevented her from reaching Amos' body. "I wanted to make Amos stop choking me, but I didn't truly want to kill him." Tears streamed down her face. "He seemed to go mad, right before my eyes. He kept saying I belonged to him and . . . I never saw anybody act so wild."

His breath coming out in fits and starts, Hank pulled the distraught young woman to her feet and put an arm around her heaving shoulders. "Come, we'd best go back to the cabin. Danny might have heard the commotion and be upset."

Despite Treasure's renewed efforts to go to the sprawled form in the shadows, Hank led her across the big flat area and on down the rocky steps that Amos had dragged her up earlier. They paused once for her to empty her roiling stomach, then again for her to finish the foul job.

It seemed to Treasure that a lifetime had gone by since she had agreed to take a walk with Amos to tell him she wasn't going to marry him and was going to relinquish all claims on the farm before leaving with Hank tomorrow. How could things that at last seemed to be settling into a promising pattern have turned into disaster so quickly? she agonized over and over, as if by repeating the question she might come up with an answer.

When they at last reached the cabin, for they had to stop often to allow Treasure's knees to firm up enough to walk farther, she whispered her thanks to Hank and staggered into her bedroom. Not even bothering to tend her bruised neck or remove her clothing, she fell upon her bed and promptly passed into a welcome blackness.

Chapter Five

Still groggy, and sore in every muscle, Treasure crawled from her bed when Hank called to her from the doorway. Pain from her swollen neck and throat made swallowing a tedious chore and brought involuntary tears. She noticed the old man's face was grim in the light from the lantern he held.

"Is it morning already?" she asked, her voice more of a muffled croak than a human sound. Trying to clear her throat, she raked back her tousled hair with bruised fingers.

"Not quite, but we need to get moving."

"Why so early?" Memories of last night's horrors cleared Treasure's mind of all vestiges of sleep. Noting that she had slept in her clothing, she hurried to join him in the front room. She glanced at the closed door to Danny's room before going on. She was relieved that before the boy went to bed last night she had whispered the good news about leaving with Hank. Phrases picked up from Blackie since her mother's death five years ago flavored her speech. "My God, Hank, what are we going to do about Amos' body!"

"Not to worry. I've taken care of that. I saddled his horse and scared him into running up the Trace toward Rocky Bluffs." When Treasure pressed for more details, Hank replied, "Stop thinking about last night and start thinking of yours and Danny's future. We need to wake him and get a move on. He knows you're coming with me, doesn't he?''

"Yes." Her thoughts ran ahead. "What will Sheriff Tadlock think when he finds Amos dead here on the place and us gone? I can't go until I tell what happened and why—''

"What good will it do for you to stay and maybe stand trial for murder?'' he interrupted harshly. At her tortured expression, he added, "I thought your main concern was to get Danny to your mama's family in Natchez so he could be educated. Is staying here and talking with the sheriff going to do that? What if they lock you up? Who's going to care for Danny then?''

"But you know why I . . . did what I did, Hank. You could tell the sheriff how Amos was trying to—''

"Who's going to believe an old peddler? Anyway, I can't be hanging around these parts to be talking to the law. I have to get started on my route or I'll not sell enough to stay alive next winter. The sensible thing is for you and Danny to leave with me so early that we'll be far down the Trace at McHenry's Stand by dark. Maybe folks will think we left yesterday before Amos got here. You can tack a note on the door telling where you've gone.''

"It's not right. I have to live with myself.''

"It's the only thing you can do if you want to make sure you live at all—or at least outside a jail.''

After listening to some more comments of like nature, Treasure awakened Danny and began packing the few changes of clothing they had.

"You never said we'd be leaving in the dark," the sleepy boy complained as he tugged on his clothing.

"We're too lucky to be going along to gripe about the hour." Treasure paused long enough to ruffle his hair and give him a quick hug. She was glad that he seemed not to notice her hoarseness. "Get a move on and go help Hank outside.''

While Danny and Hank saddled the horses, Treasure made ready to leave, pondering her situation as she worked.

In many ways, what Hank had said about the need for

her to get away made sense to Treasure's befogged brain, but her conscience nagged her. Wasn't leaving a sign of guilt? If she stayed behind and told her side of the struggle down by the river, wouldn't Sheriff Tadlock believe she attacked Amos with her knife in self-defense? After explaining what happened, she could leave without a shadow of suspicion hanging over her.

On the other hand, the sheriff might allow his old feuds with Blackie to color his judgment. Then too, as Hank pointed out, he would be long gone down the Trace by then. How could Danny and she fend for themselves along the reputedly treacherous four hundred miles? She had never traveled far from home.

Her hand and eyes dropped to the empty holster at her hip. She swallowed hard, almost grunting from the pain of the simple movement. Her knife was still . . .

"Hank," Treasure whispered when Danny and he returned and the boy went into his room. "What about my knife?" She should not have given Blackie's knife to Frank Sutter in payment for his help when Blackie was killed, she thought.

Grimacing, the old man whispered back, "Forget about it. I'll fetch one out of my supplies if you must have one."

She nodded vehemently. "I want a knife."

The one Hank slipped to Treasure after a trip outside to his packhorse was about the size of the one Blackie had made for her, but its handle was not pearl, and it didn't fit her hand right. Even so, she felt better prepared now that she had a weapon in addition to the rifle already in the saddle holster on her gelding.

"That's right, Danny," Treasure said when all was in readiness for their departure. "You sign right below my name so everyone will know you're agreeing with me."

Danny read the note aloud in a sleepy voice, " 'Danny and I have gone to Lindwood, our mother's family home near Natchez. The Ryan property belongs to Amos Greeson.' "

Taking the quill Hank had supplied, the boy signed his

name below his sister's. After watching her tack the note onto the front door, he shrugged and mounted his horse.

"I would have liked to tell Walking Bear good-bye, but I'm sorta glad we're leaving while it's not yet daylight," Danny remarked as they rode away. "I might get sad thinking how this is the last time I'll be here."

"We can't be looking back anymore, Danny," Treasure told him. "Going to Lindwood is what we hoped for, remember?"

To hide the bruises, Treasure had tied one of Blackie's neckerchiefs around her neck. One hand fidgeted now in the predawn light with the black cloth while she glanced around furtively. There was no sign that Amos' horse had returned, and she was grateful. How could she have explained its presence to Danny? She had no wish to let the boy know what had happened. They were almost at the place in the path where the rocky ledges angled up to where she had struggled with Amos.

Sensing that Danny's need for consolation was almost as great as her own, Treasure reassured him. "I'm glad we're leaving before it's light, too." Images of what Amos' body must look like by now flitted to mind and brought a wave of nausea. She willed it away, swallowing painfully. "I believe it's time for us to get started toward Natchez."

"You didn't have much of a choice, the way I see it. Not if you aim to get that little boy where he belongs," Hank remarked before riding on ahead and taking the lead while they forded the Duck River and turned southwest on the Trace. A pale golden light was beginning to outline the eastern ridges.

"I'm not a little boy anymore, Hank," Danny said when he rode up beside the old man. "I'll be thirteen in October, old enough then for Treasure to teach me to use the rifle."

As the trio rode down the Natchez Trace, never more than sixteen feet across and sometimes half that distance, Treasure agonized over the awful encounter with Amos and barely noticed the thick forest on either side of them with its budding hardwoods and occasional pines. She was blind and deaf to the scurrying of birds and furry animals seeking breakfast. Not even the beauty of blooming red-buds or huge clumps of dogwood trees covered with large white blossoms made an impression.

Danny seemed fascinated by every new view, but soon found Hank to be far more talkative than his sister. Before noon, he had given up trying to converse with her and rode beside the old peddler, leaving the morose young woman to trail behind Hank's packhorse, Daisy.

"Do you generally travel so far without stopping to call on people?" Danny asked around midafternoon, noting how deftly his gelding Buck avoided a stump in the edge of the cleared path that had gradually narrowed. There was plenty of room for Buck to travel beside the peddler's Duke, but even if Treasure had cared to ride alongside, she would not have found space enough for Vagabond to move freely along that section. "I've seen several trails leading off, like maybe to a farm."

"Sometimes I call at every farm or Indian village, and sometimes I don't. It seemed a good idea to put as much distance as possible between your homeplace and us before dark on this first day," the old man replied in his soft, whispery voice. His free hand tugged at the back of his wig after he turned to check on the solemn-faced young woman following behind Daisy.

"Why do you suppose Treasure is so quiet and sad? When we stop to rest or eat, she keeps looking back."

"I expect she's got a lot on her mind, not knowing what lies ahead. Women like to get things all settled in neat little pockets in their minds, and I expect that's what she's doing." Hank turned again and swept his gaze over the drably dressed figure. He noticed that since the sun had warmed the spring air considerably even since midday, she had exchanged the coonskin hat for a black kerchief. "She'll feel better tomorrow."

"How did you learn so much about women?" Danny asked, his tone both curious and teasing. Having spent most of his life in the company of his overly protective sister, he was enjoying having private talks with a man.

Hank pursed his mouth before answering, "I used to know one pretty good."

"Did you used to be married?"

"Yep, but it was a long time ago." He flicked a hard-eyed look at the boy. "And I never talk about it."

It was almost dark when they reached McHenry's Stand. Set back off the Trace a few hundred feet, the large, two-story building serving as home to its owner and as inn to travelers was flanked by tall cedars, oaks, and beechwoods. Behind, not far from a creek, sat a low-roofed shed and stable near a tall barn with a hayloft. Built of rough oak boards, gray from several years of weathering, the buildings blended with the twilight shadows made deeper by distant ridges.

Sniffing at the comforting smell of wood smoke drifting from one of the stone chimneys rearing up at each end of the house, Treasure allowed herself to admit how weary and sore she was and how good it was to see proof that someone truly lived along the wilderness path they had traveled all day. Barking dogs seemed a reassuring touch, too, especially when they seemed more curious than threatening.

Not that she hadn't needed the private time to get her thoughts together, Treasure mused as she followed Hank and Danny to the hitching rail underneath the trees. She still abhorred the idea that she had killed a man and wondered if she could ever stop thinking about it. But when she would swallow and be reminded of Amos' punishing hands about her throat, she found herself accepting the fact that she could have done no less and remained alive herself. Hearing Danny's boyish chatter and seeing his happy face helped, too. She was all he had now, and she would have been no help in fulfilling their mother's dreams for him had she allowed Amos to kill her.

"Any friends of Hank's are friends of ours," Burr McHenry told Treasure and Danny after they followed Hank across the front porch and into the large receiving room. A gruff talking Scotsman, Burr called through a door leading to the back part of the large ground floor,

"Trinoma, Hannah, come say hello to your favorite peddler and his young friends."

Two women, their long white aprons serving as drying cloths for their hands, came and greeted the newcomers.

"I'm glad you got here, Hank," Trinoma McHenry said after introductions were made all around. Although it was plain to Treasure that the stand owner's wife was a full-blooded Chickasaw, she wore a white shirtwaist with lace-trimmed collar and cuffs and a full skirt of dark red linsey-woolsey. "I'm down to my last spoonful of vanilla flavoring."

"And I'm needing some more needles and thread," Hannah Ainsley, the other woman, said. Pretty and buxom, the auburn-haired young woman smiled in such a way as to include Treasure. "I've had to pass down Roxanne's clothes to Cecily, she's growing so fast. She's after me to sew that length of yard goods that I bought from you last fall."

"Where are the girls and Frederick?" Hank asked. He had already greeted the three strapping McHenry sons, who had promptly left to take the horses out back to the stables for the night. "I'd like to see how much they've grown."

"They'll be along soon," Hannah replied. "They're washing up for supper." She walked over to stand beside Treasure and spoke to her then. "It's good to have another woman at the stand. We don't have many stopping with us. Hank said you were from up near Rocky Bluffs. I reckon you're pretty tired after such a long journey. Let me show you and your brother to your rooms so you can freshen up before we put supper on the table. Hank already knows which one is his."

Treasure heard the friendliness in Hannah's voice and felt better than she had all day. On the way upstairs, Hannah, plainly curious about how they came to be traveling with the old peddler, chatted with the Ryans. She showed them to two small rooms at the top of the stairs.

"When we don't have many guests, like now, we offer private rooms. We might have to put Danny in with Hank if we get crowded," Hannah said. Already she had explained that she had become a widow nearly three years before. With her three youngsters, she lived at the stand and worked with Trinoma in caring for the guests. "My boy is eight years old, and my girls are three and six. They'll be tickled pink to see Danny. Not very many youngsters travel the Trace. Or women either."

After the pretty young widow left, Treasure opened her saddlebags and took out her few possessions. She poured water from the tin pitcher into the matching washbowl and bathed, wishing she had something nicer to put on than the worn waist once belonging to her mother. When she had noticed that Hannah was as neatly dressed as Trinoma, she had felt especially unkempt. She had only one other skirt, though, and it was in no better shape than the black one she wore.

Deciding that to wear her holster down to supper would look ridiculous, she did not rebuckle it around her hips. The brawny Burr McHenry seemed formidable all by himself, but with his three sons around him, he formed a picture of absolute authority. The youngest, she reflected, was at least her age and appeared all grown up. Removing the concealing black kerchief, she brushed her tangled curls in front of the small mirror above the washstand. She felt safe and let her thoughts drift to her image in the mirror. The faded blue blouse seemed to make her hair look even blonder, and she decided that tying back her long fall of curls with one of the blue ribands Hank had brought her was a nice enough touch.

For a tense moment, she peered into the mirror to make certain that the high-necked waist hid the bruises on her neck. She couldn't help thinking how nice her mother's locket would have looked there at the spot below the neckband and grieved anew at its theft. Already having heard Danny leave the room next to hers, she went downstairs to the large room which obviously served to receive, entertain, and feed the patrons of the inn.

Because only two soldiers were staying at the stand that night, in addition to Hank and the Ryans, all of the children were allowed to eat with the guests at the huge table running across one end of the large room. Treasure thought the McHenrys' youngest child and only daughter, Dawn, a delight. She was six and showed her mother's Chickasaw blood in her reddish brown complexion and black hair. Her bright blue eyes were almost identical to those of the big Scotsman.

Had she not also met Roxanne Ainsley at the same time, Treasure might have thought Dawn was the most beautiful little girl she had ever seen. Roxanne had a headful of the reddest, bounciest curls anyone could imagine, plus dimples and a charm equal to her beauty. The six-year-old's pale blue eyes set within black lashes studied the newcomers with remarkable calm, reminding Treasure of the handsome adventurer who had stopped to have his horse shod—and later had kissed the daylights out of her. She flushed at the wayward thought and noticed that Hannah's younger daughter, Cecily, was also pretty. She couldn't compete with the vivacious Roxanne, though, and apparently accepted the fact. Even at three, Cecily was reserved like Hannah's oldest child, Frederick.

During the meal Treasure felt covert gazes washing over her from the two soldiers at the table, as well as from the McHenry sons. She was grateful that no one attempted to engage her in direct conversation. She was still too tense from all that had happened over the past twenty-four hours; her throat hurt when she spoke more than a few words at a time. Pleading fatigue, she left with Danny for her room as soon as everyone rose from the table.

Hank surprised both Treasure and Danny after breakfast the next morning.

"Nope," the old peddler told them when Danny offered to saddle the horses. "I went out to check on Duke and Daisy earlier and Duke looks bilious in the eyes to me. My rheumatism is acting up, too, so I think we'll rest here a day or two before traveling any distance."

Her head cocked to the side in doubt, Treasure remarked, "I never heard of a horse being bilious. What kind of treatment does Duke need?" She had slept far better than she had expected to and felt refreshed. Her neck and throat were still sore, but talking no longer pained her.

"I just give him lots of rest, same as I do for myself for my rheumatism." He pulled a pipe and a small pouch from his pocket and began tamping tobacco into the clay bowl. "I'm going to indulge myself with a smoke and a spell of sitting. Can you two find something to keep yourselves busy?"

"Can you afford to keep us all here, Hank?" Treasure asked after Danny left to join the children outside. She was eager to get moving again toward Natchez, but she did not want to burden the kindly old man with her problems. Not when he seemed to have some of his own that morning. One more day couldn't make that much difference, she reasoned.

"Sure. We agreed you and Danny would be paying your way by cooking on the trail and tending the horses." Hank had his pipe going then and turned toward the front porch, tugging at his red wig with one pudgy hand.

"I'll be checking on the horses today, but especially on Duke," Treasure assured him as he left.

Treasure watched the rounded figure go outside with a noticeable limp, sorry to learn the old peddler was in pain. She had noticed that his rough complexioned face had a gray look. It was strange that Blackie never had mentioned that horses could be bilious like people, she mused.

That afternoon while giving the horses a good brush down in the stable, Treasure heard Danny and the younger children coming back from fishing in the creek behind the barn. She could hear the creak of the well pulley as someone lowered the bucket in the well beside the lot fence. Off and on all day, she had seen the youngsters and even visited some with them as they wandered around the place, chattering and laughing. Danny seemed to relish being treated more like an adult than a child by them, and they seemed in awe of him, especially Roxanne. Treasure recalled with amusement the little red-haired girl's apparent worship of the older boy.

"We have an uncle who's probably the strongest and

bravest man in all Tennessee. He's coming in from a hunting trip tonight or tomorrow,'' Frederick bragged to Danny. All had paused beside the well and were taking turns passing around the gourd dipper from the bucket of water Frederick had drawn. "He always sleeps with us in our rooms when he visits.''

Treasure couldn't help but overhear, and she grinned at the way children loved trying to impress others. Only time would tell if the little boy was stretching the truth, not that it mattered one way or the other. She moved to the next stall and began currying Vagabond's tan mane.

"Why don't you stay with us instead of upstairs, Danny?'' Roxanne asked. "If I'm going to marry you someday, we might as well get to know all about each other.''

Everyone hooted, except for the pert Roxanne. "My mama told me I'd know when I met the one I'd marry, and I knew last night it was Danny. I'm going to sing and dance for him when I grow up, and he'll be my very own Prince Charming.''

"Fat chance,'' Frederick teased in the way of older brothers. "Danny's going to Natchez. He's not coming back to Tennessee.''

"He will too come back, 'cause this is where I'll be waiting for him.''

"Don't be crazy, Roxanne,'' Dawn, the little McHenry girl spoke up. "We're just six. We can't say who we'll marry yet. Anyway, probably our folks will decide for us.''

"I'll decide for myself, thank you,'' Roxanne retorted. "Even if Mama marries our uncle like she's talking about, I'll still make up my own mind about things. So there!''

A splatting noise told Treasure that the sassy redhead had stuck out her tongue at her doubting companions. Smiling at Roxanne's daring, she wondered how Danny was taking such ardent declarations from a little girl. He had played mostly with Indian children, and she didn't recall hearing such talk about marriage among them. In fact, now that she thought about it, the little Indian girls seldom ran with the boys.

Treasure was tempted to peek through the cracks, but she didn't. The noisy group moved on in the direction of the house and were soon out of hearing. All at once she felt even better about her decision to get Danny to Natchez among their mother's family and friends. She had been too protective of her young brother and kept him too close to her. From what Marie had told her about her own childhood, groups of plantation children spent long lazy hours together and became better prepared for the adult world that way.

Putting away the currycomb and inspecting Duke's eyes once more for signs of what Hank called biliousness, Treasure went inside to get cleaned up so that she could offer to help Trinoma and Hannah get the table set for supper. Before the noon meal she had learned that the women refused to accept her help in any other way. She was a guest.

The arrival of a party of four men from Nashville prevented the smaller children from being served in the main room that evening, though Danny still rated a place there beside his sister. Treasure, again wearing the long-sleeved blue waist and the matching riband in her hair, listened anxiously for talk of a murder near Rocky Bluffs. No mention was made. The men seemed interested in learning the latest news of highwaymen along the Trace. When no tale of recent attacks was forthcoming from Burr, sitting as host at the head of the table, they paid more open attention to the only young woman sitting with them.

Mindful of keen looks from Hank, one of the men leaned across the table and told Treasure in a low voice, "I'm a drummer for ladies' fine garments on my way to New Orleans. If you'd like to come to my room after a while, I could show you the latest styles in bonnets."

Treasure pretended not to understand the gleam in his eyes and responded to Hank's request for the sugar bowl to be passed down to him.

Another man sitting beside her told her *sotto voce* that he was pretending to be a cotton buyer so as to throw off highwaymen, but that he was actually a jeweler with fine gems sewn inside the lining of his coat. When he mentioned that he would reward her if she would take a walk with him outside Treasure was not even surprised. Obviously the travelers were eager for the company of any woman and were willing to pay for the privilege. Somehow she felt cheapened.

Treasure noticed that each time Hannah brought in a plate of hot biscuits or came from the kitchen to check the supply of food in the large bowls all four men eyed the young widow's nicely rounded body with interest. Treasure admired the way Hannah turned aside their implied invitations for her private attentions with cheerful smiles and good-natured rejoinders. Though Burr was openly hearing and watching all that went on, he never interfered. It seemed plain that the pretty widow needed no help from him.

Treasure marked Hannah's actions and made mental notes on how she herself might stave off further, unwanted attentions from men. This was only the first leg of a long journey, and Hank had indicated they would be stopping at several stands on their way to Natchez. Recalling that both Trinoma and Hannah told her that few women traveled the Trace, she figured that she had best be prepared for future encounters with male travelers overly eager for the company of women.

From what Treasure observed, it appeared that a woman should assume a breezy air of indifference and good humor, as if what was going on was a game with set rules for each side and that there did not have to be a decided winner. Hannah did not seem to suffer the sense of shame that she had experienced from the men's sly advances. Treasure was eager to avoid a repetition of her earlier reactions. She already had enough to keep her spirits sagging, she reflected.

A burst of noise from the kitchen area shattered Treasure's ruminations while the front door opened behind her.

"Uncle Fort!" the three Ainsley children yelled while rushing past the table to greet the newcomer. "We were watching out the window and saw you ride up," one of them exclaimed joyously.

They swarmed the lean figure stooping to gather them close. Her hands twisting together in the folds of her apron, Hannah came into the room then and walked toward the tall man. When he stood and lifted his head from the adoring trio of children, he put an arm around Hannah and kissed her cheek. Their talk was low and intimate and did not carry to the diners.

"Looks like our hunter is back," Burr McHenry said when Hannah shooed the children from the room and went on back to the kitchen. "Take a seat and grab a plate. We've got plenty of food left for you." With a sweep of his arm he gave the names of the four travelers from Nashville.

Like a stone figure, Treasure sat looking down at her plate, a warning hand resting on Danny's knee beside her. She did not want him to make any big to-do over the fact that they knew the man who apparently had just been reunited with his mistress and her children. Fortner, the adventurer, was the "uncle" that the Ainsley children had talked about out at the well, the man their mother was going to marry. Treasure reflected that a spring twister seemed to have whisked up her mind and her heart and shaken the living daylights out of them.

"Burr, I met Hank on the Trace last year, and I already know the ones you say are traveling with him," Fortner was saying by the time he pulled out a chair and sat at the table. Nodding a polite hello to Hank, he went on, "Hello, Miss Ryan, Danny. How are you two tonight?" The remembered pale blue eyes probed Treasure's puzzled brown ones, both sets asking all kinds of unspoken questions.

"We're fine, Fortner," replied Danny. "It's good to see you again." His sister's hand squeezed his knee tighter, and he hushed before blabbing all about how they happened to be at McHenry's Stand. Cripes! he thought. He had thought Treasure liked Fortner, too, and he couldn't understand why they had to act as if they barely knew him.

"Hello, Mr. Fortner," Treasure managed to say. Her

throat and neck had not pained all day as keenly as when she uttered the greeting. Her face grew flushed from the pensive looks he was sending her and her heartbeat kicked up a fuss.

Seeing Fortner's arms hug Hannah earlier, no matter how briefly, had reminded Treasure how it had felt to be pulled closely against that manly frame. Was he as surprised as she to find her in the stand where his mistress lived? She well recalled Frederick saying that their "uncle" always stayed with them in their first-floor rooms. How could she have believed Fortner was fine and upstanding when all the time he was mixed up with a comely young widow? She felt her cheeks heat up even more.

Hannah came in then with a warm smile and hot food for the latecomer, and Treasure hardly knew who said what after that. Her thoughts kept skipping back to that soul-searing kiss Fortner and she had shared on her porch only a week ago. How could she have permitted him to kiss her, much less gain such a passionate response? She must be as wanton as the men making overtures to her earlier apparently believed, she agonized.

No, that part of her studying Hannah's easy manner with the teasing men insisted, Fortner and she had done no more than play the game between the sexes. She was not wanton, merely innocent of the ways of the world outside the Ryan farm. In the last letter written to Aunt Olivia, her mother's childhood friend, Treasure had agreed that she would "save herself" for Aunt Olivia's son, Thornton, to consider as a bride until the two could meet. What could one kiss do to subtract from that saving of herself? But it should not have been given to a man with no morals, she chided.

From behind half lowered lashes, Treasure secretly watched Fortner talking and eating in the same easy manner he had shown at the cabin. Right off she had seen that he was even more handsome than she remembered. His smiles of thanks to Hannah as she poured him more coffee or brought him more food seemed replicas of those he had showered her with back at the cabin. All at once she became incensed. The man was a far cry from being a gentleman. Obviously everyone at the table but her accepted without censure that Hannah and he were lovers. She tried to swallow the hot lump punishing her throat.

There was no doubt left now in Treasure's whirling mind. Fortner was the kind of man her mother had warned her about, the kind who flaunted his good looks and charm before whatever woman he happened to be around to get what he wanted. She had been wrong to kiss him, wrong to think he was fine and upstanding...and even more wrong to feel sadness when he rode away that morning and to let her thoughts dwell upon him at times since. The man had duped her—and Danny. She hated him!

Chapter Six

Later that night in Hannah Ainsley's living quarters on the lower floor, David Fortner Copeland sat in deep thought before the fireplace. Though he was unaware that the little action had become habit over the past couple of years, the thumb and forefinger on his left hand revealed his inner agitation, for they lay pressed together, rubbing against each other periodically. Eyes narrowed and fixed on the dying embers, he puzzled over the way seeing the golden haired farrier at the stand had jolted him. That he had thought often about the tall, beautiful Treasure since leaving the Ryan farm over a week ago also grabbed his attention.

Why were Danny and she traveling with Hank Marcellus? If Hannah's children hadn't been hanging around the door waiting for him to finish eating and visit with them, Fortner would have liked to talk with the old man and learn what was going on. Not that it was any of his business, but he had not taken to the old peddler from their first meeting on the Trace last summer. He had never before tried to figure out why. Now that he thought upon it, he guessed it had something to do with his feeling that Hank was, somehow, not what he seemed. Could the same be true of Treasure and Danny Ryan?

"Heavy thoughts?" Hannah asked, coming back from the other bedroom where she had checked on the sleeping children. She smiled fondly at the handsome young man.

"Are they asleep?" Fortner asked, wrenching his gaze from the coals to her pretty face. In the soft candlelight, her auburn hair glowed warmly.

"Yes, and with smiles of contentment on their faces, thanks to you. They do love you so . . . and so do I."

Hitching up a shoulder and glancing away from Hannah's admiring eyes, he quipped, "That's one of the rewards of being an uncle to such handsome children." He reached for his saddlebags lying on the floor nearby and brought out a leather pouch that he held toward her. "I was waiting until the little monsters fell asleep. Here's some money from the sale of the farm, Hannah. I want you to ask Burr to lock it in a safe place until you need it for you and the tykes." When she hesitated and blinked hard at tears flooding her dark eyes, he pressed the pouch into her hand and closed his larger one over it. "This is the way I aim for it to be, Hannah."

"Thank you," Hannah said, weighing the bulging pouch in her hand. "You shouldn't give so much to us, Fortner. There were four of you boys, and if my Samuel were alive, his share would have been only a fourth. You've already done more than most men would have done for a dead brother's widow and children. Bringing us here where I could earn our keep and start over—"

"Enough of that talk," he broke in abruptly. "I kept plenty for my needs. We're the only Copelands left now, and we likely wouldn't be alive if we hadn't stuck together. Have you had any problems about using your maiden name?"

"None. Frederick never seemed to give it another thought,

and the girls were so little that they never had thought of themselves as Copelands, so it went easy. When I decided since Christmas that I was ready to begin a new life and accept Seth's proposal, I told him about what happened over two years ago, but only the barest facts.''

"I'm dying to meet this Seth Willows. I almost get jealous hearing the kids talk about Uncle Seth.''

Hannah laughed low in her throat and blushed. "Seth is riding down tomorrow or the next day. If he could have gotten the extra rooms for the children finished in time, we were going to be married at the stand when you came. His place is near the Buffalo River, though, and high water kept him from getting all his supplies in on time. We'll likely have the ceremony next month.''

"He must be a fine man to have won you—and he's a lucky one, too.'' Fortner had been in his early teens when his oldest brother had brought his young bride home to live, and Hannah had quickly found a place in the hearts of all the Copelands.

"You're kind to say so. Seth is kind, too, and very good with the children. He's older than Samuel would have been, but maybe that's what I need, someone settled. He has a son of his own, though he's grown and been away from home ever since his mother died a few years back. Last month Seth took all of us up to show us his place. It's really nice and looks prosperous. He grows tobacco and a few acres of corn.''

"If I go ahead with my plans and succeed, I might not get back this way for a long spell. How does that strike you?''

"You know how I pray you'll put away that notion to get even, Fortner. Nothing will bring back those we loved. Don't be shaking your head at me. I don't need another lecture, and I'll hush up. We'll miss seeing you when you go, but I don't know anybody who needs to get away from Tennessee more than you to start a life in a brand new spot. Texas or wherever you end up will be lucky to have a man like you. I'm sorry about all that happened back on the Cumberland, but I'm also sorry that things didn't work out for Sarah and you. . . ."

The thumb and forefinger on his left hand meeting again, Fortner returned his attention to the dying fire before saying in a musing voice, "Maybe Mrs. Lovelace was an even better teacher than I thought. I've thought a lot about her maxims, like how bad things happening to us have a way of turning up something good in time. I see now that I don't need a woman for keeps, Hannah. She'd only tie me down and keep me from doing what I must do."

Hannah threw back her head and laughed softly. "You sound so wise and weary. Are you sure you're only twenty-five?"

Recognizing that he had sounded bottom-of-the-jug grim, Fortner grinned at his teasing sister-in-law and noticed again how pretty she looked. Falling in love again had done wonders for her. There had been a time when he had doubted he would ever hear her laugh so spontaneously again or see those once dead eyes sparkle from happiness. His own scarred heart lightened at the outward progress both of them had made over the past two years.

"I'll try to act my age just to please you, sister dear, and ask about the pretty blonde staying here at the stand," he countered when both sobered. Earlier, before playing games with the children on the floor, he had slipped off his boots. Now he turned his chair so as to hold his stockinged feet close to the glowing embers and stretch them languorously.

"Don't tell me you've forgotten a name like Treasure Ryan. Frankly, I would've thought your innards shriveled forever if you hadn't noticed how lovely she is. I really like her. There's hope for you yet."

"What are she and her brother doing with Hank? They don't seem like they go together to me."

"She's as friendly as she is pretty. She told me that Hank is escorting them to Natchez to live with their mother's family, now that their father is dead, too. I suspect that grief has put those prickle points of pain in her eyes. I asked her if there was some lucky young man waiting for her down there on one of those plantations I've heard about. She blushed like crazy, but she never once smiled.''

His smooth forehead creasing a bit, Fortner said after a spell of comfortable silence, "So that's it. She's going down there to get married.''

Silently he added, She wasn't making that up about some rich gentleman asking for her hand. Not that anything Treasure Ryan did was his business, he reminded himself. Fortner stood then and stretched his long arms and frame, as though to remove the kinks in his thoughts as well.

A man-sized yawn seized him. He let it run its noisy course before saying, "If you're ready, I'll move the girls to your bed and join Frederick for a snooze. Up in the hills, a blanket on the ground was fine, but once I get close to a bed, I realize what I've been missing. Bear-John and the others ought to be getting here just any day, so this might be my last chance to sleep on a mattress for a spell.''

Hannah stood then and nodded her approval. She turned back the covers on the big bed. Bringing first Roxanne and then Cecily, Fortner tucked them in. He sent a loving look at each pretty face and smiled.

Before he went into the other bedroom and closed the door, Hannah glanced at the sleeping girls in her bed and, with amusement in her voice, asked, "Wouldn't all the guests who think I've been your mistress all this time be surprised at our customary sleeping arrangements?''

"No doubt about it, sister dear." He chuckled and winked before adding, "Good night.''

"Roxanne! Cecily!" Fortner called the next morning as he neared the creek behind the barn and stables. He had promised Hannah he would check on the children, though her request made no sense when he realized that she managed them alone when he was not around. If he hadn't known better, he would have suspected she was trying to keep him occupied. "Frederick!"

Shouts and laughter reached his ears then, and he walked across the last rise leading to the little patch of trees and bushes edging the small stream.

"We're here, Uncle Fort," Frederick replied. "We're fishing, but we ain't got our feet wet."

Fortner saw the merry group down by the creek then, not only his nieces and nephew, but also little Dawn McHenry and Danny . . . and Treasure sitting off by herself. Walking more slowly now that he had found the children safe, he saw that the beautiful young woman wore a shiny riband in her hair as he had noticed last night upon arrival. But today it was pink. A shaft of mid-morning sunlight fingered her honey toned curls as she sat perched upon a giant outcropping of tree roots on the bank watching the youngsters fish not far downstream. She acknowledged his presence with a polite nod. Why no smile? he wondered as his own faded from lack of response.

Once he greeted each child and bragged on the size and number of fish strung upon long, slippery willow limbs, Fortner turned toward Treasure up on the bank. She still sat with her arms around her drawn legs and her chin resting atop her skirt-clad knees. Somehow he sensed that she had watched his every movement, for the back of his neck had that prickly feeling that warned him about such things.

"When I didn't see you anywhere back at the stand, I figured you must be up in your room. I missed seeing you at breakfast," he told her, settling upon one of the several exposed roots of the fat oak trunk.

"Yes, I ate early," Treasure replied stiffly, glad that her voice sounded normal again. Her throat was improved, too, but her pulse was as unsteady as when she had seen him last night. "I suppose some of us needed more sleep than others."

As soon as she had seen Fortner follow Hannah's children down the hall to their quarters after supper the night before, Treasure had stood to go up to her room. Hank had waylaid her planned flight and questioned her at length in a secluded corner about what the men from

Nashville had said to her, as well as about how she came to know Fortner. She was exhausted by the time she got away from him and had little voice left. To her surprise and disgust she had found it hard to fall asleep knowing Fortner was with Hannah, but she had awakened at her usual early hour.

"So you and Danny are on your way to Lindwood?" Until she spoke just then, Fortner had not realized that the husky timber of her voice was intriguing, almost titillating. He felt as if a low note from a moaning fiddle might have floated by and called to something deep within him.

"You must have talked with Hank," was her answer.

Treasure had been unable to take her eyes off the self-proclaimed adventurer, so handsome and virile did he look in the crisp blue shirt unbuttoned at the top. As she had guessed might be the case if she saw him closer, the blue of his eyes did seem deeper and richer from the reflections of the garment. Instead of the hip hugging brown breeches he had been wearing when she first met him, Fortner wore blue denims with the same snug fit over his lean hips and buttocks. Not that it mattered how he looked, she warned herself. He was no gentleman, and he had a mistress. And she hated him for taking advantage of her. He had probably had more than one good laugh about the way she had melted in his arms.

"Yep, Hank seems tickled to have you and Danny along on this trip down the Trace."

Unlike Hannah, Hank had volunteered no information to Fortner about a prospective bridegroom awaiting Treasure in Natchez. The sunshine still filtered through the newly greening overhead limbs and stroked her hair, but Fortner noted that her face and eyes were in shadow. Somehow he had pictured her eyes as being golden like her hair, but he realized that without highlights, or perhaps at a closer view, they appeared a soft, shadowed brown. Or had they changed since he last looked into them a little more than a week ago?

Moving closer to where she leaned back against the tree

trunk, he said, "I was surprised to see you and Danny here."

"I'll bet you were," she retorted, her face flushing when she heard the rebuke in her voice. What business was it of hers whom he saw or slept with? Trying to remember what she could from watching Hannah quip with the diners the night before, she wracked her brain for one of the light rejoinders the pretty widow had handed out so glibly. Treasure didn't want him to know she was a backward hill woman who had clung like a fool to the first man who kissed her. "Why does everyone think a woman might not like new territory as well as a man?"

Fortner swiveled his head toward her in disbelief. Asked in that throaty way, the oft bandied retort took on an even more suggestive meaning than usual. When had she become so sophisticated? *Ah-ha!* he thought when he saw the rosy tint of her face, the trembling full lips, and the embarrassed drop of her eyes. She must have picked up such a notion from hearing Hannah fence with the guests. A spark of mischief danced in his pale eyes.

"What do you mean, pretty lady?" he asked, smiling and leaning nearer, ostensibly to pluck a blade of grass and put it between his teeth. He straightened up then and studied her lovely face from the closer view. He had been right, he saw when she lifted the tangled sweep of dark lashes. Something did look different deep in those velvety eyes, and it was more than the confusion that his baiting was bringing about. "Are you going to become an adventurer like me?"

"I might if it pleases me." She upped her chin.

Fortner's dazzling smile almost coaxed one to Treasure's face, but she refused the invitation. Why was he staring at her that way, as if he knew a secret she might like to know? Could he tell that she had come to hate him since they last met? She squinted and searched overhead for the bird nest that she had been watching a pair of mocking birds build earlier. A bright blue sky formed a striking background for the varied greens of half formed leaves on dark limbs.

Fortner took advantage of Treasure's preoccupation and looked at her more intently. Where was the fancy ivory handled knife she had worn in that holster back at her home? The one there now was the ordinary kind sold in stores and by peddlers. Instead of the shapeless, man's oversized shirt he had seen her in that first day, she now wore a high-necked waist of pink checks with her black skirt. Last night she had worn a pale blue one, the exact shade of the riband in her hair. With her face lifted while she gazed up into the oak, he gained a clear view of her neck and admired its graceful arch. Were those bruises on her silken skin or merely shadows? Deciding that the play of light and shadow was deceiving him, Fortner lowered his eyes to even more tempting sights. He could see the swells of the full breasts that had crushed against him when he kissed her and, lower, the indentation of her tiny waist.

"Since you seem confident of your skills with a rifle and a knife, you must figure you'd have no trouble fending for yourself. Is that it?" he asked when she ended her search in the tree overhead and fixed her eyes on him again. Brown with golden flecks, he noted, and definitely shadowed from within. Why?

All at once Treasure had no heart for the game. Fortner's teasing words brought back painful memories of the struggle with Amos. She rose and stepped away from the roots of the tree, stooping to brush debris from her skirt, the quick movements sending her curls tumbling forward over her shoulders and jiggling enticingly for her rapt audience of one.

"Danny," she called. When the boy turned his dark head in answer and smiled at her from a short way down the stream, she asked, "Will you be staying down here? I'm ready to go."

"Yes. I'm having a good time, Treasure." Danny turned back then to help the redheaded Roxanne get a wriggling fish off her hook.

"Did I say something wrong back there?" Fortner asked

when he followed alongside her on the worn path leading to the barn. He still chewed on the blade of grass.

"No." Treasure shook her head in emphasis, her waist-length hair dancing in the spring sunshine. The way Fortner matched his stride to hers seemed a polite gesture, but she had the feeling they were moving as a team yoked by an invisible, tenuous harness. She wished she knew how to break it. Not being in control was scary.

Before Fortner could say more, a deep-voiced, "Hya-ho there, hoss!" broke the mysterious spell linking the two on the path. He did not have to look up to know it was Bear-John McHenry, his friend since childhood.

"Aunt Trinoma told me I'd find you down here, Fort," the young man said, a friendly smile splitting his broad face as he came toward them. "She told me I'd also likely see the purtiest blond gal in the United States with you. By damn! She was right on both counts."

Burr McHenry's nephew paused to let Treasure and Fortner reach him. She noticed that the trim but huge young man had the features of one with Indian blood—reddish brown skin and black hair and eyes—but that his language and wide, engaging smile reflected a white heritage and upbringing. When Fortner greeted his friend enthusiastically and made the introductions, Treasure found herself drawn to Bear-John McHenry. She got the feeling that the April sunshine had suddenly become warmer.

"Ma'am, you'll have to forgive my lapses into coarse speech. I've been riding the trails with this hoss too long to keep my finer parts honed." Twinkling black eyes raced from Treasure's face to Fortner's, no doubt approving whatever it was they saw there. "He didn't say so, but we grew up along the same section on the Cumberland River, ma'am."

"No one calls me 'ma'am,'" Treasure protested. She had to look up to see into the faces of the young men on either side of her. For one of the few times since she had reached her height of five feet and eight inches, she felt small and feminine. It was a bit unsettling, to say the least. "Treasure suits me fine."

"Danged if it don't at that," Bear-John said, his implied compliment bringing a pleased flush to her face. "I picked up that 'ma'am' down in Natchez and thought it might impress some purty lass some day."

"This pretty lass isn't easily impressed," Fortner told his longtime friend with a glance down at Treasure as she walked along between the two men. "She's no ordinary young woman."

"Well, I can shore tell that. She looks good enough to eat all right, but that knife she's wearing looks to me like it's more than something to peel a tater with."

"Plus she's a mean hand with a rifle," Fortner added. He saw the way Treasure's lips twitched at the corners and figured she wanted to smile. What was causing her to be so guarded? One of the things he had liked about her was that she seemed so natural, so sure of herself. What could have changed her?

Bear-John asked, "And just how would you be a'knowin' what kind of hand she puts on a rifle, hoss?"

By the time Fortner finished telling how he had met Treasure across the barrel of her rifle, the trio had reached the stand. They guided her around to the front porch and paused there until the story was ended. Bear-John seemed so impressed upon hearing of Treasure's skills at shoeing horses that she found herself blushing and smiling and feeling flustered from such intense attention from the two handsome young men. None of it was fair, she kept telling herself, because she had meant not to be friendly in Fortner's presence.

Even after she went up to her room to get ready for the noon meal, Treasure was blaming her sudden dropping of her guard around Fortner on the effusive Bear-John McHenry. The man was as much a charmer in his way as his fellow adventurer was in his. It was easy to imagine they had grown up together. She guessed Bear-John knew he would likely run into Fortner at his uncle's stand, since he likely stayed around close to . . . his mistress.

When Hank returned that afternoon from his call on an Indian village over the ridges, she would ask if he might be ready to leave on the morrow. She hungered to get away from the disturbing Fortner and put him out of her thoughts for good. Out of sight, out of mind, she reassured herself.

The children hogged the conversation at the table that day at noon, and Treasure was relieved that she could sit back and be an observer. No one objected when she returned to her room to do some mending she had offered to do for Hank. It was hard, but while plying her needle she channeled her thoughts toward what might lie ahead for Danny and her in Natchez.

Late that afternoon after she bathed, Treasure again put on the blue waist and tied her hair back with the matching riband, this time changing from the black skirt into the navy one. When she went downstairs, she found that a couple of rough looking travelers had taken over one end of the large front room. Apparently noticing her disapproval of the loud, talkative men still wearing their pistols in holsters, Hank left them and escorted her over to meet the newcomers. Danny came in in time for the introductions.

"Miss Treasure Ryan and Danny, meet the Thorpe brothers," Hank told her, his soft hand on her arm. "George Henry and Juno."

While Hank attempted to carry on a kind of conversation and include Danny and her in it, Treasure covertly sized up the two men who were so openly doing the same to her. She saw little family resemblance between the brothers except for a cold wariness about their dark eyes. Neither was much taller than the old peddler, though both looked hard and wiry.

Obviously older and more outspoken, the full-bearded George Henry also seemed more uncouth. The sour, unwashed smell of a man on the trail for a spell was not new to Treasure, but she found it repulsive anyway. A black space from one or more missing teeth jumped out at her when he smiled. Right off she noticed that his smoldering eyes never lit up during his smile and that some of his remaining teeth were broken. The way his hot gaze chased over her body before settling on her face brought a feathering of goosebumps up her spine. If George Henry noticed that she offered no smile with her low greeting, he made no show of it.

Juno seemed less offensive, Treasure decided. Clean shaven, Juno had a rough complexion, but he had even, white teeth and a more acceptable version of what passed for a smile. His eyes had more lively sparkle, and his forehead, unlike his older brother's, had no unusual bulge. Though he too possessed an animal-like defensiveness about him, he seemed more at ease with himself than George Henry. Juno appeared far more interested in her face and hair than in her body, though for the life of her she couldn't figure out why that led her to judge him any less ferocious. Even with the few pluses she gave him, Juno Thorpe impressed her as being crude and threatening.

Treasure was relieved when Burr, Fortner and Bear-John came into the room from outside. When she noticed Burr did not welcome the Thorpes with the same congeniality he had shown other arriving guests, she wondered if he too viewed them as different. Soon George Henry was answering questions about a brother named Felsenthal, who had apparently died a few months ago. Obviously the Thorpes were not strangers to any but Danny and her, she mused. Even so, the other men seemed tense around them. She did not have to wait long to find out why.

Supper was a noisy affair, dominated by the sounds of the Thorpe brothers wolfing down victuals with little regard for manners. Treasure noted how both George Henry and Juno leered at Hannah and tried to gain her favor, especially when the meal was ended and some were sipping second cups of coffee. Outside darkness was falling.

"Are these men bothering you with their cute sayings?" Fortner asked the pretty young widow when she seemed fresh out of retorts. She made no answer, merely went on removing plates. "If anybody thinks it's none of my business what's said to Miss Hannah, speak up and I'll meet him outside." His pale eyes swept the Thorpes with daring and icy contempt.

George Henry swept a startled look Fortner's way, what little of his face showing above the full beard turning red.

"Ain't nobody a'figurin' to rile you, Fortner. We was jes' funnin' with your woman. If'n we was a'wantin' to get flirty, we'd be a'throwin' looks at somebody younger and purtier." His gaze shot toward Treasure's flushing, lowered face.

"Not in my place you wouldn't," Burr McHenry announced sternly. His three sons, their Chickasaw dominant features suddenly gone still, added their own stares to that of their father. "I don't stand for such. You knew my rules when—"

"Good God amighty!" George Henry retorted. "We ain't meant no harm to nobody. We know you're a hard-headed Scotsman—and that you could get your wife's whole tribe after us if'n you had a mind to. We was jes' a'horsin' 'round."

Treasure squirmed on her chair, not liking that all eyes seemed fixed on her. She had heard Fortner's stout defense of Hannah and then Burr's interference on her part, but she could think of little but an urge to escape the presence of the foul smelling—and foul talking—Thorpes. Maybe it was the hauntingly fresh memories of her brush with Amos, but she was strangely out of fight. The need to lick her wounds must not be satisfied yet, she thought.

"Danny," Treasure said privately, "why don't you go visit with the children back in Hannah's rooms while I see if I can help the women in the kitchen?"

When they reached the darkening hallway leading to the kitchen, Hannah stood stacking empty plates on a serving shelf built in a small alcove.

"I heard all that," Hannah told Treasure. "I don't blame you for wanting to leave the table. Some men are plain crude." She turned to Danny. "Go ahead to my quarters down the hall. The children are there, and they'll be pleased if you'd read them some stories. They get tired of hearing my voice."

Treasure watched Danny disappear down the hall. "Hannah, what can I do to help? I don't want to go back in there." She had purposefully not looked at Fortner as she left with Danny for fear that she might see amusement at her flight—she who had put on such a show of bravado the first time they met. During the meal she had caught his eyes upon her each time she glanced his way. Had his mistress also noticed and maybe been a mite jealous?

Hannah hesitated a moment, her pretty face showing not a trace of agitation. "Wait here until I get all these dishes carried into the kitchen. There's a big pile of towels I snatched off the clothesline before supper. I'll fetch them, and you can stand out here and fold them on the serving shelf. I don't think Burr can fuss too much about that." She patted Treasure's arm and added with a conspiratorial smile, "After all, you'll not be a guest working in the kitchen."

Shortly Treasure was left alone with the pile of towels. Since Hannah had taken away the tin plates and closed the door to the kitchen, talk from the table drifted around the corner with such clarity that Treasure could hear every word. Marie had taught her that eavesdropping was rude, but she saw no way to avoid hearing every word spoken, especially when none of the men seemed to care about being overheard.

Apparently continuing a conversation begun before Treasure was alone in the hallway, Burr was saying, "No, George Henry, I don't aim on being the law, but I'm not going to tell lies to the soldiers for anyone, either. Two of them came here asking questions a couple of days ago. I didn't like hearing their report that some killings from last year are being blamed on you Thorpes. Some bodies floated out of the swamps and backwaters down the Trace during high water, with ropes still holding rocks to the corpses. They thought they could trace the ropes to you boys."

"Horse shit!" George Henry retorted. "Ever'thin' they told was lies. The Thorpe Brothers' gang ain't never been killers, 'less'un somebody's a'tryin' to kill us. If'n that happens, we jes' leave 'em where they fall. Like I tole you earlier, our brother Felsenthal run into somebody too damn handy with a knife a while back and had to give up the ghost. These is danj'rus times. We be jes' ordinary highwaymen liftin' a few spare coins from time to time.''

Treasure paused in the folding of a towel, her heart pounding. Those were notorious outlaws sitting at the table! And Burr McHenry knew it. Why had he taken them in? And why were Fortner and Bear-John silent? Hank was old and obviously no threat to the Thorpes, but why were the two young men from the upper Cumberland taking no stand? Surely they did not accept the company of outlaws, who, from all she had heard, were likely murderers as well as robbers. She shivered.

The Scotsman's slightly accented voice went on. ''I'm not judging. I'm just telling you that you're going to end up with a widdy around your neck if you don't mend your ways. If you're ever here when the soldiers come, my boys and I will side with the law. I owed your pa a favor, but I think it's been long paid back by now. How long has he been dead?''

Treasure thought it must be Juno who answered.

''Pa was hanged five years ago. I wasn't but seventeen. It's a hard thing to have your pa strung up and then have his head chopped off and nailed to a tree. Buryin' our brother wasn't easy either.''

George Henry broke the ensuing silence with an obscene snicker. ''Don't be a'frettin', little brother. Nary one of those skokers what nailed Pa's head to that tree be around enjoyin' it now. Naw sirree, they learnt that J.Y. Thorpe had family who wasn't takin' such crap without doin' sumpin' 'bout it. An' that varmint which knifed Felsenthal learnt that family looks after family, 'specially when it's Thorpes.''

''When you talk like that,'' Burr reprimanded, ''you sound no better than the Masons or the Harps. Not so long ago such cutthroats had everybody afraid to travel the Trace. One reason I started taking in people here was because folks was scared to spend the night in the woods. The Harp brothers didn't end up no better than your pa or your brother, from all I've heard. Seems they finally caught little Harp with some of his cronies last year and hanged them down in Greenville.''

''We heared 'bout that,'' George Henry mumbled. ''We ain't mad dogs like them. We jes' lighten the loads of some what looks like they got more'n they needs.''

After a burst of raucous laughter, apparently from the Thorpes, Treasure heard Burr continue.

''You can laugh, but if the soldiers are right and somebody really can identify you as the ones doing those killings, then you're going to find yourselves kicking at space above the ground and clawing at your necks.''

''Good God amighty!'' George Henry exclaimed testily. ''We ain't come here for no sermon, Burr McHenry.''

''Our pa knows that,'' one of the McHenry boys replied in a steely voice. ''He's trying to tell you that we ain't going to protect you if the soldiers come.''

''Shore, and I understand. But they ain't enough of them prowling the Trace to keep it safe like it was a'settin' inside the walls of their fort. Anyway, jes' like always, we checked around good for strange horses before a'ridin' in here this afternoon. We'll be gone at the crack of dawn.''

''Good,'' Burr said. His tone became more that of a host then. ''What about the rest of you? Are you moving on tomorrow?''

His soft voice barely reaching Treasure's ears, Hank answered, ''I believe Duke and I are better now, so we'll likely be leaving in the morning.''

Fortner and Bear-John seemed to be conferring in low voices, but Treasure could not hear their decision until Bear-John spoke.

''Uncle Burr, Fortner and me don't figure on hangin' around much past tomorrow either.''

The scrapes of chairs and boots against the puncheon floor drowned out further eavesdropping, but Treasure could tell that the earlier tension had been released because the men's voices sounded deeper and less strident. Goosebumps had trailed up her spine when she recalled tales of an outlaw's head being nailed to a tree at the fork of the main Trace not far south of the Duck River. Some told how it hung there and turned into a hideous skull until the man's wife and sons took it down and buried it with the rest of his body. Was that man the father of the Thorpes? Her backbone was not yet back to normal, and her hands trembled while smoothing the towels.

What if somebody decided to come down the hall in search of a drink of water and caught her there listening? Treasure added the last towel to the stack on the shelf and scooted into the kitchen where Hannah and Trinoma were washing the last of the cook pots. Did they know that they had fed what was left of the Thorpe Brothers' gang?

"Burr says we can get along with the outlaws better than we can fight 'em," Trinoma answered when Treasure haltingly asked her question. "Guess they have needs like everybody else, and as long as they don't give us trouble, we might as well take 'em in."

Hoping that neither of the busy women would insist that she leave before they were ready to join the men out in the receiving room, Treasure stood back out of the way and tried to hide her disapproval. She watched Trinoma carry the dishpan out the back door and heard the splash when she threw out the dirty water. Hannah stacked cutlery, tin plates, and cups on the worktable near the door, ready for use at breakfast.

Treasure sniffed at the sharp odor of fermented potatoes when Trinoma lifted the lid from a jar of sourdough starter sitting on the cool side of the stove. She saw her add flour from a large wooden bowl and stir briskly. The familiar smell of sourdough and the sounds of the wooden spoon thwacking against the stoneware brought back memories of the times she had watched her mother tend her own starter dough, so as to be able to make yeasty biscuits for the next day's meals.

Somehow the movements of the capable women soothed Treasure's jangled nerves, and she hoped they would not decide suddenly to adhere to Burr's rules about no guests being allowed in the kitchen. Following what was obviously a nightly routine, the two women hurried about getting everything in readiness for cooking breakfast the next morning.

Hannah removed a side of salt pork from a ceiling hook in the corner and slapped it down on the chopping block nearby. An evil looking butcher knife already lay in readiness on the well-scored wooden surface. Brushing aside Treasure's offer to draw a bucket of water from the well out in the back yard, Hannah took care of the matter in short time.

"Now," the auburn-haired widow announced, her smile reaching out to Treasure, "we can join the men."

Wondering how it was that she still liked Hannah despite her apparent status as Fortner's mistress, Treasure watched her light a half burned candle in a pewter candleholder and walk with it to the door.

At the worktable, Trinoma leaned over the lantern used to light the kitchen whenever whale oil was available and turned down the wick, watching until the flame flickered out. The Chickasaw woman turned and said, "How nice of you, Treasure, to help by folding up the towels. I'm glad you waited for us."

Wide-eyed yet from all that she had overheard and was trying to digest, the pretty young blonde from near Rocky Bluffs gave a tremulous smile. She followed the wavering light from Hannah's candle up the shadowed hallway.

Treasure shrank at the thought of meeting the bold looks of the Thorpes again. Mostly, though, she dreaded reading amusement in the pale blue eyes of the adventurer . . . before they would rush to caress the face of his mistress.

Chapter Seven

"I'm glad we're on our way toward Natchez again," Treasure told Hank the next morning when they stopped to water their horses and themselves from a tumbling branch beside the Trace. Her mind had entertained so many troubling thoughts about Amos Greeson and then about Fortner that she welcomed new scenery and surroundings.

"So am I," Danny added. His dark eyes lit up. "I had a good time back at McHenry's Stand, didn't you, Treasure?"

Having returned from a brief stint behind some trees, Hank busied himself with tightening the belly band on his packhorse.

Treasure hesitated before answering. What had been good about seeing the handsome Fortner again and facing up to the fact that he had made a bit of a fool out of her? It smarted, too, when she thought of how she had been no more capable of defending herself against the crude looks and remarks from the Thorpe brothers than the ordinary woman. How Fortner must have snickered secretly at her helplessness!

"Yes. McHenry's Stand is a nice place," she responded before going to find a secluded spot to relieve herself.

Not that McHenry's Stand had seemed so nice last night, she recalled unhappily while searching for privacy. When the three women had come from the kitchen, the men were sitting near the fireplace where a small blaze cut the chill of the April evening. Treasure remembered how she had flinched when George Henry and Juno Thorpe had cast hot, knowing looks at her, looks even harder to bear after she knew they were highwaymen and probably murderers as well. Hurting her in a different way had been the private looks being exchanged by Hannah and Fortner, and she had angled her chin in defiance of all that seemed unbearable at the moment. Stiffly she had asked Hannah to send Danny up to his room soon and climbed the stairs to her own. She had seen no point in punishing herself by staying where she felt she did not belong.

Annoyed at the way Fortner kept invading her thoughts, Treasure made her way back to the branch. She knelt and rinsed her hands in the clear water before returning to the waiting horses.

The trio were soon back on the wilderness path taking them toward the Tennessee River, where, Hank told his wide-eyed companions, they would cross over it on Colbert's Ferry within the next week.

The trail climbed gradually until they were riding across the top of what seemed an endless, forested ridge. At noon they were still viewing their world from the vantage point of several hundred feet up in the crisp air.

Treasure was more aware of her surroundings than she had been on her ride down to McHenry's Stand, and she kept thinking that each new vista of green valleys sliced by serpentine streams must be more breathtaking than the last. Her body moving as one with Vagabond's easy gait, she breathed in the bracing, pine-scented air and felt attuned with all that surrounded her. Once she glimpsed a long string of small huts bordering one of the streams in single file. She smiled upon seeing that, as Blackie had told her, the Chickasaw tribe near their farm was not the only one that preferred such spacing over the usual, circular clustering of dwellings into villages. For a moment, Walking Bear's face rose to mind, and a pang of homesickness jabbed at her.

To Treasure's delight, blooming dogwood trees dotted the predominantly pine woods slanting down the steep sides of the ridge. Sometimes she glimpsed blurs of reddish pink that told her redbud trees were adding their colors to nature's glorious spring palette. More than once she lifted her face and sniffed the poignant smells riding the gentle breezes, marveling at the healing she could feel taking place inside with each passing mile. Fleecy clouds had been gathering in the blue distance all morning, but remained low on the horizon, posing a possible threat at some later time.

''What's that noise?'' Treasure asked Hank. At that point, the Trace was the width of the crest of the ridge they followed, and Vagabond moved easily between Danny's Buck and the peddler's Duke. She cocked her head and looked down the trail as far as she could see, her hair flopping across her shoulders from beneath her black kerchief.

Tugging at his red wig, Hannah replied with an amused smile, "That's John Swaney's bugle. He's the post rider. When he's traveling alone, Swaney blows it to let everybody know he's a government official so they'll get out of his way and let him alone." He, too, watched up ahead. "It's likely John will come barreling into sight soon."

Never having seen the highly regarded post rider, but aware of his heroic accomplishments in carrying mail between Nashville and Natchez in record time, Treasure and Danny exchanged pleased looks. Their youthful curiosity, along with the oxygen-charged air and its spring fragrances, brought sparkles to their eyes and huge smiles to their faces. Now that they had left all signs of civilization behind, they gave free rein to the hope that some kind of madcap adventure might be theirs.

Treasure rejoiced upon sensing a lightening of spirit, recognizing it as a true sign that she was feeling more like her old self. She had not felt so full of joy and expectancy since the night Fortner had held them captive in the cabin with his deep voice spinning tales about— She almost gasped at the unbidden memory and sent it back into hiding. The thought had raced to mind before she realized what was happening, and she tossed her curls in annoyance. Damn the man! She wasn't wasting any more time thinking of him. If she had to think of a man, she would choose Thornton Crabtree, Aunt Olivia's son near Natchez. From the plantation Merrivale, she added as her mother had always done.

"Does the post rider really make the journey in ten days, Hank?" Danny asked, his question rescuing Treasure from additional mental lashings.

"Most of the time, or so he tells. He stops at certain stands along the way and gets fresh horses, and he doesn't spend much time sleeping unless it's storming. He only visits when he has to stop for other reasons, so we'd better move into single file and give him plenty of room."

Down the Trace, a figure on a racing horse came into sight right after they formed a single line. Trying to take in the whole picture before John Swaney met and passed them, Treasure saw the tin trumpet flopping from a strap around the rider's neck. Resting against the galloping horse's withers and tied to the saddle horn was a ballooned leather pouch which she figured might hold corn for the horse. The stock of a rifle showed at the top of a saddle holster. Not until the postal rider came close enough to exchange greetings with Hank did she see the bulging saddlebags of oil-dressed deerskin emblazoned with a big seal that she felt sure belonged to the United States Government. She had heard that inside those bags were all kinds of newspapers, letters, and government dispatches.

"Wow!" This outcry came from the bug-eyed Danny after the squeaking, jangling noises of the rider and his swift-footed horse faded behind them. "I never figured on meeting the postal rider. I guess even the outlaws get out of his way."

Her sense of adventure deflating at the mention of outlaws, Treasure did not urge Vagabond forward again. Somehow, to ride behind and let her thoughts ramble seemed more appealing. She felt up to facing them now with the honesty and courage so natural to her before the encounter with Amos.

When she had gone downstairs that morning, she had been relieved to learn that the Thorpes had demanded an early breakfast and departed at the first light of day. Though she had not known who they were upon meeting them, she well recalled her awareness that they were different from any others she had ever met. She wondered now if it might not have been the air of evil about them that she had unknowingly sensed. Like the way a horse got fidgety when it smelled blood, she thought. There was no rhyme or reason for that action either, but it was a fact of nature she herself had observed. Her fervent wish was not to meet up with the Thorpes again.

Or Fortner and his fellow adventurer Bear-John, she added for good measure. She was more than ready to get on with new and better chapters in her life. Assuring herself that it had nothing to do with Fortner, she let herself imagine that Thornton Crabtree from Merrivale would be tall and good looking . . . and have pale blue eyes that crinkled when he smiled.

"David Fortner Copeland, I'd like you to meet Seth Willows," Hannah was saying about the time that Treasure, a half day's ride down the Trace, was thinking about the handsome adventurer and his half Indian friend.

Fortner stuck out his hand to shake that of the older man standing in the front room at McHenry's Stand. Hannah had made certain that the three were alone for the meeting of her brother-in-law and the man she planned to marry.

The men made the usual, offhand comments while sizing each other up, then Seth said, "I don't know if Hannah told you or not, but we're planning to marry next month." He sat on the chair Hannah indicated and watched Fortner bow to her wishes and sit on another close by.

"She told me all about it . . . and you and your place up on the Buffalo."

"I'm gonna be good to Hannah and the young'uns," Seth promised in a tone that Fortner could not doubt was sincere. "I've got a boy of my own, all growed up now and gone from home, but I fairly like having young'uns around. Especially when their mama is Hannah." His gray eyes slid over to the blushing young widow and lit up in the nicest kind of way.

"That's good to know," Fortner replied. He liked the man's manner of sitting straight and looking him squarely in the eyes. He was still trim and good looking, despite the extra years he held over Hannah, and it was easy for Fortner to see why a woman would find him attractive. Surely, he mused, if Seth Willows was as smart as his bright eyes hinted, he would know that as Hannah's only living adult relative, Fortner might appear at any time and look into the welfare of his dead brother's family. "I'm right sorry I'll not be around for the wedding next month, but I'll likely be stopping by your place every time I'm in this part of the country.''

"As her closest kin, you'll always find a welcome," Seth said with a smile. He seemed to have read Fortner's mind and obviously had no objections to the warm relationship between the in-laws. "Hannah's already told me how good you've been to them since her husband's death, and I appreciate it, too. Letting those stopping by the stand think that you have a claim on her has likely saved her much harassment.''

A mite embarrassed that Hannah had probably been praising him more than he deserved, Fortner managed no more than a mumbled, "Humph, well . . ." What could he say? He was merely doing what seemed natural.

By the time the three had visited enough to feel that they had cleared the way for the new relationship, it was the middle of the afternoon. Eager to get on his way now that the future of Hannah and the children seemed assured, Fortner went in search of Bear-John.

They bade all good-bye at the stand owned by Bear-John's uncle and aunt. Together Fortner and Bear-John had brought a bereft Hannah and her children to the stand more than two years ago. Together on that spring afternoon they waved farewell to a radiant bride-to-be, her children and her intended, then rode south on the Trace toward Natchez. They had plans to carry out, plans carefully set into motion the preceding fall.

"I usually camp here when I'm on this section of the Trace," Hank explained to the Ryans late on the second day out from McHenry's Stand.

The trail had descended gradually since mid-afternoon and no longer tracked atop mountain ridges. The area Hank indicated in a broad valley was only a few yards from the Trace and had a large, cleared area beneath a grove of hardwoods and pines. Several large, fire-blackened rocks showed that it was a popular site with travelers seeking a rest stop.

"This place looks better than the one we stopped at last

night, Hank. The branch looks like it might be full of fish," Danny said, already dismounted and leading Buck to drink from the water rushing down its rocky bed from the surrounding hills. "I think I'll give it a try after I tend the horses and tether them for the night."

Giving in to a yawn of weariness, Treasure watched her brother lead the other horses down to the branch and remove their saddles and gear. She then went about performing the tasks of getting ready to cook the evening meal. Hank stretched his rotund figure out on a grassy spot, taking the saddle Danny brought and using it for a pillow. Apparently Danny and she had done their jobs well enough the night before, for the old peddler was leaving everything up to them tonight, she mused with satisfaction. She was determined that Danny and she would earn their keep.

"Will we be seeing more cabins tomorrow?" Treasure asked, her resolution not to think about the yesterdays strengthening with each passing mile and hour. Her throat had not pained her all day, and when she peered in the little round pocket mirror Hank had given her, she could see only faint signs of the bruises from Amos' hands.

"Yeah, I'll have a couple of stops to make, so we might not make it to Colbert's Ferry for a day or two," Hank replied before he closed his eyes and dozed.

Watching Danny through the trees as he cut a long stalk of cane and rigged up a fishing pole, Treasure let the peacefulness of the campsite claim her. Everything was going to work out all right, she told herself while collecting fallen limbs for the campfire. Hank was kind and did not travel at a grueling pace. The two calls they had made with him that day down small paths to crude cabins had been pleasant experiences. That he seemed to know the Trace so well kept Danny and her from thinking about how they had left everything familiar behind. If Blackie was meant to die and leave them alone, she doubted they could've been in better hands.

The women at the second cabin Hank had called on that day had given him a haunch of fresh venison in payment for a length of calico and a spool of thread. Treasure rigged up a spit over the campfire and let the meat cook while Danny fished and Hank snored.

It was difficult to keep from dwelling on all the bad things that had happened, Treasure confessed, but she was beginning to feel more cheerful and find some good parts in her present situation. She pushed down the thought that she was wanted by the law for killing a man and replaced it with one of thanks to the Lord that she was free and was getting Danny closer to Natchez with each passing hour. After all, she kept telling herself, it had been Amos' life or hers.

After the tasty supper of smoked venison, all three confessed to being weary and made ready for the night. No sooner had Treasure and Danny wrapped up in their blankets near the smoldering campfire and invited sleep than the sounds of galloping hooves could be heard coming up the Trace. She popped up her head, relieved to see that Hank still sat on the far side of the fire. As Danny made no move, she assumed he was already asleep, dead to all sounds not involving his name.

"What's going on?" Treasure asked the old peddler, her hand fingering first her knife in its holster and then the rifle tucked underneath her bla ket.

"Guess we're fixing to have company."

"You don't seem concerned."

"Too late for that, I reckon." As if to reassure her, Hank reached for his rifle and stood.

"Ho, there! There's two of us needin' a spot by a campfire for the night," came a voice from the approaching horses, slowed now to a fast walk.

Goosebumps marched up and down Treasure's spine. The voice sounded like George Henry Thorpe's. She felt for the trigger on her rifle. Even the nearby tree frogs hushed their monotonous songs and seemed to be listening.

The horses stopped when Hank sat back down and called, "Get down. There's plenty of space."

What was wrong with Hank? Why didn't he tell them that they didn't want company? Wishing she had left on her scarf or else donned her coonskin hat to hide her hair, braided in a loose rope for sleeping, Treasure agonized as to whether she should remain covered and still or else sit up and brandish her weapons. She lay still, her rifle cradled beside her.

"Well, danged if'n it ain't the peddler and his two little partners. Howdy, Hank. We's done et, but we're shore ready to get outta these here saddles."

George Henry barely had the words out before he was standing on the ground, joined almost immediately by Juno. Treasure squinted her eyes almost closed when she saw them glance toward where Danny and she lay side by side in their blankets. Maybe they would think both of them were asleep, she prayed.

"I was hopin' to get to see the purty gal with the gold hair," George Henry said. He stripped his horse of saddle and blanket before handing the reins to Juno. Without being told, the younger brother led the animals down to the branch where the other horses were tethered and beginning to whicker and stamp their feet. "Don't tell me she's already sleepin'."

"As a matter of fact," Hank replied from where he still sat near his own blanket and saddle, "they both went to sleep some time ago."

Aware that Hank was lying to protect her, Treasure sighed with relief until she heard boot steps on the rocky ground coming close.

"I wanna see her."

It was George Henry standing over her, Treasure realized, her eyes closed tightly now. She recognized his voice, but also she could smell him.

"You'll see her in the morning," Hank said, his normally soft voice sounding hard as a rock.

"Says who?" sneered George Henry, swiveling around to stare at the old man.

Treasure heard his boots hit sharply against the rocks as he stomped back toward Hank. Her heart was beating so fast that she wondered if it might not take flight.

"*I* say so," came Hank's steely answer.

Breathing a silent sigh of relief, Treasure prayed that the old man would continue to speak so forcefully. Would he be able to fend off such ruffians if . . . Unnamed fears made her weak all over.

Apparently back from tethering the horses, Juno spoke then with undisguised disgust. "Blood and tobacco, George Henry! Let's get some sleep. The others will prob'ly be a'comin' from up the Trace in the night and a'wakin' us up. Hank's right. Tomorrow's soon enough to get another look at the gal."

The terrified young woman heard no more mention of her, only low, indecipherable words and grunts as the men apparently spread out their blankets and removed their boots. She peered up through the trees at the sky, noticing that a half moon was rising over a distant ridge. Her hand still resting on her gun, she did not fall asleep until long after she heard snores mixing with the sounds of the night callers.

Too exhausted to do more than register the sounds of horse hooves upon the rocky soil of the campsite sometime in the night, Treasure slumbered fitfully until first light. Somebody was adding fuel to last night's coals. She could hear small tree limbs being snapped, then the trunks of larger ones being dropped in place. The pungent smell of wood smoke teased and tickled her nostrils. She stirred, knowing that she must soon leave the warmth of her blanket and cook breakfast.

Men's voices broke through her semi-conscious state, and she remembered with distaste. The Thorpes had ridden in before she went to sleep and had mentioned that they expected someone to join them. Vaguely she recalled having heard horses coming late in the night. If she knew Hank as well as she thought she did, he would expect her to cook for everybody—but could the old peddler continue to control the Thorpes now that some other members of their gang had apparently arrived? Bemoaning the ill fortune that had brought the highwaymen to their campsite, Treasure sat up and searched in her saddlebags beside her bedroll for her coat and something to cover her tousled braid.

Her raccoon-lined coat a welcome barrier against the morning chill, Treasure had just tucked her hair beneath her coonskin hat when she heard footsteps coming near.

"Would you like me to bring over a burned stick so you can smear your face with soot?" a low voice asked, amusement plumping out each word.

She jerked around, not believing her ears. Pale blue eyes were laughing down into her startled brown ones. Her ears had not tricked her. It was, indeed, Fortner.

Smarting from his gibe about the soot smeared on her face when they had first met, Treasure demanded in a throaty morning voice, "What are you doing here? Are you with . . . them?" Her hand flicked disapprovingly toward the Thorpe brothers across the smoking campfire where they were going through the motions of stretching and waking up in the predawn light. Fortner made no denial. She went on lowly, her words fraught with mingling emotions, "I thought you told me back at the cabin that you were an adventurer. I didn't know that was a fancy name for highwayman."

Fortner's countenance revealed a trace of pain at her first scornful questions, but by the time she finished her brief diatribe, his handsome face wore that same devil-may-care smile that Treasure remembered all too well.

Why in thunder, she agonized, did he have to show up just when she was beginning to get the ordeal with Amos Greeson sorted out in her mind? And he was turning out to be a highwayman at that! Her insides felt shivery, and she pulled her coat closer. It didn't help the internal churning at all.

"Lots of things seem to have changed since we were at your place, if you want to know what I think," Fortner told her, his gaze sweeping her flushed face and tousled braid. He was glad to see that whatever had dulled her golden eyes back at the stand seemed no more than mysterious, deep-seated shadows now.

Rising, Treasure huffed and tried to wound him with a

look loaded with venom. "I don't want to know what you think. I don't even want answers to my questions. Please go away."

Aware that behind her Danny was awakening and greeting Fortner cheerily, Treasure stalked off toward the branch. She didn't like anything about the new situation. How was she going to explain to the boy how Fortner, the man he so admired, happened to come to the campsite in the night without also telling the boy about the Thorpe Brothers' gang and Fortner's connection with it? Getting breakfast for a hungry bunch of men was her prime concern, she assured herself, not trying to figure out one conceited, two-faced rascal who was as apt to lie to a woman as look at her.

And Fortner did do more than his share of looking, the agitated young woman reflected while splashing cold water upon her face. She had never before met anyone who seemed so determined to see clear inside her soul. Did he think he had some special claim on her because she had kissed him back? Her cheeks flamed, despite the icy drops of water still clinging there. Whether or not she relished the idea, she was going to have to tell Danny that Fortner was an outlaw and not at all the man they had believed him to be. Never would she fall prey to his devious charms again!

Thanks to the peddler keeping the talk during breakfast to the weather, the Trace, and the travelers they had met and passed, none of the men bothered Treasure with more than a few sidelong appraisals while she prepared the simple meal. In an obvious attempt to be friendly and helpful, Bear-John offered to pour coffee from the big pot sitting on a flat rock in the edge of the coals. Without a glance around or a touch of grace, she ladled up mush laced with strips of leftover venison onto the proffered tin plates with resounding plops. She then squelched Bear-John with a flinty glare and filled the cups herself. He was Fortner's friend, not hers.

"I'll help you get things cleaned up and packed away in Hank's gear," Danny told her when all the plates were emptied and the men were sipping the last of the coffee out of their own cups from their individual saddlebags.

Gratefully, Treasure accepted the boy's offer and they went down to the rock-bedded branch.

"Why are you so mad at Fortner?" Danny asked, not liking the way his sister's full lips formed a straight, tight line and took on the look that Walking Bear and he had secretly referred to as her mad mouth. Even though the sun had come out enough to warm things a little and cause her to shed her coat, she still wore the old hat pulled over her hair. He watched her scoop up a handful of coarse sand from beneath the rocks in the branch bed and scrub the last tin plate with it. As with the others, she then dipped the plate into the clear, rushing stream and brought it up clean.

"I'm not exactly mad at Fortner," she denied. "Just disappointed, I guess." Sure. That was it. She was merely disappointed that Fortner had deceived Danny and her in a new way. First the mistress. Now . . .

"I think it's a wild colt that he showed up!" Danny declared, his boyish way of elevating an ordinary pleasure into one of keen proportions bringing an indulgent smile to his sister's troubled face. "Who would've thought we'd ever see him again that day he rode off from our place? Then there he was at McHenry's Stand, and now he's here. Do you think Bear-John and him might ride along with us?"

"*He*, not *him*," she corrected before replying to his eager question. "Not likely." Treasure hesitated, wondering how long she could count on keeping the truth from Danny. After all, he was unusually bright and might have already gleaned more from conversation than she realized. She herself hated being deceived, and she did not like holding things back from the boy.

Like the business with Amos Greeson? a devious part of her brain asked without warning. *No!* That was not something she should share with a youngster. But the business of the Thorpe gang was different. What god-awful luck. If only the men had not shown up.

"You see," Treasure explained in her low-pitched voice,

"the Thorpes are two of the three brothers who've been robbing up and down the Trace over the past several years. Fortner and Bear-John—well, I . . ."

Danny added what she could not. "Fortner and Bear-John are part of their gang. They're highwaymen, too. Is that it?"

She looked into her brother's dark eyes, appalled upon reading nothing there but acceptance—and maybe even a touch of admiration. She knew it was her duty to lead the boy to view Fortner in a truer light.

"Danny, you know it's against the law to take from others," Treasure said in a stern tone. "Those men might be killers, too, for all we know. I wouldn't have told you if I hadn't known you thought Fortner was a respectable man. Not everybody is what he seems, and he's one who isn't. You need to learn that, and now is as good a time as any. We don't want to be in the company of such people when we can avoid it."

"Cripes!" Danny exclaimed, using the only word bordering on cursing that she would permit. He held Hank's tarp bag open so she could stack the clean dishes, implements, and cooking pot inside. "I like Fortner. He makes me laugh. You're being mighty hard on him when you don't even know his side, aren't you?" She sent him her don't-get-smart-with-me look, but he wasn't ready to let the matter drop. "Isn't that what you always tell me when I jump to seclusions?"

"*Con*clusions," Treasure corrected automatically before going on. Down the stream, she saw Juno and Bear-John lead the gang's horses up the bank to the campsite. If she kept tarrying, maybe the men would leave and both Danny and she would be spared another sight of the unsettling Fortner. "There's no 'side' a decent person can take if he becomes an outlaw, because there's no excuse for making such a choice." She rose and fixed a stern eye on him. "Not a word about this to anyone, not even Hank. I don't know why he puts up with them, but he does, so I reckon he has to."

Hank called down for Danny to get their horses ready

for the day on the trail. Treasure watched him stalk away carrying the tarp bag, pained at his apparent disappointment upon learning that Fortner should no longer be considered an honorable man. *You're not alone, brother dear,* she told the retreating figure silently. Something like a fist squeezed her heart for a second. She must have eaten her breakfast too fast, she reasoned.

Treasure lingered by the branch long enough for the outlaws to mount. From where she stood behind a canebrake combing out her hair and peeking toward the campsite at intervals, she saw the men send searching glances her way before reining onto the Trace and moving south. Seeing that Fortner rode alongside George Henry in front of the others did nothing to lighten the heavy feeling that still lingered around her heart. She made a note to eat the next meal more slowly.

"Why would a man like Fortner—and Bear-John, too—run with a wild pair like the Thorpes?" Treasure asked Hank as they got on their way a while after the highwaymen left. Her insides still were not settled, she realized. "They're probably going to meet violent deaths just like their brother and father did. I don't know why they would choose such a life, do you?"

His eyes studying her face from where he rode Duke alongside her, Hank replied soberly, "I wouldn't be knowing the right answers, not having met Fortner and Bear-John until nearly the end of last summer. What makes you think those two are any different than the others, and why do you care what happens to them? I thought you'd met Fortner only once before he came to McHenry's."

"That's right. I had met him only that time back at the cabin when I replaced a shoe his horse lost. Actually I don't care what happens to Fortner or his friend. It's just that I had figured he was a decent sort."

The way Fortner had sat in the cabin and laughed and told tales to the boys and her flashed to Treasure's mind. At the time something about him had reminded her of her father. She recalled how several men had said at Blackie's funeral that they had never heard anyone deny that Blackie

Ryan was a fun loving, good man at heart, out to bring harm to no one. Could the same be said about Fortner?

"And don't you think he's decent now?" Hank asked.

"Why, no, Hank." Treasure shot him an indignant look. Her lips set somewhat primly, she added, "A highwayman isn't a decent sort. Surely you don't think those ruffians are like other people."

They rode a while in silence before the old man made a response. "You tend to form opinions mighty fast, girl. I wonder how you'd take it if folks was to do the same about you." He fingered the back of his wig and gave it a good yank.

Treasure sucked in her breath and stared at his profile. Was Hank referring to her stabbing Amos Greeson and then sneaking off with him before reporting what happened to the sheriff? Before she could collect her wits and reply, Danny spoke up from behind them.

"That's what I told her, Hank. Probably there's a good reason why Fortner and Bear-John joined up with the Thorpes."

"What do you suppose it could be?" Hank turned and asked.

"I don't know, but I got a feeling it doesn't take away from what Fortner seemed to be the first time I saw him," Danny replied with ringing conviction. "I still think he's a nice man and not a natural born outlaw like the Thorpes."

"Yeah," Hank said in a serious, musing voice. "I got a feeling you're right."

A fast traveling group of horsemen came up behind them then, forcing them to end conversation and ride in single file. There were ten men in the party, and all sneaked admiring looks at the pretty young woman on the handsome gelding as they rode on by. She was too engrossed in cogitation to notice.

Chapter Eight

The campsite Hank chose late that afternoon was a lot like the one they had stopped at the night before. Instead of a branch to supply water, there was a high-banked creek of brown water.

Both Treasure and Danny had become accustomed to the routine of getting set up for the night and went about their chores with alacrity. They shared their excitement over being one day nearer Natchez.

About an hour after dark, when supper was over and everything was cleaned and put away, shots echoed from down the Trace. Danny, having pulled out his Jew's harp earlier and played a hill ballad, sent a questioning look toward his sister.

"Wonder what's going on?" Treasure asked Hank, who was returning from the creek. She had gone earlier to the stream and gotten ready for the night, as had Danny shortly afterward.

"Can't tell. Maybe somebody ran into a rattler," Hank commented as he sat down and leaned against a tree near the campfire.

"Then he must have missed a lot, 'cause I heard several shots," Danny joked. He returned the Jew's harp to his lips and, to the obvious pleasure of Treasure and Hank, brought up his forefinger to the stiff wire and twanged a pert dance tune. When the last note quivered away, he lowered the small instrument and cocked his head to listen, announcing in a voice crackling with excitement, "Uh-oh, I hear horses coming fast."

Treasure's fears came true when the horsemen turned out to be the same four men who had shared their camp the preceding night. Wondering if the overheard shots meant that some poor soul not only had been robbed, but also had been killed, she glared at them while they made themselves at home.

Already in her blanket when the Thorpes barged in on them the night before, and down by the branch when they left that morning, Treasure had never before seen the brothers' hats up close. Both men, she noted, wore black ones with tall, uncrushed crowns. Her mind whirling, she found herself recalling the one found in the shed after Blackie was killed. She knew that men sometimes replaced a favorite hat with new ones identical to those discarded or lost.

A quick but thorough look told her that no red feather lay tucked inside a snakeskin band. Even so, she reminded herself, such ruffians could have easily been her father's murderers. She had a yen to ask what kind of hat their recently deceased brother wore. She glanced at Bear-John; his hat was a light tan that called attention to his Chickasaw coloring. Forcing herself to include Fortner as a suspect, she saw again his brown hat and remembered how at her first sight of him she had believed him to be a comfortable study in browns. Ha! A pox on her first impressions.

The way some of the outlaws, laughing and talking all the while, checked and reloaded their pistols before jamming them in their holsters convinced Treasure that, indeed, they had been the ones who created the earlier commotion down the Trace. How was it that the men happened to find them again when Hank and his party had traveled behind them all day? If only Danny and she had already slipped into their blankets.

Obviously keyed up, George Henry prowled about the cleared area and barked unnecessary orders. Then, ignoring the others, he pulled a bottle from his saddlebags and plopped down onto the ground near where Treasure was sitting. Down at one end of the campfire, Hank lounged, his back propped against a broad red cedar.

"Your health, Miss Treasure," George Henry said before taking a deep swig. He wiped his sleeve across his mouth and smiled, revealing the unsightly gaps in his front teeth. "I tried to git here earlier tonight so's I could see you." When she made no reply and kept her gaze on the blazing fire, he drank again and added, "I aim to take me on a woman like you. My ma's allers tellin' me I oughter git married."

Treasure flinched. Aware that the other three outlaws were returning from the creek and settling onto the ground around the campfire, she wondered what Fortner must be thinking. She had purposefully kept from looking directly at him after her quick survey of hats, but half glances had told her that he was sitting down beside Juno directly across from George Henry and her.

Danny could pretend all he wanted to that he was concentrating on whittling a cedar limb behind her in the shadows, but Treasure knew he was tuned in to every word. She was relieved that her rifle was over with their saddles, for Danny might think he should grab it and protect her. There had been so little money for ammunition over the past few years that she had never taught him how to shoot.

"Talk, damn you, woman!" George Henry bellowed. "Didn't you hear what I said?"

"George—" Hank began, only to be cut off by the apparent leader of the Thorpe Brothers' gang.

"Stay out of this, Hank," George Henry ordered. "'Taint your business."

Feeling sorry for the kindly old man, who likely knew as well as she that he could not sway George Henry, or any man, when he was drinking, Treasure gave in to the waves of anger and indignation washing over her. "I heard what you said, and I didn't like it well enough to find an answer."

"Oh, you didn't like it, huh? You soun' like you think you's too good for the likes of me," sneered George Henry. He laughed mirthlessly and tipped up his bottle, then held it out toward her after he drank. "Try a little of this whiskey an' see if'n you might not change your mind 'bout what you like."

"Leave her alone!" Hank demanded with more force

than Treasure had ever heard him use. "You're drinking and you've got no business pestering her."

George Henry sniggered and sent baleful looks at the old peddler resting against the tree trunk. "I ain't drunk . . . yet. Juno might think he's the only Thorpe with ways to charm the gals, but I'll show you I ain't no slouch myself. And besides, how you gonna stop me from doin' whatever I damn well please?"

From where he sprawled on the ground alongside Fortner, Juno said, "Hank's right. You been a'hittin' that bottle purty good ever since Felsenthal got killed. Leave the gal be."

"Nobody's a'tellin' me what I can't do when I set my mind to it," George Henry bragged. "Not even Whitey." He shot daring looks to where Bear-John and Hank sat together at the end of the campfire and then toward Fortner and Juno directly across the way. When nobody made a comment, he returned his attention to the young woman by his side. "You ain't got big Burr McHenry and his 'breeds a'takin' up for you tonight."

"I don't need anybody taking up for me tonight," Treasure snapped, upping her chin and tucking the front strands of her unbound hair behind her ears. When she brought her arms down, an elbow brushed against the knife in her holster and lent her confidence. Since leaving McHenry's three days ago she had recaptured some of her old bravado and had no intention of running from a confrontation with George Henry any longer. She sensed it was inevitable; he was the stalker, she the prey.

Behind Treasure, the sound of Danny's whittling died. She could feel Fortner's silvery gaze upon her face far more than she could feel those of the others. A sideways glance from underneath her lowered lashes told her that he was not amused. A further sweep of her gaze around the loose semicircle gathered near the campfire showed that Hank and Bear-John were also not enjoying George Henry's determination to shower her with attention.

George Henry threw back his head and laughed, the movement showing the repulsive inside of his mouth. Twisting to face her more squarely then, he taunted, "If'n you don't need nobody a'takin' up fer you, I s'ppose you gonna give me a kiss. Then we can let ever'body know you's my woman from now on.''

"Not on your life. I'm nobody's woman, and I don't plan to be anytime soon—especially not yours," she declared haughtily. Hearing Danny's indrawn breath, she turned her head and asked over her shoulder, "Don't you expect it's time we crawled into our blankets and got some sleep, Danny?"

The boy mumbled acquiescence, his dark eyes wide and frightened.

"I shore like a woman with spirit. I do fer a fact," George Henry announced to everybody, a foolish leer upon his bearded face while he looked from one to the other. Apparently encouraged by the silence of the men, he leaned over and grabbed Treasure with the speed of lightning, managing to seize her by her left arm and yank her toward him there on the ground.

Before George Henry could bring his mouth to hers, Treasure had whipped her knife free and slashed his arm. Howling from the unexpected pain, he slapped her wrist hard enough to make her lose her grip. The knife fell with a clatter upon the rocky soil. Next he slapped her face, then twisted her arm behind her back. The action jerked her upper body forward against his. The pain shot too deeply for her to do more than lay against him without further protest. Up close he smelled even more like a polecat. Her skin crawled in sympathy with her squeamish insides.

"So," he snarled with animal-like pleasure, "you like to fight first."

"George Henry—" Hank called, his face a scowl.

"George Henry—" Fortner protested at the same instant.

"Shut up!" the angered outlaw shouted. He glimpsed movement across the campfire and behind him. In steely tones he ordered, "I'll handle this. Set back down, all a you. I hear you movin' behind me, Danny, and if'n you don't put up your knife and set your ass down over here where I can watch you, your sister's gonna be in even worse trouble." He paused until the boy returned his knife to its holster and sank back onto the ground. Cackling the laugh of one appreciative of his own feeble wit, he bragged, "This here's my business, 'lessen somebody's dumb 'nough to make it his'n, too. I aim to have a kiss from this here purty gal an' take her to my blanket."

With his hand still pinioning her arm cruelly against her back, Treasure secretly readied her missile and waited until the lowering, repulsive face came nearer. She spat then, glad to see that the spittle landed in the corner of a beady eye and nettled him in a new way.

"You Ryan bitch!" he snarled. "God amighty! I'll get you—"

Seeing her chance when George Henry loosened his hold for a second from shocked anger and blurred sight, Treasure raked his cheek with her nails, not surprised when he added yowls of pain to his string of curses. Flesh rolled up underneath the tips of her nails. Before he could fully recover from her last attack and before anyone across from them could guess what she had in mind, she had snatched his pistol from its holster and scooted a body's length away. A scared crawfish couldn't have shot backward in shallow water any faster. Her hastily drawn up knees served as a steadying place for the heavy weapon as she aimed it at her attacker.

"Get right behind me, Danny," Treasure called softly, wishing she had some way to steady her runaway heartbeat. As soon as she felt his hand touch her back, she called to the men shuffling around on the other side of the campfire, "I can't shoot you all, but I know one who'll get it between the eyes if anybody tries to get Danny or me. Think long and hard, or you'll see George Henry Thorpe with a hole in his head."

"You'd not know how to shoot even if'n that gun was loaded," George Henry drawled, his eyes beady and glued on the weapon. Not since she aimed the pistol at him had he moved.

"I saw you load it after you came into camp," Treasure informed him in a low, emotionless voice while cocking the pistol with a steady but damp thumb. Her palms had become downright wet, she noted. Inside she was no more than warm, screaming mush, but her voice did not fail her. "And don't bet on my not knowing how to use it."

Fortner's voice rose above the din of the others, deep and commanding. Crazy thoughts were pouring through his mind. He had a damned good idea that Treasure not only could shoot but would if pressured much farther. "Treasure, you don't want to pull that trigger. You and Danny back away from him and let me come get the gun. You're a nice young woman, and you don't want a man's blood on your hands. He'll not bother you any more—will you, George Henry?"

"Shut up, Fortner!" George Henry replied, his bulging forehead beginning to sweat, though the night air was chilly. "This ain't your business. What in hell do you know 'bout her? I can tell you this bitch ain't what you might be a'thinkin'. She's a killer. She done knifed a man up near Rocky Bluffs an' the sheriff is a'lookin' for her right now. An' no wonder. Her pa was that no good, cheatin' Blackie Ryan."

"Hush up about Blackie," warned Treasure, still holding the pistol aimed at George Henry's face, "or you'll get it right now." The dampness of her hands increased, and the gun felt icy cold.

Why did he mention Blackie? she wondered shakily. Had he known him? Everything was happening so fast. Adrenaline was racing through her veins, and she was once more back at the farm where her words and weapons were respected. She admitted she was even more frightened now than when Amos had attacked her because there was more involved here than her own life. Behind her, she could feel Danny tensed up against her. God! Was she going to have to kill again, to protect both of them this time? She figured that once she shot George Henry, bullets would rain upon both Danny and her. A searing lump lodged in her throat, and her heartbeat roared in her ears. Like her thoughts, the silence around the campfire was punishing.

If Fortner thought she was such a nice young woman,

Treasure wondered in spurts of delayed anger, why in hell hadn't he spoken up before now? Nothing made sense but that she was in control—for the moment. She didn't fool herself into believing that she could truly hold the four outlaws at bay and escape without harm to Danny and her, even if Hank could manage to help her somehow. She might as well be on a runaway horse that was holding the bit between its teeth. What choice did she have but to hang on until something slowed its pace? If she could come up with a way to save Danny . . . Natchez and their mother's people seemed a million miles away, and she almost despaired.

Oh, Lord! Treasure agonized in those seconds stacking up like an eternity. *What next?* The sudden blaze of a shifting log in the campfire gave her a clearer view of the motionless man glaring at her with smoldering hatred. She did not shrink, merely returned a steady, baleful look of her own. No human sounds broke the awful silence except for the heavy breathing coming from the bug-eyed George Henry. In a detached way she noted that blood from the cheek where she had scratched him still ran into his dark beard.

Fortner, no less than the others, had not believed the speed with which the flapping of a fool's loose tongue had become a violent life-or-death struggle right before their eyes. Who could have guessed that Treasure might prove to be so quick and strong . . . or so devious? He scoffed silently at what George Henry spouted about her having killed somebody, but it would have made no difference if he believed him. He had no desire to see the beautiful young woman pull that trigger and end up dead herself. His throat tightened.

Without even trying, Fortner could recall in an instant the first time he had seen Treasure behind a rifle barrel and how her eyes had raked and threatened him, like those of a cornered wildcat. Not that he had a personal stake in the matter, he assured himself, but Treasure Ryan had too much of the wilderness born and bred in her to end up defeated by the likes of the Thorpes. Whatever had her beaten down back at McHenry's Stand no longer controlled her. He had always admired spunk, wherever it cropped up, and that seemed reason enough to step in. That there might be a cause touching closer to the bone seemed too farfetched to consider.

The raw pleading in Danny's eyes reached across the campfire and almost did Fortner in as his thoughts careened. Already Juno had eased his pistol free from its holster and was aiming it at the grim-faced young woman with the golden curls streaming down her back. The second shot from Juno, if the first one didn't fell both of the Ryans, would be at her brother. With the speed and force of lightning, Fortner's mind dug and delved for a plan.

"I've got an idea," he said, breaking the silence and looking all around. His hands had become fists.

Fortner did not know how much longer Juno would remain beside him as a crouched bystander with his gun in his hand. Bear-John was tensed near the bug-eyed Hank in the center of the semicircle; both of them seemed stunned and helpless. Though Treasure did not break her stare at the man in front of her or lower her aim, he could tell she was listening. In a sudden blaze of firelight he could see a kind of vulnerable look creep around her pursed lips, but her determinedly set profile never wavered.

Fortner went on. "To keep anybody from getting killed here tonight, I'll take George Henry up on his offer for somebody else to make this his business. We'll make it a fist fight. Fair, with no weapons. What about it, George Henry? I'm making it my business what goes on between you and Treasure."

George Henry swallowed hard and scowled. "Good God amighty! How many women does it take for you? You're a stupid Injun lover, Fortner, but I ain't got no quarrel with you. This ain't none of your business. Keep it that'a way."

"Yeah, but I've got a quarrel with you," Fortner replied, thinking how the words had been true nigh on three years now. From the corner of his eye he saw Bear-John's neck stiffen in warning. "And I just made this my business. No matter the outcome of the fight, at least the little boy goes on traveling with Hank to his grandpa's place. Agreed?''

George Henry seemed to be turning over his options in his mind, but he moved only his eyes toward Fortner. "Suits me. I ain't got no hankerin' for the boy. Come to think of it, we can make the gran'pa pay to get the boy an' gal delivered to him. How 'bout that?''

"We'll get the law down on us hard and quick if we ask for ransom," Fortner said. "Let's deal with that later on. Right now I'm trying to get the matter with the girl settled.''

George Henry did not take long in making up his mind. "Awright. We'll talk about ransom later. Come hell or high water, though, the winner gets the gal till we gets to Natchez." His gaze swinging back to Treasure, he added, "But what if'n the wildcat don't go along? She's the one with the gun leveled at me.''

Treasure heard the exchanges with more than her ears. Here was a way Danny would not end up paying the price of her rashness in striking out against the outlaw. There was no telling what would be her fate, but neither Danny nor she had a lot to look forward to at the moment. If the fight was to determine where and with whom she slept during the next few weeks, so be it. She was the one who had set the bizarre scene into motion, and perhaps some kind of future might be possible now. From what George Henry had said, word must be out that she had killed Amos, and she likely would be taken back soon to the jail at Rocky Bluffs. So long as Danny kept moving southwest toward their grandfather . . .

"Hank," Treasure called, still keeping her eyes on George Henry. "Will you promise me that you'll take Danny to Lindwood, no matter what?" Surely, she agonized, if the gang decided to demand money their grandfather would pay it to have Danny and her brought to him. That they would be worth money to the gang might be the only guarantee they wouldn't be killed.

"You have my word, Treasure," came the whispery

voice, a bit higher than usual. "The fight seems the fairest way to get this mess settled without somebody getting killed."

"Who do you want to hand the pistol to, Treasure?" Fortner asked now that she seemed amenable to the plan. He had counted on her seeing that his way secured Danny's safety.

Later, Treasure would wonder if her life—the lives of everyone there that night—might not have taken a different turn had she named Hank or Fortner to come for the pistol. For some strange reason a steely part of her brain sidetracked the old peddler, her first mental choice. She sensed that to name Fortner was wrong, too.

"Bear-John," she heard herself say in a strong voice. Danny right behind her tried to whisper Hank's name and get her to change her mind, but she repeated, even louder, "Bear-John. Let him come take the gun."

His face as inscrutable as during the entire happening, Bear-John rose and, careful not to get between Treasure and the man she held at bay, circled around George Henry to where she sat on the ground. She continued to stare at George Henry as she dropped the pistol into Bear-John's outstretched hand. With a quick movement he scooped up her knife where it had fallen. Danny's arms went around her then, and she dropped her eyes and turned to hug him close.

Within minutes the obviously humiliated leader of the gang was on the other side of the campfire, angrily stripping off his shirt and flexing huge, muscular arms. He kept muttering obscenities all the while. Juno had moved over to him, pumping him up with crude remarks about how his brawn and experience would overpower the taller but far leaner Fortner.

"Here's the best place, where it's free of underbrush and big rocks," Bear-John declared, motioning to a spot away from the fire.

As soon as he had claimed the weapons, Bear-John had tucked the knife and extra pistol in the waistband of his breeches and hurried to where Fortner stood. With his usual air of calm, he watched his friend remove his shirt and wished he knew the names of the Chickasaw gods revered by his mother's people. If Bear-John had ever felt like praying, it was now. For some reason he feared his father's God might not be powerful enough to be the only one petitioned for help. Of the four Copeland sons he had known back on the Cumberland, Fortner had been the least inclined to brawl—and therefore the poorest fighter when they were growing up.

"We agreed this was to be a fair fight and only between the two of us," Fortner reminded George Henry when they eyed each other as adversaries in the reflected firelight. The memory of the man slapping Treasure infuriated him. "None of your devil's claws."

"I ain't gonna be a'needin' no help or no devil's claws to whup you fair 'n square, Fortner. That she-cat of a woman'll be warmin' my blankets a'fore this night is over, 'cause I'm a'gonna lay you out cold."

"One of us might be out cold before it's over, but I'm betting it'll be you," Fortner promised in a deadly voice.

Treasure heard the remarks about the devil's claws and suffered a mental picture of those left hanging back in the smithy's shed. As when George Henry mentioned Blackie, half formed memories of finding Blackie's body that cold January morning circled at the back of her mind. Was it because of the cloud of evil she sensed hovering about the Thorpes each time she was around them, the same kind of evil that must have permeated the shed during her father's brutal murder? She glanced at Danny sitting beside her and tried to swallow the knot in her throat. It didn't budge.

Along with the other bystanders, Treasure cast aside all thoughts outside the fight when George Henry, shorter but with heavily muscled arms and chest, bellowed and rushed at his opponent with his head lowered. The surprise missile landing in his belly brought a loud gasp from Fortner. He staggered backward, trying to catch his breath while dodging meaty fists cuffing him solidly about the head. Once he recovered enough air to push way and dance out of reach, he feinted and studied the bearded man with new regard as they moved in a rough circle, arms lifted and fists at the ready. What he saw as a fair fist fight obviously differed from what George Henry agreed to, Fortner reflected. Excitement heated his blood.

The winter that Fortner had spent trapping among the brawling frontiersmen in the wilds of Kentucky had taught him more than he had wanted to learn about the ways men could do each other in without any weapons other than their bodies. After first serving an apprenticeship as an unwilling punching bag, Fortner had moved up into the realm of habitual winner. He would have laughed had he known what Bear-John was thinking, for he could now stomp, punch, bite, and kick right along with the lowest. He always let his opponent set the pace.

George Henry grinned. "We's supposed to be fightin', not dancin' around—"

Fortner sent a quick jab to George Henry's jaw, cutting off his taunt and causing his teeth to close upon his tongue. Howling from the pain, blood streaming down his chin, the maddened outlaw lunged for his younger opponent. He hooked a meaty arm around Fortner's neck, then rained blows upon his ribcage and flat belly and kicked at his legs. Meanwhile, Fortner strained to free his neck and send another blow to the shorter man's chin, able at last to land one resounding lick against a temple.

The fighters backed off then, circling and breathing hard. His arms being considerably longer than George Henry's, Fortner feinted successfully and landed a few jabs on the man's thick chest. Grinning now despite his bleeding tongue, the leader of the gang seemed not to feel the licks.

Without warning, George Henry's fist shot an uppercut to the younger man's chin, jolting him and sending him into a weak-kneed backstep. A spark of victory leaping from his eyes, George Henry followed that timely lick with double fisted, sidearm blows to the staggering Fortner's head, first on one side, then the other. While his head reeled and his ears rang, Fortner grabbed George Henry in a restraining bear hug, a necessary ploy to remain on his feet with help from his opponent. Shortly they stumbled and fell to the ground, grunting and breathing rapidly.

When George Henry used both arms and fists like a board to slap Fortner's head so brutally, Treasure and Danny were aghast. They had seen few brawls between adults, and never one like this, where there seemed to be an invisible aura of deep-rooted hate and evil. Though she felt guilty for being the reason for the fight, Treasure entertained the wild thought that the brutal struggle might not have anything to do with her at all.

Still on the other side of the campfire, brother and sister rose to their feet and watched with a kind of horrified fascination as the men continued to roll and kick and struggle for mastery on the rocky soil. Treasure guessed George Henry's frequent use of a jackknifing leg was meant to plant telling blows on Fortner's groin. The knot in her throat was fast becoming the forerunner of nausea. Judging from the sounds of flesh hitting flesh and occasional groans and growls, she guessed both men must be meting out equal punishment.

"'At's right, big brother. Git 'im in the balls!" she heard Juno yell in gleeful tones. Throughout he had urged George Henry on with such off-color remarks. "He won't be no peacock then."

Suddenly, George Henry rolled away and jumped to his feet, kicking viciously at an apparently spent Fortner, who was only then rising to one knee. The younger man caught the boot with both hands before it landed in his face and yanked it hard while bouncing up to his feet. Even quicker than he had risen, George Henry crashed to the ground with an echoing thud, his head landing first and taking the brunt of the fall. Fortner dived onto the fallen figure, fists pounding at the bearded face with blood still streaming from the split tongue. George Henry, openly in pain and trying with no success to recapture some wind in his lungs, flailed feebly with his fists before bringing them up to protect his face from more blows.

"Enough?" Fortner asked, still astride and panting, but

keeping a fist aimed. When no answer came, he raised up in a half crouch and backed out of reach to the side.

"Throw me . . . my gun . . . Juno," George Henry called, the words coming out in spurts while he still gasped for air and tried unsuccessfully to roll over and sit up. "Nobody . . . ain't a'gettin' . . . the best a me . . . over some damn gal."

Across the way, Treasure and Danny held their breath and exchanged terrified looks. They could see the shine of sweat on the men's naked, heaving torsos and hear their struggles for breath. During the fight it had seemed to Treasure that the night sounds receded into a kind of raucous, background chorus for the bloody drama being enacted before them. Sister and brother anxiously awaited the next move arm in arm, their disbelieving eyes fixed on the three men standing nearby.

"I ain't got your gun," Juno announced. "Bear-John has it. Ask him for it."

"Throw me your'n then, you damn fool!"

"Nope. I ain't a'gettin' in what was started as a fair fight," Juno replied, upping his chin and glancing at the wide-eyed Hank. His unflinching gaze then met the disbelieving stare of his brother, panting there on the ground. "George Henry, you allers been a big'un for sayin' nobody oughten start sumpin he cain't finish." He stepped back, turned his head, and spat upon the ground.

"George Henry comes up with some real good ideas sometimes, don't he?" Bear-John asked in the sudden silence. Seemingly at ease on widespread legs, he stood down a way from Hank and Juno, a full head taller than either and with shoulders uncommonly wide, even for a man of his height. His fingers lightly touched the stock of his own pistol at his hips, then played around that of George Henry's stuck inside the waistband of his breeches. "I always admired a man with brains."

"Good God amighty!" George Henry complained, breaking the new silence. Not looking at Fortner, who still crouched warily off to his side, he bellowed from where he still lay upon the ground, "Ain't nobody gonna help me up? I'm damn near knocked clean outta my head an' don'

hardly know where I am, an' all you'ns can do is stand
aroun' a'starin' an' a'spittin'."

"My pleasure," Fortner replied, relieved that the wily
outlaw had come up with a way to let the matter lie and
save a little face at the same time. He leaned closer and
held out his hand, but he made sure that he remained out
of boot reach while George Henry struggled to his feet.

"Fair an' square," George Henry said when everybody
seemed to be waiting on word from him. Wobbly, but
moving under his own power, he retrieved his shirt and
wiped at the blood thickening around his swelling mouth.
The look he gave the men watching him was that of one
accustomed to giving orders and having them obeyed. "So
be it. Fortner won the gal fair an' square." Staring belligerently
at Fortner, he added, "Till we gets to Natchez an' hits her
gran'pa for money."

Chapter Nine

Glancing across the lazy campfire at Treasure, Fortner
raked back the hair falling across his forehead. Only then
did he become aware that he had a bloody cut up there
somewhere. It smarted; his hand came away stained.

"I don't care that Fortner may have won me fair and
square," Treasure called, bringing her hands to her hips
and glaring at the men looking across at her. "He's no
more welcome than George Henry to make a claim on
me." She had the scary feeling that she might be caught
up in the center of a tornado and that an even greater
turbulence would strike soon.

She looked at the silvery eyed winner in the firelight,
taking in the naked, sweat-oiled muscles rippling across

his broad chest and down his thick arms as he flexed them languidly in an apparent attempt to iron away kinks. She was surprised to see that even in the pale light, his exposed upper body was as tanned as his face. She marked how the dark matting on his sweaty, heaving chest dropped into a vee, then into a thin line leading downward. The fascinating line commenced again below his navel and disappeared into the tight breeches hitched low across his flat belly and lean hips, leading her thoughts down to—

Goosebumps feathered up her spine, and an involuntary shiver ruled her torso. She sensed that a kind of animal force still remained inside his tall, masculine body and that it could sweep her soul into oblivion as surely as it had fueled the defeat of George Henry. Her cheeks burning at her boldness in studying Fortner's virile form, Treasure looked at his face then and saw the blood trickling down his temple. Fortner seemed to be studying her with like interest, and she felt new blood rushing behind that already heating up her face.

"You done talked turkey, gal, an' you ain't a'backin' out now," George Henry said.

"I never said I wasn't going to honor my word," she retorted, her head tilting in defiance and setting her curls to dancing in the firelight. She hated the fact that her unexpected breathlessness showed when she spoke, but she was grateful that the light was too faint to reveal her blushes. "Even to outlaws. I wasn't the one who started this fracas, so I never had much choice."

"Don't get uppity. You ain't a bit better'n us," was George Henry's quick reply. "Outlaws is outlaws, no matter how you look at it. An' nobody can get hung but one time, if'n he killed one or a hun'erd. That goes fer you, too."

"Enough talk," Fortner said, moving toward where Treasure stood close to Danny. How he wished he could know what was going on behind those golden eyes fixed so fiercely upon him. The crazy thought came that if they had been in complete darkness, her assessing eyes likely would have glowed the menacing green of a cornered animal. Even crazier, the idea titillated him in the same wild way that her husky voice did, and he felt taller and more manly than he had a right to. And challenged all over again. God, but she was beautiful! "I won the fight, and I have a say about what happens to the prize."

"If'n you don't take her, by God I will," George Henry declared.

"Give 'er to me, Fortner, if'n you don't want her and Hannah both," Juno said, his lewd laughter joining that of his older brother. "I'll make it worth your while." Catching Treasure's horrified glance, he winked at her and licked his lips.

Treasure's eyes narrowed. She had forgotten how Juno had seemed flirty that night she had met him, as if he thought he was attractive to women. Her chin angled higher. She had also forgotten about Hannah. Would Fortner hand her over to another man because of the auburn-haired widow back at McHenry's Stand? Or for a sum of money? Matters could go from bad to worse, she realized. Her heartbeat sped up to an even more punishing speed while the Thorpes gibed.

Tension had been building ever since George Henry sat down beside her earlier, Treasure agonized anew. The fight had not resolved it completely, merely set it into new rhythm with her at its core. The seriousness of her predicament had not escaped her for a second, but she had chosen not to dwell upon it during the vicious fight. Now the time of reckoning had arrived. She knew that she had lied through her teeth when she said that Fortner was no more welcome as victor than the smelly, gap-toothed outlaw. She swallowed hard.

The man who, according to the unwritten rules of the wilderness, had won the right to control her was handsome and clean. With candor she admitted that at times Fortner seemed to possess some of those finer qualities she would have sought in a man were she seeking a husband. Still, she wasn't ready to face the moment she lost her freedom, without even the dubious benefit of marriage vows, to a highwayman . . . and her virginity as well. What she had written Aunt Olivia about saving herself until she could reach Natchez and meet her son Thornton might as well have been penned on the wind.

Treasure recognized that she had reached a crossroad the night she left Amos sprawled upon the rock and that nothing would ever again be the same. Never had she dreamed, though, that her life would become linked with Fortner's and that he would have mastery over her. An inner trembling, begun when she had released the gun to Bear-John, threatened to turn her into a mass of weeping, pleading womanhood. She gulped and stood her ground, willing that none of what tore through her mind with dizzying pace would show.

Smiling now from only a few feet away, Fortner said with maddening calm, "Treasure, I think you should choose between George Henry and me. Since Juno put in his bid, you can consider him, too. That way you'll always know you made the final choice. Tell me, Treasure. Which man do you choose?"

Treasure sucked in a deep breath and tried unsuccessfully to dislodge the persistent lump in her throat. At least Fortner was not tossing her aside like so much leftover mush or accepting Juno's offer of payment. The others had hushed and were moving toward them while Fortner spoke. They stopped now, as if not to miss a word of this surprising new development. She could see the Thorpes exchanging amused looks and grinning. Surely they must know there was only one answer. It had taken only a Tennessee minute for her to make up her mind.

Lifting her eyes to the blue ones impaling her with their silvery gaze, Treasure said without hesitation, "I choose you, Fortner." When a look she suspected was smugness raced across his bruised face, she drew herself up taller and added, "That is, if you'll give your word to find Danny and take him to our grandfather in case he and Hank travel slower than we do. I expect you to take me to him as well, ransom or no."

"Agreed." This was said after a brief pause followed by an assuring wink at the solemn-faced boy. "Did everybody hear that?'' Fortner asked in a louder voice, not breaking his new, encompassing look at her. God! What a woman, to stand there and put conditions on her choice, as if she had any bargaining power in the matter. Not for the first time he admired her spirit. In spite of all that had taken place she was not giving in without having a final say. Grinning to himself, he picked up her rifle from beside her saddle and placed it beside his own. Treasure Ryan was no ordinary woman.

Answering shouts and laughter from the other outlaws told the bemused Fortner that no one would forget that on this night, before all of them, Treasure had chosen him. If all went as he hoped and expected, her voiced decision would help keep down possible trouble over her company as they traveled to Natchez. He had hoped that after a private talk with George Henry, he could dissuade him from demanding money from Mr. Lindsay for the return of his grandchildren. He was too relieved to have removed the Ryans from the earlier volatile situation to quibble over ransom now.

"A bottle and the bones for a good game," George Henry announced. "We'll see if'n Fortner's luck holds out with dice, too." He was soon passing around a bottle of whiskey.

"What does all of this really mean, Treasure?" Danny asked after Fortner left them to take the men up on their offers of drinking and gambling. He saw Hank tugging at his wig and coming toward them.

"I guess it means that I'll be like a . . . common-law wife to Fortner until we reach Lindwood," she explained, tears swelling her words. They lurched out like a death sentence. Would he truly release her then? She had known defeat before, but never like this.

"Are you unhappy about it? Is that why you sound like you're crying on the inside? Isn't there something we can do to make everything like it was before?" His love and concern for the one who had mothered him most of his life shone in his eyes.

Proud that not once had Danny reverted to the behavior

of a twelve-year-old and asked what was going to happen
to him, Treasure hugged her brother close. She determined
that he must not know the depth of her fear and concern
for him. Just as Hank reached them, she included the old
peddler with her eyes and explained to the boy what had
happened between Amos and her on top of the big rock
beside the Duck River.

"So that's what George Henry was talking about when
he called you a murderer," Danny said after he digested
all that his sister had told him. "I can't believe that Amos
treated you so ugly. I guess I shouldn't have gone off to
bed and left you with him." For a moment he looked
teary-eyed.

"Nonsense," Treasure said, pleased that the boy managed to blink back the tears before they spilled over. "You
couldn't have known any more than Hank and I did that
Amos was going to become a lunatic."

Hank spoke softly. "What's done is done."

Treasure was glad that the outlaws were too busy drinking and rolling dice on the other side of the campfire to
hear what was being said. Someone had thrown a pile of
tree limbs on the campfire and had it blazing high again.
Night callers chorused incessantly from all sides of the
encompassing forest.

"Treasure," Danny insisted, "you didn't have any choice
about stabbing Amos, just as you didn't have one tonight
when George Henry grabbed you. You're not a murderer
when you're protecting your own life, are you?" When
she gave no answer, he turned to Hank. "Isn't that right,
Hank? She's not a murderer and an outlaw, is she? She
didn't go up on that rock with Amos planning to kill him."

Hank, apparently fatigued and harried from all that had
gone on that night, replied in little more than a whisper,
"She might not be a murderer when you put it like that,
but I guess she's an outlaw if the sheriff is looking for
her."

"Everything will work out, Danny," Treasure said in
what she hoped was a confident note. "You'll be traveling
with Hank now, but I'll have to ride with Fortner . . . and

the other outlaws. Now that Hank's rheumatism is acting up so often, he'll need you to help him with the cooking as well as with the horses. We may not see each other until we reach Lindwood, but we'll make the best of it.''

She motioned to their bedrolls over in the shadows. "Let's get your blanket and saddle and put them beside Hank's. I'll have to wait and see . . . where Fortner wants me to put mine later.'' Frightening mental images zigged across the back of her mind, and she sneaked a glance across at the vociferous men. Maybe Fortner would stay up so late drinking and gambling that he would pass out and not bother her.

Sister and brother walked over to where their belongings lay underneath a low-limbed pine.

"Fortner isn't a bad man, Treasure,'' Danny said after he picked up his bedroll and saddle. "You've always said I'm a better judge of people than most. I believe he'll keep Sheriff Tadlock·from catching you and taking you to jail and then see that you get to Lindwood all right. Grandpa Lindsay won't mind paying money to get us; Mama always said he was rich.''

Treasure smiled grimly at the boy's blind faith and innocence. She had mothered him too closely. Had she ever been as young and trusting? It seemed to her that for a long time she had borne burdens too heavy to let the girl inside her run free. Or maybe there was not one living there anymore. That she had learned well to fend for Danny and herself when Blackie all but deserted them after Marie's death was little consolation now. Wasn't it that same self-taught, fiery independence of hers that had landed her in such a precarious spot—and the innocent Danny as well? A taste of bitterness flavored her mouth.

"Danny, you're probably right,'' she agreed with little hope that she spoke the truth. "Keep believing in Fortner. If the last two nights are signs, we're likely to be running into each other long before we get to the end of the Trace. Don't worry about me. You know I can take care of myself.''

A final hug and whispered good night and she watched

her brother walk over to a far tree where Hank was already spreading out his own blanket. Did she imagine it or did Danny really move more like an adult? She had to believe that Hank, or maybe Fortner if pressed in an emergency, would keep their promises to deliver him safely to Lindwood. If she couldn't believe that, she had nothing at all to look forward to.

Treasure gazed up through the pine branches at the overcast sky, not surprised that no stars or moon showed. The man in the moon would have hidden from mortification had he seen all that had been enacted there that night, she reflected with bone-tingling awe. Not to mention what was yet to take place.

Her heart jumping and her throat filling ever fuller, the miserable young woman sank upon her blanket and stared across at the carousing men on the other side of the campfire, burning brightly now from the added fuel. While she was braiding her hair to keep it from tangling while she slept, the highwayman with pale blue eyes flicked a look her way. Had she not known better, she could have sworn that his gaze held a wondering sadness akin to her own. Her breath got caught back in her throat. Her cheeks heated up as if a wayward tongue of flame from the blazing fire had curled out and licked them. She did not recall how long she sat in numb stupefaction on her blanket before she keeled over and fell asleep.

Though fatigue and sleep blurred her acuity, Treasure was aware when, late in the night, another blanket settled upon the ground next to hers. When the quiet figure flipped part of his blanket upon hers, then stretched out close behind her and became still, she tensed. She knew it was not likely that she recognized Fortner by smell, but how else could she have known for certain it was his blanket covering hers? Warily she waited for a touch or a word from the one who had won the right to claim her. Nothing came.

Treasure soon heard snores drifting from across the campsite. Bullfrogs no longer complained down in the creek, and the insects sang with less frequency and volume than before she had fallen asleep. Night winds soughed through the thick pine branches overhead. Within moments, the breathing coming from behind her evolved into an easy, regular pattern. When it appeared that Fortner had no plans to force himself on her and had snuggled down for the night, she permitted herself to sink back into the welcome pit of sleep.

While the others slept, David Fortner Copeland lay behind Treasure and gave his thoughts freedom to wander back to earlier times on the Cumberland River, where he was born and reared along with his three brothers. Tonight's events, for some unknown reason, had jolted him into examining how he happened to be traveling along the Natchez Trace as a member of the Thorpe Brothers' gang.

David, as Fortner was called while living at home, was fourteen when a violent storm felled a tree on his father, John Copeland. His widowed mother, Agatha, and her four sons continued to eke out a meager living on their farm beside the upper Cumberland River near a small settlement called Brashear's Town. Both from the serving class in England, Agatha and John had married young and come to the colonies as indentured servants. Once they retired their indebtedness, they followed Daniel Boone through the Cumberland Gap and settled in the river valley along with others fleeing the growing unrest in the seaboard colonies in the 1770's.

Occasionally highwaymen from the Trace south of Fort Nashborough traveled as far north and east as the area around Brashear's Town to elude lawmen or soldiers pursuing them. Once there, they demanded food, supplies and horses from the poor farmers in exchange for their lives. More than one barn or house was burned when some brave settler attempted to defend his belongings from the ruffians.

Samuel, David's older brother who had married Hannah Ainsley and brought her to live with his mother and brothers a few years earlier, forced an unruly gang off the Copeland farm in 1800. David and Jocephus were at work in a back field that day, but Hiram, the youngest at sixteen, seemed entranced by the outlaws and their big talk. Hiram sneaked off the next night to join up with the gang, named after J.Y. Thorpe, the merciless father of three sons riding with him.

After nearly two years, Hiram returned to the Copeland farm, eager to put behind him his reckless life as a highwayman. Thinking he had outwitted the gang, he brought with him a bag of gold coins taken from a group of merchants traveling from Natchez to Nashville on the Trace. Welcomed by his family, Hiram did not confess that he had kept the loot from the robbery and that he had claim only to a portion. He did tell that J.Y. Thorpe had been caught and hanged soon after Hiram joined up with the Thorpes. Ever since then the oldest son, George Henry, rode as trail leader of the robbers.

The afternoon after Hiram's return, David, twenty-three and the second oldest Copeland son, rode into Brashear's Town to have supper with the Methodist preacher and his family. Reverend and Mrs. Lovelace had played a vital role in the lives of the Copelands.

Not only had the couple extended Christian fellowship and kindness to the widowed Agatha and her children, but also Mrs. Lovelace, educated in Virginia, served the community as teacher. An excellent student, David had not attended her classes for a number of years, but he had often dropped by the parsonage to borrow books to read. Each time he had seen the Lovelaces' young daughter Sarah over the past year, both at church services and at the parsonage, he had become more and more drawn to her. Sarah was femininity as David dreamed of it—fine featured, blue-eyed with innocent wonder and frail, with an apparent need to lean on a strong shoulder. *His* broad shoulder, he sensed with a deep-rooted need of his own to offer it to the right young woman.

On that night over two years ago as David returned by moonlight to his home several miles up the Cumberland, he made plans. He would take the preacher aside and tell him that with his permission, he wished to speak to Sarah about courtship, with marriage to take place when her parents thought her old enough. After supper that night, she had allowed David to hold her soft, small hand while they sat in the porch swing in the darkness. Listening to her high, sweet voice and teasing giggles, he had felt his heart swell with anticipation that Sarah cared for him, at least a little.

David's musings died when he topped the last ridge before reaching the valley where the Copeland farm lay. The house and the barn were burning. Riding hard, he saw men dashing to their horses. As he got closer, he halted in an attempt to identify the culprits, knowing that his rifle with powder enough for no more than two shots would be useless against the several men he saw. One man off to the side seemed to be gesturing and giving orders, and David saw in the light from the burning buildings a sight that he knew he would never forget—a stocky rider with shoulder-length white hair falling from beneath a dark hat.

"Whitey," a man bawled in a frantic voice, "let's get the hell outta here afore somebody sees the fires! We ain't gonna find that gold now."

In turn the one called Whitey yelled a high-pitched, "George Henry!" to a man down by the barn, and all wheeled their horses about and thundered away. David recalled George Henry as a name his hotheaded brother Hiram had referred to when he returned home the day before. The Thorpe gang, apparently under new leadership of a person called Whitey, must be the villains destroying his family's property, David reasoned. Had the gang not ridden away at that moment, and had the troubled young man not believed that somewhere the family lay hidden safely in a ditch or in the woods, he would have dashed after them and at least made use of the two shots he had.

When David called loudly and searched in the areas near the burning barn and house, but found no signs of life, he rode to the nearest neighbor for help. Robert McHenry and his half Chickasaw sons, Gray-Son and Bear-John, returned to the farm with the grief-stricken young man.

By dawn they were able to enter the smoking ruins of the house. On the floor lay the charred bodies of Agatha and her three sons; the metal parts of their nearby guns showed they had tried to defend themselves. Fearing to find his sister-in-law Hannah and her three young children dead also in the root cellar beneath the kitchen, David rejoiced at finding all alive, though in shock and varying degrees of hysteria. Having played in the root cellar as a child, David knew how each word spoken in the house above carried to the earthen walled cellar. Hannah's eyes told him that she had heard far too much, and he feared for the sanity of the pretty young woman.

Robert McHenry and his wife took in the suffering Copelands. When Hannah and the children were able to travel, David, accompanied by his lifelong friends Bear-John and Gray-Son, escorted them southwest of Nashville to live with Robert's brother and family. Burr McHenry, owner and operator of a farm and a stand for travelers on the Natchez Trace, took in the widowed Hannah and her children. His wife, Trinoma, welcomed the company of and assistance from another woman.

The terrible happenings up to that point devastated the young man who had come riding home from an evening spent with his sweetheart and found his mother and brothers victims of a cruel bunch of highwaymen. Hard to accept also were the losses of buildings, equipment, and livestock the family had struggled to obtain. Only the sight of the children and Hannah had kept him from charging off like a madman to seek those responsible.

By the time Hannah and the children were able to travel, the grieving young man had banked his blazing hatred and begun planning how best to find and punish those murdering his family. Brashear's Town had no sheriff, and overworked lawmen down in Nashville made little effort to assist outlying areas in bringing criminals to justice. With no real taste for the job at hand, David Fortner Copeland became Fortner and took on the task as his own.

Fortner moved restlessly beside the sleeping Treasure, his left thumb and forefinger renewing acquaintance while his mind moved backward. Not since he had escaped alone to the mountain wilds that first winter of his bereavement to trap and earn money had he permitted such hurtful memories to surface. Why now, he agonized, when his every bone ached and his head whirled from too much whiskey?

Though he had relished inflicting pain on George Henry during the fight, David Fortner Copeland doubted he would ever feel avenged until he meted out even harsher punishment to the one called Whitey, the true boss of the Thorpe Brothers' gang. Obviously in command that miserable night at the Copeland farm, Whitey somehow still delivered orders to the Thorpes in secret—of these points Fortner was certain.

Bear-John and he had tried all the past summer to worm their way into the gang, not succeeding until the fall right before the Thorpes broke up for the winter. More than once they had heard the brothers mention the elusive Whitey and his plans for the gang, but the newcomers had yet to meet him. In time, Fortner consoled himself. In time, now that the gang had reunited for the new season of crime, he would confront the elusive Whitey and the entire group and reveal his identity—right before he killed them all. Now that Hannah and the children no longer needed him, what else did he have to live for but to avenge the deaths of his mother and brothers? He could bide his time.

Beside him, a stirring from the young woman lying wrapped in her own blanket, then covered again with an edge of his to make it appear that they were sharing one, snagged his thoughts. He sniffed at a subtle fragrance that tried to remind him of that night he had kissed her, then dismissed it as being no more than that of a spring wildflower floating upon the night breeze. His having stepped in and taken a hand in Treasure Ryan's life had nothing to do with his soul searching, he assured himself. Nothing at all. His goals were fixed. There was no slot for a woman, not after having had his heart broken by Sarah Lovelace. Once he escorted Treasure to Natchez, he would be through with his new responsibility.

Except for Hannah, Fortner now viewed women as too

vain and superficial to rate a vital place in the new life he planned for himself. Not that the capable, headstrong Treasure was like any young woman he had ever met before, still . . . He must remember to ask her why George Henry said she had killed a man, though the idea was preposterous. He rearranged his head against his saddle. Women had their uses, he admitted with a warm appreciation for his past successes with the fairer sex, and he had a virile young man's needs. Outside that . . .

Giving in to a shuddering yawn, Fortner firmly vowed to put a stopper on the rest of what had driven him away from Brashear's Town. Enough self-inflicted punishment was enough. Not one image of Sarah Lovelace, fickle Sarah who had not waited for him to return from his winter of trapping, rose to haunt him. His weary body became heavily still and his breathing deepened. He reminded himself that he had no desire to emulate the martyrs he had read about in the Bible that Reverend Lovelace had given him years ago, the one lying now in his saddlebags. Sleep blotted the jagged edges of thought and fatigue into soft, black nothingness.

Twittering birds roused Treasure soon after daybreak. Surprised that she had slept so long and so well, she blindly poked out her arms in a luxurious stretch. When an arm bumped a solid form, she sat up in alarm. Curled up to her back was Fortner, his blanket covering not only him but her as well. Vaguely she remembered then that he had settled beside her in the night. Not so vaguely she wondered if anything had taken place in the night that she should remember.

"Quit pulling my blanket," Fortner mumbled, one eye squinting balefully up at Treasure before popping shut again. Good Lord! His head felt like a drum being pounded by an energetic Chickasaw at a festival dance. Come to think of it, he reflected, the rest of him didn't feel a hell of a lot better. His mouth felt downright rusty.

"You look like something the dogs dragged up and had too much sense to eat," Treasure retorted.

Eyeing the bruise above his temple, she noted that it was purplish and swollen. She was so relieved that he had not demanded she surrender to him in the night that she felt she owed him something in return. He might be handsome and appealing in his easygoing way, but he was an outlaw, and she needed more time to get used to the idea. Then, perhaps . . . She knew that she would have no choice but to give in. Her pulse skipped and tried to run away as it had last night when all she could think about was how it might be to know a man in the Biblical sense. She had thought of such things a few times over the past year, but never before had she had a face to put on the man's body. It was scary.

Leaning over for a better view of his injury, Treasure said, "I want to take a look at that place on your head."

"I'm in no mood for kissing," he teased when he sensed her nearness and felt her breath fanning across his cheek. Was that her hair giving off the same fragrance that he had sniffed during the night? He could get in the mood easily.

Treasure jerked back, her face flaming. Anger fueled her pulse. "Neither am I, you jackanapes!" Some movements were beginning to show underneath the blankets across the way. She would need to start preparing breakfast soon. "I was merely trying to see if I can doctor your face."

"You must be feeling guilty for being the cause of its being banged up."

"Why would I feel guilty? I didn't ask you to jump in and take on George Henry, you arrogant polecat. You're lucky he didn't stomp the daylights out of you—and luckier that Juno wasn't holding his pistol when he asked for it." She shuddered at that last thought. What if— But he had opened his good eye by then and was watching her. She saw that the right one, underneath the ugly bruise, was almost swollen shut and would likely be black before nightfall. The partially hidden eyeball lent him a decidedly roguish air. "In fact, it seemed to me as if you'd been looking for an excuse for a long time to give him a good whipping."

As far as Fortner was concerned, last night was ended. He had no wish to think upon it again. For Treasure to have sensed that his pummeling George Henry had brought him a special kind of pleasure led him to think again that she was certainly no ordinary woman.

"Are you always so bright-eyed and chipper when you first wake up?" he complained. His head ached.

"Always," Treasure retorted, reaching into her saddlebags for her scarf or coonskin hat.

He groaned at her answer and brought his hand up to test why the vision in his right eye was blurred. He felt like bloody hell, with one of its fires trapped inside his head.

"Don't hide your hair under that damned hat or ugly old kerchief," Fortner ordered when he realized what she was doing.

"Is that one of your rights, to tell me what I can or can't wear?" She whirled to hurl a haughty look at him so quickly that her long braid flopped forward over her shoulder.

"It's the only one I've asked for, isn't it? I'm not too bashful to speak up for what I want." His rakish, one-eyed gaze slipped down from her flushing face to the opening of her half buttoned shirt. The sight cooled some of the fire in his head, but ignited one below his waist. A half smile turned up the corners of his mouth when her fingers flew to button the top buttons and hide the tantalizing view of cleavage.

She didn't know why, but Treasure felt that Fortner must have guessed how she had fretted over what was going to happen when he came to sleep beside her in the night and was laughing now at her groundless, naive fears. No doubt he never had intended to couple with her. Her face flamed anew. Why should he? He had the pretty Hannah to hold in his arms.

Treasure never had understood why Fortner challenged George Henry last night and offered her a way out of the deplorable situation, but she had suspected all along that it had little to do with her being a desirable woman in his eyes. Only now did she give form to the suppressed thought that Fortner might have acted from an innate decency that she had sensed within him upon their first meeting. There was no reason to think that he found her desirable, or even attractive, and planned to make her his woman. All that he wanted from her, she reasoned with new understanding, was her talent for tending to his other needs on the Trace.

Grateful that Fortner, for whatever reason, had prevented George Henry from being the one who joined her in the night, Treasure bridled her tongue. Marie's advice to her daughter had been for a woman to gain her way with honeyed words and actions and leave the force to shrews and ambitious men. Well, she had used force and lost. Now for the honey. Besides, what difference did it make what he thought of her looks? When some secret voice threatened to rise up and point out the difference, she squelched it. Logic told her she was lucky that Fortner had no interest in her body. She believed in logic.

"You're right, Fortner. You've been downright gentlemanly about not making any demands," she conceded with a ladylike politeness learned long ago from her mother and summoned forth when needed. "And I appreciate it. I truly do. I'll remember not to cover my hair again unless it's raining." If he was going to be that easy to please, perchance he would return her rifle and her knife to her if he believed that she was accepting her fate gracefully.

Suddenly the dawn held more promise than Treasure had expected possible. She mustered a small smile. "As soon as I finish up with breakfast I'll get out my medicines and tend to that wound on your head." After all, she doctored horses and other animals, why not the highwayman, too? The animals offered her no more than appreciative looks, whereas the outlaw might reward her with her weapons and, thus, her freedom. "I'll bring a wet cloth from the creek and lay it on your right eye. It'll likely make the swelling go down."

Stunned at the instantaneous change in the beautiful young woman, Fortner lifted his throbbing head and watched her swing off toward the creek, her black skirt whispering against the dewy crop of weeds springing up in the clearing. He had expected her to parry remarks as she had done upon first awakening, even lash out about having to travel with him now instead of with Hank and her brother. Somehow he had not expected that she could be so easily tamed. She must be up to something.

But, Fortner reminded himself as he stretched, then grimaced from the pain of sore muscles and limbs, hadn't he noted from their first meeting how Treasure seemed free of that infernal love of trickery most women seemed bent on practicing in order to hoodwink men? Despite the aches and the soreness, he felt better already. Obviously all that Treasure Ryan had needed was to meet up with a forceful man like him.

Later in the morning, Treasure lost her hopeful attitude. Saying good-bye to Danny was tearing her apart.

"Don't fret about me, Danny." Treasure forced herself to sound serene. Hank had announced that the boy and he were branching off the Trace to call on one of his customers. The outlaws waited impatiently at a short distance. "You take care of yourself and help Hank. If you get to Lindwood first, tell Grandpa Lindsay that I'm on my way."

"I will," Danny replied. When Treasure leaned from her horse to plant a kiss on his cheek, he slipped one arm around her neck and patted her shoulder. "Don't be thinking about what happened with Amos. You did what you had to do. Hank says we'll likely be running into each other down the Trace. Fortner will watch out for you. Good-bye, Treasure."

Treasure stiffened but kept to herself the thought that she wasn't planning to depend on Fortner for anything. "Good-bye, Danny, and you, too, Hank."

Until she lost sight of them, Treasure watched her brother follow the old peddler down a narrow trail in the dense woods. Danny was so young and so unprepared for the world, she agonized. She called herself all kinds of names for petting and spoiling him as she had. Would he be able to cope with whatever lay along the way to Lindwood? It never occurred to her to wonder about herself.

Chapter Ten

"Don't you ever give up, Treasure?" With a bent forefinger, Fortner tipped the front of his hat back to his hairline and studied the lissome young woman riding beside him. As always, the view was rewarding.

He had learned a lot more about Treasure over the past three days, he reflected, other than that she was stubborn. She was, as he had thought upon first seeing her honey colored hair that day at the smithy's shed, the most naturally beautiful young woman he had ever seen.

Sometimes Fortner caught himself imagining how she might look all dressed up in elegant gowns like those worn by the women he'd known in Natchez last summer. The image always staggered his imagination and stirred up private fires he had no intention of letting burn out of control. He didn't like thinking about it, but he couldn't forget that Hannah had suspected a man awaited Treasure in Natchez. He had no right to step into that part of her life, not when he didn't want her for himself. He kept telling himself he didn't. The forgiven, but not forgotten encounter with false little Sarah Lovelace had convinced him that he was better off to remain fancy-free. Any woman was trouble, and Fortner sensed that Treasure Ryan might give the word new meaning.

Half amused and half angered at her persistence, Fortner put aside his musings and continued. "I've told you for the past three days that I'm not giving you your knife or your rifle until I think you need them.''

"You don't trust me," she accused, raking him with a sideways look from behind half lowered lashes.

Treasure had been surprised, but the pattern of that first night she had become "his woman" had not varied. The four highwaymen always sat up late drinking and gambling while she fell asleep in her blanket in whatever secluded place nearby that Fortner selected. To her further surprise, none of the others seemed unduly interested in what the two of them did. She surmised that all believed, however wrongly, that she had become Fortner's woman in the fullest sense of the word.

Only when the gang traveled and Fortner rode beside her did Treasure get much chance to talk privately with him. She had learned much about him over the past three days. For sure, he was handsome and well-mannered, even when angered, as now. Another thing she had learned and come to accept was that he apparently had no more interest in making love to her than he had evidenced on that first night after the fight.

Accepting the obvious facts that he must be madly in love with Hannah and did not find her pretty or desirable rankled far more than the preferred, objective part of Treasure's brain cared to admit. Sometimes that feminine part of her stirred up a fuss and tried to tempt her into using wiles to salve her wounded feelings, but logic always won out. She told herself that just because she was spending more time tending her hair and peeking into the little pocket mirror Hank had given her did not mean she was trying to attract Fortner's attention. After all, he had forbidden her to wear her kerchief or hat, hadn't he?

Treasure was aware that the pale-eyed highwayman still watched her a great deal—did he suspect that she hoped to escape?—and that he seemed to enjoy teasing her, but she figured that was simply his way. She no longer feared him or looked upon him as anything but an outlaw. Well, she reflected with inherent candor when she recalled how he had stepped in and rescued her the other night, she guessed she did think of him as a kind of friend . . . sometimes. This wasn't one of those times, though. He had not responded to her earlier attempts to win him over with dulcet words and disposition. She had lost patience with dissembling.

Fortner seemed to be amused about something as he sat with careless ease atop Brutus and let the conversation die, and she couldn't resist needling him. She was getting nowhere with her repeated requests to get her knife or her gun back.

"I thought your sore head was on the outside and that it would heal. I see now that I was wrong to waste my time doctoring it," Treasure said.

Smarting from her sly dig, Fortner shot back, "Maybe I'm a sorehead because you don't appreciate what I did for you the other night. Did you ever think of that?"

"Never. You volunteered to fight George Henry. I didn't need your help." Inside, she knew she lied.

"The hell you didn't!"

Each day Treasure seemed to get prettier, Fortner mused while his gaze drank in her tall, slim body there on her light tan horse. And sassier, he added with a private grin when he recalled what she had done late yesterday afternoon during an attempted holdup on the Trace.

Snatching his thoughts back to the moment, Fortner prided himself upon having made his stand about her leaving her hair uncovered, for the sight of the blond curls tumbling about her face and down her back pleased his eyes as well as something deep within. Maybe, he mused, all of it connected with his mysterious need at times to fix his eyes and mind on things beautiful. Why he sometimes longed to touch the silky cloud of gold fell into another category, one that he chose to ignore.

Fortner leaned toward her and asked mischievously, "Would you rather be up front riding beside George Henry or Juno?"

Treasure did not deign to answer. Instead, she upped her chin and studied the sky through the overlapping trees. All day dark-edged clouds had been drifting together until the late afternoon sun lay completely hidden.

"Hold up!" George Henry called, halting his horse and waiting for the others to ride up. "We'll backtrack now an' lift some of that gold from them cocky Kaintucks we met on foot back yonder. If'n we can't take it legal-like in a frien'ly game, we'll have to get rough." He fixed critical, beady eyes on Treasure. "I ain't a'lookin' for no trouble outta yore woman like yestiddy, Fortner."

"No problem," Fortner assured the gang's leader in a tight voice. "I'll keep her with me in the background."

"See that you do, even if you have to tie 'er up— 'specially her mouth," was George Henry's curt reply. A grimy hand swiped at his untidy beard. "Come to think on it, it might be better to leave you'uns behind to set up camp. We'uns might be gone a spell if'n we get a game a'goin'."

Treasure's eyes widened as the four outlaws stared at her. She might be amply covered by one of Blackie's denim shirts tucked into her old black skirt, but somehow she felt terribly naked and vulnerable. Even Bear-John, she reflected, who was always nice to her, seemed displeased with her. No doubt none of them could forget what she had done yesterday afternoon during a planned robbery.

Treasure recalled that twilight on the preceding day was the only time the gang had attempted to rob anyone and met resistance since she had become Fortner's woman three nights ago. The intended victims, six casually dressed men, had proved more able to protect themselves than George Henry had expected. As he had done each time a holdup was planned, Fortner had ordered her to remain hidden in the woods until he came back for her.

Treasure had borne up well until yesterday afternoon when gunshots boomed and made her panic. What if Fortner were to get shot . . . and die? she agonized from her hidden spot in the woods. She rationalized that she had no weapons and no hope that any of the other outlaws would refrain from claiming her body. To hell with orders! Without examining the wisdom of her actions, she had yelled Fortner's name and urged Vagabond toward the sounds of the melee. The appearance of a screaming young horsewoman galloping from the dim forest with a cloud of pale hair streaming behind her had spooked both the robbers and their victims.

Too well Treasure remembered how her unexpected screams and Vagabond's hurrying hoofbeats from behind the outlaws had ruined Juno's careful aim at a fleeing traveler. Smoking pistol in one hand, Juno had turned his head, jerking his highstrung horse's reins in disbelief. The horse had reared up, spilled his cursing rider into a sump, and taken off through the woods as if chasing after the outlaw's stray bullet.

The scene kept replaying in Treasure's mind. George Henry, seeing Juno lying facedown in the mud hole and apparently fearing he had been shot, had yelled for help and rushed to his brother. By the time Treasure had ridden up, Fortner and Bear-John had pulled back from the chase and gathered around where an irate George Henry was pulling the still cursing Juno from the soured mud hole. Meanwhile, the six travelers had continued to light out down the Trace toward Colbert's Ferry, all of their valuables still intact.

Now, under the hard-eyed scrutiny of the gang as they made plans for the new robbery attempt, Treasure flushed at the memory of how angry the four men had seemed last night. Out of necessity they had made camp near the foul smelling sump while Bear-John helped Juno chase down the runaway horse. She was nervously serving up a tasteless rabbit stew to a silent Fortner and George Henry by the time the two fuming outlaws had stalked into the campsite leading the exhausted animal.

Treasure had no difficulty in recalling how she had not been able to fall asleep readily last night, not when she fully expected Fortner to upbraid her again in private when the inevitable gambling ended. Loud voices had intruded every so often and she had gathered that George Henry was losing and being an ass about it.

"I'm outta money and you know it, Fortner," George

Henry was saying when Treasure had lifted her head to see what was causing the latest ruckus. "And it's your fool woman's fault for scarin' off those men. I never heared a nobody who wouldn't take valuables jes' the same as money."

Fortner's words had not reached her ears, for his back was turned, but she had watched him shrug and hold out his hand for the bearded outlaw to drop some object into it.

Before settling back down, Treasure had seen George Henry jerk his head toward where she lay in her blankets and say, "I 'spect your woman might give you a' extry roll an' tumble for joolry like that. Be shore an' give it to 'er."

His overheard words had angered Treasure, but she had shrugged them off as one more example of his crudeness. It was plain to her that if Fortner had any jewelry he would save it to give Hannah on his return trip. Besides, she had no wish to own stolen goods.

She recalled confessing silently that she knew even less about men than she had believed when Fortner slipped into his blanket behind her last night with his usual silence. Not until now had anyone made reference to her apparently unforgivable behavior of the afternoon before. Rumbles of thunder in the distance echoed her inner uneasiness.

"George Henry thinks it best that you and I stop down the Trace a piece at a spring we know about. Since it looks like rain, we'll set up camp," Fortner said, his explanation jerking her back to the present.

Treasure nodded. She wondered why he didn't lambast her about her stupid behavior yesterday. Not until last night had she realized she could have gotten everyone, including herself, killed.

She watched the others ride back up the Trace, a frisson of fear for the unsuspecting Kentuckians they had met a short while earlier nipping her. There were only four in the party that Fortner had explained were flatboatmen. They were walking back to their homes in Kentucky, he told her, after floating down the Mississippi and selling their goods and their boats in New Orleans. Carrying only a skinny blanket pack on their backs, and dressed as they were in filthy shirt and trousers of black canvas, they gave no inkling that they had anything worth stealing, Treasure thought.

George Henry's brag to Burr McHenry that the Thorpes took only the extra money travelers could spare was as big a lie as she had suspected when she overheard it. *Hell and damnation!* she thought, letting one of Blackie's expletives become hers. By bucking George Henry, she had gotten herself into one god-awful sticky situation. The only good thing she could think about was that Danny was safe with Hank, traveling on ahead of the gang toward Natchez. She guessed they might have already reached what Hank called Colbert's Ferry.

"Stop your woolgathering—or whatever," Fortner teased. Often he noted the same sadness deep in her lovely eyes that had befuddled him back at McHenry's Stand. Was it only normal curiosity that led him to want to question her about it?

Fortner watched the pensive looks shadowing Treasure's face as she rode beside him into the woods. Her usually sunny disposition had come as a surprise. Never before had he spent so many uninterrupted hours in the company of a young woman, and he would not have been surprised to find her moody, sulky, and demanding. Treasure was none of those, he realized with something he figured was akin to gratitude.

Was she afraid of the approaching storm? Fortner wondered when she made no response. Not likely. Could she be having misgivings about being left alone with him for a spell? Surely she knew by now that he had no intentions of forcing himself on her. The unbidden image of the lissome Treasure in his arms rushed to mind, and he scolded himself for his weakness. More and more, now that he was with her constantly, he kept remembering how her lips had tasted that night he had kissed her back on the Ryans' porch and how her body had felt pressed against his. Now here she was riding beside him, so damned beautiful and cocky and so much fun to banter with. . . .

Willing his thoughts to sanity, Fortner pointed to several dark indentions low in the sheer rock cliff ahead. He waited for a distant roll of thunder to end before speaking. "There's the spring I remember. Several small caves are close by in case the storm gets bad."

Without the need for further words, they reined up and dismounted when they reached the stream fed by the spring bubbling from the rock cliff. After letting the horses drink their fill, they stripped them and gave them brisk rubdowns before tethering them downstream. Treasure watched Fortner take their saddlebags to what looked like a small cave or a protected spot underneath a drooping overhang of limestone.

"Now that we've got a fire going, I'll see if I can shoot a squirrel or two so you can make another tasty stew," Fortner said, breaking a long but companionable silence. He squinted up at the overcast sky where clouds continued to build and darken. "It shouldn't be completely dark for a couple of hours yet." He couldn't remember having been around any other young woman who didn't think it her right—or duty—to keep up a constant stream of talk, no matter on what topic.

"I'll come along," Treasure surprised him by announcing. She followed him into the woods, hurrying so as to walk beside him and look up into his face. "If you'd let me have my knife and my rifle I could be a lot of help. It's going to be too dark to hit a target before long. I'm a good shot."

So she was back to trying to regain her weapons, Fortner mused. "I figured you for a good shot, Treasure, but I don't care to end up in your line of fire. I'll handle the guns."

"What about the knife? Are you afraid I'll use it on you and run away? Where would I go?"

From listening to the gang and recalling Hank's references, Treasure knew that they were nearing Colbert's Ferry and that there was a stand across the Tennessee River. Maybe, just maybe, Hank and Danny were still at Colbert's Stand, and she could reach them . . . if she only had a gun. Now that she saw Fortner was apparently true to his mistress and had no desire to make claims on her, she doubted he would wrest her away from the old peddler in front of those at the stand. True, she had given her word, but what did that mean to outlaws like Fortner?

Fortner suspected ridicule in her tone and retorted, "The reason I don't give you your weapons has nothing to do with my being afraid of you, if that's what you're getting at. And I believe you're too smart to try running off on your own."

She tossed her hair in annoyance and looked up at him. "Then at least let me have my knife. My holster flops around all day except when you let me keep it while I'm cooking or eating."

Fortner drew in a huge breath of exasperation, then let it leak out slowly. "All right, but you'd damned well better use if for the right reasons, or I'll—"

"Or you'll what?"

"Try me and see."

"I'll pass, thank you. All I want is to get to Lindwood and be with Danny and my family." Molasses could not have made her voice sweeter, she exulted. She needed Fortner to keep his promise to see that both Danny and she arrived safely at Lindwood—unless she could manage to escape and reach Danny and Hank at Colbert's Stand up ahead.

"And you'll do anything to get there, won't you?"

Fortner was tempted to add that he knew what really drew her to Natchez was the man she was going to marry, but he couldn't bring himself to say the words aloud. The lucky man was probably as rich as Croesus and owned a plantation as fine as her grandfather's. For the umpteenth time he reminded himself that Treasure was nothing to him except an obligation.

From inside his belt he drew out her knife and handed it over. In a near whisper, now that he had spotted a couple of squirrels chasing up a tree in the distance, he threatened, "Remember that I can take it back as easily as I gave it."

"Thanks, Fortner, for your faith in me." Hoping the edges on her softly spoken words cut him, Treasure took the knife and jammed it in the holster on her hip, then studied him again from beneath half lowered lashes. Why was it that every once in a while he sounded bitter and accusing? What went on behind those fascinating blue eyes? Not that she intended to hang around long enough to find out. "You're not going to let me have my rifle anytime soon, are you?"

Ignoring her question, he readied his own rifle and continued on through the darkening woods with quiet steps, his eyes fixed high in the gum and beech trees in search of a small bulge on a limb. Treasure helped him look in the fast fading light. A hunter alongside her father since childhood, she knew that the tree limb he sought would have either a wreath of fur curling over it or a furry tail hanging down. In the greening trees, both could see giant nests of dried sticks lodged tightly in networks of branches. The narrow little valley was squirrel country. She walked right beside him, as careful as he not to step on a snake emerging from hibernation or to put a foot on a fallen limb and snap it.

"Look!" Treasure whispered, grabbing Fortner's arm in her excitement and pulling on it for him to halt. "Aren't they beautiful?"

Fortner stopped and leaned over enough to follow her pointing finger. A doe and her fawn were drinking from the stream down the way. Treasure's hand felt warm and natural on his arm. His initial look at the animals veered quickly back to her animated face, as if to remind his befuddled brain that a far more beautiful sight lay closer. Pleasure pinked her cheeks and added prickle points of happiness to her golden eyes when she glanced up to make sure he also saw the deer. Her hand still gripped his forearm, and he could feel her excitement transmitting itself through her touch.

Fortner had noticed before what pretty teeth Treasure had, and as close as he was he now thought them perfect. But no more perfect than the tilted nose he was seeing from a birds-eye view after she returned her rapt attention to the animals. He was sure that she was unaware that she still held onto him or that a breeze dipping from up high brushed some of her sweet smelling hair against his arm as she smiled at the scene. No part of him was unaware, though. His very pores seemed alerted.

That same gust of wind playing in Treasure's hair must have wafted their scents to the alert doe then, for the animal lifted its dainty head and scuttered off into the forest, its lifted tail a white beacon for the spotted fawn bounding behind its mother on coltish legs.

"I don't guess I'll ever get used to such a sight," Treasure explained when she realized she still held his arm. Feeling silly and strangely flustered, she dropped her hand.

All at once she remembered that morning back at the cabin when their hands had collided during the handling of the coffeepot. She had felt the same rushing of hot blood all over her body then. Absurd. Both incidents were nothing but absurd overreacting on her part. No matter that the young man was handsome and had saved her from death—or perhaps worse—at the hands of the Thorpes, he was an outlaw. She refused to allow the memory of their kiss that night on the cabin porch to surface. She walked forward, wondering why she was a step or two away before he moved.

Once more they became a team of hunters in search of food. Good luck, a touch of wiliness on Treasure's part and Fortner's expert marksmanship soon brought them what they sought. Laughing and talking about the way she had dashed noisily around the far side of the trees and sent the squirrels scurrying to the side where Fortner awaited with rifle at the ready, they reached the campsite with three fat fox squirrels. Already ecstatically pleased with themselves and in high spirits, for some unfathomed reason, they bragged then on their sense of uncommonly good timing—the firewood had burned down to a hot bed of glowing coals, perfect for cooking.

Later, after cleaning and setting the meat on to simmer,

they settled onto the ground to await the arrival of the gang . . . and the approaching storm. Already the air was cooling and bearing the damp, earthy smells of a spring thunderstorm. Gusting winds danced and played whispering melodies high in the limbs of overhead trees, all but drowning out the natural singing of the stream flowing from the spring. Only the protection from the rock cliff reaching straight up some thirty feet kept the wind from playing havoc with their campfire. A few pesky spirals of smoke did manage to dart out toward them from time to time, but an obliging breeze always showed up and whisked them away before the smoke could do more than smart their eyes or tickle their noses.

"Why do you run with this pack of no-good outlaws?" Treasure asked, not sure Fortner would answer, but too full of the question to deny it life any longer. It seemed a perfect time for frank talk. They had been together three days.

Fortner, sitting cross-legged nearby, turned to look her full in the face. "Does it bother you that I do?"

She licked her lips self-consciously, for he was staring at them in a way that seemed out of the ordinary. "Yes." Whatever made her bring it up? Now he'd be asking why she cared.

"Why do you care? You'll not have to be around me anymore once we get to Natchez." He saw her face flush. Had she noticed how his gaze lingered on her pretty mouth? How was it that her full lips always seemed so pink and moist? The way she held them frequently hinted at what she was thinking, almost as much as her eyes did, he realized with a start. Strange. He never had noticed that in anyone else.

"I don't care what you do," she lied, one hand fidgeting with the hem of her old black skirt where it covered her drawn up legs.

As quickly as a rumble of thunder broke the silence, Treasure recalled how at first she had disapproved of Fortner being a highwayman because she hadn't wanted the impressionable Danny disappointed. Also, she hadn't liked being shown how far off she had been with her first impression of the self-proclaimed adventurer. It still angered her when she remembered how the term adventurer had seemed to match what she glimpsed in his pale eyes back at the cabin that first day—something far-seeing, promising, and infinitely appealing. Not that the elusive qualities had disappeared, she reflected, but everything seemed so different now that she had learned he was a highwayman.

From the way Fortner's silvery gaze kept sweeping lazily over her face now, she guessed that she would have to find some kind of answer. "It's just that you don't seem like an outlaw. And neither does Bear-John."

His lips pursed thoughtfully a moment. "Are you judging us? Don't tell me you've never read the Bible."

She blushed, but with anger at his refusal to answer more than his use of sarcasm. "I don't see how an outlaw can deny he's breaking more than man's law. And what would you know about what's in the Bible?"

"Maybe more than you could guess," he replied quietly. Then he returned to what really bothered him. "What about you? George Henry keeps saying you're an outlaw and no better than we are. Why have you never called him to task for saying that you killed a man? It's not true, is it?"

Treasure stiffened from his first word and looked into the fire. She wished she could take back her line of questioning. His steely gaze had made demands that she wasn't sure she could meet. Did Hannah find it as hard to sidestep his questions as she herself did? Remembering the pretty widow and her obvious claims on Fortner sobered her into facing up to truth.

Maybe, she mused with a heavy heart, she *was* as much a culprit as the highwayman awaiting her answer. Had not Hank also implied as much that day on the trail when she had criticized the Thorpe Brothers' gang? Her mind whirled in rhythm with the overhead branches swaying rapidly in the wind with little moaning sounds suggesting struggle.

"Yes," Treasure replied. "I did kill a man."

Fortner's senses reeled from shock. He hadn't known

what to expect, but it had not been admission. She was so young, so obviously innocent . . . His mind rushed back to when he had seen her at McHenry's Stand. She had seemed withdrawn, quite different from the brash young woman who had shod his horse and then eyed his gold with raw hunger. Was he at last going to learn what had happened after he left the Ryan cabin that wrought such a change in her?

"Do you want to tell me about it, Treasure?"

Her words slipping out huskier than normal and her eyes frequently seeking and gaining understanding from the pale ones watching, Treasure summed up the awful story of Amos Greeson and herself, even threw in a brief account of Blackie's sordid death. Her low-pitched voice spun out the threads of what had fashioned her into a tightly wound ball of doubts and fears interspersed with determination. His ears tuned into the nuances in her soul stirring voice. In quiet, resonant tones, he asked the right questions, enabling her to reel back in a looser, less tormenting version of what obviously haunted her.

A spellbound listener, Fortner never removed his gaze from the lovely face that was undergoing telltale changes at each new revelation in the glowing firelight. At times his heart pained him and blotted out coherent thought. At others a part of his mind raced ahead in search of elusive answers he felt he already knew through sensory methods alien to logic. He could not dispel the notion that somehow he held a key to unlock some of the doors closed to the troubled young woman. But where? What? Not until he came up with something concrete would he dare give her hope. He knew too well the suffering that could result from false hope.

By then the fire was almost too low to light up the massive cliff towering in front of where they sat side by side. Nightfall was a comforting curtain behind them. As far as they knew, the music of the wilderness night singers had either not begun or else was being drowned out by the increasing gusts of wind and nearing rumbles of thunder and crashes of lightning. Both seemed to have blocked out consciousness of anything or anyone but the other. If it was past the normal time for the gang to have returned, neither registered such mundane knowledge. The little world that they inhabited for that intimate space of time was theirs alone.

Treasure couldn't imagine why, but one part of her felt better for having told her worries to the attentive young man beside her. On the other hand, another part of her seemed raw and unformed, hardly recognizable. Had it come into being while he shared her burdens and made them lighter, or had it been born when she admitted that she was a fugitive from the law?

She had noticed how the gang sometimes paused around the campfire at night to listen for approaching horse hooves and exchanged concerned glances, but she had never before realized she had as much to fear from a surprise visit from soldiers or lawmen as they. Her stomach churned in protest at a new identity that she could no longer deny. Outlaw. She swallowed at the gorge rising in the back of her throat. Treasure Ryan was an outlaw, just as Fortner was.

Having added more limbs to the fire while Treasure rose and stirred herbs into the stew, then set the coffeepot on a flat stone in the coals, Fortner waited for her to sit back down beside him. "Is this Sheriff Tadlock looking for you right now?"

She nodded. "That's what George Henry said the night of the fight." She looked down through a rush of scalding tears at her hands, knotted in her lap. Calling up all the control she could muster, she squelched the tears. Self-pity was not her style, and neither was accepting sympathy from one she had so recently met. What was happening to her? It was so unlike her to spill out her woes to anyone. Had telling so much about herself been a mistake?

"How do you know you killed Amos Greeson if you passed out?" Fortner asked after deep thought.

Treasure recalled coming to with an agitated Hank bending over her before answering. "Because Hank told me I had. And my knife was gone, and he lay so still when we left the rock.''

"But you don't remember actually knifing him hard enough to deal a death blow?'' When she shook her head in puzzled denial, he explained, "It seems unlikely that anyone passing out would have the strength to stab hard enough to kill.''

"Just because I can't remember doesn't mean I didn't kill him, though. If it hadn't been for Hank, I would have ended up in jail, and there's no telling what would have happened to Danny. I'm not sure anyone would have believed me when I told what happened. Everybody around Rocky Bluffs owed a lot to Amos. I always heard he had a foul temper, but I never heard anything about him acting so out of control as he did that night.''

"It seems a plain case of self-defense to me, Treasure,'' he assured her. "The man apparently had some kind of seizure and went crazy. You must stop punishing yourself about something that's over and done with.''

His compassionate tone soothed Treasure, and she chided herself for having doubted the wisdom in confiding in him.

"Fortner,'' she said after sifting through all that yet clouded her mind, though in a less threatening way, "I guess you're right. But George Henry is right, too. I'm an outlaw just like all of you, and not one whit better. I'm hoping you'll be able to talk George Henry out of asking Grandfather Lindsay for ransom. I see more than ever that it's a good thing it worked out for Danny to travel on to Natchez with Hank and not be around the Thorpes.'' Almost shyly, she cut her eyes toward the solemn-faced young man and sent him a half smile. "I thank you for making that possible.'' When he seemed not to hear her and continued staring at her face with a wondering gaze, she flipped her hair back from her face and invited a lighter mood. "Do you suppose George Henry will let me take part in the next job if I promise to keep quiet? Everybody deserves a second chance at becoming a successful outlaw, don't you think?''

Fortner chuckled, relieved that she was choosing to tuck away her sadness and, at the same time, release him from whatever kind of spell had sneaked up on him. From within the framework of those unbelievably thick lashes, her amber eyes met his with charming impishness. Her smile was a shade tremulous, but served only to make her lips more tempting. He admired the features of her lovely sculpted face there in the firelight and thought that he might never forget the way she looked at that moment, threadbare, ill-fitting clothing and all. Who would have ever guessed that one so young and beautiful bore such heartache?

A part of him wanted to lash out at everyone who had hurt her and forced her to withdraw behind a facade of bravado. She tried too hard to fight the whole damned world—when not everyone was against her. He sensed, from a wisdom he hadn't known he possessed, that she would have to learn to bend and become more like the deep-rooted trees freeing their tops to dance with the wind overhead or she would break. The thought of Treasure breaking was even more unbearable than the awesome one that she was going to be destroyed that night when she aimed the pistol at George Henry. He had not even known her then, whereas now . . .

Fortner turned off such thoughts and asked, "Why did you come tearing up the Trace after us like that yesterday afternoon? Didn't you realize you could have gotten hurt?"

Flashes of firelight sparking her eyes with gold, she replied with candor, "I was afraid you'd been shot." Oh, Lord! Why had she told him that? He might think she was reading something special into their relationship when he had made it plain there wasn't and never would be. Always there was Hannah in the picture. Not that she wanted more than this casual friendship they seemed to be building, she assured herself. After all, she wasn't going to be around long if she could help it. Since she couldn't take the words back, she tried diluting their meaning by adding, "And I didn't know how I'd get to Natchez if you were killed."

Fortner winced. That was the nexus of the matter. She was bent on getting to Natchez so that she could marry. That was all he meant to her, a means to insure that she reached Natchez . . . and a bridegroom. The thumb and forefinger of his left hand met and rubbed together. She was as full of determination to reach whatever goal she set as the approaching storm was full of violence. Nothing could stop her or the storm. What else could he have expected from a beautiful young woman? Fortner questioned hotly. How long would it take before he let the well-learned lesson soak in?

Hoofbeats and yells signaled the arrival of the Thorpes and Bear-John. By the time the men had tended their horses and stashed their bedrolls in one of the larger caves, lightning was streaking the dark sky overhead. Hurriedly all ate the squirrel stew, first one and then another telling Fortner in between bites how they had won all the Kentuckians' gold in a dice game and then left the men getting set for a stormy night in the forest.

"For oncet I ain't a'hankerin' for no gamblin' after supper," George Henry announced after he cleaned his plate.

"Me neither," Juno said, rising and looking overhead. "I'm a'headin' for a cave right now."

Within a short time Bear-John finished a private talk with Fortner and followed after the Thorpes.

Treasure, down beside the stream, hurriedly finished cleaning up after the meal. Taking advantage of the dim light coming from the campfire and hiding behind a clump of leaning willows, she used her handkerchief and washed away the grime of the day on the Trace. Afterward, she hurried toward the small cave where Fortner had stored their gear earlier.

The lightning and thunder were directly overhead by then, and little drops of rain already were splattering the dying campfire and sprinkling Treasure's hair and clothing. Dashing to catch up with her before she reached the ledge, Fortner came from downstream and put an arm around her to guide her on the climb. No matter that his touch seemed to brand her, she felt relieved. Going alone into the dark cave held little appeal.

Chapter Eleven

"What are you doing?" Treasure asked when Fortner released her arm and left her standing at the edge of the dark little cave. She was a bit breathless, and she blamed it on the rapid, steep climb in pelting rain. The protected area seemed to be shaped a lot like a giant powder horn, she noticed, with the front end not quite as large as Danny's bedroom back at the cabin.

"Looking for a candle." Fortner continued to search in his saddlebag lying on the hard ground.

Turning to peer out at the increasing rainfall, and trembling from the sudden chill of damp garments and hair, Treasure thought how nice it was to have shelter on such a stormy night as this one promised to be. A few harsh gratings of flint against steel, followed in a brief time by a flare of golden light, told her that he had found his candle.

"I don't believe we're sharing our cave with any varmints," Fortner said after stepping deeper inside and holding up the wavering light while looking about.

"I wonder how far back that hole reaches," she remarked, seeing for the first time that earth formed the floor of the cave and reached on out of sight through an opening not much larger than a horse's head. She shivered and hugged herself, glad that her knife once more rode in her holster, but not feeling very brave when she acknowledged fully the thought forming: snakes and bears liked caves for protection, too. Only a gun would suffice against such formidable foes.

As if reading her mind, he turned and said, "I suspect any snakes in there would have crawled out after the noise I made stowing our stuff here earlier. Plus I plugged up the hole pretty good, and I sleep with my pistol by my hand."

When Fortner brought the candle closer, Treasure could see big rocks, such as were lying around on the ground, piled back in the hole. She breathed easier. She knelt and pulled her mother's old black shawl from her saddlebag and draped it over her upper body, wriggling her shoulders in appreciation for its familiar, comforting warmth. Then she reached for her blanket and unrolled it in the center of the cave.

No doubt others had spent nights there, Treasure mused when she sat down on her blanket and gave the place a thorough look. Overhead were smudges of soot, and a blackened spot of dirt near the front opening showed where at least one fire had been built recently. Rain was falling so hard by then that it had a roar of its own, one separate from that of the nearly constant rumbling of low clouds. She had the bizarre feeling for a moment that the two of them might be caught up in one of those clouds instead of settling down inside the cave.

"Why do so many women braid their hair at night?" Fortner asked, flipping his blanket next to hers and then gesturing toward her hands where they were dividing her long hair into three sections at the back. In one liquid, masculine motion, he sat down cross-legged, facing her.

"How many women have you watched get ready for sleep?" she countered, stopping to send him a haughty look designed to tell him that he didn't truly own her and that she didn't have to answer him. On the other three nights she had slept near him, he had been with the other men around the campfire while she made herself comfortable for sleeping. She wondered if she would ever get used to the way his eyes took on a silvery look in shadow and in darkness. Could it be the contrasting black lashes framing them that made them appear so mysterious?

Fortner grinned like a rogue and winked at her. "Thirty-seven, before you."

"What does Hannah think about that, or have you told her?" she quipped, giving in to the urge to smile at Fortner's ridiculous answer. How was it he could make her smile when she didn't even mean to? What she had feared would become a blackened eye had not progressed beyond a slight discoloration, and she saw that even that was no longer noticeable, especially in candlelight.

"Hannah doesn't have anything to do with what we say or do, Treasure, and I'll thank you to leave her out of our conversations." Had he not known better, he would have suspected he glimpsed a spark of jealousy in those wide eyes before she smiled. She was merely trying to needle him. There was an air about her that seemed different, but he wasn't eager to figure it out. Mystery went well with the stormy night. "Looks like I'll have to give orders about leaving your hair alone at night, too." He stretched out one leg to push off a boot against the toe of the other, leaning back against his arms and grunting when it didn't move at first try.

"What an asinine remark. You can't tell me what to do about such things." If he weren't acting so smarty, Treasure huffed, she would offer to help him get his stupid boot off.

Just then the top boot loosened, though, and he sat up and tossed it near his saddlebags in the corner with a loud thunk.

Turning back to her, Fortner asked, "What if I asked polite-like? Would you not braid it then?"

"Why would you care? Did some woman with braided hair get the best of you?" Treasure watched the way his arm and shoulder muscles rippled beneath his damp shirt as he leaned down to remove the other boot and add it to the first one.

"You'd like it if I said yes, wouldn't you?" he teased, returning his attention to her while his fingers untied his neckerchief and loosened the top buttons on his shirt.

Treasure had not forgotten how manly Fortner's body looked on the night of the fight, but she was unprepared for what the closer view did to her. Mesmerized by the sight of his casual movements as he went on making himself more comfortable by pulling his shirt from the waistband of his breeches and unbuttoning the rest of the buttons on his shirt, she felt her face grow warm. Always in the mornings she left her blanket before he did, and she had no idea in what state he slept. Surely he wasn't going to remove his breeches! From where she sat upon her blanket, she forced her eyes to the candle stub he had stuck between two rocks behind them and then pretended great interest in the eerie shadows dancing on the inwardly curving walls.

While admiring the graceful, feminine movements that Treasure's hands made when she once more began separating her hair, Fortner felt a compulsion to run his hands through those golden curls that she was getting ready to hide in a thick rope down her back. His fingers itched with a longing echoed in some crazy way deep inside. There was something disturbingly intimate about the shadowy cave holding only the two of them safe from the thunderstorm raging outside. All day the thought of how it would be to touch her had skipped in and out of his mind. Each time it appeared it stayed a little longer.

"Turn around," he ordered gruffly. "If you're determined to plait it, I'll do it for you."

When she froze, her eyes hidden behind lowered lashes fanning darkly against her golden skin, he moved behind her and stopped her hands with his own. A crashing bolt of lightning nearby echoed deep within the cave, no more startling than Fortner's reaction to touching her hands and her hair. He felt he might be catching fire down in his groin—and he had not even kissed her! What was wrong with him? he wondered in frustration. He didn't usually have such problems in controlling that basic urge.

Treasure suffered no unnatural fear of storms, but the double shock of the eerie lightning and Fortner capturing her hands with his set her entire body trembling.

"Don't be afraid of the storm," he said as he turned her toward him and gathered her into his arms.

"I'm not afraid of storms." She stiffened against him

and pushed away. Her pulse was jumping and frolicking like mad. The remembered smell of saddle leather and virile young man blended disarmingly with the sweet fragrance of spring rain and usurped her breathing pattern. The air seemed fraught with—her mind struggled for the right term. She almost gasped when it came. Maleness. Aroused maleness.

"Then don't be afraid of me," Fortner murmured. Fixed on him, her eyes were wide and luminous. She couldn't seem to hold her lips still. Something was frightening her.

"I'm not afraid of you either."

Despising the way her breath came out so rapidly, Treasure suspected that she knew what it was she feared. Herself. When she was being totally honest, as now, she confessed that she still sensed that the man so near exuded a mystifying kind of power capable of overwhelming her private will without half trying. And it had a lot to do with that air of maleness permeating the small cave. Was it any wonder she was wary?

"Why push me away, then?" Fortner closed the small space between them by leaning his head nearer hers.

"I don't like being mauled by . . ." Treasure had meant to add "by an outlaw," but her tongue became lifeless. His face was so close now that she could see the dark rims around his pale irises. He had been unusually nice to her all afternoon, and she had no valid reason to wish to hurt him. In many ways she owed Fortner far more gratitude than she had shown; but kissing a man whose touch unnerved her as much as his did was hardly a way to express gratitude, she reasoned. Even as she mulled over the entire situation, she found that she hated facing up to the new realization that she was an outlaw herself and hardly in the position to be hurling insults.

A tiny muscle twitching in his cheek, Fortner studied her in the silence, then finished her statement. "Mauled by an outlaw, is that what you meant to say?" When she sucked in a breath and hid her eyes behind those incredibly thick lashes, he figured he had hit upon the truth. Her rebuff stung far more than he cared to admit, and he wanted to get back at her. "You're wanted for killing a man, and yet you hold yourself higher than me. What a little hypocrite you are!"

Before Treasure did more than part her lips for indignant denial, Fortner had captured them with his own. She struggled against his close embrace at first, but his kiss dampened her wish for resistance. Giving in to the temptation to cuddle closer to his warm, hard body and savor his manly smell and taste suddenly seemed the most natural thing in the world.

Fiery, moist, and deliciously supple, Fortner reflected with wonder when her lips softened beneath his. They tasted even finer than he remembered, some part of him exulted. Her shawl had slipped to the ground when he turned her toward him. Now, with her arms around his neck, he could feel the curves of her breasts through the thin, damp fabric of the man's shirt she always wore. Did that mean she wore nothing underneath? The thought of what those feminine mounds would look like in the wavering candlelight fired both his imagination and his passion into dangerous realms.

Why didn't she push him away? Treasure asked herself when the kiss lasted on and on, growing in intensity with each passing moment. To feel herself being hugged so close to the half covered chest she had only recently admired triggered a new kind of feeling deep within. She felt like a warm mold of butter, all soft and melting from the heat of a merciless sun.

Except for her breasts, she realized with a sinking sensation. Something just as crazy was happening to her breasts. They were heating up and growing firmer everywhere they touched against his bare chest. She had the feeling that if she were to remove her shirt her breasts would flame at such searing contact.

What his mouth was doing to hers was unthinkable, Treasure thought with a trace of panic. That first kiss back at the cabin had been no more than a provocative sample. She couldn't seem to get enough of the taste of him. That remembered male essence was blending wondrously with the excitement of the storm raging outside the cave; the combination was feeding the tumult swelling within her body.

When Fortner felt her lips open farther beneath his, he sent his tongue exploring the soft underside of hers, unable to stop its heated foray past her teeth into the warm velvet of her mouth. Sensation overwhelmed him when she moaned low in her throat and seemed about to wriggle from his arms. The movement of her unbound breasts against his skin as she settled back against him and hugged him closer shot the spark of fire in his groin into his bloodstream. At the rate his heart was beating it took only a second for his entire being to ignite. His hands rewarded themselves with a trip through the mass of her golden hair, settling after a while at the sides of her head. His thumbs stroked her silken temples while his fingers memorized the shape of her ears.

All the while Fortner pushed aside those thoughts he had entertained from the first time he had kissed her, but even more so since he had been around her so much lately— those thoughts about how he had no wish to add a woman to his plans for the future and how getting involved with Treasure Ryan would inevitably lead to trouble. From the first he had sensed she was no ordinary young woman. Not once did he recall that somewhere a man waited to claim her. Maybe the storm whisked away that sane part of him with the identical force it was using to tear green leaves from the tops of the tortured trees out in the night.

As ruthlessly as Fortner's resolves sailed away during their passionate embrace, Treasure's followed suit. She hardly heard the roar outside, for the one inside her body controlled all of her senses. When his hands left her head and fumbled for the buttons on her shirt, she leaned away from his kiss and looked into his eyes and face. His lips, wet from their glorious meeting with her own, were fuller and etched with what she could label only as an appealing manly tenderness and vulnerability.

Smiling up at his handsome face, she traced the shape of

it with gentle forefingers, delighting in the illusion of power it gave her to hold him as if transfixed with nothing but two fingers. A zigzag of lightning close by appeared to make up her mind and give her direction. Her eyes hiding behind lowered lashes, she unbuttoned her shirt herself and then peeked up at him from behind those tangled sweeps of silk. She shivered at the way his gaze bathed her face and neck with heady washes of silver before settling into the valley between her firm breasts.

"You're the most beautiful woman I've ever seen, Treasure Ryan," he told her in the huskiest, most thrilling voice she ever could have imagined. With trembling hands he slipped the shirt off her shoulders and tossed it aside. The full view of her naked breasts and shoulders brought a gasp of need to his already full throat. With a heartfelt moan of pure happiness he gathered her close to him again and once more took over her honeyed mouth.

Treasure never had dreamed any young man might think her beautiful. For Fortner to tell her so, both in words and with looks, set her heartbeat to an even more furious rate as they kissed with increasing passion. Never before had she, owner of what she deemed a logical mind, suspected such overpowering feelings could dominate a person's body. Being the uninhibited child of nature that she was— though her logical side tried to keep that knowledge from her—she felt no compunction about giving in to what felt so right. Some inner voice whispered that had it not been right, she never would have allowed the situation to develop.

Besides, she reassured herself, Fortner had been so considerate and gentlemanly by rescuing her and then making no demands upon her that whatever was consuming her was likely gratitude. *Is it not love rather than gratitude that is melting your bones and snuffing out your brain?* came the demanding question.

But Treasure had slammed the door on logic by then and didn't pay attention to anything but Fortner's caresses. She was too busy sighing at the amazing discovery that Fortner seemed to like kissing her throbbing breasts and turning her nipples into tight peaks with his tongue. Not to mention how much *she* enjoyed what he was doing, she marveled, giving in to the thrills racing up and down her spine from his touch.

Tossing her hair back and laughing low in her throat, she sent her eager hands to slip his shirt off his shoulders and trace in lazy patterns the shapes of his muscles from his arms to his chest. His skin felt wonderfully smooth and good. The way the dark curls matted the upper section of his chest fascinated her. Dared she tell him he was beautiful?

"You feel as good as you look," Treasure confessed in her throaty way, leaning to initiate a kiss while her hands went up to play at the base of his neck. She had forgotten that the texture of his hair was so crisp and different from that of her own. Every masculine aspect she was discovering delighted her all over, and she shivered with anticipation. She entertained the wild notion that each caress was as volatile and unique as each streak of lightning flashing outside.

Fortner did not recall undressing Treasure or himself. The fury of the storm exploding out in the darkness caught them up in its violence. It seemed that suddenly they were standing before each other without clothing, gazing with wonder upon their splendid nakedness there in the small cave. Weird shadows still danced on the rock walls, but they were shrinking and losing their force, just as the storm outside was beginning to do. The stub of candle was burning low, in direct contrast to the fires burning inside the two who were standing and drinking in the delectable sights before them.

His eyes reflecting his awe of her beauty, Fortner reached out and brushed her nipple with a tender thumb. "You're beautiful all over, darling."

The velvety endearment plucked at something secreted in Treasure's heart and almost set it free. Her thumb matched his movement, her eyes widening when his nipple also turned into a tight knob.

"So are you, Fortner," she murmured in a voice she hardly recognized. She tried to add an endearment of her own, but she found that saying his name came close enough.

Having grown up on a horse farm, Treasure was not surprised to see the firm evidence of his arousal springing up from its nest of dark curls. What surprised her was the sudden heaving of her heart, the devastating loss of breath, and the dewiness collecting in her womanhood, as if her body might be preparing for what she knew was nature's tumultuous way of joining male and female.

He reached his arms around her and cupped her buttocks in his hands. She did likewise, her golden eyes mirroring her ecstasy at the way, when she nestled against him, his fervid tumescence pressed against her skin down low and created a tantalizing new storm of fire racing within her veins.

For a space of time too small to gauge, Treasure wondered why it was that back on the horse farm the mares shied away and teased the fierce, strutted studs when they were so obviously ready for mating. How could they prolong the exquisite agony if it resembled her own in any way? As for herself, she had no desire to move one inch away from the man setting her body ablaze with his caresses in the dying candlelight. In truth, she wondered restlessly how she would stand it if he didn't claim her soon. All she could think of was how achingly hungry and impatient she was to take him inside her and become one with him. He had stolen her breath and captured her sensibilities. To hold back a moment longer seemed pure insanity.

Sensing that her body craved his now in the same way that his craved hers, Fortner gathered Treasure close and lay down with her on his blanket. Their kisses burned with new intensity when they at last lay together in delicious, naked splendor, their trembling hands and bodies touching in the uninhibited ways of passionate lovers. One minute she was shocking him with her innocence, the next she was casting his senses into another world from her uncanny knowledge of how to create new thrills. Never before had he held such an extraordinary woman in his arms.

Fortner entered her with a wild appetite, one unlike any he had ever possessed. This fiercely keen hunger was tempered with the desire to give the woman he embraced more than pain and frustration at her first introduction to making love. And somehow he knew that he succeeded in blunting the pain for her, holding her so tenderly and murmuring his need of her in such a way as to lead her to seek the ultimate he whispered about instead of settling for the slicing hurt. She surprised and pleasured him with her eager response. There in his arms she knew the joyous secret of shared passion between man and woman. Wildly she joined in Fortner's driving rhythm until the inner conflagration flared high enough to explode and fade into a withering nothingness.

Not until they lay spent and nearly asleep in each other's arms did Treasure think about how she truly had become a woman. Had she not been so fatigued and gone ahead and completed her thought, as was her custom, she would have been appalled. She had become more than just a woman. She had become a highwayman's woman.

The first light of morning awakened Treasure. For a brief moment she wondered why she was naked, but her movements soon told her that she was not alone underneath the blankets. Then the memory of the night's lovemaking flashed to mind and she closed her eyes again.

How could she bear facing Fortner? Now he must suspect what she herself had not wanted to admit last night, but recognized now as clearly as she did her name. She was in love with the man she knew only as Fortner, a confessed outlaw, in love with a man who loved not her but his mistress. And one who had not seemed unduly attracted to her until last night during the height of the storm. A worse realization was that Fortner was exactly the kind of man that her mother had warned her not to love.

Hell and damnation! How stupid could she get? Treasure writhed silently and would have moaned aloud if she had been alone. No doubt any other woman would have served his needs as well as she, she agonized with self-deprecation. She was no better than the trollops she had read and heard about. Sailing closely behind that degrading thought came another: She was also an outlaw fleeing a sheriff.

What a fool she had been to tell Fortner all about herself and learn nothing at all about his past. Who was he, really? She knew little about him except that she loved him madly. Had he perhaps made love to her only because he'd had needs and she was handy? Treasure swallowed a bitter taste back in her throat and glanced at Fortner as he lay sleeping on his side with his cheek resting against an open palm.

By not giving in to the desire to confess how handsome he was and what a magnificent, tender lover he was, she fed her instinctive need to regain her former bravado. Damn him for being so male and so sure of himself! She would make sure that he never found her vulnerable again, she vowed while slipping from the blanket and putting on her clothes in the pale light.

It was then that Treasure saw her rifle lying alongside Fortner's in the corner with their other belongings. He must have forgotten to put them beside him last night before he fell asleep. Her face colored when she realized the reason.

Stealthily Treasure moved toward the guns, slapping at the unruly mop of curls left free all night. Fortner's breathing sounded deep and regular from behind her, just as it had when she left him.

What if she took both of the rifles, Treasure wondered, maybe found his pistol when she got nearer and slipped away with all the weapons? She had already spotted the powder horns. A quick look outside indicated that the day would be fair, once the sun came up. The outlaws hardly ever stirred until sunrise. If their talk was true, she could likely be down the Trace to Colbert's Ferry before dark. Holding her breath at her good luck, she knelt and reached out toward her rifle.

"Don't move!" came a steely voice from what she had believed was a peacefully sleeping man.

Treasure whipped her head about, shocked to see that Fortner, still underneath his blanket, was propped on an elbow and was using his free hand to aim his pistol straight at her.

"Get away from those rifles and powder," he ordered, sitting up and motioning with his pistol.

Transfixed, she watched the blanket crawl down his naked torso and then puddle somewhere low across his folded legs. Never had he looked so masculine or so formidable. "Are you going to shoot me if I don't?" She glanced back at the rifles and wondered if she stood a chance at grabbing one and turning it on him before he could remove the safety and shoot.

"Don't try picking one up," he said in that maddening way he had of seeming to read her mind at times. He clicked off the safety, the sound loud there in the cave.

Treasure's eyes and head reacted as if they were connected to that little piece of metal, for they jerked back toward him in rhythm with its sound. She straightened up, brushing impatiently at the long curls straying across her face. It dawned on her that it was his fault she never had braided her hair last night and that it was now full of tangles. A more pressing thought was that she never before had looked down the wrong end of a gun barrel. She swallowed hard.

"You wouldn't shoot me, would you?" Treasure hated to hear that her voice sounded ascensive and weak.

"Walk over here slowly, and no tricks."

Trying to recapture some dignity, but nevertheless keeping her eyes glued on that formidable gun barrel, Treasure took two steps in Fortner's direction. In the dim light she saw a suspicious shape on the ground behind him, one not in her view until she moved his way that very moment.

Her hand dropping to her knife holster, she said in no more than a loud whisper, "There's a rattler coiled behind you." When he grinned in disbelief and quirked a dark eyebrow, she hastened to add, "I wouldn't lie about this, you arrogant jackass. Freeze!"

Fortner narrowed his eyes and studied her face. Damned

if he didn't believe she was telling the truth. Either she was or she was getting ready to hurl that blasted knife at him. He swallowed at a sudden thickening in his throat. If the snake was as close as her horrified gaze indicated, he wouldn't have time to turn and shoot before he could be struck. Besides, his thoughts ran on like wildfire, he had recalled before he picked up the pistol that he never had loaded it last night. He felt his hackles rise. The varmint must have crawled out from the little passageway at the back of the cave.

Getting Fortner's attention had been Treasure's first goal. Now she needed to take at least two more steps to reach an angle where she could throw her knife with full force. So far the snake seemed content to lie coiled upon the cool, damp ground. It appeared that its triangular head was directed toward Fortner's naked backside. She knew that speed was as essential as skill. If she could keep from detracting the snake's attention from the motionless Fortner, perhaps she could at least cripple it enough to prevent its deadly bite on his unprotected back.

Sliding her knife from its holster as slowly as possible, she set one foot in front of the other with more caution than she could ever remember taking. She realized that dawn was spreading more light with each passing moment, and that the partial darkness in the cave was helping conceal her movements. In the folds of her skirt, she nervously palmed the knife until the sharp point lay in position between her thumb and fingers, all the while wishing that she had her old pearl-handled blade. It seemed forever before she got her body lined up with her feet and gained the clean angle she needed. Neither the snake nor Fortner had moved.

Swallowing at the gorge rising at the back of her throat, Treasure brought up her right arm rapidly and hurled the blade in the end-over-end way Blackie had taught her. At the same instant the knife quivered through the air beside him, Fortner lunged forward and rolled, removing himself as a near target for the dreaded fangs.

"I got him, Fortner!" she cried, her eyes fixed on the snake's head. "I got him!"

Treasure couldn't remember when she had felt so proud of what Blackie had taught her, unless it was the first time she had killed a snake that way, back when she was about Danny's age. Shuddering at the lethal sound of the rattles on the snake's tail writhing against the dry dirt, she watched the diamond-marked body twist and turn. It wasn't going anywhere though, for the feared head was pinned firmly to the packed earth by her blade. She turned to see Fortner slipping into his breeches over in the corner.

Sending her a weak smile, he picked up his rifle and walked over to make sure the snake was dead. For good measure he whacked the head with the butt of his rifle before retrieving her blade and sticking it inside the waistband of his breeches. He guessed the snake was almost as long as he was tall. The thought of how much venom it must have stored up during the winter staggered him. Had it perhaps slept near the two of them all night? Or had it not crawled near the blankets until after Treasure arose? Whatever the case, it was a close call. Grim-faced, he slipped the long gun barrel under the still writhing but decapitated varmint and slung it out of the cave.

"Treasure, has anybody ever told you that you're damned good with a knife?" Fortner asked when he turned back to finish dressing. "Thanks. You saved my life!" She had returned to the corner and begun brushing her hair while he went about making sure the snake was dead and getting rid of it. He wiped the blade and held the handle out toward her, wondering why she was keeping her distance and watching him so covertly. "I don't want you ever to be without this thing again."

Treasure took adequate steps to take her knife but moved backward while jamming it into her holster. Bringing her hand from where it had lain hidden in the folds of her black skirt, she brandished Fortner's pistol and aimed it at him.

"Thanks. I believe we might be even now, and I'll be on my way—without your fine company."

"You're acting crazy," he protested, taking a step toward her and holding out his hand. "Give me the pistol. You don't want to shoot me."

"What makes you so sure?" If he dared bring up last night she would do her damnedest to shoot so close to his head that his ears would ring all day. "You were going to shoot me a while ago, weren't you?"

"Did I say I was?"

"Don't aggravate me, Fortner. I've got my mind made up that I'm going on down the Trace without you or your friends."

"I don't want you trying something so foolhardy." He took a step in her direction. Did last night mean nothing to her other than an introduction to making love? "Give me the gun and go get breakfast started."

"You'd better stop if you don't want to get shot." Why was he testing her so? It was clearer than ever that she needed to get away from this man who had gotten next to her skin and her soul. He was not good for her. Wasn't what happened last night proof enough? He had used her body, and she had done more than let him: she had enjoyed every wonderful moment. "You can cook your own breakfast from now on. I'm leaving."

He squinted across at her and cocked his head. "Is it because of what happened last night?" When her face grew still and her lips trembled a bit, he said, "I can make sure that won't happen again if you won't try to run off by yourself. There are plenty more like George Henry out there on the Trace between here and Natchez. You might not get away from the next one." Noting her hesitation, he added, "We can forget last night ever happened and go on being friends, can't we? You need me to look after you. Besides, you're too good a cook for me to lose you now."

Fortner didn't bother to examine the way his words were affecting him on the inside. All he wanted was to calm Treasure and get the notion of running away out of her mind. True, she was no ordinary woman, but she was no match for a black-hearted scoundrel determined to best her. Whether she cared to admit it or not, she needed him to protect her until she reached her grandfather. Why was she being so stubborn?

"I never intend to let what happened last night happen again anyway, so I don't care what you say," Treasure retorted, her face flushing. "I'm leaving, even if I have to shoot off your toe." It seemed mighty easy for him to say they would forget all about last night, she fumed. What about her feelings? She had learned far too much about him and herself last night ever to forget it. Damn him! All he cared about was hanging onto his cook. How right her mother had been to advise her to avoid entanglements with handsome rogues like Fortner. If only she had heeded that warning!

"Actually," Fortner drawled, "it'll be hard to shoot a man's toe off when the pistol isn't even loaded." He was near enough to grab her then, and he felt the starch go out of her when his arms went around her. With one hand he wrenched the pistol free, broke open the chamber to show her it was empty, and tossed it onto his blanket.

"You devil!" she snarled, as mad as a wildcat backed into a corner. "It wasn't loaded when you pointed it at me either, was it?" She could read the answer in his eyes. Knowing he had been laughing at her all along fueled her anger to greater heights. "How could you be so mean and lowdown and...downright nasty?" She pummeled his broad chest with her fists and tried to kick him. "Get your hands off me, you no-good scoundrel, you lying outlaw!"

"Not until we call a truce." He caught her hands in his and stilled them, aware that touching her even in that way satisfied some secret part of him. He didn't blame her for calling him names. He had a few in mind that he figured he deserved that she hadn't used. "I promise I'll not lay a hand on you if you'll promise you won't try to run away again."

She looked up at him. He was so much bigger and stronger. . . . Was there no way to escape him? She knew she was licked—for now. Back to dissembling. "Honest Injun?"

He grinned, recalling the phrase from some of Danny's

and her teasing banter that night back at the cabin. Fighting down the urge to brush the stray lock of hair from her forehead and kiss the daylights out of her pouting lips, he freed her hands. Treasure's beauty and impetuosity so fascinated him that he did not notice she never repeated her part of the bargain.

Unaware that he called up the same soft, bass tone that he had used when he had called her darling the night before, Fortner replied, "Cross my heart and hope to die."

Chapter Twelve

George Henry led the way that afternoon to a hidden spot near Colbert's Ferry. After they arrived late in the night, he announced that they might camp there for a day or two and watch whoever crossed the Tennessee River.

By the next afternoon, the gang had forced money from three small parties of travelers without incident. Announcing that he was running low on whiskey and that he wanted to meet up with Whitey, George Henry declared that it was time to go on down to the ferry and cross over to Colbert's Stand.

The Thorpe Brothers' gang had not traveled the scant mile to the ferry before they met trouble, trouble posing as two well-dressed men accompanied by a black man riding toward Nashville. Having spotted the travelers in the distance, George Henry turned and, as usual now, ordered Fortner to send Treasure into the woods.

Chafing at having to take orders, even indirectly, from the repulsive leader of the gang, Treasure obeyed. She was soon leaning against the trunk of a pine tree and venting her anger to her horse, Vagabond. Gunshots and shouts from up the Trace told her that something drastic was happening. The robberies earlier that day had taken place without gunfire. Her heart pounded harder when she tried but could see nothing from her hiding place in a pine thicket.

Treasure knew well that it was illogical for her to be praying for Fortner to be unharmed, especially when only two mornings ago she had tried to escape from the cave. But then, her reasonable self pointed out, neither had it made sense for her to save the man that same morning from an almost certain lethal snakebite when only seconds earlier he had been holding a gun on her. To make matters worse, she'd had no inkling that the blasted pistol wasn't loaded.

The memory of the farce in the cave fired her temper, and Treasure wondered if she would ever get over it. She kicked at a pine cone, barely aware that Vagabond shied and jerked on the reins in her hand. Fortner was a worthless scamp with a warped sense of humor . . . she kicked another pine cone, sending it sailing into a stand of wildflowers . . . and he had not a scrap of respect for her.

Treasure's conscience nagged her at her last thought. Not once over the past two days had Fortner mentioned anything that had taken place in the cave, and she had to give him credit for that. Still, she groaned, how was it that she was unlucky enough to have fallen in love with the handsome highwayman?

Tightening her mouth in self-loathing, Treasure cocked her head to listened. Someone was coming! Her uneven heartbeat sped up. The sounds of horses racing down the muddy Trace neared. Treasure abhorred the thought that one set of hooves might not belong to a handsome gray gelding with black points. Snatching at any inanity to think upon, she wondered why she never had asked Fortner why he called his horse Brutus. Though she had been with him for a week now, there always seemed to be so much to talk with him about and so little time. . . .

"Oh, Fortner," she murmured with a little catch in her

low voice when she descried his proudly held shoulders as he leaned low over Brutus and galloped toward her.

"Well, Fortner," Treasure said after he came closer and reined up Brutus. There was no need letting him know how much the sight of him, safe and sound, lifted her heart. He was conceited enough as it was. It had not taken an entire week with him to find that out. "I see you made it back." She turned then to greet his half Chickasaw friend riding close behind him. "It's good to see you, too, Bear-John." Her fear had abated, but now relief was making her knees as weak as curds of whey. "Was anybody killed?" Her eyes had searched Fortner's face and form from her first sight of the two men in the distance. Both of them appeared to be unharmed. "What happened?"

"One of the men put up a fight, and George Henry's shot hit him in the shoulder. The black and the other man lit out up the Trace toward Nashville." Dismounting quickly in the loose-limbed, rhythmic way that Treasure admired, Fortner removed his saddlebag. He turned toward her then where she stood holding Vagabond's reins bunched up in one hand, her eyes wider than usual as they studied his face solemnly. "George Henry and Juno will stay in the woods tonight while the three of us ferry across to Colbert's Stand and see if any soldiers happen to be there. Sometimes soldiers hang around Colbert's, and they might have gained a description of us from that bunch who got away the other afternoon . . . after you came tearing out of the woods screaming like a banshee."

Treasure saw the glint of devilment in Fortner's pale eyes and knew that he was enjoying the hell out of calling up the memory of her impulsive interference four days ago. She felt her cheeks warm up.

Without pausing more than a moment, Fortner admired the pretty way her face grew pink and then continued. "Bear-John will send a signal when it's safe for the Thorpes to cross the river and meet us on down the Trace tomorrow."

"But if we go to the stand and some of the men who got

away did give descriptions to any soldiers there, won't they recognize you?'' Treasure asked. Letting her concern for his safety push aside her initial impulse to point out that today she had followed orders down to the letter, she noted that Bear-John had also dismounted and was poking his telltale black neckerchief into his saddlebags.

"I doubt it," Bear-John reassured her with that open smile she had come to associate with the big black-haired man. "We always wear something over our faces."

Treasure marked how Bear-John no longer seemed upset with her about her reckless action of that afternoon, which she kept trying unsuccessfully to forget. During one of the frequent private exchanges between the two friends, had Fortner told him why she had acted so rashly and come charging up the Trace from her hiding place? He probably had, she reflected; it was likely both had gotten a good laugh about her fear for Fortner's safety. Whatever the reason, she was pleased that Bear-John appeared friendly once more.

Fortner sent appraising eyes over Treasure. A breeze played in her golden curls, and he congratulated himself for the hundredth time upon having insisted that she leave them unbound. Though she was unusually tall—and delightfully curved underneath the worn, shapeless shirt and black skirt, he mused with instant recall of their making love in the cave—she looked, somehow, like an innocent young girl. Her beautifully sculpted face seemed abnormally pale in the shadowed forest now that the flush had receded.

"Are you all right?" Fortner asked the tawny-eyed young woman, unaware that a new note warmed his voice. When she tossed her long hair back from her face and nodded affirmatively, he went on. "Can you help us pull off a little charade to keep the law from tying us to the gang? They'll be looking for four men traveling together. Nobody saw you close enough that afternoon you rode out after us to tell what you look like. Besides, it was almost dark, so the three of us can probably ride right in without anyone giving us a second glance. George Henry and Juno will wait for a signal before crossing over to Colbert's Stand.''

Despite his preoccupation with Treasure's looks and her ready agreement to go along with his plan, Fortner kept recalling that George Henry had said he hoped to meet up with Whitey across the river. Would he at last get to meet the unseen leader of the Thorpe Brothers' gang?

Twilight was fast becoming night by the time the ferry-man had wound the last screaking turn of cable guiding the rickety ferry ashore from the eastern side above the Tennessee River.

On the unsteady trip over the rushing currents, Treasure had held her horse's reins and soothed it with soft words and gentle pats to its nose and velvety muzzle. She was hoping with all her might that Hank and Danny might still be at the sprawling stand that she could make out on the darkening western shore. Maybe there was some way that Hank could help her get away from Fortner since there would be others around. But, she agonized, if soldiers or lawmen happened to be at the stand, she might do well not to call attention to her plight, being an outlaw herself.

Within a short time Treasure stood with Fortner inside Colbert's Stand, looking around the large receiving room with open curiosity. Perched on the bluffs above the Tennessee River as it was, the large building commanded a sweeping view of the river and the forested banks. The stand lacked the spit-and-polish look of McHenry's, she mused. She had seen no signs that Hank and Danny were around.

''You and your woman get last room upstairs,'' Sly Colbert told Fortner in basic, barely accented English.

Sly's black eyes raked curiously over the couple, but his copper-toned face remained impassive. Wise and wily, as his nickname indicated, the owner of the ferry and stand made no show that he had ever seen the tall, blue-eyed young man. A Chickasaw who had been married long enough to a woman of both French and Chickasaw blood to have several grown children, Sly Colbert had learned the ways of the white men so well that he usually came out on top of any dealings with them.

"Fine," Fortner replied. "I'm David Ainsley, and," turning to gesture toward Treasure, "this is my bride."

From where she stood waiting not far behind Fortner in the receiving room, Treasure shot a derogatory look at his broad back. Ainsley! Not only was she going to have to pass as his wife, but she was going to have to do so under the last name of his mistress! Mr. and Mrs. Ainsley? She swelled with indignation. The man knew how to make her feel worthless.

Bear-John came in from tending the horses and whispered to Treasure that he had found out at the stables that Hank and Danny had gone on down the Trace only that morning. After he turned to speak with Sly, he learned that he would have to sleep in the barn.

"The place must be filled with travelers," Bear-John remarked, accepting the assignment without protest. "Or maybe a bunch of soldiers?"

"Soldiers return here at night all this past week," Sly said. "They work on Trace south of here. Storms blew over many trees in winter." He put away the ledger in which he had been scribbling. "Preacher coming tomorrow."

Fortner and Bear-John exchanged glances, then Fortner said, "Since it's Saturday, I guess folks from around here will be coming tonight to have some fun before hearing tomorrow about the pitfalls laid out by the devil." When Sly nodded in agreement, Fortner went on. "Are there any women around here who might sell me a dress for my wife? We lost some of our belongings when we forded a creek. I'd like her to have something pretty to dance in."

Treasure sucked in a breath. The rogue could make a lie roll out as smoothly as a lizard glided across a rock. What gave him the right to decide that the clothing she owned wasn't pretty enough to wear to a gathering of hill folk on a Saturday night? Only a guarded look from Bear-John before he went back outside kept her from spouting her protest. Aggravated at the thought that while Fortner talked on with Sly Colbert she had no choice but to remain silent, she let her mind skip back to the times when Blackie had taken his family to such shindys as the one scheduled to take place that night at Colbert's Stand.

How handsome her father had looked in his best white shirt and red cravat on those rare occasions, Treasure recalled with keen pleasure. Blackie's hair always shone in the lantern light like the silky wings of ravens, and his teeth flashed so often from laughter that the young Treasure had no trouble finding her father among all the other frolicking couples. Curtsying before Blackie at the beginning of each dance was her lovely mother, Marie, before she became ill and disheartened, back when her eyes yet held dreams in their lovely depths. Marie, petite and with pale, blond hair and blue eyes, would always represent the epitome of feminine beauty to her daughter.

When Fortner left and followed Sly Colbert into the back part of the stand, Treasure walked over to stare into the fireless fireplace, calling up the happy sounds and sights of those bygone Saturday nights in Rocky Bluffs. She hadn't thought of them in years, she realized with a heartfelt sigh.

With her head resting against the split log mantel, Treasure remembered it all. The high-pitched calls of the fiddles had seemed directed only to the handsome couple that appeared almost like strangers to their admiring young daughter sitting on a quilt beside little Danny, who was usually asleep by the time the dancing began. As if transformed by the night and the lively hill music, her parents had become fantasy figures in the young Treasure's worshiping eyes, figures coming to life in her mind's eye just then as she gazed blindly at the cold ashes in the fireplace. So gallant were Blackie's attentions to Marie, so flirtatious were Marie's smiles to her handsome partner, and so lightly did their feet make the dance steps on the hard soil that their daughter had often felt she might be standing outside her own dream watching it unfold. And always the banjo sang.

To Treasure's surprise, the memory was not painful or mocking, as it had been when she had last let it surface a few years ago. Somehow it now brought her a remarkable comfort.

Caught up as she was in reverie, Treasure had no idea how pretty she looked in profile when Fortner returned to escort her up to their room. A gentle smile curved her full lips, and as she turned to meet his gaze, her eyes glowed with a kind of happiness that he had never noticed before. But not for long.

"Why did you use Hannah's last name . . . Ainsley?" Treasure asked, refusing to look directly at the blue garment hanging over his arm. She was shocked that Fortner had been able to get a dress, but even more shocked that it seemed to be an uncommonly pretty one. Were those ruffles around the bottom edge of the skirt? "I feel disgraced enough that you dared claim we're married without your using—"

"Calm down and hush up. You know I couldn't use my own name, or yours either. Do you want to call attention to us?" He turned to see if anyone seemed unduly curious, but no one else was around. He had thought she would be pleased that he had found something pretty for her to wear, and she was as riled as he had ever seen her. If a more cantankerous woman existed than the fiery-eyed blonde staring up at him, he fumed, he had yet to meet her. "I told Sly we're newlyweds. Do you think a bride would be quarreling with her husband in a public room?"

"She would if she was married to you!" Treasure stuck out her tongue at him, crossed her arms over her breast, and whirled back around to face the cold fireplace.

"Come on. We're going to our room." Fortner was proud that his voice came out quietly but firmly and gave no hint of his agitation and disappointment. Leaning over, he took the dress that Sly's wife had sold him—for a sum he suspected was exorbitant—and stuffed it between her folded arms and her breasts. "I'm sorry now that I even bothered trying to get you something decent to wear tonight. You're not worth the trouble you cause." He wheeled around, picked up their saddlebags near the front door, and started upstairs.

Treasure held back her retort, for through a window she could see some soldiers crossing the front porch. Clutching the blue garment, she hurried to catch up with Fortner before he disappeared up the narrow stairway.

When the silent couple reached their room, Fortner found a candle and lighted it. Treasure saw the set of his jaw and recognized it as a sign of anger, but she shrugged and looked around the small room. She eyed the double bed, recognizing the Wedding Ring pattern of the faded quilt which her mother had once described to her. How ironic, she reflected while glancing over her shoulder and noting that Fortner's attention also seemed glued to that dominating piece of furniture. The grim look of his jaw had softened.

"I'll fetch some water so we can clean up before going down to eat and then dance," Fortner said.

"Dance? I don't care to dance. You should have talked with me before you asked about a dress. I'm perfectly satisfied with my clothes and the way I look in them. I don't need anything fancy when I'm not going to be dancing anyway." She flipped her waist-length hair haughtily and went over to look out the narrow window beside the bed.

"You might as well get that burr out from underneath your saddle blanket, Treasure. We're going to be questioned by those soldiers. You agreed to go along with my plan to convince them that we're a newly married couple traveling to New Orleans. Whether you like it or not, you're going to wear the dress if it fits at all. If you don't want to dance with me, fine. We can at least listen to the music and pretend we're a married couple."

Fortner snatched up the large pitcher from the washstand and left.

Treasure whirled around then and gave in to her desire to hold up the dress and look it over. Made of a shiny blue cotton trimmed with double ruffles at the neckline and on the brief puffed sleeves, it had a full skirt gathered onto a waist cut into a vee, both front and back. And more ruffles edged the bottom of the skirt, she realized with delight as her eyes swept on down the length of the gown. It was as pretty as any gown she had ever seen and showed no signs of wear.

The excited young woman rushed to stand before the small mirror over the washstand. Yes, the blue did seem to be the shade of one of the ribands that Hank had given her. She could see only her top half in the mirror, but when she draped the dress across her bosom, she liked the way the two rows of small ruffles bordering the scooped neckline made her look womanly, even with Blackie's old shirt showing underneath it.

Oh, my! Treasure thought with a touch of panic as she stared at her image in the mirror. She had never owned a dress since she had become grown, and she couldn't imagine how she was going to feel having her neck and part of her breasts exposed. Maybe it wouldn't fit and she would be wearing her blue waist and navy skirt after all. Instead of cheering her, her final thought brought a little sigh of wistfulness.

"You can wash up first," Fortner told Treasure when he returned with the pitcher of water. Whistling softly, as if only for his own ears, he filled the large basin on the washstand and then busied himself with his saddlebags in the corner. Though he made no comment about it, he saw that the dress Mrs. Colbert had told him was too small for her and too large for her young daughter was lying across the bed, all spread out on top of the colorful quilt and looking even prettier than he had thought. So his spirited "wife" had been more interested in what the dress looked like than she had pretended, he reflected with secret amusement.

"Couldn't you go back downstairs while I bathe?" Treasure asked peevishly.

"I could, but I'm not. The room down there is full of soldiers. I would rather wait to talk with them when I have my 'bride' along. They won't be as apt to ask so many questions when they see such a 'happily married' couple traveling along the Trace to make their new home in New Orleans." Treasure turned her back and began unbuttoning her shirt. "Don't be so modest. I've seen naked women before ... counting you."

"I know," she retorted, stung that he would refer to her undressing before him in the cave in such a casual manner. She noted with pride that she was learning to talk with him about all manner of things now without that infernal heat rushing to her cheeks and making her feel like a fool. "I believe you indicated that I'm number thirty-eight."

Determined that Fortner not see how unsettling she found his presence during her toilette, Treasure stripped to her chemise and used the clean cloth to wash away the day's grime. Some alien noise reached her ears. She paused, but did not turn around. It came again, and she almost doubted what she was hearing. She stopped all movement. Yes, the rascal was humming as if he had not a care in the world! She could feel his gaze on her back from time to time, and once her own eyes collided with his in the small mirror. She made sure that didn't happen again, though, for something in those silvery depths set her pulse racing.

After Treasure relinquished her place before the washstand, Fortner, still humming at intervals, went about shaving and getting cleaned up while she exchanged her shift for a clean one and searched for her blue riband in her saddlebags.

From a distance Treasure had watched Fortner shave his face beside the streams where they had camped, but, she reasoned, that was different from having him perform the manly ritual right in the same room with her, with his shirt off and his breeches barely hanging onto his lean hips. Without meaning to, she found herself captivated by the ripple of his naked muscles as his arms moved slowly to accommodate his careful maneuvering of the long razor blade. The little scraping sound of the blade against his dark beard followed by periodic splats of discarded lather and whiskers against the side of the basin reminded her of the many times she had watched Blackie shave. It wasn't the same, though.

Even the smell of Fortner's shaving soap was different from her father's, Treasure reflected. She sniffed. Spicier. More fragrant, somehow. And then he was splashing an even spicier liquid upon his face with his hands, the little slapping sounds loud yet intimate there in the small room. The lotion smelled a lot like what Blackie had always used, she decided, but with something different added. Lemon? No, more like piney woods.

She inhaled the fragrance and realized that the manly scent, though stronger now, was the same one she had smelled that first time he had pulled her close back at the cabin, the same one she had smelled faintly during their lovemaking in the cave. Treasure welcomed a less punishing thought: How many highwaymen bothered to carry good-smelling soap and lotion in their saddlebags?

"Does the dress fit?" Fortner asked after he finished shaving. He no longer hummed, but his tanned face wore a decidedly pleased look. He tucked a fresh white shirt inside clean brown breeches, then carelessly tied a blue patterned neckerchief around his neck and walked to where she stood struggling with the dress on the far side of the bed.

"How can I tell when I can't get the blasted thing fastened in the back?"

Laughing low in his throat at the charming picture she made as, with tangled curls spilling all over her face, she struggled to reach behind to fasten the gaping bodice, Fortner said, "Let's see if I can help."

While he fastened the hooks, Fortner reveled in the close view of so much exposed, pale, satiny skin. She was holding up her hair obligingly, and he saw for the first time the captivating indentation at the base of her hairline. Unable to restrain the impulse, he bent and kissed the tantalizing spot after fastening the final hook.

"Stop it, Fortner! Who told you that you could do that?"

Treasure had flinched from the unexpected touch of his warm lips at the nape of her neck. Her heartbeat had not been steady since he had returned with the pitcher of water, but now she felt breathless and her stomach felt fluttery. She flounced off to stand before the little mirror over the washstand and brushed her hair with far more energy than was actually needed.

"The devil in me said it might be fun," he replied with a straight face. "And that sucker was right!" Over in front of the washstand, she lifted her chin but made no comment. "You see," Fortner went on in a teasing, unhurried voice, "there's both the devil and an angel living inside me, and I never know which is going to pop up and take over." He saw her eyeing him suspiciously in the mirror while she pulled her brush through the long mass of golden curls and he grinned. Was that a hint of a smile on her full lips?

"I have news for you." Treasure could hold down the big smile trying to claim her mouth, but she couldn't fight the one inside. How could Fortner come up with such farfetched ideas? She had had no inkling that a man could speak to a woman about anything beyond his everyday world and basic needs. But here was this outlaw called Fortner, always surprising her . . . and amusing her as well, she admitted. "There's no angel living inside you, or even close by—not that I've been able to tell during the few weeks I've known you."

Treasure's attention fell then to her dress. Jumping Jehoshaphat! The neckline was so low that the top halves of her breasts were exposed. Cautiously she leaned over a bit, keeping her eyes on the image in the mirror. "Hell's bells!" she muttered, forgetting for a moment that she was not alone. "One false move and I'll be falling out of this thing."

"And what a pretty sight that'll be," Fortner said, chuckling and then letting out a soft, suggestive whistle.

"Oh, you—you devil! You weren't supposed to be listening."

Treasure's face and all of her exposed skin flushed hot and pink—and, she agonized, after she thought she had conquered such telltale signs of her inner feelings! Despite her frustration she joined in his low laughter. She guessed she *was* being a bit ridiculous. Now that she paid more attention to the fit of the dress, it was obvious that the bodice fit too snugly for her full breasts to escape. With that comforting thought she turned sideways and admired the smooth fit of the blue cotton while continuing to brush her hair. She had seen that the skirt did not quite cover her ankles, but then she was unusually tall. It was unlikely that any dress could have been found to fit her perfectly.

"The devil may be ruling me now, but when I come and help push you back inside the dress, I'll be all angel."

Treasure hooted. "I'll bet!"

The memory of his hands upon her breasts in the cave almost stole Treasure's breath and did manage to turn her nipples into tight little knobs. She was glad they had both agreed that there would be no repeats of that night's lovemaking. In time, she promised herself, she would be able to bury the disturbing thoughts of how it had felt to be in his arms. Just as she would get over being in love with him, she added with vehemence. He was far from being what her mother had assured her was the only kind of man who could make a good husband.

Not that Fortner would ever be interested in marrying her, Treasure reminded herself. He had Hannah Ainsley waiting back at McHenry's Stand. Down in Natchez perhaps some true gentleman would find her appealing and propose—like Aunt Olivia's son, Thornton Crabtree from Merrivale Plantation. For some reason the thought did not lift her spirits as it once had.

Fortner was still trying to control his pleasure upon seeing how utterly beautiful Treasure looked in the second-hand dress. It couldn't have looked prettier on her if it had been made for her, he decided from where he was sitting on the bed. Damned if the ruffles encircling her pale breasts and shoulders didn't make her look like a woman dressed up to please some man. To please him, he amended, and only him, since he was the one who had bought the dress for her.

Each time Treasure lifted her hand to brush through her long hair, Fortner admired the way her full breasts moved and rippled in the poorly lighted mirror. Never before had he watched a young woman get herself all prettied up, and he confessed that he found the little ritual fascinating. Not until she stopped and pulled the top section of her hair back to her crown did he realize that she was going to tie the curls there with a length of blue riband. A smile lifted the corners of his mouth as he recalled how at the Ryan cabin that first day he had wanted to replace the ugly black strip of cloth holding back her lovely hair with a riband. How out of character for him to be having such crazy thoughts! Then *and* now. What was wrong with him?

"You'll be the prettiest woman at the dance." Fortner's words floated out as soft and warm as the candlelight.

"Thank you, but I doubt that. If I look nice, I guess I have you to thank." Recalling her anger when he had first mentioned buying her something pretty to wear, Treasure turned to face Fortner with a flourish of full skirt and ruffles. "I do appreciate your getting the dress for me, and I'm sorry I was curt. I hope you're not going to be ashamed to be seen with me now."

"Shame never had anything to do with it," he assured her, his eyes telling her all kinds of private reasons for wanting to buy her an attractive dress—so private, in fact, that he would not dare admit them to himself. David Fortner Copeland was not yet ready to examine what he truly felt for Treasure Lindsay Ryan. He rose and walked toward her. "I like to see women looking pretty, that's all."

"Like Hannah?" *Drat! Double drat!* Treasure scolded herself inwardly. Why had she mentioned his mistress' name again when it seemed he might have forgotten about her for a spell?

"Why do you keep bringing up Hannah's name?" When she tried to turn back to the mirror, he caught her arm and backed her against the wall, playfully, but as effectively as if he meant to do her bodily harm. "Are you jealous of the ladies and your highwayman?'' His voice was low and teasing.

The way Treasure stood, so still and wary, with her eyes hiding behind the sweeps of tangled dark lashes, tugged at Fortner's heart. He had almost forgotten how much pain the beautiful young woman had endured. It was time to tell her about his sister-in-law and—

Treasure flipped Fortner's arm off hers, interrupting his thoughts and reminding him that he had forgotten her willful spirit as well. If he had not maneuvered her so close to the wall when she tried to move away from him she would have put some distance between them before replying. She was blocked in by the washstand and the handsome outlaw. Her eyes blazed in the wavering candle-light, and her chin lifted, but her words slipped out coolly in her usual husky tone. ''Don't be thinking so highly of yourself. Why would I be jealous? You're not *my* highway-man or *my* anything else ... only someone to get me to Natchez.''

Fortner acceded to the hateful truth that had eluded him for a brief spell: Some man awaited her in Natchez.

''Since we've become friends, it seems you would want me to have someone waiting for me somewhere, seeing as how you have a man expecting you in Natchez.'' He saw her lips part and her dark eyebrows lift quizzically. ''You told me about him that night we sat on your porch, remember?'' He wasn't about to repeat Hannah's suspi-cions that Treasure was on her way to get married in Natchez.

As her fingers twirled a long curl falling forward over her bare shoulder, Treasure replied, ''That's hardly the same as you having a mistress, though. My mother's girlhood friend has a son a few years older than I. She always hoped and dreamed that Danny and I could go to her home near Natchez and live the kind of life she had lived before eloping with my father. She kept telling me that I should be mistress of a fine plantation—if you can imagine such a thing.'' She let out a nervous little laugh and darted a look up at Fortner to see if he might be laughing. He wasn't. "Aunt Olivia, my mother's friend, keeps writing me about how much she hopes that when I get to Natchez, he—Thornton Crabtree—and I will like each other and maybe get married. That's all there is to that. I might not care for him at all, and he might hate me on sight."

At each revelation of the facts, Fortner's smile grew all out of proportion to what he was learning. The last statement sobered him though. "Oh, the man won't hate you on sight." Like a drop of rain lingering on a lofty tree branch, Treasure's remark that her mother thought her daughter deserved to be mistress of a plantation clung somewhere in Fortner's mind. Also like the drop of rain, her words would crystallize and claim his attention only in their own good time. Right now all he wanted was to bask in Treasure's amber gaze. He could imagine the look washing over the unknown Thornton Crabtree's face when he met the beautiful blonde, and he knew it would not resemble hate. "It's more likely he'll fall in love with you."

"Great. I'll send you a letter and tell you all about it. Then we'll each have somebody special, won't we?" His remark about their being friends had not gone unnoticed. In fact, it still rankled, even spiced her next remark with a trace of irony. "That will give us one more bond to strengthen our friendship, won't it?"

"Treasure, I can't tell you all the details yet, but you might like to know that even though Hannah is special to me and that I love—"

"You don't owe me any explanations about Hannah, and I don't want to hear any." Treasure heard herself utter that vile lie and wanted to bite her tongue. Hell's bells! Now she was going to have to hear how madly in love he was with the auburn-haired widow. She lowered her eyes and turned her head as she fluffed up the ruffles on her puffed, off-the-shoulder sleeves, her hands busy first on one side and then on the other. She wished that Fortner wasn't standing so close and that she could move about the room without having to touch him to get out of the little corner. She was feeling far too warm all over.

"Hannah Ainsley is my sister-in-law, the wife of my dead brother. She's the only woman I love, but I love her only as a sister. Hannah is engaged to marry a farmer who lives near McHenry's Stand. For reasons I can't disclose yet, she and I needed everyone to think that we were lovers. There's a lot about me that isn't exactly what it seems." Why was Treasure apparently more concerned with arranging the damned ruffles on her sleeves than listening to him? Hell! He might as well give up ever trying to understand her. He had thought she would at least show some interest in the truth about Hannah's identity.

"Well, well," she said after finding enough breath to speak. "So Hannah is your sister-in-law? That's a pretty tall tale." Dared she believe him? For sure, she wanted to. If Hannah was in love with a farmer, what could have led her to go along with such a deception? What was that bit about everything not being exactly as it seemed? How hungry she was to know all about him! She allowed herself to look at Fortner then. He really was too close for comfort. And far too handsome. "You certainly had me fooled."

"No more than you had me fooled into thinking that this Thurston Crabtree had proposed to you." Could her eyes seem so free of guile if she were not being truthful about the man in Natchez? Although he wasn't sure he wanted Treasure for himself, it pleased Fortner to know that she was not in love with anyone.

"Thornton, not Thurston. The man's name is Thornton Crabtree." Was the devilish Fortner deliberately using the wrong name just to aggravate her? As hard as Treasure tired, she could detect no sign of dissembling deep in his smoky eyes. Her thoughts ran to a subject more telling: Fortner apparently did not love her, or else he would have told her when they made love—but at least he was not in love with another. Somehow that scrap of knowledge made her head light.

Stepping back then, Fortner bowed half mockingly and

offered her his arm. "Now that we know a little more about each other, shall we go down and act the part of loving newlyweds?"

Treasure slipped her hand inside the crook of his elbow, disconcerted by the unsettling feeling in her stomach—like fluttering butterflies. "How do newlyweds act?" She looked up into his handsome face, admiring the smooth tanned skin and the fine shape of his nose and drinking in the manly fragrance of the lotion she had watched him splash on. "Have you ever been married?" She held her breath for his answer.

"No, but I've been around people who were. They treat each other special." He opened the door, liking the way the ruffles on the bottom of her skirt whispered against his breeches legs as they walked out of the room arm in arm. A lantern hanging near the top of the stairway spilled soft light into the narrow hallway. Never before had her hair looked so much like a golden cloud of silken curls as it floated down to her tiny waist. His fingers itched with longing to touch it.

"Do you mean, walking along with the woman holding the man's arm . . . like this?" She could feel the muscles beneath his white shirt sleeve bunch up, and she wondered if she might be holding his arm too tightly. Even when she lightened her touch, though, her fingers told her that his arm remained tense.

"Yes." Fortner stopped. "And maybe with him reaching to brush back a stray curl from her face . . . like this." His fingers felt as if they were all thumbs in their clumsy attempt to clear her forehead of the silken wisps. He loved the way she lifted her face to him so trustingly and the way her eyes looked in the poorly lighted hallway, sparkling and mysterious. If he had not been in the room and known better, he would have suspected that she had rubbed something pink and shiny on her lovely lips.

"And her straightening his neckerchief . . . like this." Treasure released his arm to use both hands for the little wifely task. The combined fragrances of his shaving soap and the spicy liquid used after shaving assailed her nostrils and played havoc with her breathing that time. She fought down the crazy impulse to tell him that he smelled good enough to taste. The force of his gaze added to the warmth that she could tell was flooding her cheeks, but she did not dare look higher than his mouth. Her fingers trembled as they rearranged the blue-patterned fabric so close to his face. Why had she never before noticed that his top lip was a tiny bit smaller than his bottom and that laugh lines formed little half moons near the corners? "With the bridegroom's neckerchief folded just right, people won't think he's unkempt and forget to notice how handsome he is."

They walked together again, her hand once more resting on his arm before Fortner went on with their little game. "No doubt the wife would be the first to laugh if the husband told a joke, and the husband would watch the wife all evening, even when they weren't together. That way he could knock the hell out of anyone who tried to touch her because she looks so beautiful." Treasure preened mockingly and gave him a flirty, sideways look from behind half lowered lashes that almost did him in. "Also he would be able to dash to her side quickly in case she fell out of her dress."

"You're plain naughty, Fortner. And I believe you really are a devil." She giggled and blushed, almost losing pace with his long-legged stride when she looked up at him. He truly did have the most incredible eyes. Who ever heard of pale eyes and black eyelashes?

"I know." He leaned down and whispered close to her ear. "And you love it, don't you?"

"I do not!" His breath feathered into her ear and reached clear down to the butterflies, fanning their movements into more exotic motion.

"I can tell that you do, Treasure Ryan."

"You cannot!"

A silence cloaked them then while both wiped the secretive smiles off their faces there at the top of the stairs.

"Fortner, what shall I call you, and what will you call me?" A secret voice cruelly reminded Treasure of the endearment he had called her the night they had made love in the cave: darling. Just remembering it for that brief second made her feel breathless. Fortner kept looking at her in the strangest way. Did she really look as pretty as he said she did? Something about the way his eyes brushed lazily over her made her *feel* downright beautiful, she admitted. Not that it made a lick of sense, she added.

"You'll call me David and I'll call you Lindsay," Fortner whispered so that neither of the men entering the long hallway behind them would hear. Voices from the receiving room below indicated that there would be a large number of men there. Every last one of them would want to steal her, he agonized.

"I like the name David," Treasure whispered back. Was that his real name?

"And I can accept Lindsay for one night." Fortner remembered her telling him that her father had insisted she be called Treasure instead of Lindsay. And he was glad.

"But I don't like the name Ainsley." Even now that he had offered what sounded like a reasonable explanation of his relationship with the pretty widow, Treasure could not welcome any reminder of her earlier jealousy of Hannah. Had her logical self been in charge she might have wondered if Ainsley was Fortner's true last name. Logic had stayed behind with her father's old shirt and her worn black skirt and the wonderful news that he was not in love with another woman.

Fortner put his hand over Treasure's where it rested upon his arm and whispered one final instruction before leading her down the stairs. "You don't have to like the name Ainsley; just make sure you answer to it while we're here at Colbert's Stand."

Chapter Thirteen

"I can't believe so many people have come since we arrived," Treasure said to Fortner when they went outside to the large front yard after the evening meal. Her hand had rested in the crook of his arm until they paused to look around. She was too keyed up to remain still and keep her hand in place. There was so much to see and hear!

The cleared area in front of the two-story stand had taken on a festive air, Treasure noticed with a silent wish that Danny could be with her. The thought of how her young brother's dark eyes would have sparkled brought a warm smile to her already animated face.

She could see several women in the clusters of simply garbed hill folk standing and talking beneath the lanterns hanging from tree branches here and there. Excited young children and dogs chased each other among the groups of adults standing about, their laughter and playful barks blending with cheerful adult voices. The older children—those nearer Danny's twelve years, Treasure judged by their size—seemed engrossed in a quieter game beyond the smooth grassy area, where several torches blazed. Already night insects were forming circles around the nearby lanterns, but the torches were too far away for her to see those that she knew must be humming and circling there.

"Not many of the settlers in these parts can pass up the rare chance to hear the traveling preacher give a sermon tomorrow," Fortner said, breaking their companionable silence there at the edge of the front yard. While Treasure had been drinking in the sights and sounds, he had searched the various groups for any signs of lawmen and found none.

"Well said, hoss," Bear-John said with a good-natured laugh as he came to stand beside the couple. "And nobody with middlin' good sense wants to miss the chance to shake a leg to some mountain music tonight. I'm feeling an itch myself." He kept looking around the dimly lit area as if seeking a particular face.

Treasure nodded her agreement, not needing the men's explanations. The noisy, happy scene was too much like the rare ones back in Rocky Bluffs when she was a child, like those she had recalled earlier while waiting for Fortner to get her a dress. Still not accustomed to seeing the beruffled blue skirt rippling around her ankles, she patted the full gathers at the snug waist and looked down at the pretty sight.

On the broad porch of the stand, jovial musicians were tuning up their instruments, the discordant sounds sliding out and bumping into each other in such a way as to suggest that they might never blend harmoniously. Treasure smiled, for she had faith that when the group decided the time was right to perform as a band, the notes would meld and become a rollicking mountain melody. She turned around to watch, happily leaving the two old friends to their talk about horses and soldiers and lawmen.

Two lanterns created a bright circle of light for the motley group of five men on the porch who were getting ready to entertain the gathering crowd. Treasure counted two potbellied gourd fiddles and one regular fiddle, obviously hand carved of a dark wood that she suspected might be walnut. One of the fiddlers appeared to be holding a wad of tobacco in his pouched cheek—and then she recalled that Blackie had told her long ago how the fiddlers often softened their reserve strings by holding them there until a replacement was needed. Even now that she was grown the thought of placing in one's mouth the gut from a cat, wild or not—even cleaned and boiled—did not set too well on her full stomach. Not that she was overly finicky....

Over to the side of the three fiddlers a man was rapping against his denim-clad leg the largest harmonica Treasure had ever seen. She watched him bring it up to his mouth, his work roughened hands cradling the instrument as if it were something sacred. Within moments practice scales in rich bass tones floated out upon the night air and brought chills to Treasure's sensitive backbone. Then it seemed clear to her why the musician held the harmonica with such apparent reverence.

Treasure had almost forgotten how much she missed hearing Danny play his Jew's harp until she saw one of the men put aside his blow jug and pull out a Jew's harp from his shirt pocket. If only Danny could have been there to share all of the excitement, she thought again. A new twinge of sadness tugged at her when she remembered that Hank and he had not left Colbert's Stand until that very morning. She cheered herself by thinking how it would be easy for the gang to overtake the slower traveling peddler and Danny once the Thorpes ferried across the river and they all started toward Natchez again.

"Look, Fortner," Treasure exclaimed when a newcomer joined the musicians already on the porch. She unconsciously clasped her hands in anticipation of what the spring evening promised. Maybe it was because the night air was warm and carried the sweet smells of freshly trampled grass and wildflowers, but it dawned on her that it was the first day of May. May had always seemed to herald a new beginning. "Can you believe it? There's going to be a banjo, my favorite instrument."

"I like a banjo, too, but I believe the fiddle is my favorite," Fortner said. During supper he had been proud of the way Treasure had acted her part as a newlywed. Each time he had turned to say something to her she was watching him and pretending fond interest in what he had to say. He was pretty sure that none of the five soldiers staying at the stand had any inkling that the two were not Mr. and Mrs. Ainsley, newlyweds on their way down to New Orleans. There were so many extra guests that a second table had been set up in the receiving room, but Fortner felt quite sure that not a single person had been unaware of the beautiful blonde. The blue dress set off her tall slenderness the way he had imagined it would, and he felt an inordinate measure of pride at being the man claiming her attention.

"Here she comes now," Bear-John announced. His face was wreathed in an even larger smile as he watched a petite young woman come out the front door.

"Who is she?" Treasure asked, having turned along with Fortner to see who was warranting Bear-John's obvious approval. She admired the black-haired young woman's swaying, beruffled red calico skirt. "I saw her serving the tables at supper and figured she must be one of the Colberts. She's beautiful."

"Isn't she, though?" Bear-John replied. He hurried to meet the young woman and walked with her back to join Treasure and Fortner. In an admiring tone he introduced her. "Celeste Colbert, the daughter of Sly and Mary Colbert."

Her bronze skin plainly showing her predominantly Chickasaw blood, the newcomer nodded to the couple. Tight black curls escaped from the long braid hanging down her back and framed her delicately shaped face. "Everyone calls me Star, but since my mother is half French, she first named me Celeste." Tilting her small head and cutting her pale eyes up at the towering Bear-John, she added, "When we met last summer, Bear-John learned from my brother that Celeste is my true name, and now he won't call me anything else."

"When we met last summer, you hadn't become sixteen yet, and your pa wouldn't let you take part in one of these shindys. I've already asked him if I can claim the first and last dances tonight. As well as lots in between," Bear-John said. "Is that all right with you?" His smile showed no greater pleasure than the one that Celeste returned when she demurely nodded her assent.

While Treasure and Fortner watched the pair stroll farther out in the yard, a couple of the grown Colbert sons came by. Obviously spruced up and eager to join in the night's festivities, they paused to visit.

"Are you having a good time, Mr. and Mrs. Ainsley?" Mark, the older Colbert son, asked.

"Oh, yes," Treasure answered for both Fortner and herself. Hearing the false names did not diminish her happiness. She couldn't remember when she had smiled and laughed so much, she mused. Had it all begun when she put on the pretty blue dress?

"Don't reckon you ran into that Thorpe Brothers' gang on the way down here, did you?" asked Matt Colbert, the second son.

"Never did," Fortner replied.

"Guess it's a good thing, too, for more'n one reason," Mark said. "A bunch came ridin' in here a few days ago upset and twisted all outta shape. The Thorpe gang had waylaid them back up the Trace a piece, and just as they were ready to turn over their money something weird happened. They told about how the Thorpes are being chased now by some pale, ghostlike woman with hair as long as she's tall floatin' behind her. They said she screeched and carried on like a banshee and scared the outlaws as much as them. All hell broke loose, they said, and everybody scattered in a hurry. Sounds like the work of the devil—or so some folks what heard it said."

"Sounds to me like something somebody might have made up," Fortner said, his lips moving until he pursed his mouth as if he were deep in thought. Actually he was fighting down a grin. He quickly looked down at Treasure, noticing that her eyes looked stretched wide and fixed on some repugnant, faraway subject. He might be amused, he reflected, but she sure as hell was not. He crooked his arm and offered it to her, but she seemed unaware.

"Yeah," Matt said. "They said she rode a horse the same color as her hair and, pardon me, ma'am," he said to Treasure. When Fortner nudged her with his elbow, she nodded a stiff permission for Matt to continue. "She didn't have a stitch of clothes on. Two what saw her said she could'a been a witch or even a real ghost for all they could tell. The other four said she was more like a beautiful avengin' angel, what with her eyes all shiny gold like her hair and shooting sparks right and left." When the couple stared at him, apparently too stunned for words, Matt added, "Pa says he never heard of the Thorpe gang killin' any women, not even when they had several men ridin' with 'em a few years back and were causin' a lot more ruckus than they have lately."

"I don't know much about what the Thorpes have done, but I don't believe I would put too much faith in such a wild tale as those men told," Fortner said, doggedly refusing to let surface the grim memory of his mother's charred, bullet-marked body. "Likely somebody got to drinking and letting his imagination run away with him."

"That's what Pa said, too," Mark said, sending disapproving looks at his more talkative brother. Then, with polite nods of their dark heads toward the rigid, suddenly mute Mrs. Ainsley, the Colbert sons moved on to mingle with the other guests.

"Take my arm, Treasure," Fortner whispered as soon as they were alone again.

Treasure clutched his arm then, sagging against him. "My God! They know, don't they? They know I'm—"

"No, they have no idea—nor do the other Colberts— that Bear-John and I joined up with the Thorpes last fall. When we came back through here we weren't traveling together. Nobody here knows we have any connection with the gang." Fortner could feel her body trembling, and he longed to put his arms around her.

"I wonder why those men made up such a lie about my not having on any clothes?" Treasure asked, her face flushing at the exaggerated account of her being naked when she rode up the Trace screaming. And with sparks shooting from her eyes!

Hoping he might gain at least a smile from her, Fortner countered, "It made a hell of a better story that way, don't you think?" Low laughter shook his shoulders. He saw no need in letting Treasure dwell upon the negative aspects of the bizarre tale. He had been enjoying her soaring spirits and fine humor, and he had no wish to see them disappear.

At first Treasure wanted to slap Fortner's laughing face, but the more she thought about it, the more she could see the humor in the whole situation. Besides, the night seemed too fraught with enchantment to dwell upon anything but the handsome highwayman. A giggle escaped first, then, after she let her eyes meet his, a full belly laugh rolled out.

Before Treasure and Fortner squelched their laughter, the musicians ceased their tuning and practicing and struck up a few lively chords which evolved into a spirited song. Instantly from the groups came several couples hand in hand to answer the musical call. They moved out into the open yard, their feet stomping upon the hard, grassy soil and their faces wreathed with smiles.

From the sidelines the people who were not dancing added to the merriment by clapping their hands and tapping their toes in time with the mountain melody. Treasure laughed up at Fortner when a good-natured male voice called from the shadows, "Wahoo! Swang that purty little woman one more time!"

The boisterous children and dogs slowed their games at the sounds of the rollicking music and settled down upon quilts lying beneath the lanterns. A kind of magic cast its spell over the bucolic scene on the western banks of the Tennessee River.

"Come dance with me, wife," Fortner said.

The name had slipped out without his notice, but it did not escape Treasure's attention. A smiling Fortner captured her hand where it rested upon his arm, then reached for the other, but she slid it behind her back and tried to back away from him. Wife. Obviously the term meant next to nothing to him. He was merely keeping up the game of pretense. And doing a damned good job, Treasure thought grudgingly.

"I've already told you that I don't plan to dance." The way his eyes sent a silvery invitation along with the voiced one set Treasure's heart to jigging on its own. Inside, each speck of her seemed to reverberate with the tantalizing rhythm coming from the tinkling banjo. Ringing clear and happy, almost like a sparkling waterfall tumbling down a tall rock, it called to her hungry spirit with promise.

"Tell me, Treasure," he said, leaning low so as to read

her luminous eyes, "is it because you don't want to dance with me or is it because you don't know how?"

"It's because I don't know how." Treasure could not deny to herself how much she longed to be claimed in his manly arms before all the people there. At the supper table she had sensed the respect that the other guests had for the handsome man posing as her husband; and she had basked in the attention they gave her as his companion. What was it about Fortner that seemed to pull people toward him and make them want his approval? She had not once thought of him as an outlaw all evening—until the Colbert sons had come by and told that farfetched tale about her wild dash up the Trace. And now, as surely as the musician blowing into the empty whiskey jug was marking the tempting, lively beat, she was going to let Fortner talk her into trying to dance. She would fall on her face. She knew it. If only she could get away.

"Trust me," Fortner said softly. He held out his free hand, and, as though in a trance, she placed hers in it. "I can tell you're feeling the music." As if to prove it, he laced his fingers with hers and moved both their hands in time to the rhythm. When she realized that his hand wasn't moving all by itself, she looked up at him and nodded. He put her left hand on his shoulder, then rested his right hand at the back of her small waist. "All you have to do is let your feet have their way. Follow me, Treasure. First, a heel"—she looked down at his foot, angling her own to rest upon its heel like his—"and a toe . . . then a step, step, step . . . and away we go!"

And with those carefree words, Fortner heeled and toed Treasure amidst the other dancing couples. Before they had moved very far she found, to her amazement, that he was right. All she had to do was let the rhythm dancing inside direct her feet. Fortner's strong arm around her waist and his hand holding hers guided her in the right direction. Suddenly she was free.

With her long blue skirt whirling, Treasure gave in on successive tunes to the compulsive urge to become one with the singing banjo. *Plink!* She felt as if her heart had a million strings being plucked by magical fingers. *Plank!* She felt as if her tickle box was in tune with the happy banjo, and she laughed for the pure joy of being seventeen and alive and dancing with the most handsome young man she had ever seen. The man she had fallen in love with, the one who kept whispering to her that she was the most beautiful woman there.

Plinkety plank plank! His teeth flashing white as he smiled down at her, Fortner winked at Treasure in a shamelessly flirty way. His deep laughter joined hers then as if they shared the most delightful secret in the world. *A heel and a toe!* she exulted. And the night was only beginning.

After each of the first three dances, Fortner hugged the starry-eyed, breathless Treasure close when others seemed headed in their direction to claim a dance. The time came, though, when the men did not turn away politely. Realizing that there were so few women there, and none so beautiful as Treasure, he relinquished his "bride" with open reluctance.

From the sidelines Fortner saw what he had felt when she was in his arms. Treasure was a light-footed dancer with a natural feel for the music. Around and around her various partners whirled her, and each time Fortner admired the way the blue dress belled out from her tiny waist and showed her pretty ankles. Her bouncing hair seemed to pick up new curls from the night's damp breeze, and it shone like a beacon to the man who watched from the sidelines.

Though her smiles and bursts of laughter might not have been as frequent or as vivacious as those she had delighted him with, Fortner reflected with honesty, Treasure still smiled and gave each partner a glimpse of her carefree spirit. Why did it bother him? he wondered while he sipped on corn whiskey and found that he could think of little else. After all, he did not own her—as she had been quick to point out on more than one occasion. And he had no wish to—as he had told himself even more frequently.

Fortner walked over to the refreshment stand set up earlier by Sly Colbert and his sons and asked for a refill of the potent corn whiskey. He guessed that he should be doing more than watching Treasure and sipping on the colorless brew from the Colbert still, but he relished spending such a rare, relaxing evening. There were no raucous Thorpes to be gambling with around a campfire and no reason to pretend to be anything except what he was.

"It was nice having you and your wife at our table tonight, Ainsley," Sergeant Canfield said after fetching himself a cup of whiskey and joining Fortner underneath a large, thickly branched cedar tree. "I enjoyed dancing with your pretty wife a little while ago."

"That's good," Fortner replied, remembering just how much the good looking young soldier had seemed to be enjoying it. Once he had suspected the sergeant might be holding Treasure far closer than necessary, but . . . He forced himself to concentrate on other matters. "Did I hear you say at supper that you and your men had come down from Nashville last week by way of Rocky Bluffs?"

"That's right. We've been sent out on detail to clear the Trace of fallen trees and such, and we followed that loop on our way here. Do you know the place?"

"Yes, I've been through Rocky Bluffs. Seems like I recall there's a storekeeper there named Amos . . ." Fortner deliberately left off Amos' last name.

"Oh, you mean Amos Greeson," Sergeant Canfield said with a knowing smile. "Amos is a peculiar sort, to say the least. He rules that little spot like a backwoods tyrant."

Fortner swallowed hard. He had no wish to make the man suspicious, but he had to know. "How was old Amos when you were there last week?"

"He said he was fit as a fiddle," the sergeant replied. "But if you asked me, he had done more than run into a wildcat in the woods to get all those scratches on his face and neck. Even had some cuts on his hands, and some weren't completely healed."

"Do you think Amos had been hunting and was jumped by a wildcat?" Fortner asked, working to keep his shock from showing in his face or voice. Amos Greeson was alive! Treasure had not killed him with her knife. Something strange was going on. Hoping to glean more information without appearing overly interested, he tried for a casual tone. "I didn't know he was a hunting man."

"Frankly, I don't believe he is, anymore than I believe that was a real wildcat that cut him up." Sergeant Canfield sipped on his whiskey, then added with a big grin, "All of us suspected that Amos might have run into a wildcat all right, but one with a knife in her hand."

"I guess if it happened that way, Amos would have the law on her and lock her up—or else they would be finding some dead woman's body." Fortner sucked in a breath and held it while awaiting the man's next remarks.

Sergeant Canfield laughed. "You must not know him as well as we do or you'd know that Amos is too big a coward to do anything but talk a good game." He sipped his brew and continued, apparently pleased that someone wanted to hear what he and his friends had learned. "We've come through Rocky Bluffs often enough to learn how everybody around there knows all about Amos' business. They seem to talk about it with everyone but him, so we jawed a spell with the men who were hanging around outside his store. They said nearly the same thing as you about how Amos surely would have the law on anybody who dared attack him. They had asked around and found that Sheriff Tadlock wasn't out looking for anybody, so they were about to decide they won't ever get to know who cut up the old skinflint. One said he thought at first it might have been that Indian woman living with Amos who looks after his kids."

"Maybe it was the Indian woman who did it," Fortner offered when the sergeant slowed down to savor some more of the Colbert moonshine. The need to learn that Treasure Ryan's name was not going to crop up consumed him.

"No. The Indian is just as curious as everybody else. She said Amos came home one morning just before daylight, all bloody and half out of his head. Till she saw the cuts, she figured Amos had had one of his temper fits and passed out and maybe fallen off his horse somewhere. She didn't have any better explanation than anyone else." The soldier brought his cup up to his mouth and drank again before ending his tale. "No doubt Amos Greeson met his match and isn't eager to let anybody else know it."

Fortner smiled feebly, hardly aware when the young man slapped him on the back in a friendly way and went to join his fellow soldiers beneath a far tree.

What the hell was going on? Fortner wondered, his eyes following Treasure among the dancers. Why did she think she had killed Amos when obviously she had done no more than slash him up a bit? He tried to recall what she had told him. Hadn't she said that Hank was the one who told her that Amos was dead? Could the old peddler have been mistaken? After all, according to Treasure's account, it had been dark, and both Hank and she must have been frightened half out of their wits.

Still, Fortner mused, something about the affair didn't ring true—like where had George Henry heard that Treasure was wanted for murder and that the sheriff was looking for her? From what Treasure had told him about the old peddler's long relationship with her family, he couldn't believe that Hank would be sharing such news with outlaws . . . or anybody else. George Henry had let it slip that he'd had recent contact with Whitey, likely since they had left McHenry's Stand. Had the elusive boss of the Thorpe Brothers' gang told the lie about Treasure? Obviously it was a lie, or else the soldiers would not have found Amos alive last week when they stopped in Rocky Bluffs.

Fortner knew that when law officers in rural Tennessee were looking for someone, they shared their information with the military at Fort Nashborough and gave them the authority to help in their searches. Why else would Bear-John and he be scouting ahead at Colbert's Stand for George Henry and Juno, except to avoid running into soldiers who might take them back to Nashville for questioning and possible arrest?

Should he tell Treasure what he'd heard? Fortner wondered, imagining how happy she would be to learn that she had not killed Amos Greeson. After one more swig of moonshine, he decided that it might be better to wait and share the good news with her after they returned to their room. It was likely she would get excited, and he had no wish to call special attention to them there in the crowd. *Besides,* some sneaky inner voice whispered, *if she learned she wasn't an outlaw, she might turn all of you in and gain her freedom from you. She had already tried to escape once, hadn't she?*

The familiar tall figure of Bear-John came into view then, and Fortner admired his friend's grace as he danced with the pretty Celeste Colbert. He wondered if the way they gazed into each other's eyes meant that something was brewing between them. By damn, he thought as he finished his second cup of whiskey, they did make a handsome couple.

When the music stopped and one of the musicians announced that they were taking some time off to rest, Fortner headed toward Treasure, who stood talking with her recent dance partner, Mark Colbert. Thoughts of Amos Greeson had disappeared along with the moonshine.

"I'll claim my wife now and find her something to drink," Fortner said to the young man. He watched Mark walk away before he turned back to Treasure. Her face was flushed and her long hair was tousled a bit. He thought she never had looked prettier . . . or more kissable. "You've been having a good time, I see."

"Yes, I have," Treasure replied in that husky tone that seemed to Fortner to reach right out and caress his ears on its way deep inside him somewhere. "Have you been watching, or have you been dancing with some of the other women?"

Smarting a bit that she obviously had not given him a glance or a thought since he relinquished her to other partners four dances ago, Fortner felt an urge to remind her that they were far from being strangers. Two cups of corn whiskey had stirred up that inner devil he had told Treasure about, he told himself when the word jealous came to mind. His gaze raked openly across her exposed shoulders and the swells of her full breasts before he leaned close to her ear and whispered, "How could I take the chance on not being on hand if you popped out of your dress?"

Treasure felt as if the heat of Fortner's gaze on her skin had penetrated all the way into her bloodstream and created a problem for her heart; it seemed to be skipping up and down in search of an escape route. Lifting her hair off her warm neck with both hands, she huffed and pretended that she thought he was awful, but she couldn't keep a smile from curving her lips. She let her hair fall then and brushed back the tiny moist curls clinging to her forehead and temples. "I see the devil in you is still in control."

Feeling especially light-headed—from the whiskey, he told himself—Fortner put his arm around her small waist and guided her toward the refreshment table. She nestled against him as they unhurriedly walked in step, and he felt much taller than his six feet and three inches. "Frankly," he told her when she looked up at him through her thick lashes, "I'm a lot more fun when the devil's in charge."

"Maybe I should be the judge of that."

Then the talkative, fun loving crowd mingled around them and private talk died as the hill folk asked their names and told their own. The music and dancing had knocked down earlier barriers, and Treasure felt that she might truly be among friends. For a brief moment she wondered if the approving looks and smiles might not turn into frowns and snarls if everyone learned that Fortner and she were outlaws, not seemingly respectable newlyweds, Mr. and Mrs. Ainsley. The thought marred the evening's beauty, and she pushed it aside.

Easy conversation among the other couples and the Ainsleys filled the time as all moved closer to the refreshment table. Earlier the Colberts had served the children who were still awake and sent them back to their pallets underneath the trees. The men tried to talk about their hunting and planting, but the women refused to be outdone. They laughed and flirted and wheedled them into talking with them about the fine music and the dancing yet to be done on the rare, festive occasion.

When it came Fortner's turn to order refreshments, Bear-John and Celeste had joined Treasure and him. The two men bought cups of blackberry wine and pieces of plum cake with raisins before escorting Treasure and Celeste over to sit on the edge of the porch. For all four the time flew while they ate and drank and talked of nothing serious at all, judging from the frequent bursts of lighthearted laughter. They confessed surprise when the musicians once more took their places on the porch. Not wanting to miss a single dance, they hurried out to the open area.

The tinkling, driving music led the whirling dancers onward while the torches down near the river burned out, unnoticed now that the moon had risen and was lending its silvery light to the scene. The whale oil in the lanterns hanging in the trees sank lower in their bases. Only the moon on the horizon and the stars spreading out across the canopy of night sky grew brighter with each passing hour—unless it was the flare fueling Treasure's love for Fortner, or, perhaps, the similar flame burning, unrecognized, deep inside Fortner's heart for the beautiful blonde with the golden eyes.

"Look," Fortner told Treasure as they waited for the music to begin again. His arm still encircled her waist possessively. Someone from the porch had hollered that the last song was coming up after the musicians rested a few minutes. "There's the Little Dipper."

Her eyes following where his hand pointed northward toward the constellation in the velvety sky, Treasure nodded, too moved by the awesome brilliance overhead, the evening's fun, and the man with his arm around her waist to speak. Though they stood surrounded by other couples, she had the uncanny feeling that Fortner, she, and the sky occupied a special private patch of the world. In a crazy kind of way she felt that she might be glowing right along with the dazzling stars and that they might be calling to each other to look down at the young woman standing beside the Tennessee River with her beloved.

"And over there," Fortner went on after a sweet silence in which they both gazed upward, "is the Big Dipper. Strange, isn't it, that we should be looking at the same star that the Book of Job calls Arcturus? I wonder how many thousands of other people have seen the constellations and also found strength in knowing that they're always there." He wondered, too, why it was that feeling Treasure leaning lightly against him as he hugged her close with one arm seemed as natural and reassuring as looking up and finding both of the dippers on a clear night.

Treasure had eyes only for Fortner by the time his deep voice died away. He spoke of the Bible as if he knew it well, she mused wonderingly. She had no false illusions about her limited knowledge of the world outside the Ryan farm and the books there; but she sensed, and not for the first time, that the handsome man she gazed at was far more complex and serious than he had led her to believe.

Earlier that night he had told her about his sister-in-law, Hannah, and that he could not say more about himself yet. What else was there to tell? she wondered with a sudden, aching need to know everything about the highwayman. She was falling more in love with him with each passing hour.

Surprised at the turn of her thoughts, Treasure realized that it no longer seemed important to her that Fortner had broken laws and might continue to break them. All that he was—even though she had no knowledge about what that might encompass—she loved. Nothing else mattered.

Tired but happy when the music and dancing ended, the revelers at Colbert's Stand made their way to varied places to sleep away the small portion of remaining darkness. No one cared to miss the next glorious occasion: the traveling preacher would be arriving around noon the next day to extol the glories of Heaven and to condemn the fiery pits of Hell.

Families traveling from distant cabins in the hills slipped

into bedrolls alongside those of their already sleeping children. The low-limbed trees surrounding the edges of the front yard of Colbert's Stand offered protection from the rising night winds blowing moisture up from the Tennessee River. The travelers fortunate enough to have found rooms at the stand trudged inside and found their beds. Some paid a small fee to throw bedrolls on the front porch. Many, like Bear-John, walked the short distance to the large barn behind the stand and climbed up into the well-stocked hayloft.

Treasure and Fortner, still in a daze from the magic of the night, wandered down a moonlit path leading to the river. Holding hands and looking more frequently at each other than at the moon-drenched scenes around them, neither felt the need for talk. As if the earlier sounds of the band had frightened them away or, perhaps, made them ashamed to intrude now on the peaceful silence, night callers were few.

Midnight was long gone by the time the starry-eyed couple stepped gingerly around the people sleeping on the shadowed porch. They almost broke into laughter when one man let out a monstrous snore and flopped over directly in their path. With a warning forefinger held against her smiling lips when she looked over her shoulder at Fortner, Treasure led the way as they entered the empty, dimly lit receiving room and tiptoed up the stairs to their room.

"No need to light a candle," Treasure said after Fortner closed the door to their room.

"I agree."

Pale moonlight streamed through the open window beside the headboard of the bed. Treasure walked over to see the stars, not wanting to think about going to sleep. The thought that Fortner might climb into the bed with her made butterflies start up in her stomach. Maybe he would just throw his bedroll on the floor. The bothersome situation of how they would manage the obviously limited sleeping space had loomed in her mind ever since the band had stopped playing.

Not that the insane rhythm pulsing through her body had slowed one bit, Treasure agonized. It seemed that the singing banjo still echoed within her. She pulled her thoughts back to more solid matters and noticed that the stars seemed paler now that the moon had added its brilliance to the heavens. Even so, the stars still twinkled upon the dark overhead dome, and she again felt an eerie kinship with them. Who was watching whom?

Chapter Fourteen

"Did you have fun dancing tonight?" Fortner asked, moving to stand behind Treasure as she stood looking out the window.

"Oh yes, Fortner." Treasure turned to look up at him. "Thank you for the dress and for teaching me to dance and—"

Fortner's lips drowned out the rest of what she might have said. Treasure stepped close to his tall, manly frame and gave herself the treat of answering his sweet lips; it seemed the proper ending for such a perfect evening, she reasoned. She admitted to herself that she had been more than a little disappointed that during their silent, leisurely stroll down by the river Fortner had not kissed her.

After this one kiss, she promised the tiny protesting part of herself, she would insist that he throw his bedroll on the floor and sleep there. No matter that she intended to fall out of love with Fortner as quickly as she had fallen in love with him, she would allow herself this final brief embrace. Her blood heated up alarmingly as his lips alternately softened and pressed against her own. She felt again the furious fluttering of the butterflies that had claimed her stomach earlier. Her arms must not have gotten the message that Treasure intended to end the kiss right away, for they crept up his white shirtfront and around his neck.

Like honey, Fortner thought when his lips first tasted Treasure's. Like honey and nectar and all the delicious things his besotted brain could imagine. He thought back to how light-headed the moonshine had made him earlier in the evening and knew that what now set his senses reeling was a far more intoxicating brew. He was drunk, all right—drunk on moonlight and fragrant silken skin and long blond hair and laughing golden eyes. Drunk on Treasure.

The way her curves melted against the planes of his body turned Fortner's thoughts away from his original intention to kiss her good night and unroll his blanket on the floor. While strolling with her in the moonlight he had meant to tell her what he had learned about Amos Greeson, but his mouth had refused to form the words. What if, afterward, she were to stalk away and report to Sergeant Canfield that she was an innocent woman held against her will by a highwayman? Later. He would tell her later, he promised himself again.

Without much difficulty, Fortner squelched all thoughts but those of the beautiful Treasure in his arms and how the taste and the feel of her were wreaking a welcome devastation within. His tongue traced the soft inside of her full lips, then searched further in to the remembered velvety depths when she moaned low in her throat and opened her mouth more fully to his.

Treasure did not know how long they stood in rapt embrace, so lost was she to the wonder of Fortner's tender mouth and his strong arms holding her close. The manly fragrance and texture of his skin excited her, reminding her of the wondrous differences between man and woman. Her breath came in spurts, linked somehow with her erratic heartbeat. Hearing her beloved's chaotic breathing laboring to match up with her own titillated her anew.

When she felt his fingers lifting her hair and then

fumbling with the hooks on the back of her dress, a licking tongue of searing flame replaced the swarm of butterflies inside her stomach and slithered enticingly to invade her womanhood. Stepping back and gazing up at Fortner when the dress was freed, Treasure worshipped him with marveling, star-kissed eyes as he tenderly slid the puffed sleeves down her arms, the ruffled bodice whispering down and over her full breasts, her slender rib cage, and then her small waist. When he freed the sleeves and the bodice, the pretty blue dress rippled over her hips and down to the floor with a little feminine sighing sound.

"This promises to be one of my best ideas," Fortner said, his pale eyes as warm and mysterious as smoke in moonlight.

"I think you may be right." Treasure's voice was huskier than Fortner had expected and worked a finer magic on him than at any earlier time. She stepped free of the dress encircling her feet and kicked it aside, her eyes knowingly flirting from behind half lowered lashes and never leaving his.

With her golden hair and luminous face limned by the moon's glow, Treasure looked as if she might be some ethereal beauty visiting from a mythical world, Fortner thought with awe. The fire building in his groin leapt and set his pulse to an even faster pace. And as they were naught but very real lovers of delightful flesh and blood and boundless passion, they exchanged dazzling smiles of promise before Fortner leaned reverently to lave the tops of her breasts with a spate of warm, moist kisses.

Then, his silvery gaze drinking in each newly exposed part of her, he gathered the lower edge of her shift in both hands and slowly lifted it over her long shapely legs . . . her curving hips . . . her tiny waist . . . her voluptuous breasts . . . and, at last, her head, surprising and delighting her with a kiss upon her lips the moment that her face was free. With roguish aplomb he kept his mouth on hers and sailed the garment across the moonlit room with one hand.

If any inhibitions still lurked within—and she doubted that any did—Treasure sent them flying with her shift over to the darkened corner. She moaned her pleasure and pressed her naked breasts against Fortner's solid chest, kissing him back with matching fervor. Her senses reeling, she felt his hands sliding her underdrawers down and off. As earlier that evening when he had shown her how to dance, she felt free, ecstatically free, but in a far more delicious, earthy way.

He lifted her in his arms then and cosseted her, slowly twisting his upper torso from right to left and back again, while gazing down at her as if she might be his most precious possession. The feel and the sight of her lissome body so close in his arms satisfied Fortner's inexplicable love of natural beauty. Never had he dreamed of holding such perfection, even for a brief moment.

Fortner stooped and, with one hand, yanked back the Wedding Ring quilt and eased Treasure onto the white sheet on the double bed. As if he had all the time in the world and had chosen that particular way to please himself, he then began to strip one shapely leg and foot of a stocking and a shoe. His warm hands lingered upon her smooth bare leg and foot and worked some kind of soothing magic on both Treasure and him as his fingers gently massaged away the kinks left from so much dancing.

"Hmmm, Fortner," Treasure murmured, watching him with a satisfied expression suggesting that she might be purring. "That feels heavenly." She didn't tell him that each touch from his fingers stretched all the way up her leg to her heart or that she felt she might melt and turn into jelly gone bad from too much heat.

"We must be getting close to the right territory then," he replied in a velvety whisper, bending his dark head to plant a kiss on the arch of the well-shaped foot he held.

Not once did Fortner's enchanting gaze let Treasure forget that he adored each inch that his hands caressed.

"Beautiful," he murmured at intervals, pausing to smile up into her enraptured face. Then, "Perfect."

A marvelous ache joined the swelling blaze in Fortner's groin. With the same sensuous movements he rewarded her other fair limb, unaware that he was giving far more erotic pleasure than he was gaining.

Treasure sank back against the soft pillow in the throes of bliss, her insides turning into a useless pool of warm pulsating wetness that threatened to drown her. She heard the sounds of her shoes falling to the floor when Fortner removed them, but mainly she heard her heartbeat pounding mercilessly in her ears, in her chest, and throughout her entire body. And she was still hearing the leftover rhythm of the lilting banjo echoing deep within her vulnerable heart.

"No," Treasure said when Fortner removed his own shoes and socks and stretched out beside her, reaching to pull her into his arms. She tried to push him away, but her hand refused to put firm pressure on that lean manly cheek; it merely lay there, as if it had found a home.

"No?" He studied her love swollen lips and her eyes. Were they not sparkling warmly with what he had suspected was passion? Removing her hand from where it was heating his cheek, he turned it palm upward and kissed it before looking at her again. His mouth went dry with fear that Treasure might repeat his promise made back in the cave not to try making love with her again. What if she asked him to honor it? "No?"

"No. Not until you take off your clothing. I can't wait to feel you naked against me." Treasure held her breath at her impulsiveness and wondered if she might be part wanton. But Fortner chuckled then and leaned over to plant a loud kiss on a saucy, uptilted nipple, and she knew that she had pleased him . . . as well as something wild and yearning within herself.

Quickly Treasure rose to her knees on the bed. She reached behind his neck and began untying the blue neckerchief that she had so carefully smoothed earlier that evening. She was leaning so close that the backs of his hands brushed against her naked breasts as he fumbled with the buttons on his shirt. Unexpected thrills raced over her and stole her breath. Her nipples, already tight little buds, tingled anew at each seemingly casual contact with his busy hands.

"Let me," she begged when he would have shrugged off the white garment without her help.

Remembering the thrills he had given her when he had removed her own clothing, Treasure unhurriedly slid the sleeves down over his robust, muscular arms. She exulted in the way he gazed at her so adoringly and let her have her way. At each opportunity she deliberately let her pulsating breasts brush against his furred chest. Smiling and sending him flirtatious looks between each movement, she leaned to kiss the smooth swell of his well-muscled forearm, recalling as her lips moved on down his powerful arm to his hand how those manly muscles, arms, and hands had combined to save her from the despicable George Henry. And earlier that awful night, she recalled with renewed awe for the handsome man watching her, his sharp mind had come up with the way to save her life and Danny's.

Oh, no! a secretive voice scolded Treasure. *Not tonight. No memories tonight that remind you that your beloved is a highwayman with perhaps a brief time to ride the Trace and remain alive—and a man who has never said that you are special to him, much less that he loves you. Tonight is the last time you can allow yourself to get lost in Fortner's arms. You well know that he is not the kind of man who will ever marry you and make a good husband. Didn't your mother tell you so?*

By the time Treasure's mind had skimmed over that voice's warnings and kicked it into a hidden corner, she had taken off Fortner's shirt and breeches. Laughing lowly, she flung them to find resting places atop her own garments somewhere on the floor in the shadows. He stood and slipped off his underbreeches and lay down beside her, moving into her welcoming arms with a deep growl of masculine pleasure.

"Darling," he whispered, not suspecting that some part of Treasure awaited that endearment and snatched it into her heart for safekeeping before the last resonant syllable faded in the moonlit room.

Fortner doubted that he would ever forget the way Treasure snuggled against his nakedness and offered her honeyed mouth to him. Searing passion washed over him anew as their tongues met and caressed. His hungry hands filled themselves with the remembered shape of her firm, warm breasts. Though it did not come as a full-fledged thought, he sensed that whereas he had *seen* beauty when he had cradled Treasure in his arms and looked down at her, he was now *feeling* beauty within every sensitive part of his body.

His tingling hands became lost in her glorious cloud of hair, and his heart expanded when her fingers crept through his own hair and then lingered at his ears. Short of breath but brimful of desire for the lovely, long-limbed young woman in his arms, he gave his hands license to explore all the provocative silken hills and valleys that he embraced. Woman. Treasure was all woman. His woman! he exulted, stealing a moment to examine what that term might truly mean. Was he in love with her? Or was he merely bewitched?

The moon sailed along its destined course on the western horizon while the lovers basked in its pale light in the small room of Colbert's Stand. Fevered caresses and kisses guided them with certainty to that ultimate union that both had courted from their first kiss upon returning to their room, courted sometimes provocatively, sometimes tenderly, and sometimes with an underlying fierceness fraught with their unrecognized needs to hear and speak the words "I love you."

Treasure felt the smoothness of the sheet against her back when Fortner turned her to receive him, but the remaining part of her senses dwelled upon the feel of his throbbing manhood as it touched the velvety opening to her womanhood. The inner beat pulsing throughout her body ever since the music and the dancing had begun directed her hips to tilt invitingly and plead for Fortner to become a part of her once more.

When her beloved entered her gently but masterfully and she felt no pain this time, Treasure felt like celebrating and cried out and moved her head restlessly against the pillow. She nipped at his lips with her teeth and clasped him closer with her arms, eager for his pressing member to meet the center of that moist mass of womanhood that had been waiting in trembling need. Her softness enfolded his firm length, and for an exquisite moment he lay still and deep within her. They became one in a kind of molten ecstasy. He moved a little, then returned to her core. She welcomed him again and embraced his lean hips with her legs so as to absorb more of him. The inner music that Treasure had captured earlier swelled right along with the scintillating heat reaching out from her center as she joined Fortner in the glorious rhythm of love that he had shown her that night in the cave.

And all at once the brilliance that the panting lovers sought burst over them, filling both with a piercing light and joy that catapulted them skyward. Together they soared to one of those distant stars Treasure had imagined might be watching them beside the Tennessee River. She wondered if, for a brief time, Fortner and she might not be inside that star . . . no, they had somehow become that star and they *were* the celestial brilliance swelling majestically until the heavens could no longer contain it.

The explosion burst without a sound until the lovers cried out in jubilation. Even as their star disintegrated and fell into oblivion, a kind of harmony reaching beyond what Treasure had clutched inside all evening escorted the breathless lovers back to earth, back to the bed, back to splendidly satiated arms and legs and bodies.

As when they had walked beside the river and had felt no need for words to maintain communication, Treasure and Fortner lay within each other's arms and welcomed the comforting blanket of sleep.

Shortly before the tender pink of dawn, Treasure awoke from a vaguely frightening dream. She was lying with her back to Fortner, who lay on his side facing her with a protective arm flung across her. Ever since she had chosen to be his woman a short week ago after the fight with George Henry, Treasure mused, she had awakened to find them in similar positions—except that no separate blankets enwrapped their bodies now. And both were still naked. Memories of their impassioned lovemaking claimed her attention, and she smiled at the memories of erotic caresses, both from Fortner and from herself.

Pushing tousled curls from her eyes, Treasure turned to admire the handsome sleeping face in the pale light. Her slight movement brought an aching awareness of the scratchy but mesmerizing feel of the dark masculine hairs on his arm resting on her naked shoulder. An involuntary shiver claimed her. What was she going to do about the way she loved Fortner? she wondered with a stab of sadness for all that might have developed between them if they had not been running from the law.

Treasure allowed herself to imagine that they were free from such troubles as dodging lawmen. Had Fortner perhaps fallen in love with her a little and held back telling her since it was apparent that they could have no future together? If that were true and they could begin anew as merely a young man and a young woman, without the stigma of being outlaws, would he ask her to marry him? No, she admitted with growing sadness as she glanced at his handsome features again. He did not love her, for he would have told her so even if they had no future as a couple.

Trying not to disturb Fortner, Treasure inched from under his arm and padded on bare feet to the open window. The moon was low on the horizon, but its glow yet bathed the heavens and reflected there in the small room. The stars were fading fast, but she noted that one seemed still wondrously radiant.

A smile hovered at the corners of her mouth when she recalled how she had wondered if the culmination of their passionate lovemaking might not have carried them up to a star and left them shimmering there for a brief time. She sighed at the fanciful thought, sending her toes to press hard against the rough wooden floor and remind her that she existed in the real world now. When a breeze floated in to dance in her hair and send chill bumps down her naked back, she tiptoed over to the corner and sorted through the pile of clothing until she found her shift.

Returning to the window once more after donning the shift, Treasure thought of how she had so foolishly vowed that she would get over loving Fortner. After their evening of dancing and having fun followed by the glorious love-making, she admitted that she was making hopeless promises to herself. Fortner had become as much a natural part of her as that distant star was of the heavens.

"Are you looking for a falling star?" Fortner asked, propping his head against his opened palm and looking across at Treasure. She seemed to blossom in the celestial light, he thought as his gaze rested on her shift-clad curves and the golden cloud of tangled waves and curls reaching to her waist.

Treasure, startled, turned to look at him. "I tried to be quiet so as not to wake you." How was it possible that he looked even more handsome with his hair all tousled and tumbling across his forehead?

"You didn't make a sound, but I must have sensed you were no longer beside me." Like a flash of lightning across a stark, midnight sky, it dawned on Fortner that he was in love with the beautiful young woman with the golden hair and eyes. He sat bolt upright and tried to still his racing pulse. When had this crazy, undesired thing happened to him? He had a mission of revenge to accomplish; there was no place in his life at that time for a woman . . . or for love. Even in his agitated state of mind he realized that vengeance and love could not exist side by side. Willing himself to become again that blind person who had refused to acknowledge what had attracted him to Treasure from the beginning, he struggled to recapture the light conversation. "I asked you if you're looking for a falling star."

"Maybe. My mother used to tell me that if you see one, you can make a wish and it will come true."

"Have you ever seen one and made a wish that came true?"

Treasure shook her head, a section of her hair sliding forward to rest across a breast. "I don't believe in such things." *But I wish I did,* she added silently, returning her gaze to the heavens.

Fortner laughed low in his throat, bending to find and pull on his underbreeches. "What's to lose? What would you wish *if* you believed and *if* you saw a star falling?"

Treasure tilted her head and brushed back her mussed hair impatiently, her eyes still fixed on the sky overhead. "You'd laugh if I told you."

"No I wouldn't. Tell me." Fortner rose then and walked near her at the open window.

"I would wish that I wasn't an outlaw—or you either."

"Is there any special reason why?"

Treasure turned her face to his, knowing that when she did he would be awfully near, for the space before the window was rather close. "Yes. For one thing, it seemed so right last night to be with those friendly people and acting as if you and I were free and belonged. I hated knowing that they might be afraid and would likely despise us if they knew what we really are. I would have liked it if we were able to join them this afternoon when the preaching takes place." His pale eyes seemed completely silver, Treasure mused, except for the dark pupils and the outer rims of the irises. She wondered about the pained look deep inside them. Hoping to soften some of the hurt that her words may have caused, she added in her husky way, "Not that I think of you as an outlaw anymore, Fortner. Somehow you've become just plain Fortner to me, and it doesn't matter what you are on the outside or what others think about you."

She struggled for the courage to tell him of her love but failed. Those words would bring nothing but a laugh from a carefree man like Fortner, and her vulnerable heart could stand only so much. Being near him during the preceding evening had kept her on a high note so long that she doubted she could ever again function on a normal level.

She refused to think again about their making love in the night, for to do so would lead her into debilitating thoughts that she dared not explore right then—not when he was so close and looking at her in such a mesmerizing way.

Fortner cleared his throat, so touched at Treasure's soft declaration of faith in him that he felt guilty as hell about having held back the truths that could make her wish come true. He hated himself for having given in to his selfish wish to keep her with him one more night. At least now he recognized that what he felt for Treasure was love and not merely admiration or desire. The thought served only to stab his conscience more cruelly for having deceived her . . . and himself.

The young woman gazing up at him seemed destined for the grandiose future that her mother had dreamed for her and not for what he could offer, Fortner thought with a new and painful clarity. That drop of truth waiting to splash into his world had fallen. It seemed achingly clear now that Treasure belonged on a huge plantation as its honored mistress. She bore the proud carriage and beauty and intellect for such a challenge. Even after he satisfied his need for revenge he would not be in a position to provide her with a home and security such as she deserved. Out West, where he was heading as soon as he put the business of Whitey and the Thorpes behind him, there would be little security for a man seeking land to clear and farm, much less for his woman.

Fortner reached out and touched Treasure's hair, letting his fingers comb the waves and curls back from her face tenderly in the way that they had itched to do ever since he had awakened and found her standing by the open window.

"Thank you for no longer thinking of me as an outlaw," he said, moved deeply by both her words and his searing thoughts. "I take that as a compliment."

As Treasure stood with her back to the window and allowed his fingers to winnow leisurely through her hair, Fortner tried to ignore his erratic heartbeat and reassemble the thoughts that had seemed so right last night. He had figured it best then not to reveal what Sergeant Canfield had told him about Amos until he could talk with George Henry and learn the source of his obvious lie about Treasure being sought as a murderess. Somehow he had hoped that George Henry might get himself crossed up in a lie and lead Fortner closer to the long awaited meeting with Whitey. He had nothing to go on except a hunch, but he had a feeling that the elusive Whitey had fed the false information to George Henry. But why and where would he have heard it? his restless mind asked yet again.

Questions would have to wait, Fortner decided. The needs of the beautiful young woman looking up at him with trusting, star-filled eyes suddenly seemed far more important than his own need to ferret out Whitey and have a showdown with the entire Thorpe Brothers' gang. He must set her free and should not even have waited this long.

"Your wish has come true, Treasure. You're not an outlaw," Fortner said, watching the way her beautifully sculpted features took on a doubting look. "Sergeant Canfield told me last night that Amos Greeson was very much alive when he and his men rode through Rocky Bluffs last week."

"How can that be?" Treasure managed to ask, her voice breaking and trembling with unspoken hope. "Hank told me he was dead." Could it be possible that she was truly free, no longer bound to obey the outlaws for fear of being turned over to lawmen? She shook her head, disbelieving. "Hank wouldn't have lied about something like that."

"Maybe he didn't know he was lying," Fortner reassured her, taking her into his arms and holding her trembling body close. The feel of her curves covered only by the thin shift sent tremors up and down his body. "You said it was dark on the rock and that Hank seemed as upset as you were."

The enormity of what Fortner was revealing did not burst upon the shocked Treasure until he repeated all that Sergeant Canfield had said. She pulled away from his embrace and pushed at him with her hands, her eyes sparking with fury. Searing waves of anger washed over her and she trembled. Another more punishing thought was that there was no longer any need to travel with Fortner, but she rebelled against giving it credence. Anger made a lot more sense to her right now.

"You reprobate! Why have you kept it from me all this time? You knew how I longed to be free. You must have known this since the earlier part of the night. I saw you talking with the sergeant while I was dancing." Treasure slapped Fortner, more furious with him than she had ever been before. The sound of the healthy smack seemed to reverberate in the small room.

"I deserved that, Treasure." He held out his arms and took a half step toward her.

"Don't touch me! I despise you! You deliberately kept this news from me so that I would fall into bed with you, didn't you?" Her heart was writhing from agony and disappointment. No, it was breaking into a million pieces. The welcome news that Amos still lived and that she could no longer be labeled a killer paled beside the raw pain from her roiling anger and hurt. "By jingo! I was wrong to think of you as anything but an outlaw. Only you would pull such a low-down trick." Scalding tears formed and she brushed at them with both hands. "Damn you, Fortner! How little you must think of me to treat me with no respect." A loud hiccup punctuated her heartfelt sob. The truth reared its despicable head then. She never would see Fortner again after today.

"Please listen, Treasure," Fortner begged when she shoved past him after another hiccup and threw herself facedown on the bed. He went to stand beside it, aching to touch her heaving shoulders but fearing that to do so might upset her more. "I hadn't meant to tell you all about myself until I had all my problems taken care of, but I see now that I have no choice but to explain everything." Her sobs and hiccups stopped.

"I don't want to hear anything you have to say." She lifted her head, sure by then that she wasn't going to bawl in the way she had done as a child when she had stubbed her bare toe on a sharp rock. But the pain was far greater, far more difficult to bear, she realized. How could she go on never hearing his voice again? She wondered if she might not be bleeding on the inside, but her pride urged her onward. "You'd do nothing but lie."

"I've never lied outright to you," he denied, sitting on the side of the bed.

"Does it matter now?" Treasure looked at him, struck by the grieving set to his normally smiling mouth. He looked pale and washed out, rather like the stars that she had noted were fading in the sky at the approach of dawn.

Yes, Fortner realized with sinking heart. It mattered far more now than ever. He knew now that he loved her. "It matters a great deal what you think of me, and if you'll sit back against the pillows, I'll tell you all about me . . . and how I'm not an outlaw either."

"Not an outlaw? Another one of your lies!" Treasure hooted, slapping her tousled hair back from her face with both hands. "I may be only seventeen, but I'm not an utter fool. I've seen you take part in robberies, remember?"

"You've never seen me shoot at anyone, have you?"

"I've not seen that many attacks, not from my hiding places in the woods," she retorted bitterly. "This is a stupid conversation. I'm getting dressed and going down to ask the Colberts to awaken the soldiers." Why prolong her agony? She scrambled toward the far side of the bed, saying over her shoulder, "I don't have to stay with you any longer. I'll ask some of the soldiers to escort me down the Trace until we overtake Hank and Danny—while the others take you four robbers to Nashville."

"Wait and hear me out." Fortner leaned toward her, surprised that she paused. Was she planning to grab her knife from the saddlebags? If she but looked, she would find her rifle lying with his own and his pistol. Somehow, though, he did not believe that earlier wild recklessness still ruled Treasure. She was obviously seething with rage, but he could not blame her. "I'm sorry about all of this."

"Sorry? I'll bet. Don't push me, Fortner, or I'll scream and wake up everyone in this stand." Her eyes added a fierce warning of their own.

"I'm not going to hold you here, but it seems you owe me the courtesy of listening to what I have to say before you go storming off for help." Fortner took it as a hopeful sign that Treasure had not yet stooped to the floor to find one of the weapons. Was she already learning that force did not solve everything?

"I owe you something?" Treasure hissed, new anger building on the old. "What could I possibly owe you?" At the pained expression on his face, she calmed a bit. She recalled how Danny and she likely would have been killed had not Fortner interfered and then whipped George Henry that fateful night. She acknowledged that she might be indebted to him for his heroic actions, but she couldn't forget that Fortner had had no qualms about seducing her in the cave. *Hold it, girl!* an inner voice scolded in scornful tones. *You were more than a little willing to fall into the handsome highwayman's arms. And you're already grieving at having to leave him.*

Her temper deflating at the jarring truth, Treasure sighed. "I guess I do owe you a chance to explain whatever it is you have to say. Not that it's going to change my mind about getting as far away from you as possible." She raised her chin and flipped her hair over her shoulders, meeting Fortner's pale gaze with open defiance. Separation from him would be good for her, she promised herself. Then she could forget more quickly how desperately she loved him.

"You'll be free to go as soon as I speak my piece. Put the pillows behind your back and get comfortable."

When Treasure cautiously did as he asked, Fortner settled against the footboard. He began his revelation at the time when his youngest brother had left home to join up with the Thorpe gang, led then by J.Y., the father of the three brothers. Noting that Treasure had calmed down and watched and listened with puzzled interest, Fortner told how his brother had returned within a couple of years with loot from a robbery and declared that he was home to stay.

"J.Y. had been hanged by then, and the Thorpes had

evidently gone crazy in their determination to strike at those who had killed their father,'' Fortner said in a detached manner, steeling himself for the most painful parts of his story to come.

''Was that when George Henry became the leader of the gang?''

''He's not really the leader. The true boss is a man called Whitey whom no one except the Thorpes ever sees.''

''I've heard Juno and George Henry mention more than once how their other brother Felsenthal was killed, but I've heard the name Whitey only a time or two. Why would anyone keep on flirting with death that way—even if he has no respect for the rights of others?'' It occurred to her that she desperately wanted to ask why Fortner had chosen the life of an outlaw. She hushed so that he could continue.

''I have no idea what drives them, but I know what drives me to ride with them.''

Treasure listened, wide-eyed, while Fortner told how his mother and brothers had died that terrible night beside the Cumberland River. She did not miss the mention of Sarah Lovelace, whom he had gone to see that night, but she allowed him to continue the gruesome tale without interrupting to ask where Sarah was now and if she still claimed a portion of his heart. Tears glistened on Treasure's cheeks long before Fortner reached the part about how Bear-John and his family had helped him rescue the terrified Hannah and her young children from the root cellar beneath the charred ruins of the Copeland home. When his true name fell from his lips, Treasure took the name David Fortner Copeland into her heart, down to the secret spot housing the endearment ''darling.''

''How awful that you had to wait until last fall to be taken into the gang so that you could avenge the deaths of your mother and your three brothers,'' Treasure said, her voice huskier than normal from her earlier tears. ''What do you plan to do? Why haven't you told lawmen what you know about the Thorpes?''

Then Fortner explained why he had begun passing as the

adventurer called Fortner and why he was determined to wait until he met up with the mysterious Whitey before making the Thorpes pay for their cruelties.

"You know that you could be killed, Fortner." Shivering, she recalled how evil George Henry had looked and sounded that night when he had yelled for Juno to throw him his pistol—even after he had agreed beforehand to a fair fight with Fortner. If she had not chosen the formidable Bear-John to hold the pistol she had snatched from George Henry, would Fortner already be dead? The thought that both Danny and she might be dead as well followed closely behind.

"If my death insures the deaths of those killers, I must accept it as my fate."

Biting her bottom lip to stop herself from blurting out that she could not bear the thought of Fortner being killed, Treasure looked beyond him at the daylight now streaming through the window. Was there some way she could help him find out about Whitey? Maybe there was no reason to leave Fortner right away . . . at least not today. "What now?"

"If you'll agree to keep quiet about all I've learned from Sergeant Canfield and ride on down the Trace with me until we meet up with Danny and Hank, I think I'll stand a better chance of coming face to face with Whitey. George Henry is liable to get spooked if we tell all we've learned about you not being wanted by the sheriff. I can't promise that the Thorpes won't still demand ransom money for Danny and you, but I'll keep my vow to see that no harm comes to you on the way to Natchez."

Treasure considered Fortner's words very carefully. Here was a way to ease the pain of leaving him later on, when she would have more time to prepare herself. Could she trust him to do what he said? More telling, could she trust herself to put him out of her heart if she stayed with him? "You've not been able to talk George Henry out of asking for ransom?"

"No. He's determined to demand money for turning Danny and you over to Mr. Lindsay." Fortner rose from the bed and began pulling on his shirt. "He thinks I'm crazy to plan on delivering you to your grandfather." Inside, that inner devil he had told Treasure about agreed.

Treasure began getting dressed, too. "But you do plan to leave me at Lindwood, don't you?" She almost crossed her fingers and made a wish that he might say something romantic, like, "I love you and I don't want to leave you anywhere." Logic overruled, and she did not. As Fortner had just told her, he was a man bent on carrying out a private mission. The only reason she was with him at all was that, as she had suspected from the beginning, he was too honorable to allow a decent young woman and her innocent little brother to be killed or molested by real outlaws. What a gigantic mess!

"Sure. I'll leave you at your grandfather's plantation safe and sound, just as I promised." Fortner wondered how he might indicate that Treasure was special to him without revealing that he was in love with her. His brain seemed especially one-tracked when it came to thinking about Treasure, he reflected. He supposed that the best course to take was to assume the teasing, friendly manner they had begun sharing after the first day of traveling together. Any other kind of relationship would tax his overflowing heart too heavily. "I wouldn't want to disappoint old Thurston Crabtree."

"Thornton. His name is Thornton Crabtree, and he's only a few years older than I am." Fortner's bantering tone told Treasure clearly that whatever had taken place between them last night and that night back in the cave held no place of majesty in his heart, as it did in hers. He probably made love to dozens of women when he rode up and down the Trace, she agonized. Now that she knew he was no true highwayman, she still detected no sign that he was interested in marrying her and settling down. Adventurers were no more likely to be good candidates for husbands than outlaws, she decided. She was tucking her shirt into her black skirt by then and searching on the floor for her shoes. "Will Sarah Lovelace be waiting for you to return to Brashear's Town after you finish your . . . business with the gang?''

"Hardly. She married the new Indian agent that first year after the fire, while I was away hunting in the mountains." How could he have ever thought that he loved that prim sickly girl? Fortner wondered. He did not have to look at Treasure to recall how fine and brave and vibrant— He cut off the list. It would take an entire morning to name all of Treasure's qualities that had led him to fall in love with her, plus another morning to list all the reasons why he must never speak of his love to her. She was so young and impressionable, she might misjudge the passion he had kindled in her and think it was love. He had been wrong to give in to his overwhelming desire for her; now he must free her to seek what she so richly deserved. If he made sure that they never again made love, he reasoned, then she would never entertain any thoughts that he might care deeply for her.

Treasure sneaked a glance at Fortner. Was that a glimmer of pain deep inside his pale eyes? Had Sarah spurned him and made him suspicious that all other women might also be fickle? She had listened to women talking the few times that she had attended the revival meetings at Rocky Bluffs, and it seemed logical to her that Fortner might well be a man who had lost faith in women. Perhaps if she showed him that she was not of the same cut as Sarah Lovelace . . .

No, Treasure assured the faltering part of herself, she would be better off to get away from Fortner as soon as possible and oust him from her heart. She had shown weakness a few minutes ago when she had allowed herself to grieve over having to leave him today and then jumped at the first feeble excuse to stay with him. She would not falter again. Noticing that Fortner was getting his gear in order, she began gathering up her own belongings and putting them into her saddlebags.

Treasure was no more surprised than Fortner when she heard herself saying in a few moments, "I think that for me to keep on traveling with you might be, as you say, helpful in your dealings with George Henry and Juno. There's no point in getting George Henry riled or suspicious by telling him he was wrong about me." She might be newly free in one way, Treasure reflected with sobering wisdom, but in another she was more a captive than ever before.

Fortner felt blessed that Treasure seemed too intent upon folding the ruffled blue dress and slipping it gently into one of her saddlebags to see his expression. He was certain that written somewhere on his face, as plain as day, were both relief and joy that the woman he had fallen in love with was not planning on stalking out of his life . . . yet.

Suddenly feeling ten feet tall, David Fortner Copeland longed to grab Treasure and kiss her breathless. Instead, he went on with his packing, substituting a low humming as a mighty poor second for kissing.

Chapter Fifteen

Treasure, Fortner, and Bear-John traveled south on the Trace for the next two days, expecting to find the Thorpe brothers waiting around each curve.

On the Sunday morning after the dance, Bear-John had secretly signaled for George Henry and Juno to cross over the Tennessee River on the morning's first ferry, while even the soldiers were sleeping late. By sneaking the outlaws behind the stand and the barn, Bear-John had guided them onto the Trace without anyone seeing them. When the Thorpes had not appeared by the end of the second day, Fortner and Bear-John pulled long faces and worried in private if perhaps George Henry had become suspicious of them.

Treasure was too happy about not having the repulsive Thorpe brothers along to give the matter much thought. Fortner and she had recaptured their easy manner and mutual admiration, and she basked in his attention without allowing herself to delve too deeply into her reasons. Her only voiced complaint was that she longed to know if Danny was all right.

"Ho, there!" George Henry called out on the second night out from Colbert's Stand.

From where they sat around their campfire, Treasure, Fortner, and Bear-John had heard horses approaching from the south. They exchanged looks of apprehension upon recognizing the leader's voice.

"Ho, yourself!" Fortner replied, peering out into the darkness. Though he needed to retain close contact with the Thorpes in order to find Whitey and complete his vengeful plan, he admitted that the past two days without the outlaws had been downright pleasant. He calculated that they had traveled close to fifty miles.

George Henry rode into view then, with Juno following closely.

"Juno an' me done et," George Henry announced after he dismounted and handed the reins to his younger brother. His beady eyes swept the three sitting on the ground while Juno nodded to all and disappeared in the darkness with the horses. "How y'all been since you lef' Colbert's Stand? Have you done any good, or has that damn fool woman been a'holdin' you back?"

"We've had a little good luck," Fortner replied, warning Treasure with a covert glance that she should not let George Henry's derogatory comments offend her. He himself was not about to admit that the three had done nothing but laugh and talk and ride southward. One of the gang's rules was that only those who took part in a robbery shared in the loot—except for the tenth always handed over to George Henry for Whitey. His money pouch flush from recent poker games, Fortner had no qualms about forking over a few coins to prevent George Henry and Juno from learning that Bear-John and he had pulled no holdups.

"How about Juno and you? We were getting worried that something had happened to you."

"Have you seen Danny and Hank during the past two days?" Treasure asked, forgetting that she had promised herself from the beginning not to address the Thorpes unless forced to do so.

"What makes you ask a fool question like 'at?'" George Henry asked, removing his hat and narrowing his eyes at her.

"Bear-John learned back at Colbert's Stand that Hank and Danny had been there until the morning before we arrived," Treasure replied lamely. George Henry's scrutiny was unsettling; she had forgotten how revolting his unkempt beard and gap-toothed mouth were. "I was hoping that since you've apparently been south on the Trace, you might have seen them and could tell me if they're both all right." Now that Fortner had told her about how the Thorpes had murdered his family and burned his home, Treasure found it even more difficult to be civil to the disagreeable man.

"What makes you so sure we been south?" George Henry asked in a quarrelsome tone. Frowning, he reached inside his loose jacket and brought out a small bottle.

"I happened to notice which way you came from," Treasure remarked, sorry now that she had even tried to talk with the bad-tempered outlaw. She watched him uncap the bottle and tilt it against his repulsive mouth.

"Tell yore woman not to be noticin' nothin' about us, Fortner, or I might have to up the ransom we gonna ask from her gran'pa." George Henry stared at Treasure assessingly before turning his attention to Fortner. "Are you still sayin' you gonna let her stay with ole man Lindsay? Whitey says it's up to you whether or not you pay us the money or the ole man pays it. Frankly, if'n I was you—"

"Yes," Fortner interrupted quickly, "but you're not me." He had no wish for Treasure to hear what was likely to be filthy talk, nor did he care to listen to George Henry make sly remarks about the woman he loved.

Fortner realized that his patience was running out. He wondered how in hell he had remained calm enough to refrain from grabbing his pistol and blowing off George Henry's head the night he had slapped Treasure. Seconds later, Fortner recalled, he had had little chance to help Treasure by killing her tormentor, for by then she had snatched George Henry's pistol and Juno had pulled his own weapon and aimed it at her and her young brother across the campfire. Though he had not known then that what drew him to the beautiful blonde was love, he well remembered his panic when she was threatened.

From long practice, Fortner quashed his hatred of the outlaws and went on. "I still plan to deliver Treasure to her grandfather—after we meet up with Danny and the peddler at Locust Creek between Washington and Natchez, the way we planned." Fortner squinted across the lazy campfire, sensing that George Henry was feeling unusually pleased with himself. "You've had a meeting with Whitey some time during the past two days, haven't you?" When George Henry stared at him as though surprised at Fortner's deduction, Fortner went on in an aggrieved tone. "You promised me you'd take me with you the very next time you met up with Whitey." How much longer would he have to keep up this charade? "Don't tell me you're still trying to test Bear-John and me."

George Henry laughed and took another swig from his bottle. "Naw, I ain't a'worryin' over you and that half-breed. It jes' didn't work out for you to go with us to meet Whitey this time."

Disappointed for Fortner that he had missed out on meeting with the secret boss of the gang and that she had not learned any news about Danny, Treasure left the men and slipped into her bedroll over in the shadows. All that she could do, she fretted, was to believe that Danny was faring well under Hank's protection. She tossed and turned long after the four men began their customary drinking and noisy gambling.

Glittering stars spattered the overhead canopy of black sky in patterns as old as time. Tree frogs screeched monotonously for rain from the surrounding trees, and the air of the May night had no more than a breath of chill as it caressed Treasure's face. Not in keeping with her usual self, the restless young woman had no thoughts for her surroundings.

Treasure kept remembering how nice it had been last night when her only company was the amiable Bear-John and Fortner. Maybe it was because she had truly longed to remain at Colbert's Stand long enough to visit again with the hill folk and hear the preaching, but after they had eaten, she had spoken about some of the bizarre happenings at religious revivals that she had attended near Rocky Bluffs. To Treasure's delight, Fortner had begun spinning yarns about revivals and traveling preachers in much the same way that he had told tales about Daniel Boone back at the Ryan cabin. Falling out of love with the handsome adventurer was not an easy task, she mused ruefully just before she fell asleep to the tune of his bass voice across the way.

During the next two weeks, the weary pattern of riding all day and taking to the woods when George Henry decided to rob travelers almost wore Treasure down. She kept thinking that it would get easier for her to ignore what she knew was taking place out on the Trace while she waited in the forest. It didn't. Ever since she had killed the rattlesnake in the cave, Fortner had allowed her to keep her knife. Now that he had returned her rifle as well, she knew that she should be feeling more secure while hiding in the woods. She didn't, though, for she could not see what dangers Fortner faced during holdups.

Treasure suffered acutely each time a robbery took place until Fortner again came riding through the woods for her. What if he were killed, or what if lawmen appeared and arrested him? There was no way for anyone to tell that Fortner or Bear-John were not as evil as the Thorpe brothers, she reflected, not when they wore kerchiefs over their faces and took part in the holdups along with George Henry and Juno. She thanked God that no gunfire had been exchanged during any of the ten or so robberies carried out since they had left Colbert's Stand. No doubt all of those traveling between Nashville and Natchez had heard of the numerous killings on the Trace and valued their lives too much to resist attacks.

The nights were no easier to bear, though Treasure suffered from a different kind of anguish then.

George Henry apparently feared for the group to stop at any of the few stands they had passed, and each night found them camping beside the Trace. As hard as she tried to gain a glimpse of familiar horses somewhere near the stands when they would ride by early in the mornings or late in the afternoons, she never saw the ones belonging to Danny and Hank. She reasoned that Hank could be down any one of the numerous trails they saw branching off the Trace now, but she was starving for word that Danny was safe and well.

Treasure's need to share with her brother the wonderful news that she was free and that she had not killed Amos seemed to grow larger each day. Hank would be pleased, too, she reminded herself. She shied away from thinking about how she might explain tactfully to the kind old peddler that he had made a grievous mistake in declaring Amos dead on that awful night.

In campsites with little cleared area, Fortner sometimes threw their blankets so near the campfire that Treasure could hear the men talking while they gambled, even though she had no particular desire to. She would tense up each time one of the Thorpes became overly curious about Bear-John and Fortner and what they had been doing before they showed up on the Trace late last year. Though she had at first worried that Fortner or Bear-John might drink too much and become loose tongued, she put aside that fear after the first few nights of listening to their responses. Neither seemed prone to tell more than he had to.

Finding herself more and more mysteriously attuned to Fortner's resonant voice, Treasure lay in her blanket in the partial darkness imagining the exact expression claiming his handsome face while he spoke or laughed with the other men. Though she had met him only four weeks earlier, she had learned far more about the blue-eyed adventurer than she realized.

After a resonant rumble of laughter the young woman listening from across the campfire visualized the way Fortner's teeth sparkled behind his sensuous lips. An amused hoot of disbelief at someone's tall tale made her recall the way his dark eyebrows lifted in unmatched arches when he openly doubted something. Was it his left or his right eyebrow that angled higher? She tried to remember, not sure even after she gave it some thought. A quick, bass rejoinder to another's joking and Treasure thought about Fortner's ready wit and his apparent love of teasing and the way his pale eyes twinkled with mischief.

Only in her dreams did Treasure relive their two nights of lovemaking, for she was determined to conquer her love for Fortner and view him in the same way that he apparently viewed her: as a friend.

"We'll be entering Choctaw country today after we ford Line Creek," Fortner told Treasure one morning as they rode behind Bear-John and the Thorpes. He gestured toward the countryside that had turned from steep hills to gently rolling forest land since they had crossed the Tennessee River on Colbert's Ferry some two weeks earlier. "We've left your mountains behind for good."

"I've left a lot more than mountains behind." Treasure had noticed the changing topography, but she had not mentioned it. More often than not lately, George Henry insisted that Fortner ride up front and talk with him, and at those times she trailed behind the four men. She kept telling herself that she did not mind, not when she was working diligently to forget how much the charming man meant to her. The May sun invaded the newly greening leaves of the trees edging the Trace and created extra sparkle on Fortner's uncommonly pretty teeth as he smiled at her in that way that often stole her breath away. Sunlight danced in his pale, black-fringed eyes. "Are the Choctaw like the Chickasaw?"

Fortner thought for a moment, moving his hat to rest upon the back of his head. "Not really, though I've heard that a long time ago they belonged to the same tribe. The Choctaw tend to like farming and living in peace a lot more than the Chickasaw seem to."

Thinking of Walking Bear and the Chickasaw village of his people over the ridge from the Ryan cabin, Treasure smiled with fond remembrance. "Will there be Indians all the way to Natchez?"

"Yes, though not many Choctaw live as far south as Natchez. I've been told that the Natchez Indians who gave their name to the town no longer exist as a tribe."

Fortner was pleased that he had managed over the past two weeks to keep his hands off Treasure. Only late in the nights when he slipped into his blanket beside hers did he touch her deliberately—and that was always with her blanket serving as a barrier. Even so, he gloried in snuggling up to her back and throwing his arm across her blanketed shoulders as she slept. More than once he had lain awake after the campfire burned to mere coals, too engrossed in tantalizing thoughts about the beautiful blonde to fall asleep. The fragrance and texture of her hair drew him like a magnet, and he often awoke before daybreak with his nose buried close to the golden braid that she fashioned for sleeping. At such times Fortner exercised more willpower over the abiding passion stirred by his love for Treasure than he had ever believed possible. He would turn away from all that tempted him and spend the remainder of the night with his back to her.

"How much longer before we reach Natchez, Fortner?" What Treasure wanted to ask was how much longer would she be able to see him, talk with him every day and feel and hear him sleeping beside her every night. Sometimes she dreamed that as she slept those manly arms hugged her close. More than once she had even fancied that Fortner's face had lain close to hers during the night and that he had stroked her hair. Upon awakening in the mornings, she occasionally found him deep in sleep with his arm thrown across her. But usually he lay facing away from her.

Treasure didn't know what had Fortner so deep in thought right then, but she doubted it had anything to do with Indians. He seemed not to have heard her question. Lately he seemed so preoccupied that she sometimes wondered if he even knew what the two of them talked about.

Was he still worried that George Henry wasn't going to take him along the next time he met Whitey? Treasure wondered as she lifted a hand to stroke Vagabond's tan withers. Because of her own wish to see Blackie's killers punished, she had felt a special kinship with Fortner ever since he had confided in her the reason why he rode with the Thorpes. She realized that the feeling had nothing to do with her love for him, yet she welcomed one more bond with the tall brown-haired man riding alongside her on the worn trail.

At times Treasure was tempted to fill in all the details about Blackie's death for Fortner and ask his opinion, but she held back. The brief account she had given the night of the storm had not come easily. Besides, she would admonish herself silently when they had a few moments alone and she felt the need to tell him all about it, Fortner already bore more than his share of knowing about man's inhumanity to man.

"How much farther to Natchez?" Treasure asked again, certain when Fortner started in surprise and turned to look at her that he must not have heard when she asked the question the first time.

"We can be in Natchez in a week if we keep traveling at this pace." Fortner tried to read the expression in her eyes, but he got lost in their amber depths. The beautiful blonde had become dearer to him with each passing day, he agonized. How could he bear to give her over to her grandfather? Or to Thornton Crabtree and all the other unmarried plantation owners who would swarm around her and try to win her hand? The questions squeezed his heart painfully and stole some of his pleasure in gazing at her.

* * *

"Hold up!" George Henry called late that afternoon after they had been in Choctaw country for several hours. When all stopped their horses, he continued. "Yonder's some Kaintucks a'comin' down the way. They ain't been outta Natchez long an' ought'a have a goodly pile from tradin' in N'Orleans."

"Ain't we gonna gamble with 'em?" Juno asked. "Danged if'n I hadn't rather take their money that way." When George Henry glared at his usually silent and subservient brother, Juno added feebly, "Ain't no lawman gonna get us for jes' plain gamblin'."

"Are you a'gettin' a yeller streak down your back?"

"Naw. I jes' think gamblin' beats robbin'." Juno's face flushed, but he returned George Henry's measuring look without flinching.

"Sometimes I wonder 'bout you more'n I do 'bout Fortner and his 'breed frien', little brother." George Henry's musing statement brought a new tension to the group. His small eyes raked the solemn faces turned toward him before he went on. "I aims to meet up with Whitey soon an' we ain't gonna mess aroun' gamblin' with no Kaintucks tonight." Apparently satisfied, when no further protests came, that he had reestablished his role as leader of the gang, George Henry shielded his brow with a grimy hand and peered toward the bearded men walking in the distance. " 'Pears they got rifles at the ready, but they ain't but three of 'em." He turned to Fortner. "Get your wild woman outta sight."

At Fortner's secretive wink and nod in her direction, a stony-faced Treasure reined Vagabond off the Trace past a small stand of cane growing beneath sturdy oaks and cottonwoods. Wild woman? She huffed inwardly at George Henry's demeaning term. Not since the night of the dance after they had heard the woefully inaccurate account of how she had charged naked out of the woods had Fortner teased Treasure again about her actions. It seemed to her that George Henry could not resist reminding her at every opportunity. What infuriated Treasure more was that the repulsive outlaw never commented on the fact that ever since that one instance some three weeks ago, she had obeyed orders to the letter, never venturing back toward the Trace until Fortner rode into the woods for her.

Realizing that the tall underbrush and the slender cane hid both horse and rider from view, Treasure stopped before she had ridden as far into the woods as she usually did. She noted that twilight was already deepening the natural shadows of the forest. As always while she waited during a holdup, her heart hammered and her throat filled with a hot, tight knot. She prayed that this might be one of the last times that Fortner would have to go through the motions of being an outlaw.

The exchange between the Thorpe brothers a few moments earlier puzzled Treasure, and she wondered if perhaps the younger man might be less evil than George Henry. Now that she thought about it, Juno had made no effort to aid George Henry the night of the fight when George Henry had asked him for his gun. Juno could not have known for certain that Bear-John would choose to stick by Fortner and not lend a hand, yet Juno had refused to take his brother's side and had even pointed out that the fight was George Henry's, not his.

Well, Treasure decided after entertaining her jumbled thoughts, there was no understanding the Thorpes. She wasn't even sure that she cared to. Hadn't George Henry mentioned only moments ago that he would be meeting up with Whitey soon? Surely this time Fortner would get to go along.

While Treasure let her mind ramble, the four horsemen had ridden on down the darkening trail to meet the Kentuckians. Before their horses' hooves had stilled Treasure heard gunshots. She slipped her rifle from its saddle holster and made ready to fire, trying desperately to hear all that was happening on the Trace. Knowing that she was disobeying orders, but too fidgety to stand by blindly, she guided Vagabond close enough to the men to be able to peek through the dense underbrush yet far enough away to remain hidden. The fading light distorted her view, but her mouth dropped open at what she saw and heard.

Evidently the men traveling on foot had prepared for such an attack and had deliberately kept part of their group out of sight in the bordering forests. The three Kentuckians had suddenly become eight or ten, Treasure realized with renewed fear for Fortner's safety. They were yelling and chasing their attackers back up the Trace with volleys of rifle shots. Eyes wide, she watched the four would-be robbers gallop past her hiding place with a thundering of horses' hooves. His body leaning low over Brutus' head, Fortner trailed behind the others. She breathed a little easier, figuring that the Kentuckians had given up.

At that moment, Treasure espied a bearded man darting from behind a tree not far down the way and aiming his gun at the last rider, Fortner. Fighting back the scream tearing at her throat, she urged Vagabond forward through the brush, pointing her rifle at a fat pine not far behind the running man. When the Kentuckian heard the commotion and the shot exploding so near him, he wheeled about and fired instantly at the barely visible horse and rider crashing toward him through the undergrowth. He hollered out in terror, as if he might have seen a ghost. Within seconds he was sprinting back to join his fellow travelers down the Trace.

"She's here!" the man yelled hoarsely to his companions, not taking the time to look behind him. "The 'venging angel we heard 'bout done come. Take to the woods!"

The knapsacks on their backs flopping, the Kentuckians disappeared into the thick, dark forest.

"My God! That looks like Vagabond standing on the Trace. Can that be Treasure lying on the ground?" Fortner exclaimed when Bear-John and he rounded the curve not long after the Kentuckians took to the woods. He kneed Brutus into breakneck speed.

Fortner and Bear-John had ridden back down the Trace to find the place where they had seen Treasure ride into the woods less than half an hour ago. George Henry had ordered them to scout for the Kentuckians, but Fortner's chief thought all along had been to lead Treasure out of the forest, for night was falling fast. At the blurred sight before him, his mouth filled with a terrible, bitter taste, and his heart swelled with unnamed fear. Not until he had leapt from his saddle and was kneeling to turn Treasure over and feel her pulse did the searing knot in his throat lessen its hold. "Oh, God!" Fortner scanned her expressionless face, and the knot retained its fierce grip on his throat. "Treasure's been hurt badly."

"I thought when I looked back that I saw her come tearing out of the woods and shoot at a man who was aiming at you," Bear-John said, jumping off his horse to join Fortner where he was already kneeling over Treasure's prostrate form and talking to her. "Everything was happening so fast I couldn't be sure, though." Absently Bear-John palmed the skittish Vagabond's reins and knelt beside his friend, grimacing at the sight of the unconscious young woman. "Damn it to hell! Somebody shot her, and it was probably that same man I glimpsed before we went around the curve. How bad is she?"

"Treasure," Fortner called for the second or third time, sickened at the sight of blood seeping through the left shoulder and sleeve of her shirt. Her face seemed far too pale, though he realized that the fading light gave him a false picture. "Oh, darling, you've been shot," he murmured as he unbuttoned her shirt and sent his hand exploring above her shift.

Relieved that the wound seemed to be high on her arm and not in her chest area where it might have penetrated her heart or lungs, Fortner crooned encouragement to the unconscious Treasure. He swiftly completed his examination and found no other injuries. It bothered him that she had made no response to his words or his presence. How long had it been since he and the others had ridden past this spot to escape the Kentuckians' surprise attack? Surely not more than fifteen minutes. Tender fingers searched through the long mass of curls for bruises on her scalp, finding a large lump below her crown. "Treasure, you must have fallen from Vagabond and hit your head."

"How bad is it, hoss?" Bear-John asked again. Since Fortner had fought George Henry over Treasure three weeks ago, Bear-John had suspected that his friend was smitten with the lovely blonde, but he had not realized how deeply he cared for her until he saw the stricken look on Fortner's face—and heard the deep emotion in his voice.

"She seems to have been hit right at the top of her arm, and it's still bleeding. She must have gotten knocked out when she fell from her horse." Fortner took his handkerchief and tied it over the gaping wound, then cradled Treasure against his chest. She started and moaned when he picked her up and called her name again and again.

"Fortner?" Treasure asked, not believing that he had come back and was holding her so closely. Suddenly cold all over, she shivered when she recalled the man pointing his gun at Fortner's back. She peered up at his beloved face in the gathering darkness and tried to smile, but the pain in her left arm cut too deeply for her to manage more than a lopsided grin. "I'm sorry if I made another mess of things, but that man—"

"Shhh," Fortner said softly. He hugged her closer. She could have been killed or wounded far more seriously than she apparently was. "Bear-John told me that a man was aiming at me. I heard what sounded like two shots going off at the same time, but when I wasn't hit, I kept riding." His voice grew thicker. "I had no idea you weren't safe deep in the woods and that you had been hit instead of me. This time you should have screamed, Treasure. I would have come back and helped you."

"The noise was so loud that Vagabond reared up, and I guess I was too addled to hang on. That's the last thing I remember," Treasure said so huskily that Fortner had to strain to hear. Only then did Treasure notice that Bear-John's concerned face was leaning into the limited circle of her vision. "Bear-John, I'm sorry. At least I didn't scream like a banshee this time."

The big man grinned and reached to pat her hand. "There's nothing to be apologizing about. You probably saved old hoss' life by getting that Kaintuck's attention. I'm sorry you had to get hurt doing it, though."

"We need to get Treasure to a place where she can rest and start getting well before we head on toward Natchez, Bear-John," Fortner said when Treasure sighed feebly and closed her eyes again. "She's lost a lot of blood, and the knot on her head is the size of a goose egg. If infection sets in—" He could not go on. He had seen brawny hunters die from infected wounds during that winter he had trapped in the Cumberland Mountains.

"What about the Choctaw village off the Trace back yonder?" Bear-John asked.

"That'll have to do," Fortner replied, forcing himself to recall that a path had led off through the woods less than a mile back. *Treasure!* his mind kept screaming, *I love you. You're all I care about in this world. It's my fault that you're hurt. I can't let you die.*

"Can you manage, or do you want me to go with you?"

"I can manage. You need to get on back to where George Henry said Juno and he would be waiting. Tell them what happened. He said he would be starting down the Trace at daylight to meet Whitey. We'll have to stay behind a day or two. If Treasure and I don't catch up with you before then, we'll meet you . . . we'll meet you somewhere close to Lindwood," Fortner said. He was already standing and getting ready to mount Brutus with the drowsing Treasure in his arms.

"We agreed earlier that we'd be meeting Hank and the boy outside Washington near the bridge over Locust Creek, remember?" Bear-John asked, noting that it was unlike Fortner to be as rattled as he apparently was now. He must be truly in love with Treasure and half out of his mind with worry. "Let's plan to meet there since it's right close to Lindwood."

"Good idea." Why had he been unable to recall such a simple plan? Fortner ignored the voice inside that reminded him why. Hell, yes! he wanted to yell back. He knew that he was crazy in love with Treasure, but now was no time to be letting such a forbidden thought loose in his scrambled brain. What if he got carried away and blurted it out? Finding Treasure wounded and unconscious made Fortner more aware than ever of the dangers his beloved had to endure simply because she rode with outlaws. He should have given her up to the soldiers back at Colbert's Stand so they could have escorted her down the Trace to travel with Danny and Hank, he agonized. He should not have coerced her into staying with him until they reached her grandfather's plantation. Guilt seemed to have lodged permanently inside Fortner's love saturated heart. It smarted.

Reaching out his arms, Bear-John said, "Here, hoss. Let me hold Treasure until you're in the saddle, and then I can hand her up to you. She's not likely to get jostled so bad that way."

Fortner placed the half complaining Treasure across his lap when the big man lifted her up to him. Then Bear-John looped Vagabond's reins in the straps of Fortner's saddlebags and led the way up the Trace on his own horse. Treasure relaxed against Fortner's shoulder and gave in to the waves of blackness that kept washing over her as they rode toward the path leading to the Indian village nearby.

"Am I dreaming?" Treasure asked later that night, snapping awake suddenly as if she had been floating for a long time and had landed back on earth with a jar. She realized that she lay upon a narrow, low bed of some kind and that her left arm throbbed. Suddenly there was Fortner's anxious face bending over her, and she felt better already. Something leapt within his silvery eyes, and she wondered if it might be relief that she was better now and that he could rejoin the gang and resume his search for Whitey. She slid a sideways look toward a smelly fire smoldering in the center of what appeared to be a small, circular hut made of skinned logs and roughly planed boards. A tall, conical top with a hole in its center sucked up most of the slowly spiraling smoke, but not all. "Where are we?"

"We're in a Choctaw village beside Pigeon Creek."

Fortner tenderly brushed back her hair and laid his palm across her forehead, frowning when he felt too much warmth there. "Chief Iron Hand took us in when I brought you here earlier tonight. This hut once belonged to his mother and won't be used again until his son marries."

He reached over and filled a gourd dipper with water from a stone pitcher sitting nearby on the dirt floor. Someone had done a good job of cutting the top from the bulb end of the dried gourd and honing its edges to acceptable smoothness, Fortner reflected. The slender golden neck of the hard-rinded fruit was long and straight and fit into his hands easily. "Drink some water and then tell me how you're feeling now that I've gotten you bandaged and you've had a long rest."

Treasure tried to sit up, but pain radiated throughout her body from the piercing source at her upper left arm. Gratefully she accepted Fortner's proffered arm slipping behind her and holding her up. She took the dipper with her good right hand and drank before attempting to reply. "I don't feel worth a hill of beans, Fortner, if you really want to know. I'm not left-handed, but if there's a snake around here you'll have to kill it yourself."

Fortner chuckled, delighted that Treasure was feeling more like her old sassy self. "I promise to take care of all varmints without any help from you." Seeing her smile, even weakly as she was, lifted his spirits more than he could have imagined. He kept one arm around her while reaching for a smaller gourd dipper with his free hand. "Drink some of this herbal brew that the medicine man brought. He says it's good for fighting fever and infection in that nasty wound on your arm."

Treasure rolled her eyes in mock disgust upon smelling the vile concoction, then drank, screwing up her face with distaste when she handed the gourd back to the grinning Fortner. She pointed to the dipper holding water and, when he handed it over, she grabbed it with her good hand and drank from it thirstily. The herbal brew might help with fever and infection, she thought fuzzily, but having the handsome adventurer so near and so attentive seemed far more necessary to her well-being.

Fortner's close view of Treasure's lovely face and tousled hair in the dim light fed his climbing spirits. He returned the dipper to the pitcher and treated himself to more worshipful gazes at his beloved. The light was so dim and her mind so out of focus from her fall that he knew she could not read what lay within his eyes. He reveled in not having to conceal how much he loved her. "No doubt you took a nasty fall from Vagabond after the man shot you. Do you want to tell me what happened?"

"No, but I will," Treasure replied, closing her eyes as he gently lowered her back to the bed and removed his arm. She wished she had the courage to ask him to keep it there. "I wasn't deep in the woods as you meant me to be, but I don't care how much you tease me about not doing what I was told. That man was trying to shoot you when I distracted him by shooting behind him and riding Vagabond out on the Trace." *I love you, Fortner.* She moved restlessly on the narrow bed, despising herself for letting the thought surface. *Hell's bells! Why can't I run you out of my heart?*

"Both Bear-John and you told me something about that when we found you on the ground," Fortner said. "I thank you for saving my life—again—Treasure."

"You would have done the same for me," she mumbled huskily, already tempted to return to that soothing oblivion where her arm and her head did not throb. "I've always heard that's what friends are for." When Fortner made no reply, she opened one eye and fixed his depressingly sober face with a teasing look. "Or at least you would have if the angel in you happened to be in charge, wouldn't you?"

"You bet I would." *Darling. Even the devil in me would not let any harm come to you.*

Fortner cheered up a bit when he watched Treasure give in then to her obvious weakness and her desire for sleep. It was all right that his beloved thought of him only as a friend, he consoled himself after recalling her words. He could not have borne it had she declared that he was more than a friend—not that he dared dream she might ever love him. What future could there be for an adventurer and a fine young woman like Treasure Ryan?

Fortner jerked awake in the predawn light. Earlier he had stretched out on his blanket beside the low platform serving as Treasure's bed. Now she was moaning and flailing her arms and legs. Alarmed, he sat up and reached over to restrain her wounded left arm.

"Lie still, Treasure. If you keep moving that arm the bleeding is likely to start up again." He noted that the bandage he had looped and tied across the upper part of her left arm showed no new bloodstains, and he sighed with relief. When his free hand tested her forehead, Fortner frowned. His gaze moved to her beautiful face. What he saw in the pale light of approaching daybreak displeased and frightened him. Her breathing appeared shallow, her lips were dry, and her skin looked flushed. His heart grew heavy with the unwanted knowledge that fever was raging throughout her restless body.

Shortly after Treasure had awakened around midnight and first drank the bitter concoction Fortner offered her, Manatee, the medicine man, had returned. He had brought a neatly cut piece of chamois and an earthenware bowl of water containing aromatic herbs and roots. His face smeared with white and red paint, Manatee had chanted some monotonous phrases while shaking two brightly painted gourds with rhythmic insistence above and below the sleeping young woman. Next he had performed a more elaborate ritual around the inside walls of the small hut before adhering to Fortner's insistence that he alone would care for the wounded woman during the remainder of the night.

Fortner lifted the protesting Treasure's head and coaxed her into drinking more of the herbal concoction that Manatee had assured him would keep down infection and fever. She pushed at the hands and arms trying to assist her, never opening her eyes and never letting on that she recognized Fortner's soothing voice. Depressed anew that

Treasure mumbled incoherently and seemed lost in some dark world known only to her, Fortner almost despaired and left to seek help from Manatee or the Indian woman, Waneeta, who had assisted him upon their arrival. What if his selfish need to care for Treasure himself led to her losing ground instead of gaining it?

Recalling his mother's treatment of him during child-hood fevers, Fortner dipped the chamois in the scented water, squeezed out the excess, and bathed Treasure's face and neck. He thought how Chief Iron Hand had shown Fortner to the empty hut and then sent his son's wife, Waneeta, to offer her help. When he was attempting to cleanse and bandage the gunshot wound through the fleshy part of Treasure's arm, Fortner had welcomed the soft-voiced Waneeta's assistance in removing the unconscious young woman's shirt and cutting away the left section of her shift. He was not yet ready to turn over her complete care to another, he realized as one hand brushed silky tendrils of golden hair back from her heated forehead.

Fortner gazed at Treasure while he bathed the exposed skin of her upper breasts and shoulders and thought that she looked especially beautiful and vulnerable lying on the low bed made soft with bearskins. The twin semicircles of dark lashes charmed him anew and made him long to see her light brown eyes with their intriguing flecks of gold. How often had he feasted on the sight of Treasure as she so ably rode Vagabond beside him on the Trace? he wondered. Or as she leaned over a smoking campfire preparing food, or crinkled her eyes and laughed at his jokes in her bubbling, deep-bellied way? He realized that the list of questions was both endless and torturous.

Stirring up warring feelings of love, guilt, and anguish, Fortner's emotions lashed at him with what seemed an unrelenting fury. As he continued washing Treasure's pale, fevered skin gently with the scented chamois, he silently cursed the man who had shot his beloved. The thought that the brave young woman had deliberately drawn the man's fire to prevent Fortner himself from being the target ripped at his insides like poisoned talons.

With the next breath Fortner cursed himself for having left Treasure hiding in the woods alone—for ever having suggested that she leave Colbert's Stand with him. The soldiers there would have taken charge of her and escorted her safely to find Danny and Hank. He never would rest easily, he promised himself, until he delivered her, safe and sound, to her grandfather. Mr. Lindsay could provide her with the fine home and protection she so amply deserved until she married a wealthy planter...like Thornton Crabtree.

Treasure's welfare loomed inestimably in Fortner's newly shaken mind as his most pressing goal, insidiously nibbling away at earlier vows of revenge, without his conscious awareness that such a telling action was taking place. All he knew with certainty was that his misery swelled with the increasing morning light that inched through the open entryway into the Choctaw hut a bare mile off the Natchez Trace.

Chapter Sixteen

"No, no," Treasure murmured after a period of what Fortner had taken to be peaceful sleep.

Welcoming the increase of morning light there in the hut, Fortner lifted Treasure's head and urged her to drink some water from the gourd dipper. She did not protest drinking, but afterward she seemed upset over something private.

Treasure's voice came out thick and huskier than normal. Her lips moving with obvious effort, she shifted her head against the blanket covering the bearskins and grimaced. "Don't go near the hat, Danny."

"Don't fret," Fortner murmured when she repeated her request and seemed to be awaiting an answer. "We'll get rid of the hat. Go back to sleep."

As if Fortner's voice had begun a sensible dialogue, Treasure replied, her eyes still shut, "Never saw such a feather. Looks evil. Don't touch it! Get away from it!"

"I'll take it away." He tried to soothe her troubled brow with the damp chamois, but she brushed off his hand.

"Do you see that double vee cut in its tip?"

"The feather has a double notch out of it?" Fortner asked agreeably, wondering if Treasure had slipped back in time or if she was in the middle of a dream. Perhaps if he gave what seemed logical answers to her nonsensical questions she would return to a more peaceful sleep. "Tell me about it if you want to."

"Are you crazy? Don't you see it there on the ground? It's black and dusty. Papa must have knocked it off the man's head when they fought."

"Yes," Fortner said, hoping to pacify her and slow her renewed thrashing. "Now I see that the hat is black and has a black feather with a double vee."

"No!" Treasure's eyes popped open, staring at something only she could see. She seemed unaware that Fortner leaned over her, watching her intently. "The feather is red . . . like hot, fresh blood. Papa's blood was black and cold. The man who killed Papa in the shed—he left it behind."

Treasure shuddered and closed her eyes again, fretting and mumbling incoherently.

Murmuring soothing sounds, Fortner thought about her words while he continued to wipe the fragrant chamois across her face from time to time during the next hour. Gradually her skin became cooler, and he felt certain that the fever was breaking.

Back on that stormy night after Treasure had told him about her fight with Amos Greeson, she had said that her father, Blackie Ryan, had died violently; but she had not related any of the details. He had not wished to insist that she talk about something that so obviously upset her, but now he wished he knew more about how Blackie had died. It appeared that Treasure was reliving some awful experience during her fitful sleep. Something about her babblings set his mind to working in baffling ways.

"The devil's claws will point him out," Treasure said in a harsh voice after a long period of silence. Again her legs thrashed about and she appeared newly agitated. She seemed unaware that she moved her wounded left arm as freely as she did the other.

Fortner grabbed her arms and held them gently but forcibly against the blanket. "What devil's claws? They'll point out whom?" he asked, remembering the ones he had seen hanging from a peg in the smithy's shed on that morning when she had replaced Brutus' lost shoe. The pointed brass weapons had made him think of a set owned by George Henry Thorpe.

She apparently had not heard him. "Treasure, are you talking about the devil's claws in the smithy's shed?"

"Of course," Treasure replied as if Fortner must be a simpleton not to know as much as she knew. "Don't you see them hanging on the post? They have to be what slashed Papa's face and neck and killed our dog."

"Where did you find the claws?"

"Danny found them on the ground beneath a low shelf."

"Why didn't the sheriff take them?"

"Danny and I never told him. He didn't care who killed our papa." She smiled a grim smile and half opened her eyes for a moment. "But Papa's knife got him." Tears slid down her cheeks then, and she said in a little girl's voice, "Oh, Papa, I hope you slashed him up good. How you must have suffered."

"Shhh," Fortner whispered, stroking her forehead and hair with gentle fingers. Whatever she was recalling was punishing her dreadfully, he agonized with compassion. "Don't talk anymore. Go back to sleep." He tenderly wiped away the tears sliding down her cheeks, relieved that her skin now felt pleasantly cool beneath his touch. Not until Treasure calmed down and seemed to be sleeping peacefully did he move outside the hut, his face troubled anew at the garbled bits that she had related.

Waneeta, wife of Chief Iron Hand's son, knelt with some other Indian women beside a campfire not far away. When she saw the tall white man duck his head to miss the top of the low entrance to the hut and come outside, she stood and brought him a cup of coffee.

"Thank you, Waneeta," Fortner said, pleased to find coffee in the Choctaw village. He was not surprised, for he knew that the village was no more than a two-day ride from Tokshish, the tiny settlement around the home and office of the Indian agent, John McIntosh, where bartering took place. Not until Chief Iron Hand and his people showed their command of good English and acceptance of white people in their midst had he realized what a blessing it was to have sought aid at that particular village. Despite treaties to the contrary, some Choctaw showed an open distrust of white men who came into their midst uninvited.

The delicious smell of the fragrant brew placated Fortner. The first few sips helped loosen some of the tension he felt ever since he had seen Treasure lying on the ground last night. He glanced around in the morning light; there must be some twenty huts scattered beneath the soaring pines and oaks, he realized. In the distance he saw large cleared areas and wondered if they might not be the fields for growing the corn, squash, and other vegetables for which the Choctaw were known. "The coffee is fine. I hadn't expected any, and I'm truly grateful."

"Chief Iron Hand trade corn and gourds with white men," the young woman replied with obvious pride in the talents of her father-in-law as leader of the village. She kept her eyes downcast demurely. "How is wife this morning? I heard talk coming from hut. She is better, yes?"

"I hope so," Fortner answered, thinking that if Treasure's fever stayed down for most of the day he could give a more positive answer. "I appreciate your help last night."

"I bring food and fresh leaves and bandages when she wakes. She is very beautiful, your wife," Waneeta said, a hand smoothing her knee-length deerskin skirt. She fingered the edges of the matching overblouse as she added, "Her hair is like gold silk of young corn."

"You're very kind." Had he been wise to tell her that Treasure was his wife? Fortner agonized. He had done so to protect her, but hearing the term made him feel guiltier for having kept Treasure with him and placing her in such a perilous situation. A good husband would have used better judgment than he had shown in making decisions about the welfare of his wife along the wilderness path. What if the man's shot had killed Treasure? What if the Indians had turned on them last night and not offered the needed sanctuary?

Waneeta smiled at the man apparently lost in troubling thoughts and returned to where the other women were stirring the contents of large kettles sitting in the edge of the fire.

Before Fortner had finished drinking his coffee outside the hut the medicine man joined him. Not that he figured he would ever become appreciative of the strange sight, but Fortner did not stare at the old man's tattooed face. Last summer when Bear-John and he had first traveled the Trace, he had learned that it had long been the custom among the Choctaw for some of their medicine men to have black dots tattooed in lines fanning out from the corners of their mouths to their ears, and sometimes on down their necks. No one had offered any reasonable explanation for the unique practice, and Fortner had all but forgotten about it until Manatee appeared in the morning light.

"Evil spirits gone yet?" Manatee asked. His wizened face was free of the paint striping it last night, and his knowing eyes showed concern. "Wife sleep well?"

Eyeing the strange assortment of seeds, animal teeth and bones strung on a leather necklace hanging low on the medicine man's coppery chest, Fortner replied, "She's sleeping quietly now, but a fever made her restless just before dawn."

"The way of evil spirits," the old man said with an

emphatic, sapient nod, his graying braids flopping against his shoulders. "They attack in the dark when the soul is walking with the Great Spirit. I talked with the Giver of Breath last night and asked him to stay near the white woman."

"Thank you." Fortner thought of the Bible he had slipped from his saddlebags last night before stretching out on the ground beside Treasure's bed and of the comfort that the familiar feel of its shape in his hands had lent him. Did it matter how a man gained solace, so long as he knew that there existed a power greater than he to which he could appeal? He doubted that any of the traveling preachers with their fiery rhetoric would agree with him, or even the mild-mannered Reverend Lovelace back at Brashear's Town where he had grown up, but the idea reassured him in a singular way.

By noon Treasure had awakened and felt like sitting up long enough to eat the fish stew brought by Waneeta. Fortner left her in the kindly Choctaw woman's care and went in search of Vagabond and Brutus to check on them. Last night Chief Iron Hand had told him that he was sending someone to tether the horses beside Pigeon Creek on the far side of the village. He found the animals munching tender green grass along the banks of the small stream and gave them pats and rubdowns before tending to his own needs.

Aware that downstream a group of boys practicing spear throwing in the shade of a clump of black willows watched his every move, Fortner stripped and bathed in a partially secluded pool. Afterward, he ducked under and reveled in the feel of the cleansing cool water against his lithe, naked body, then rose to his feet with a great splashing sound and vigorous shakes of his head to shed the dripping water. With his fingers he raked back his wet, shoulder-length hair, deciding to leave it free of its habitual leather thong tied at the base of his neck until it had dried somewhat.

"White man have horse muscles," one of the boys said after Fortner had pulled on his boots and breeches and started back toward the village, his shirt thrown over a damp arm.

Fortner chuckled as he approached the wide-eyed boys, all appearing to be about twelve years old, Danny's age, he reckoned. He recognized that the youngster was paying him a compliment. Sending the several boys a mischievous smile, he flexed his arm and chest muscles. "Not horse muscles. Tennessee muscles."

"Tennessee muscles," a few said in unison, looking at each other in consternation. They shrugged and whispered then in Choctaw, obviously not familiar with the place called Tennessee or Fortner's brand of wit, but terribly impressed anyway.

Assessing the bright-eyed youngster who had spoken and who had not once dropped his solemn gaze, Fortner said, "My name is Fortner. What's yours?"

"I am called Long Arrow, the grandson of Chief Iron Hand." Like the others, he wore only a breechclout and had excellent posture.

"Is your mother named Waneeta?" He saw that the boy was handsome, with intelligent dark eyes and long black hair. Like most of the Choctaw Fortner had seen, Long Arrow had a small but graceful body. "She has been helpful to my . . . wife."

His coppery face breaking into a near smile, Long Arrow said, "Yes, and my father answers to Charlie Toskin. We saw you bring the sick woman in last night." He sent a sly look at his several companions gathered around, then asked with a touch of deviltry of his own, "Can Tennessee Muscles throw a spear?"

Grinning, Fortner tied his shirt around his middle by its sleeves and held out his hand for the weapon. "I never have, but I'm willing to try."

Fortner took the long, polished shaft and balanced it across his opened palm, then examined the sharpened flint tip fastened to the end with thin strips of tightly wound leather. He could hear the youngsters tittering and whispering, and memories of Daniel Boone's visit to his home when he himself was still a boy rushed over him. Later the boys, if they were like his brothers and him at that age, would exaggerate the size of Fortner's chest and biceps and work their arms furiously in patterns they believed would help their own muscles develop faster. Forcing himself to look and sound serious, he commented in a man-to-man tone, "You have a good weapon here, Long Arrow. Where would you like me to aim it?"

"All of us can hit the second mound of dirt down the way, and our fathers and big brothers can reach the next one." Long Arrow's arms had folded across his bare chest after he gestured at the grassy mounds some three feet in height and circumference. His friends copied his cocky stance, their smooth copper faces alight with admiration and interest. "Only the chief hunters and warriors can bury the point in the last mound and make the spear stand up."

Fortner heard the unspoken dare. Wondering just how much of an arc would be required to reach the distant target, he eyed the farthest mound. Many times as a youngster he had thrown long sticks, but never one weighted at the end with a stone. He held the shaft between his thumb and fingers in the way that he had seen the boys do, then reared back and sailed the spear through the soft May sunshine.

Boyish cheers rose when the shaft buried itself in the center of the dirt forming the most distant mound.

"Will Tennessee Muscles take part in our tourney tomorrow before sunset?" Long Arrow called after Fortner bade them all good day and headed toward the village in the near distance. "There will be horseback contests, too." When Fortner took another step and made no reply, he added, "Not many white men get asked to go up against fierce Choctaw warriors."

Fortner turned back. "We'll see how my . . . wife is doing then. If she's better, perhaps I'll take part." He had again shied away from the word wife. Saying it was not easy, but dwelling upon it only threatened to bring back the unsettling thoughts he had entertained earlier about how foolish he had been to bring the beautiful blonde with him down the Trace. Not at all like a husband good enough for Treasure Ryan.

Fortner knew it was as crazy and childish as the way the boys had ogled his well-muscled chest and arms, but he liked the idea of Treasure watching him compete with the Choctaw braves... and perhaps cheering him on. The playful thought allowed him to entertain the hope that by tomorrow afternoon Treasure might be well on her way to recovery from her gunshot wound and her fall from Vaga-bond. He walked more quickly through the village now.

"Where's Waneeta?" Fortner asked when he stooped and entered the assigned hut and found Treasure alone. He had not finished buttoning his shirt before he rushed inside, and the sight of Treasure smiling at him in the smoky, shadowy interior made him forget about everything else but her. Her teeth and eyes seemed to be beckoning beacons of enchantment. Her crudely altered shift was gone, and both of her shoulders were bare now except for a partial fall of golden curls over one of them. A wide band of blond buckskin covered her breasts but left a strip of satiny bare skin above the black skirt. He licked at lips gone dry. "Are you still feeling better?"

"Oh, yes. Waneeta brought me some water—some plain water without all those messy leaves and roots in it—and helped me get clean. She said I'd be more comfortable without what was left of my soiled shift and offered me one of her garments." Treasure looked down ruefully at the unusual band covering her suddenly tingling breasts, aware that Fortner had been staring at her as if he had never seen her before. "And I suppose I am covered better now. Someone called to Waneeta, and I told her to run along, that I figured you'd be back shortly."

The welcome sight of the handsome Fortner almost overwhelmed Treasure. Though she knew she was feeling stronger than before, she was still weak and trembly. She felt tears smart behind her eyelids for no reason at all except the joy of seeing and hearing the man she loved so madly. She saw then that only one or two buttons held his shirt together over his furred chest and that the shirttails were barely tucked in on one side of the waistband of his blue breeches. He looked almost like a young boy caught in the act of ignoring the basic rules of decency—almost like Danny at such times, she thought with a rush of tenderness.

Playfully she asked, "What have you been doing? Running from the Indian maidens or running to them?" His puzzled expression and questioning eyebrows amused her, and she giggled. "You're as bad as Danny on his worst days, Fortner. Don't you know that you're not fully dressed and that your hair is all wet and mussed?"

"Oh," Fortner said, laughing softly when he looked down and realized then that he must indeed present an unsual picture. "I took a dip in Pigeon Creek after I found our horses faring well. I guess I was in too much of a hurry to come see about you to pay much attention to the way I look." Quickly he finished buttoning his shirt. With a hand slapping his damp hair back from his forehead, he went to where their saddlebags lay on the other low platform serving as a second bed.

"Your bandage looks different," Fortner remarked as he reached into his saddlebag for his comb. "Did Waneeta change the dressing on your arm?" He pulled his comb through his thick brown hair, turning to look across the small hut at Treasure propped up on the bed. Waneeta or someone else must have replenished the wood in the small fire burning evenly out in the center of the hut, he realized. At the moment the smoke was trailing a straight path upward to the little hole in the center of the roof. He knew that mosquitoes and gnats likely would be gnawing on them already if the smoke was not surreptitiously chasing them away.

"She did. Waneeta's been very nice to me."

"How did the wound look, and how's the knot on your head?"

"The wound is terrible, from what I could tell. I need eyes where my ears are to see it properly. And the bump on my head is still there."

"You say it looks terrible?" Fortner frowned, dropping

his comb atop his saddlebag and tying the customary leather thong around the back portion of his damp hair. "Isn't your arm healing yet?" He walked to stand beside her bed, concern for her wrinkling his forehead.

"Waneeta said it seems to be healing, but it still looks awful to me. Of course there's no light except what comes in the doorway and the hole in the roof. It ached and smarted when I tried to brush my hair." She waved the brush in her good hand languidly. "I got so tired I just gave up. It's plain I won't be going anywhere today."

"Let me finish brushing it for you," Fortner said, motioning for her to move back enough for him to sit on the edge of her bed. "I may not be very good at this, but at least I can get the snarls out of the places you can't reach with your good hand. You'll have to tell me if I get too rough around that bump." He reached to take the brush, bothered far more than he cared to be by the touch of his fingers on hers. He took a deep breath. Being so close to her was intoxicating. And there was that tantalizing strip of bare skin above the band of her skirt. "Can you sit up for me?"

Treasure sat up, not sure if her injuries from the preceding night caused the sudden weakness washing over her entire body or if the nearness of Fortner triggered the unsettling reaction. At first his handling of the brush was too light and shaky to remove the tangles, but soon he managed to send the bristles deep enough to bring a semblance of order to her waves and curls.

"Does it hurt when the brush touches the knot back here?" Fortner asked, slowing the movements of the brush and using a finger to test the bruise below the crown of her head. He scolded himself for noticing the silken texture of her hair as much as the shape and size of the nasty bump he had found last night. He was supposed to be taking care of her, not allowing himself to be enchanted by her many charms. With considerable effort he pretended that the fragrance of her hair was not affecting him at all and proceeded with his delightful task of turning her tangled hair into pretty order.

"It hurts a little when you brush over the bump," Treasure conceded, pleased at his concern for her welfare. The intimacy of his fingers exploring her scalp satisfied her unspoken desire to be someone special to Fortner. She knew better than to hope that he might fall in love with her. He must have hundreds of important things to do, yet he seemed interested in nothing except seeing to her needs, she mused with foggy minded wonder. What did the medicine in the little gourd have in it to be making her feel so heavenly?

Treasure was relieved that she had her back turned toward Fortner so that he could not see the beatific look that she suspected was transforming her features, a look that had nothing at all to do with getting the tangles out of her long hair. Secretly she sniffed at the heady smell of virile young man straight from a dip in clear, fresh water. Close to her ears she could hear his breathing, could sometimes feel it feathering across her ears and neck in little uneven patterns. She got goosebumps from remembering how on two other very memorable occasions he had been so near that his breath had made delicious claims on her skin.

Was it the herbal brew that Fortner and then Waneeta had insisted she drink that was making her heart thump so wildly? Treasure asked herself sternly, trying to be objective. Confessing then that she knew she was lying to herself even to let the question form, she studied her hands where they lay knotted together against her black skirt.

Too well Treasure knew what caused her inner unrest. It was having Fortner so close and having him brushing her hair with long, rhythmic strokes. Only because she was ill and not in total control was she allowing him to affect her that way, she reassured herself. Nothing had changed. She still must fight to erase her passionate love for him and replace it with simple friendship—and she would. She had to! Friendship was all a man like him wanted from someone like her; he had no interest in marrying and settling down. In an effort to control her seesawing emotions, Treasure caught her lower lip between her teeth until she felt a pain as keen as that radiating from the wound on her left arm.

"You need to lie down and rest now," Fortner said when he sensed Treasure's agitation. The past few moments of brushing had not been necessary, he reminded himself. Laying her brush on her bed, he stood and watched her do as he had suggested. "I'll not be far way, and I'll be checking on you. Get some sleep."

"What did you do all day while I slept like a lazy pig in the sun?" Treasure asked that evening when she awakened and found Fortner bringing her a bowl of aromatic food.

"I visited with Chief Iron Hand and some of his warriors." Fortner had determined after each peek at her sleeping form during the day that when she woke up he would avoid such intimacies as the hair brushing episode of that morning. Determining to keep his hands off Treasure was one thing; adhering to his vow was another, far more punishing endeavor. "Sit up and drink your medicine before you eat the stew Waneeta sent."

Treasure found that she felt strong enough to rest her feet on the deerskin rug beside her low bed when she sat up and watched Fortner fetch the medicine. Her right hand brushed back her hair from her face, and she was pleased when winnowing fingers told her that she had not mussed it much as she slept the day away. She was even happier that the troubling dreams of that earlier fevered sleep had not returned. "How much longer will I have to drink that vile mess?"

Fortner handed her the small gourd. "Until it's all gone. I'm sure Manatee's brew is what has helped keep your fever down. Maybe you'll not have to have another dose at all tonight."

Treasure did not talk any more until after she had dipped the horn spoon several times into the wooden bowl and taken the edge off her hunger. After bringing a couple of small tree limbs from outside and adding them to the little fire in the hut, Fortner settled upon the deerskin rug that

Waneeta had brought on one of her visits to check on the sleeping Treasure.

"Don't you have something to eat, too?" Treasure asked, pausing with the curved, polished piece of deer horn in midair.

"Only a spoon like yours," Fortner answered with a sigh and a mocking tone of self-pity. He stretched out full length on the large deerskin near her bed and angled an arm and hand into a prop for his head before returning his gaze to Treasure.

Remembering her few visits to the Chickasaw village over the ridges from the Ryan farm, Treasure held the bowl out toward Fortner. "Sit up and eat. I forgot how Indians sometimes put the family's food in one bowl. Why didn't you remind me?"

"I was enjoying watching you eat." When her eyes showed her distress in the reflected firelight, he went on. "Actually, I ate earlier with Chief Iron Hand and his son, Charlie Toskin."

Treasure took another bite then, lifting her shoulders and tossing her hair in open disdain for his cruelty in teasing someone who was ill. Her expression changed instantly to one of discomfort.

"Is your arm hurting, Treasure?"

"Yes," she replied with a rueful little laugh. "It serves me right for trying to act haughty, though."

"You could never be truly haughty—not even when you become the mistress of a Mississippi plantation."

"What makes you say that?" She looked down at the tasty mixture of corn and beans and venison, no longer hungry.

"You told me back at Colbert's Stand what your mother dreamed for you, and I happen to agree with her. You'll be a grand lady when you marry your Thurston Crabtree." Fortner could not imagine why he had steered the conversation in that direction.

"Fortner, you're trying to rile me. You know damned well the man's name is Thornton. And he's not *mine!* I never should have told you anything about him or what my mother said." Treasure leaned over and set the bowl and spoon on the hard, dirt floor. She stood, a bit wobbly in the knees and not nearly so sturdy anywhere as she had expected. Her stomach flipflopped, and her head felt both heavy and light at the same time.

"What are you planning on doing?"

"Walking around to get my strength back, that's what." Oh, she didn't like thinking that they likely would be parting within the week! She was angry that Fortner had forced her into thinking about Natchez. "What are you planning on doing when you leave me with Grandpa Lindsay?" she asked after she had managed to reach the open entryway and decided that she would have to return to the bed and sit down.

"After I get everything settled with Whitey and the Thorpes I'm heading across the Mississippi to see what's out West. Rumors in Nashville were that the expedition led out last year by Captain Lewis and Lieutenant Clark to explore the Louisiana Purchase is meeting little resistance from the Indians. Imagine what kinds of sights they've seen! And I hear there's lots to see out in the Spanish area called Texas, too. There's a whole new world out there, and I'd like to be a part of it."

Fortner's enthusiastic words sliced at Treasure's heart as she returned to sit on the side of the bed and look down at the self-proclaimed adventurer. She flinched from the dreamy, faraway look in his blue eyes; it apparently focused upon a new life, one without her. "Papa told Danny and me about the Lewis and Clark party when they left Saint Louis last year. The idea of traveling in the unknown frightened me." But that was before she had met this lovable brave man, Treasure realized. The idea bore instant appeal now that she could envision herself going along with him. "Won't you miss what's left behind if you wander so far away?" *Will you miss me . . . a little?*

"I might . . . at first." He pursed his lips thoughtfully and felt his thumb and forefinger meet and rub together. *I'll miss you, darling. Forever.*

"Will Bear-John be going with you?" *Ask me to go.*

Treasure noticed the way Fortner's left finger and thumb slowly moved against each other and realized that she had seen him indulging in that little habit before. But hadn't it been when he was obviously troubled or in deep thought? Certainly he hadn't sounded troubled when he spoke so enthusiastically of his plans for the future. And there was little doubt that he had not already given those plans plenty of thought. Maybe she had been wrong. Maybe the action revealed nothing about his inner state of mind.

"Bear-John hasn't decided yet if he wants to go." *If you didn't deserve the kind of life waiting for you in Natchez, I'd beg you to marry me and go along.* The forbidden thought of having Treasure beside him forever almost stole his breath away, and he cursed himself for his weakness.

"I suppose going West is what an adventurer like you should do."

"You're right. And just think of all that lies ahead—all kinds of wildlife and places maybe no white man has ever looked at before." Fortner suspected that both his thoughts of leaving Treasure and those of the life he spoke about contributed to the sudden stirring in his blood.

But Treasure chose not to think about the exciting new life of which Fortner spoke. Instead, she focused on the present, on something he had said earlier.

"Fortner, I forgot that George Henry said he was supposed to be meeting up with Whitey right away. Do you suppose it might be today?" Her conscience nagged at her. "Maybe we can catch up with them before the meeting. You've waited so long to see the man, and now you're stuck here with me and missing out on facing Whitey at last. I'm so sorry I've been such a bother. Maybe we can leave in the morning."

Fortner sat up, folding his long legs tailor fashion. "We'll not be leaving until you're far better than you are now."

"I feel horrible about this. Why didn't you leave Bear-John to look after me so you could go ahead with the Thorpes?"

"I never gave any thought to going on without you."

The serious look in his eyes and the tone of his deep voice revealed total honesty. He never had considered leaving her behind at the Choctaw village.

"You must have forgotten about the plans to meet with Whitey." And yet he would go West without her, Treasure reminded herself when she tried to read something extra into his statement. She scolded herself for being foolish.

Fortner was silent for a moment. "Let's just say that I did have something on my mind that seemed far more important." Hoping that his timing was right, he said after a while, "You must have been having an awful dream before dawn this morning when your fever was so high. Do you remember talking about a black hat with a red feather?"

"No." Treasure's eyes flickered with partial memory. "But I do recall I dreamed about Danny and me finding Papa dead in the smithy's shed back in January. I told you about it when . . ." She paused, not liking to recall any part of that stormy night when they had first made love in the cave, not when Fortner was so near and so obviously trying to look into her very soul. Folding her legs underneath her full skirt, she leaned back against the wall.

"You didn't go into detail, though, about finding the hat you talked about this morning . . . or the devil's claws. You merely said your father was killed in a fight. Will you tell me all about it? I've an idea that I want to try out on you."

Sending Fortner puzzling glances throughout, Treasure recounted how her young brother and she had seen the strange hat that cold morning when they had returned from the Chickasaw village and found Blackie dead with his bloody knife clutched in his hand. Then came the telling of the easier part; while Danny and she were cleaning one day, the boy had discovered the brass devil's claws beneath a low shelf.

"You figured that by hanging the claws on the post you might tempt someone to identify them or, perhaps, claim them," Fortner remarked when she finished.

"Yes, that's right," Treasure replied, not surprised that she felt better about the whole miserable business from having explained it to this wonderful man watching her with compassion. She had felt the same way after she had recounted the awful business with Amos Greeson. From where she sat upon her bed, Treasure cocked her head to one side and asked, "Did you see the evil looking things when you were there?"

"Yes. Did you leave them behind?"

She nodded. "They're still there, unless Amos took them now that he owns everything. Danny and I told him what we found, and he agreed that if anyone showed interest in them we ought to send for the sheriff right away. Amos said nobody in our parts used such things."

"Was Amos the only one you told?"

"Yes. That day you came I kept trying to see if you noticed them, but I never caught you looking."

"Did you suspect me of being one of your father's attackers?" A flash of his white teeth in the dimly lighted hut revealed his amusement at her fears on that spring morning. A soft chuckle followed.

"Yes—but only at first. You see, it just didn't make sense for someone like you to show up at our place. Hardly anyone except for the people who live in the area uses that loop of the Trace." Treasure thought for a moment. "It still seems strange that you decided to travel that way." In her mind's eye she could still see the beauty of the distant dogwood blooms on that day Fortner had ridden up. Inside a voice was asking: *Would she have been better off if he never had come to the Ryan farm that April morning?*

"Do you recall the Thorpes mentioning that they had a brother, Felsenthal?"

Treasure nodded, her smooth forehead creasing at his seemingly unrelated question.

"Felsenthal Thorpe was wearing a black hat with a nipped red feather all last fall while Bear-John and I rode with the gang." When Treasure's eyes widened in surprise, he continued. "And I saw George Henry use some devil's claws in a fight down in Natchez, and he used them to threaten some men at other times. That day while you were shoeing Brutus, I thought that the claws looked a lot like George Henry's.''

Forgetting all about her wounded arm, Treasure pulled her knees up close to her chest with both arms and shuddered. "Are you saying that the Thorpes might be the ones who came to the farm that day and fought with my father after he shod their horses?" Her teeth captured her bottom lip to hold it still.

"Yes. I think it's extremely likely, because George Henry is the one who told me about Blackie Ryan having a blacksmith shop near the Duck River—and that's how I knew to take the road up to your cabin that morning after Brutus threw the shoe. I was told that Felsenthal never recovered from wounds suffered in a knife fight, and I heard George Henry bragging about getting a grand price for some horses he had come upon."

Treasure gulped and brought a fist up to her trembling mouth for a moment. Tears threatened to fall. In a tightly controlled voice she said, "How ironic that the same men who left my father dead and ransacked our cabin are the ones that I've been traveling with." She took a deep breath before completing her thoughts. "They've known who I am from the start. Could that be why they decided to make Grandpa Lindsay pay to have Danny and me delivered to him—to get back at us for Felsenthal's death?"

Fortner shrugged and looked even more serious. "Could be. Those Thorpes don't think like anybody I ever met."

"By jingo!" Treasure exclaimed, her eyes showing as much anger as her low voice. "They killed our dog, too, and stole the horses . . . I knew I should have killed that George Henry the minute I got the gun away from him!" Her right hand clenched into a tighter fist.

"Maybe, but you're not a killer, Treasure. By the time you had thought it over it was too late without getting both Danny and you shot. You did the right thing." But had *he* done the right thing?

Fortner again wondered at his remarkable self-control in not firing at George Henry the instant he slapped Treasure. Had his way truly been better? He still had not met the elusive Whitey so that he could fulfill his need for revenge, and he might never get to now that he was not traveling south with the gang. If he had not interfered further, soldiers from Colbert's Stand already would have escorted Treasure to travel with Hank and Danny. The last thought triggered another question. "Do you think Hank's the one who told the Thorpes the lie about you killing Amos Greeson and being wanted by the law? I can't figure out any other way George Henry—"

Instantly on the defensive about her old friend, Treasure didn't let him finish. "I told you back at Colbert's Stand that Hank's been a friend of my family for a long time and that I resent you even thinking such a thing. He has to get along with the Thorpes and all the other outlaws on the Trace or he couldn't make his trips every year. He would do nothing to harm Danny or me." Her lips pouted and her eyes flashed with indignation before she gave in to fatigue and stretched out on the bed. She slid a sideways, accusing look at Fortner. "Even if he were tempted to do such a thing, Hank would have nothing to gain by telling such a lie. Surely you can see that."

Fortner lifted a hand as if to ward off a blow. "All right. Calm down and get some rest. I'll see if I can come up with a better idea."

But try as he could during the silence that followed while he rose and added fuel to the fire, Fortner could not erase the thought that had crossed his mind upon first meeting the old peddler last fall. Hank Marcellus was not what he seemed.

Chapter Seventeen

Sitting cross-legged on the ground between Waneeta and Bitonka, wife of Chief Iron Hand, Treasure drank in the sights and sounds around her on the following afternoon. Little girls dressed in brief leather tunics and little boys wearing miniature breechclouts romped around the edges of the chattering crowd with their dogs. A noticeable excitement laced the air.

So many smiling Indian women had come to welcome and meet the blond stranger accompanying Waneeta and Bitonka to the tourney field that Treasure's memory had been left with a wealth of friendly, coppery faces but only a dearth of names. Now, along with almost everyone of all ages from the huts behind them, she waited for the next event to take place on the large grassy field just outside the Choctaw village.

Treasure had rested well on the preceding night, and both Fortner and Waneeta had deemed her fit enough to attend the long-planned contests taking place late that afternoon. Not understanding why Fortner had dashed off without an explanation at midday, Treasure had welcomed Waneeta's assistance in brushing her long hair and tying it back with a blue ribbon. The kindly Indian woman had also helped her slip on her blue waist over the strip of buckskin across her breasts.

Soon after arriving at the tourney, Treasure had watched the youngest warriors vie with each other in bouts of running, jumping, and wrestling. She saw that a number of horses were now being led into view across the field. Right off she noticed that the short-legged, stocky Indian ponies appeared quite different from the long-lined, high stepping horses both Fortner and she rode. She took a second look. Yes, that was Brutus standing among the smaller ponies. None wore saddles.

"Waneeta," Treasure said to the pretty Indian woman who had shown her so much kindness ever since Fortner had brought her there two nights ago. She had already told Waneeta how much she admired her long black hair that fell in a shining curtain in the May sunshine. "Is Fortner going to compete in the horseback contests?"

"My son, Long Arrow, says your husband will throw spears and enter horse races," Waneeta replied, her hands reaching up to adjust her dangling earrings of gaily painted circles of wood. "Long Arrow says he will do well against Choctaw braves, for he has what he called Tennessee muscles."

Treasure laughed merrily, thinking of Fortner's love of deviltry and imagining how the boy must have come up with such a ridiculous description. Fortner had told her of meeting Waneeta's son and his friends yesterday and how they had reminded him of Danny. How her younger brother would have loved being in the Choctaw village! Treasure thought for perhaps the tenth time. Before she could agonize further, the two men conducting the activities walked from the low platform where Chief Iron Hand and his council members sat.

"What are they saying?" Treasure asked. Though nearly all of the Choctaw language sounded identical to that of the Chickasaw Indians around whom she had grown up, Treasure recognized few words. The Chickasaw from the village near the Ryan farm had always preferred communicating in and perfecting their English. The same seemed true of the Choctaw. Blackie had told her once that a major reason for the Indians of the area to master English was their need to understand negotiations with government officials about land purchases and peace treaties. She had no wish to dwell upon anything so serious and put away her thoughts. "Tell me what they're going to do now."

This time Bitonka answered. "Next they throw spears." Like her daughter-in-law and almost all of the other Choctaw women, Bitonka wore her straight hair long and unfettered except for a beaded band reaching from her forehead to the back of her head. "Boys aim from a line closer to target; braves throw from farther back."

"Oh, my," Treasure fretted when she espied Fortner taking his place among the dozen or so Indians moving to a marked place far from the target. Though she had glimpsed him once in the distance during the earlier contests, it was the first time she saw him this close since midday when he had told her to rest in the hut and left.

She craned her neck for a better view. "I can't believe that Fortner knows anything about throwing a spear. I wonder why he's down among the braves who've been winning at shooting their blowguns and their bows and arrows?"

The way the afternoon sun reflected off Fortner's tanned, bare chest and arms started a satisfying humming inside the fascinated young woman watching him. The little inner rhythm stepped up a pace when Treasure saw that he wore only a leather breechclout as the copper skinned Indian braves did. He moved then, and she smiled upon seeing his flat belly, thick thighs, and powerful calves that she had so admired when they made love.

Scolding herself for her wayward thoughts and her skipping heartbeat, she noted that Fortner was broader in the shoulders and taller by a head than any of his less solidly built competitors. Though Treasure had seen earlier while they competed on the field that many of the black-haired Choctaw braves were well-muscled and handsome, none had pale blue eyes and the heart-stopping smile belonging to the dark-haired man who had stolen her heart. A kind of fanciful worship transformed her light brown eyes into a warm, dazzling gold.

"Do not be afraid. Your husband showed giant skill yesterday," Waneeta assured Treasure. "My son told me to bet on him to win."

"Bet on Fortner?" Treasure smiled, favoring the sound of husband in reference to the one she loved in spite of her resolve not to. "Do people usually bet on these contests?" She looked around then and recalled that there had been quite a bit of frenzied activity in between the varied contests as some men moved in and among the large crowd gathered there. "What do they use for betting?"

Chief Iron Hand's wife laughed then and said something in Choctaw to Waneeta before addressing Treasure with a big smile. "White woman should come during one of our stickball games. Choctaws bet trinkets, bags of corn, flints, whatever they have of value. Betting on ballgames is high as sky. In my time, I see whole villages lose year's crops.''

"How horrible!" Treasure looked from the smiling, weathered face of Bitonka to the younger, prettier one of Waneeta. "What do they do then?"

Bitonka's smile grew wider, and she shrugged while smoothing her beaded buckskin skirt down over her legs. "Grow more bigger crops the next year and bet again."

"I don't think I could care enough for the outcome of a ballgame to bet on it," Treasure remarked, more aware than ever of the differences in the seemingly carefree Indians that she had known and her logical self. She was too honest to deny, though, that her father—and obviously Fortner, as well—would have had no trouble understanding the urge to risk everything he owned on something as elusive as the results of a ballgame or a roll of dice.

"Choctaw ballgames—*baggataway*—bring all the tribes together," Waneeta explained. Her dark eyes sparkled from apparently fond recollections. "Men use two short sticks with nets like cups on end to hold and throw ball against goalposts. After their game, they let women play. Perhaps you and husband can come back for game at next moon."

Her blond tresses swaying against her back and shoulders, Treasure shook her head. "Thanks, but we'll not be coming back this way after we reach Natchez."

Pushing away the thought of Natchez and the time when she would have to leave Fortner, Treasure concentrated on the new games of skill beginning. She wondered if the loud, good-natured cheers and groans accompanying the contestants' efforts all afternoon might not have depended on whether the spectators had bet for or against the bronzed athletes.

Soon it was time for the young men at the farthest point to aim their spears at the target. Looking like a fat wheel with no hole for an axle, the target appeared to be made of dried and closely packed field grasses bound into its circular shape by strips of leather. A shiny green leaf marked its center.

Treasure became tense and rubbed lightly at her bandaged arm when Fortner was the only one left to throw a spear. When he stepped forward, she saw that he was barefoot like his competitors and that he appeared at ease in the scanty covering apparently favored by the Choctaw warriors. The thick mat of dark chest curls made Fortner stand out among the sleek-chested braves almost as much as his lighter skin and greater height. As far as she could tell, no other man's spear had penetrated the exact center of the target. She didn't dare hope that he might win, but she found herself counting on him to do well.

At least in the benevolent eyes of her heart and mind, Fortner was doing well, Treasure thought while her eyes drank in the beloved sight of his tan virile form covered only by the scanty breechclout. Her hands clasped together in half prayer, she watched the handsome man balance a spear in his hand, then step back behind the line in that surefooted way of his. With his muscles rippling in perfect rhythm, Fortner ran lightly up to the line, leaning his torso back gracefully before sending the long piece of polished wood on its arching path through the late afternoon sunshine.

During the sudden hush, in which Treasure realized she was holding her breath, she heard the swoosh of the airborne spear, then watched with wide-eyed wonder as it landed in the center of the leaf. It stayed there, quivering for an instant.

"Wah! Aii-eey!" came bursting from the Choctaw, large and small. Whistles and rhythmic handclaps followed. Four hollowed tree sections covered tightly with deerskins added their monotonous sounds when the drummers pounded them with their sticks, as they had done at the end of each preceeding contest.

"Hurrah for Fortner!" yelled Treasure, releasing the captured breath. She jumped up in her excitement and pride and clapped her hands wildly. If her wounded arm protested she did not know it. Her wondering eyes had veered from Fortner only briefly to watch the arc of the spear, and now they returned to him. He was smiling and watching her over the heads of the braves crowding around

him and obviously congratulating him. Somehow she sensed
the force of his silvery gaze and dazzling smile as though
he might be standing beside her. She felt sure she was
imagining that his look signaled that he had performed his
marvelous feat only for her approval.

The crowd took up the English equivalent of their earlier
cries, and Treasure could hear hurrahs drowning out her
own. Fortner had pleased more than the person posing as
his wife.

Horse racing came next, to be followed by what Waneeta
told Treasure would be a tourney relay carried out by the
braves on horseback. She did not worry about Fortner and
Brutus winning those events, for she well knew that both
the rider and his horse were superior.

Sure enough, the handsome gray with the stockings and
points of black raced around the course with ease, its rider
still wearing only the breechclout and riding without a
saddle with the same careless grace as the Indians. The
final race called for three laps around, and Fortner again
smiled across at Treasure when he was hailed as winner
once more. The smile she returned was just as magnificent. He was wonderful! There was nothing at which her
beloved did not excel.

The Indians in charge of the contests hurriedly drove
two posts into the ground. Set about twenty feet apart at
one end of the grassy field, each had a crosspiece fastened
upon it about six feet from the ground. Treasure watched
as the men hung what looked like large rings over the
crossbars.

Waneeta explained, "They put seven circlets of hard-
ened leather on the crossbars of poles in ground. The top
four horsemen from final race make two teams. Team try
to be first to remove loops with jousting sticks and ride
back to starting line. Take off loops one at a time."

Treasure nodded her understanding, watching Fortner
and one of the braves sitting on their horses, talking and
examining a long stick handed to them. She assumed that
was the jousting stick with which the two riders would
remove the circlets from the crossbar of the tall pole driven

in the ground on their side of the field. Close by Fortner and his relay partner, the second pair of riders appeared to be looking over their stick and making plans about how they would snare the rings from the crossbar of the other pole.

"Your man won the horse races. He will take the jousting stick and go first," Bitonka said, picking up where Waneeta had left off. Apparently happy to share her knowledge with Treasure, the wife of Chief Iron Hand adjusted her short cape of curly feathers woven together by strands of supple bark. "He sticks pole through loop and races back with the ring on it and rides out to get a second one. They not stop till they have all seven circlets of leather. Much excitement. Biggest bets of the day are made on this last contest."

"The other team will be trying to do the same thing, only faster—is that it?" Treasure asked. Both Indian women nodded their approval of her understanding, then fixed their attention on the four contestants.

Treasure could feel and hear the excitement building. Probably most of the bets were being placed on the team Fortner headed, she mused with an admitted headiness. For a crazy moment something displaced her logic, and she wished she had something to wager. There was no doubt in her mind that Fortner would win. She sent him a warm smile and waved her hand when she realized that his silvery gaze from across the field was fixed on her. The cocky smile and jaunty wave that Fortner returned made Treasure think of a daring, prankish boy showing off. When had she ever loved him more? she wondered with renewed awe at the way he affected her.

A stick rapped on a drum and they were off! Leaning low over the handsome gray with the flying black mane, Fortner was first to leave the starting line. Treasure joined the crowd in cheering, unable to make herself sit back down. She watched as Fortner deftly slipped a leather ring upon the tip of his long stick, circled the tall pole, and raced Brutus back to his waiting partner. The brave from the other team was far enough behind him for Fortner's partner to take the proffered stick and dash off on his pony before the other Indian had barely received his partner's stick. And so it went, to Treasure's—and most of the vociferous crowd's—utter delight.

Clinging to Brutus' back with as much skill as an Indian accustomed to riding bareback, Fortner had brought the stick and fifth ring to his partner a full two lengths ahead of their opponent. The waiting Choctaw brave let out an exalted war whoop as he took off for the sixth and next to last ring; victory seemed certain for Fortner and him. Treasure's heart had pounded harder at each segment of the fast relay, for Fortner and Brutus formed a magical pair of thundering speed and masculine precision.

Only one circlet of leather dangled from each of the crossbars then. With his upright stick holding the six rings already claimed, an exuberant Fortner urged Brutus forward again. He sensed, though he had no time to look her way, that Treasure was not missing a single moment of his remarkable feats. The final round of the relay found the gray several lengths ahead of the opponent's spotted pony.

Treasure, standing and cheering throughout the relay race, watched with disbelieving eyes. Without warning, Brutus dug in his feet only a short way from the pole, obviously no longer interested in the game of speed. As quickly as a bird of prey swooping down to earth, Fortner's body sailed over the head of his motionless horse, flipped over in the air and fell to the grassy ground. His opponent, yelling victoriously, passed him and his temperamental horse. Gasping for breath, Fortner craned his head enough to watch the Indian remove his seventh and final loop of leather with his stick, then wheel his pony around quickly, spurred on by the wildly laughing and cheering bystanders.

Scrambling up from his inglorious fall, Fortner watched the brave on the other team race his pony down the last stretch to the finish line.

"Damn you, Brutus!" a disgruntled Fortner scolded when he recovered enough breath to speak. He sent a murderous look at the watchful horse standing right where it had balked. "I should have known not to trust you after you'd had two lazy days. When will I learn?"

Fortner stooped and picked up the fallen stick with the six circlets of leather still on it. He waved it aloft before jumping back upon the gray's sleek back. Smiling deridingly at his formerly exalted opinion of himself and his imagined prowess, he slipped the point of the stick through the last ring on the crossbar and rode the prancing Brutus back to the finish line at a sedate pace. Already the winning pair of braves were accepting boisterous congratulations from the Indians rushing out to the field.

Treasure sat on her bed that night, ready for sleep. She had drunk the last of the herbal concoction brought that first night by Manatee, the medicine man. Waneeta had helped her put on a fresh bandage soon after she brought the evening stew.

Looking across to where Fortner lay facedown on the other low bed in the hut, Treasure asked, "Are you sure you don't want me to rub liniment on your back, Fortner? Even if it is horse liniment I took from Papa's shed—"

"I'm sure," he replied before she could go on.

"You don't have to sound cross, you know." Treasure had thought Fortner would have regained his normal good humor long before now. She had realized that he probably felt like a fool for a moment right after the fall, but why had his winning the relay been so important to him? He had won the spear throwing contest and the horse races. Plainly the Choctaw held him in high esteem for his accomplishments.

Fortner said in carefully enunciated words, "For the third time, I'm telling you that I'm not sounding cross. Go to sleep. Remember that we're leaving at the break of day."

In the wavering light coming from the small fire in the center of the hut, Treasure gazed at Fortner's bare back and shoulders. He had lain on the bed and appeared to be dozing ever since he had come to the hut holding himself stiffly erect. Having seen her father more than once when he had taken a tumble from a horse and wrenched his back, she had recognized the peculiar gait. When she had mentioned it, though, Fortner had become angry and refused to admit that anything bothered him. He confessed to being only tired and sleepy.

"You really were magnificent out there this afternoon," Treasure called softly as she stretched out on her blanket thrown over the padding of bearskins. She fought back a little giggle trying to surface. At least he had been until Brutus balked. For fear he might be able to tell that she was smiling, she sobered before she added, "I was proud of you."

No sound came from the other bed for a long while. "Thanks," Fortner muttered as he inched his body over painfully to lie on his aching back.

"At least now I won't have to ask you to explain why you call your horse Brutus, will I?"

Fortner almost smiled at the irony of it all. All he had wanted to do was impress Treasure with his athletic ability. A foolish action brought a foolish ending, he reminded himself. Her understanding that Brutus had turned traitor on him and balked through no fault of his rider lightened Fortner's mood a degree—but no farther. "No, you won't. I guess I'm luckier than Julius Caesar—at least I'm not dead. Get some sleep."

Fortner paid close attention to Treasure's color during the next day as they once more started down the Trace toward Natchez. By mid-afternoon she appeared pale, though she denied that she was overly tired or bothered by pain in her arm.

"I've never stopped here," Fortner said when they halted beside the Trace in a small clearing surrounded by a giant canebreak beneath tall swamp oaks. It would be a while before dark, but he decided that to push on to the camping site he had in mind was unwise. He did not wish to overtax Treasure on her first full day out of bed. "With so much cane growing here there must be a stream close by. I'll check it out while you get down and rest."

Treasure nodded agreeably and allowed him to assist her

in dismounting. She made herself ignore the way she relished the touch of his hands on her, even for that brief moment. "Thanks for helping, but my arm isn't paining me when I do things for myself today."

Back in his usual jovial mood ever since awakening that morning free of the excruciating back pain, Fortner replied, "That's good to hear, but you need to use caution. Infection could still develop." He congratulated himself on being able to step away from her as soon as she stood safely on the ground. Glancing down at her hips to make sure that her knife was in her holster, he said, "Wait here. I won't be out of hearing range."

Fortner moved on then to separate the thickly growing stalks of cane with his hands and feet and form a narrow path toward the stream that he felt must not be far away. When he found what seemed to be a shallow running branch, he knelt, sniffed, then filled his hands. The water was clear with a sweet smell. He lowered his mouth and drank. A noise behind him brought him to his feet with his rifle in hand.

"Treasure, why didn't you stay behind?" he scolded when he saw her picking her way through the skinny path he had made through the cane. "All kinds of varmints live in canebreaks, and it's easy to get lost in one this thick and tall."

"I can see why, but I followed your path. Besides, I was thirsty." Treasure ignored him and knelt to drink from the stream, splashing the cool water on her warm face afterward.

Within a short time Fortner had watered the horses and made a suitable campsite for the night while an abnormally placid Treasure sat with her back against a broad tree trunk. A trio of what looked like businessmen passed by on the Trace headed toward Nashville, but they paid scant attention to the man building a campfire down in the small clearing in the canebreak.

"It's still a while before dark," Fortner said. "Maybe I can catch a perch or two in the branch for our supper and we won't have to use up the dried meat that Waneeta gave us. I'm good at cooking fish. You can keep on resting and tell me all that I'm doing wrong." After flashing her a smile, he went to his saddlebags lying on the ground in search of line and a fishhook. Aggravated that the small packet must have fallen to the bottom of the flat, deep pouch, he began stirring objects around, finally removing some and placing them on the ground.

"What's that?" Treasure asked when she saw something shiny fall to the ground from his saddlebag.

"What's what?" he replied absently. With a triumphant smile he held up the small packet containing his precious fishhooks and line.

Treasure rose and walked over to where he knelt. "It looks like a piece of jewelry . . . a locket on a chain." The surrounding cane and the trees overhead already put the area in deep shadow, though the sun was an hour or two away from setting. Her heart jumping in fits and starts— and not from his nearness this time—she knelt beside him and picked up the familiar piece of jewelry. It was her mother's locket, the one that had been taken from the cabin the day Blackie had been killed. She asked sharply, "Where did you get this?"

Fortner stopped repacking his saddlebag and looked at what she held. "Oh, that," he replied with a shrug. "I won it off George Henry one night in a poker game."

Treasure recalled the instance when George Henry had laughed sneeringly and told Fortner that whatever he had forfeited in place of money might make a good gift for Fortner's "woman." Rare tears of self-pity at the cruelties she had suffered formed, and she blinked hard to keep them back. She felt ill all over. "Why haven't I seen it before?"

"Why would I show you everything in my saddle-bags?" Her accusing tone angered Fortner for some reason, and he felt he was being put on the defensive unfairly.

"If you truly won it in a poker game, why didn't you give it to me as George Henry suggested? I remember what he said that night when he insisted you take some jewelry to cover a bet." Her face, already too warm for the past hour, flushed hotly when she recalled how she had not known then that Hannah was his sister-in-law and that she had been jealous of her.

"Maybe you shouldn't be eavesdropping when—"

"Eavesdropping?" Treasure burst out. "How can you call it eavesdropping when I had no choice but to sleep where you told me to sleep?"

Fortner gave her an appraising look. He had figured she was feverish and that was why he had stopped to make camp so early, but . . . What else was bothering her? Her eyes looked like a thunderstorm about to break and her face was no longer pale. "You can have the damned thing. I wouldn't have figured you'd want stolen goods."

"Then you know it's stolen!" Treasure let loose the tears. "Are you sure you weren't with the gang that day back at our place when my father was killed?"

"What in hell are you talking about, Treasure? You know as well as I that anything either of the Thorpes has is bound to be stolen." He reached then to hug and comfort her, for the sight of her anguish had dispelled his bad temper and called up compassion.

Treasure slapped at his hands and backed away. Doubts and fears tumbled inside her like an unleashed fury. What was she to believe when her mind seemed so fuzzy and not at all like her own? So many strange things had happened to her during the past few weeks that she wondered if she might not be caught up in a suffocating nightmare. "Don't touch me! And don't pretend you don't know this was my mother's locket and that it was stolen from the cabin the day Blackie was killed."

Fortner stared at the small round locket in Treasure's hand, then at her tortured features. "My God! After all we've talked about, all you've come—" Fortner stopped abruptly, startled that he had almost told Treasure what she meant to him. "We've become friends, haven't we? How can you still suspect I had anything to do with what went on that day at your place?" He fought the mightiest of inner battles to keep from hugging her close and confessing that he loved her madly, that he was seeking revenge against the Thorpes now for the death of her father as well as for the cruel slayings of his own family on the Cumberland River. Having won the mental clash with considerable effort, he cleared his throat and said, "Likely fever from your wound is coming up now that it's close to dark, and you're not feeling like yourself."

Treasure heard his words—we've become friends—but mostly she heard the restored warm tone of his resonant voice that so often wrapped around her heart unexpectedly like a welcome blanket. She looked down at the gold locket and chain in her hand. Fortner was telling the truth. She was forgetting how the two of them had pooled their information and figured out that it must have been the Thorpes who had been at the Ryan farm that January day. Taking in a shuddering breath, she willed the tears to stop. "You're probably right, and I'm sorry."

Fortner gave Treasure a level look. "Keep the locket. I had no idea it belonged to your mother." He spread out their blankets near the fire. "Why don't you stretch out here and rest while I catch us a fish or two? You can call out to me if you need me. I'll be on the other side of the canebreak."

Treasure sank onto the blanket, watching silently as Fortner laid her rifle near her and then picked up his own. She closed her eyes. Her false accusations against Fortner troubled her conscience, but she gained some solace from remembering that he had seemed to understand her unsettled state of mind.

After a short sleep Treasure roused. It was still light, but she felt threatened by something. Had the horses whinnied nearby? She saw nothing unusual when she sat up and looked over at them. They were grazing and flipping their tails at bothersome gnats and horseflies. Was there something about the darkening giant canebreak in the fecund setting behind her that bothered her? The air seemed heavy with moisture and strange scents. Earlier she had noticed that wet, earthy smell and attributed it to the swampy setting. Picking up her rifle, she looked all around.

"Fortner?" Treasure called, rising and starting through the canebreak toward the little stream. She used her rifle to part some of the soaring stalks of cane that had already sprung back straight in the marshy soil since Fortner had walked back to the branch to fish no more than an hour ago. Unless she missed her guess, some of the cane would measure three or four inches across a joint cut near the ground. The tallest stalks would likely measure fifteen feet. Such large cane as she was seeing must supply the Choctaw with their blowguns and their musical instruments with fingering holes cut in their sides, Treasure reflected. "Fortner?"

"Yes?" came his reassuring voice from somewhere not too far to her left. "I'm cleaning fish, but I'll be there soon." Treasure took another cautious step down the narrow opening in the tall cane. Mosquitoes swarmed her face and neck, causing her to shake her head vigorously and mutter, "Damn!" Behind her, Vagabond nickered, then Brutus. "I'm coming to where you are."

From somewhere off to her right, maybe in the area of a high-limbed oak reaching out over the canebreak, Treasure heard an alien sound. Was that what had awakened her? It sounded like a snort or a grunt, but she had no idea what made such a noise.

"Wait there," Fortner called from a closer range in front of her. "I'm on my way."

Then, for the first time Fortner heard what Treasure heard. Hanging his game bag containing the small fish around his neck, he cocked his rifle and searched blindly through the thick stand of cane. His hackles rose, for he recognized the sound.

Of all the wild animals that sought canebreak, Fortner knew well that the wild boar was the most deadly. Only once before had he actually faced one of the squatty wild hogs and seen its long, keen tusks ready to gore dogs and humans or disembowel a horse. The deadly tusks were not the only physical difference between wild boars and domesticated ones, Fortner recalled with distaste. They had a massive shield of muscle covered with long stiff hair that projected upward in a triangular shape behind their necks and reached two-thirds of the way to their hips. Only by shooting a mature boar through the brain could it be killed quickly.

"Be quiet and stand still, Treasure," Fortner called. He couldn't see her, but her last movements had sounded directly in front of him. "There's a wild boar in the brake off to my left, and he can kill you if I don't find him first. Ready your rifle, but stay still. If you have to shoot, aim between his eyes or his ears. They like a chase, but they can't see well." As he talked, Fortner scanned the green prison.

Cautiously, Fortner moved to his left toward the renewed sound, doing his best to imitate it. He had been told that often young boars ran off old, crippled ones and that the displaced breeders wandered alone in dense canebreaks needing the concealing cane to help them fend off predators. As he had heard no other suspicious sounds while he fished during the past hour, he was hoping that what seemed interested in Treasure was no more than a lone boar.

Two more steps and another imitating grunt—and Fortner heard the cane popping in protest. As he had hoped when he made the sounds, the animal was heading toward him now instead of Treasure. With the noise and rush of a whirlwind, the boar crashed toward Fortner, its grunts turning into angry bass squeals. Fortner, his rifle ready, aimed at a spot between the large ears upon the enormous head. Backing up hastily before preparing for another shot, he watched the powerful jaws become slack, the small, mean eyes roll, and the short legs collapse beneath the stubby-haired body.

"I got him, Treasure!" Fortner shouted. "Call out and I'll come to you."

Treasure called his name with outward thanksgiving and leftover fear from what could have taken place . . . and with love. But she didn't wait. She gauged Fortner's location by the waving tops of the tall cane and met him, hugging him around the neck and clinging like one of the yellow jasmine vines creeping up the side of a nearby tree.

* * *

"Are you ready?" Fortner asked Treasure. In the past hour he had cooked the fish and hurried her through her supper while he made ready to leave the campsite.

"Yes." Treasure was already in the saddle, her rifle in her hand.

"There's a little light left, and there'll be an early moon." Fortner led the way out onto the Trace. No travelers had come along since the trio passing soon after they had stopped near the canebreak. "I've traveled at night a lot. If you're truly rested enough to go on, we'll make it. Don't fret."

"I feel fine, and I'm not fretting. I'm just sorry we had to break camp and leave because of that horrible dead boar."

Treasure shuddered at the memory of the rust colored carcass with its powerful jaws armed with four white tusks, two short stubby ones protruding from the upper lips and two long, daggerlike ones curving from the lower lips. Its ears looked as large as Fortner's hands, she recalled with a shudder at how close both Fortner and she—maybe even their horses—had come to being attacked by the squat monster. Fortner had had no trouble convincing her that spending the night near the canebreak would be foolhardy, despite his earlier thought that she had needed to stop traveling earlier than usual. The boar was too old and gaunt to warrant skinning and saving the meat. Nocturnal animals would scent the carcass and descend upon it, and might even attempt attacks on the campers and their horses.

An uneventful two hours later, Fortner led the way into a higher, cleaner clearing beside the Trace. As he had predicted, an early moon had shed light along the deeply shadowed path and, meeting no one, they had made good time.

"This site is much better," Treasure conceded after Fortner had built a fire and gotten the horses tethered beside a small creek near them. Overly tired from the long day and the draining experience with the boar, she lay on her blanket with her head resting on her saddle. Tearing her gaze from the leaping flames of the campfire, she looked up at Fortner where he sat near her. "I'm glad the gang wasn't here waiting for us." She yawned and stretched, pleased to note that her left arm did not pain her afterward.

"That doesn't mean they won't show up later, though," Fortner mused aloud. His thoughts had weighed heavily after they left the first campsite. More than ever before he felt that travel in the wilderness was fraught with too many dangers for a young woman.

Treasure lifted her head from her saddle, cocking her head in the direction from which they had come about an hour ago. She heard an eerie sound, almost like the remembered moan of a wintry wind rounding a corner of the cabin back in the Tennessee hills.

"What's that I hear?" Try as she might, Treasure could not distinguish the noise. It seemed both a human and an animal sound now that it was nearing, a bit like a deep-voiced moaning or chanting. She noticed that Fortner was leaning his dark head toward the swelling sound and looking puzzled. A ripple of fear washed over her.

Fortner peered up through the trees. "With such a bright moon tonight, I guess what we're hearing is the singing of a coffle of slaves."

"Slaves?" echoed Treasure. "What's a coffle of slaves?"

"A train of black workers being moved together."

Treasure frowned her disapproval, then gulped in fear. "What are slaves doing on the Trace? Will they bother us?" Her actual knowledge of slaves was limited to her mother's pleasant accounts from her early years spent at Lindwood. She had heard of several uprisings since her mother's death, though, and of subsequent deaths of whites trying to suppress the blacks. Several years back she had figured out that Marie's memories had sometimes been flavored with romantic distortions.

"Judging from the sounds, there might be forty or fifty of them being marched down for auctioning off in Algiers, across the Mississippi from New Orleans. And no, you have no need to fear them, for they're coffled—manacled—and then tied to each other with chains or heavy ropes.

They've likely been brought straight from Africa to the ports of Carolina and could not speak English or know where to find a hiding place if they managed to escape.''

"Do you mean the poor things have walked from the Atlantic Ocean clear across the United States to here?'' The maps in her geography book flashed into Treasure's mind, and she shook her head in disbelief. "How cruel!''

"From all I've heard, they'll not be resting for very long periods until they reach Natchez and are herded onto a ship headed for New Orleans. Right now they're part of a big business. If you wished to buy one, you'd have to take the entire coffle. Until the slave dealers reach the slave blocks where owners of cotton plantations buy great numbers, they're not interested in making deals with anyone.''

As Fortner explained what he knew about the traffic in slaves on the Trace, the sonorous bass strains of men's voices kept getting closer and sounding more like grieving than singing to the sensitive Treasure. She suspected that a jarring sound floating to her ears every once in a while through the forest might be coming from chains, and she shuddered. Buy a slave? Take away a person's freedom, the very thing that she had been exulting in having ever since learning that she had not killed Amos and wasn't an outlaw? She shivered all over, repulsed at what she had learned.

"Don't they stop and sleep at night?" Treasure asked. "And why are they singing?''

By then both Fortner and she were watching the light of a swaying lantern coming into view. They were camped no more than fifty feet from the Trace.

"On a bright night like this,'' Fortner said, "they'll probably walk till midnight and then stop a spell until daylight. Some say that the blacks are less likely to try escaping or attacking if they're bone tired. The chanting of their African tribal songs started out as their idea, I've heard. Then when the slavers figured out the poor devils couldn't be whispering in their native tongue and planning revolt if they were singing, they started insisting on it to keep the blacks peaceful.''

The two sitting beside their campfire watched a man on horseback come into sight out on the Trace. He held a lantern perched on his saddle horn and peered at the campers while his horse ambled by. He did not seem as interested in the man and woman staring at him as the horrified Treasure was in his group.

What appeared in the semidarkness to be dozens of black men walking close together in pairs followed behind the equestrian, and Treasure heard more clearly those soul stirring strains of foreign song which had earlier seemed to be no more than a loud hum. She could see the whites of eyes darting glances toward the campfire, as well as an occasional gleam from scantily covered black muscles on perspiring arms and legs. Some beautifully plaintive, high notes began soaring above the sorrowing bass at intervals then, blending with tremulous pathos, tearing at Treasure's tender heart and bringing unbidden tears to her eyes. She was not surprised to see that smaller figures, which she took to be women and children and the owners of the high voices, followed the larger group of black men.

Throughout the mournful passage, Treasure heard the dissonant clank of chains as a kind of sorrowful counterpoint. Bringing up the rear were two more horsemen with lanterns, leading packhorses.

"They looked like a group of mourners on their way to a funeral," Treasure said after the haunting notes faded into nothingness and night callers once more could be heard. She added huskily, "Their own."

"Not a nice side of our society, is it?" Fortner asked in the ensuing silence while both stared into the fire. He tried not to think about what lay ahead for Treasure when she reached Lindwood and faced up to living with slavery. Even with his aversion to slavery, Fortner realized that the economy of the Mississippi Territory and neighboring regions of the South could not prosper as they were if they did not utilize slave labor. "Not all masters are cruel to their slaves, though, and maybe those we saw will end up on good plantations with kind owners."

Treasure shook her head, suddenly fatigued and not

wanting to think about anything. How paltry her own brief fears of losing her freedom for an imagined crime had been. Though imprisonment might never be as devastating as slavery, she glanced at the man she loved and ached with the knowledge that Fortner might continue playing the role of outlaw so well that he ended up behind bars—or without his handsome head on his shoulders. She felt that a heretofore unknown sadness had seeped into her own secret pool of sorrow and would ever be with her.

The weary and disheartened Treasure had just stretched out on her blanket when she heard hoofbeats racing up the Trace. Lifting her head to watch Fortner as he readied his rifle and waited, she moaned when she heard a familiar voice.

"Ho, there!" George Henry Thorpe called while riding into the clearing. "Look here what we done foun'," he said to Bear-John and Juno, who reined in behind him. "Fortner and his wild woman done started out to jine up with us agin."

Chapter Eighteen

For the next five days Treasure went through the motions of living the life of the lone woman riding with four men down the Natchez Trace. Her arm healed rapidly. She cooked what was given her to cook, washed what had to be washed for Fortner and herself, and hid in the woods whenever a holdup was taking place. To her vast relief she heard no gunfire during the few robberies.

Most of the time she rode Vagabond and gave free rein both to her horse and her thoughts, for more and more George Henry claimed Fortner's time and attention as they traveled. Often, while trailing behind the four men, she thought about how June was fast approaching—as was Natchez and the end of her journey.

The gunshot wound on Treasure's arm healed without problems, leaving an angry pink scar about the size of her palm. With each mile leading her closer to her grandfather's plantation and the inevitable parting with Fortner, her heart took on a kind of illness of its own. She doubted that the secret wound would heal with no more than an outward show of smooth pink skin marking what had once been a bloody, ragged wound. In fact, she had little hope that her inner scars would ever lessen.

Treasure stared at the familiar sights of brilliant blue skies and bold pink dawns, but saw instead the paler blue of Fortner's eyes and the rosy tones of his sensuous lips. When fleecy clouds banded together overhead or on the horizon, she found his handsome face reflected there, sometimes in marvelous profile, sometimes in blurred images of partial features—his straight nose, his strong chin, or perhaps his forehead with darker strips above for the sweep of his brown hair and below for his expressive eyebrows.

When dappled light danced like quicksilver through the overhanging trees with their new crop of fresh green leaves, Treasure thought of the way Fortner's eyes and teeth flashed when he smiled and laughed. The breezes of approaching summer kissed her face and hair, whispering secrets into her ears; she imagined they might be the tender lips of her beloved playing their former magic on her and murmuring endearments.

With each passing day the musing young woman became more attuned than ever to the adventurer's resonant voice, to its every nuance and subtlety. Sometimes she found herself reeling in its sound to secret places, as if to capture the euphony inside forever and keep it for playing over and over for her private pleasure after he had left her at Lindwood.

All that awaited her at the end of her journey was good and noble and what she had longed for since Blackie's death, Treasure told herself during those final days on the journey: Danny, their mother's family, and a secure future for her young brother and herself. The dream that their mother had yearned to see materialize was near fruition. Her battered heart kicked up a fuss and bled anew each time she entertained that thought.

It was late on the fifth day after Bear-John and the Thorpes had found Fortner and her that Treasure sensed Lindwood must be near. Gray moss bearded giant trees. The Trace had become a washed out road with pinkish, bare banks sometimes soaring straight up for twenty feet on both sides, sometimes no more than four. The more frequent paths off the main trail and the worn condition of the Trace told her clearly that traffic was much heavier in that area; Washington and Natchez must be near. Her mother had told her that Lindwood lay between the two towns.

"Are we coming into Washington?" Treasure asked Fortner when he rode back to join her. Her thoughts jumped ahead to Danny. She recalled that Fortner had told her of seeing Washington Academy from the Trace on his previous trips through the area, and she wanted to see what the school looked like. Thinking of her young brother perhaps attending it someday lifted her sagging spirits.

"Yes, but we'll be taking a loop around it to avoid being seen," he replied. He motioned to a log bridge up ahead. "We'll cross Locust Creek and then take a loop around Washington so we won't be noticed. There's a campsite not far from your grandfather's place that we'll be using."

"Do you think Danny and Hank will already be there?" Treasure asked, smiling at the thought of seeing her brother again. She had missed him sorely.

"I wouldn't be surprised." Seeing Treasure smile dampened Fortner's mood. Why wouldn't she be smiling, he agonized, when she would soon be where she longed to be—where she deserved to be. A gleam of gold drew his attention to the locket she had worn ever since he had given it to her that afternoon after they left the Choctaw village. Such pretty things should always be hers.

"I thought sure we would see them somewhere along the way." Treasure paused to coax her horse into picking its own way across the crude bridge, the likes of which neither Vagabond nor its rider had ever seen. The horses' shoes clanked jarringly on the barely planed logs, and a rumbling, hollow sound echoed up from the shallow stream several feet below, reminding Treasure of thunder.

"So did I," Fortner mused aloud, once they crossed the bridge and calmed the shying horses. They followed the three men off the Trace down a small path through thick woods. "Last fall it seemed that we ran into the old peddler every day or two."

"You never did get to see the man you wanted to meet, did you?" Treasure turned to ask in a near whisper. She slowed Vagabond so as to keep their talk private. They were traveling in single file now, and moss laden limbs snatched at her hair. Mosquitoes appeared in swarms from the moss and thick underbrush, and horseflies buzzed around the horses. The air seemed so heavy and thick with moisture that she felt it might have fingers and be touching her exposed skin in an insidious way. She recognized that she was feeling irritable and that physical matters had little to do with it. The thought of leaving Fortner on the morrow was slicing up her insides.

"No. If George Henry met up with Whitey again since you were shot, he did so while we were at the Indian village," Fortner replied in a low voice. "I decided against bringing up his name since George Henry seemed to be gaining some kind of pleasure out of refusing my request."

"Fortner, what will you do? You can't ride back up the Trace with Juno and him, not if you go ahead with your plans to head West before winter." Treasure had accepted that there was no future for her with Fortner, but she wanted him safely away from law officers who might arrest him and put him in jail . . . or hang him. The West seemed the best answer.

"I'm thinking that I'll get lucky in Natchez. Each time the Thorpes reached Natchez last year while Bear-John and

I were scouting them, they headed for a section called Natchez-Under-the Hill. That's where they finally took to us last fall before their last trip up to Nashville. It's likely that George Henry will take me to meet Whitey while we're staying at the Silver Slipper.''

"The Silver Slipper? What's that?"

"A hotel with a gambling hall.''

"What are you two whisperin' 'bout back there?'' George Henry called. "Here lately it seems y'all got a pow'rful lot to chin about." He had slowed his horse and let Bear-John and Juno go on ahead. "We ain't got no time for lollygaggin'.''

Treasure and Fortner said no more and followed the beady-eyed outlaw off the path into a clearing beside the creek.

"Danny!'' Treasure exclaimed, reining in Vagabond and dismounting when she saw her beloved brother rubbing down his horse. Tears thickened her voice. "Oh, Danny, at last.''

His dark eyes obviously watching for her and lighting up when she appeared, Danny smiled and hurried to greet his sister. They met underneath the low limbs of a magnolia tree, laughing and hugging.

"Treasure, it's good to see you again,'' Danny said. He stepped back from her frantic hug, his face reddening but looking especially happy.

"How've you been, Danny? I never thought it would be weeks before we would see each other." Treasure wanted to brush back the lock of black hair drooping across his forehead, but she had noticed the way he had ended their embrace so hurriedly, and she had no wish to embarrass him further. His face seemed to have firmed up and matured, she noticed. There was a new, deeper note to his voice. Danny appeared much too independent to suit the one who, since his birth twelve years ago, had never spent a night away from him until last month when she had become Fortner's "woman." Had her brother changed as much as she had since they parted? "Tell me all about what Hank and you have been doing. I want to hear everything. Have you been well?''

Hank came over then and greeted Treasure. ''Danny's a right good hand on the trail,'' the old peddler added in his soft, husky voice. ''And he ain't bad at striking up a bargain with those who wanted to buy, either.'' He sent an approving wink at the boy while pulling at the back of his red wig with a pudgy hand. ''I'm going to miss having him around to help me out.''

Returning to where the other men stood talking, Hank left the sister and brother for more private visiting. They wandered through the late afternoon shade toward the creek, exclaiming over the lush forest and exchanging news of all that had happened during the weeks since they had last been together. Neither paid any attention to what the men up in the clearing were doing.

Almost an hour passed before Fortner walked to where Treasure and Danny still talked, sometimes earnestly and sometimes teasingly.

''Hank will be back soon, and it'll be time to go,'' Fortner said when the Ryans looked up from where they sat on the grassy bank of the creek in the fading light.

''Go? Are we going to Lindwood tonight?'' Treasure asked, her surprise apparent in her voice. She had thought to have one more night with Fortner. She hadn't even planned how to tell him good-bye yet. Her stomach felt weighted with lead. ''I figured we'd not be leaving until morning.''

''Hank has gone to inform Mr. Lindsay that Danny and you will be waiting for him at the end of the road leading up to the house—if he meets the terms. I have no doubt that he will.''

Treasure turned to the inquisitive Danny. ''Danny, George Henry went ahead with his plan to ask Grandpa Lindsay for money to deliver us to him.''

''Do you think he'll pay it?'' Danny asked. ''After all, he never has seen us. How will he know we're who we say we are?'' He swiveled his head around and peered up at

Fortner. "Why is Hank letting the Thorpes do this—and why are you? I thought you were finer than that, Fortner."

"You were wrong, weren't you?" Fortner replied grimly. "I can't answer for Hank. No doubt he needs to get along with the Thorpes as much as I do."

George Henry walked toward them then, swaggering and grinning in his gap-toothed way. "Come on, you Ryan brats. It'll be time to go soon." He taunted Fortner with what was obviously an earlier question, "Are you shore you ain't gonna come up with the money for your wild woman and keep her?"

"I told you all I wanted was to accompany Danny and Treasure and see them turned over to Mr. Lindsay. I promised them I'd do that, and I intend to keep my word."

"You ain't takin' them all by yourself," George Henry retorted, an ugly smile twisting his bearded face. "Hank an' Juno will be ridin' along. Bear-John will stay here with me till you'uns get back with the money."

Everything began happening too fast, Treasure reflected. All at once Hank had returned and was conferring with the men. Then Fortner was throwing saddles onto the backs of Vagabond and Brutus, and Danny was readying his horse, Buck, for the ride to Lindwood.

With Danny following him, Hank rode ahead up the narrow path through the forest. Juno brought up the rear, leaving Treasure and Fortner no chance at all for private conversation. Darkness was falling fast, but the trail was easy to follow.

"I can't see more than a white blur up through the trees," Danny turned back to say to Treasure. His eyes were wide and questioning. "I guess that must be Lindwood."

"Hush up," Hank warned, readjusting his wig where hanging moss from drooping branches had ruffled it. "Old man Lindsay might have sent for the sheriff in spite of what I told him the Thorpes would do if he did. We don't want no surprises."

Beside a moss-festooned oak marking the curving road up to the large white house in the distance, a gray-haired man stood beside a horse watching the riders approach in the twilight.

"Mr. Lindsay," Hank called, motioning for all but Danny to stay back some thirty or forty feet. "I'll bring Danny up first—if you got the money."

"I have it, you blackguard peddler," Percy Lindsay drawled. He held a long-barreled rifle at an upward angle, its stock resting against his thigh. "I took your warning and didn't send for the sheriff—and I won't until I find out that you're trying to palm off some vagrants on me as my daughter's children. One shot from me and my slaves up the way will be down here in a flash." He called out loudly, "Are you with me, August?"

"We sho' is, Massa Percy," came not one masculine voice from hidden places among the trees, but several.

"You won't be needing any help, Mr. Lindsay," Fortner called from where he waited with Treasure and Juno. The old man's voice did not reveal any fear, but Fortner imagined that he must have at least given thought to the matter of being attacked for the money he had been told to bring. The last thing Fortner wanted was an exchange of shots where Treasure or Danny might be hit. His right hand fingered his rifle resting in its holster.

"Shut up!" Juno ordered Fortner. "Leave it to Hank, like George Henry said Whitey wanted it."

Treasure gulped. Should she show her mother's locket and hope the gray-haired man might recognize it? It never before had occurred to her that their grandfather would not believe that Danny and she were the children of Marie and Blackie. She stared at the dim form that was obviously her grandfather, her heart pounding mercilessly while her fingers fondled the locket. She watched Hank and Danny approach the formidable figure and dismount. Their words were too low for her to hear, but she thought she detected a pleasant tone in her grandfather's voice. He must have recognized that Danny was a younger version of Blackie, she exulted.

Torn between wanting to stay with Fortner and wanting to meet her grandfather, Treasure felt a flood of emotions and disjointed thoughts wash over her. Why was it that she had a sudden, uneasy feeling about the old peddler? After all, she reasoned, Hank was only making sure that Danny and she were united with their grandfather . . . as Fortner was. She was almost in a daze by the time Hank called out for Fortner to bring her forward.

"So you're Treasure," Percy Lindsay said when the lovely blonde dismounted with the ease of one accustomed to riding.

"Yes, sir, I'm Treasure Lindsay Ryan," she answered, her words barely more than a husky whisper. Even the feel of Vagabond's reins in her sweaty palm seemed alien.

"I can see that Daniel is the spittin' image of Blackie Ryan, but you don't look much like my Marie." Percy Lindsay studied Treasure closely in the poor light as Fortner took her arm and guided her to stand beside Danny and Hank in front of the gray-haired man. In a voice warm with feeling, he said, "There's something about the way you carry yourself, though, that tells me you're Marie's child."

Percy Lindsay reached into a pocket of his breeches and brought out a small bag. "When my grandchildren come stand beside me and start up the path to the house with their horses, I'll throw you these gold pieces," he said to Hank and Fortner.

Hank moved beside Treasure then. "Good-bye, Treasure," he said, leaning to put an arm around her stiff shoulders for a brief hug. Unseen by anyone, his hand moved down to her holster and removed the knife he had given her from his pack. With the same stealth, Hank replaced it with another.

Treasure was hardly aware that Hank was telling her good-bye, much less that he had made an exchange of knives before moving away from her. All that she could focus on was the pale-eyed man holding her arm and the pain of searching for words of farewell.

Fortner freed Treasure's arm and gently pushed her forward, murmuring, "Good-bye, Treasure. I'll never forget you."

Lost in a maelstrom of emotion, Treasure moved along-side Danny like one in a trance, away from Fortner and Hank. She felt as if she might be trying to walk in water, so leaden were her legs and feet. Darting from the gray falls of moss draping the limbs of the huge trees, mosquitoes whined around her face. The falling twilight lent its share of eeriness to the scene, and when Danny took her hand, she clutched it as if it might be the only real thing around her.

Treasure heard the swish of the bag of coins sail through the air behind her, heard the thud of someone catching it as Danny and she walked on past their grandfather up the road he had indicated. Leading their horses, Danny and she started up the curving path. The tightly packed soil muffled the sounds of the horses' hooves. Looming ahead was the white house Danny had pointed out earlier. She almost stopped and cried out in protest when Percy Lindsay's next words floated to her on the still air.

"If I ever lay eyes on any of you three hanging around my grandchildren," Percy Lindsay said in a harsh tone, "I'll shoot you on sight." He leveled his rifle then. "There can be no thanks to culprits who take advantage of a situation as you've obviously done in delivering these poor orphaned children to me. Get off my property and stay away from my family!"

"But Grandpa," Treasure protested then, turning back to intervene and explain that Fortner was not a culprit, that he was the one who had saved her life, and Danny's as well. Later she would explain that he was no outlaw, but now she had to make the old man see that Danny and she were indebted to Fortner and that he should be as well. "You don't understand—"

"I understand more than I care to understand," Percy Lindsay retorted in a deep voice accustomed to being obeyed without question. "Not another word from you. Get on to the house, both of you. August will take your horses and escort you up there while I stay behind and make sure these degenerates leave."

Treasure saw then that Hank and Fortner had mounted

their horses and were riding off behind Juno down the darkening path in the woods. None looked back. The thought that she never had told Fortner good-bye kept torturing her.

"Thank you, Bitsy, for offering, but I prefer to get ready for bed by myself," Treasure said later that night to the young slave waiting for her in the large bedroom. Someone had told her that it had once belonged to her mother. She watched the pretty young woman leave and returned her friendly wave before stepping up the little stairs to the tall four-poster bed. With a sigh, she plopped down on the soft mattress and lay back with her arms flung out to the sides, looking up at the frilly tester reaching almost to the high ceiling. Though Marie had described it often, Treasure was still shocked to see such decoration over a bed.

After the evening meal Danny and Treasure had spent a few awkward hours with the people who lived in the huge mansion. Treasure knew that it would take more than one evening to get the entire story told about her and her brother's lives in Tennessee and to get their kinfolk straight in her mind. She had heard her mother speak often of her younger brother, Robert, and she recalled that Aunt Olivia from Merrivale had written that he was a lawyer now. She hadn't known that Uncle Robert and his wife, Rebekah, and their two young sons lived at Lindwood, though.

Never had Treasure heard of Percy Lindsay's brother in Mobile, so meeting her visiting cousin, Caroline Lindsay, at supper had been a big surprise. Then there was Cyril Wood, the young man who tutored Uncle Robert's sons. And there were so many slaves serving in the rambling mansion that she wondered if she would ever get their names and faces straight. She was glad to note that none seemed to be mistreated or visibly unhappy.

Treasure, impatient with her thoughts, sat up and stepped down the two steps of polished wood leading from the tall bed. Danny seemed to have fit into the Lindsay household far easier than she on their first night there, she mused. What was wrong with her not to fall instantly in love with such a place of grandeur and beauty, the very one that her mother had told her about again and again? Marie had not exaggerated about Lindwood's luxury.

Treasure glanced over at the large wardrobe standing against one wall, admiring its gleaming wooden surface with ornate carvings on the feet and panels. A low, armless rocker upholstered in the same rich fabric as the drapes at the windows seemed a perfect place to sit and sew, and she could picture the young Marie passing her time there with her needle. In front of the fireplace sat a small sofa covered with rose colored satin. Beneath the worn soles of her rough shoes, the only ones she owned, Treasure felt the velvety texture of the lovely rug decorated with woven pink and mauve roses.

Over in the corner a freestanding mirror as tall as the young woman staring at it winked and beckoned in the steady light from the many candles sitting about in brass holders. She sucked in her breath at the wan-faced image staring back at her and lived again the awkward moment when her Aunt Rebekah had insisted that Treasure wear one of her proffered dresses down for supper. The blue waist and navy skirt did look out of place in the luxurious bedroom, Treasure confessed now that she had won out and worn her own clothing. She had been unable to bear the thought of wearing the blue dress Fortner had given her—not when the mere sight of it threatened to bring tears for all she had lost. Could she ever wear it for anyone but the highwayman?

Not that anyone downstairs had batted an eyelash when Danny and she showed up after their baths looking clean but still wearing their bedraggled garments. Her mother's family couldn't have been more loving and gracious had they been expecting Danny and her to come and make their home at Lindwood, Treasure admitted with honesty and a bit of embarrassment at her obstinate refusal to borrow Aunt Rebekah's clothing. She promised herself silently that tomorrow she would not be so stubborn.

Arms folded across her breasts, she wandered over to one of the two large windows in her second-story bedroom and stared blindly out into the night. The muted sounds of people passing in the hall and closing bedroom doors gradually ceased as she had let her mind rove. Lindwood was settling down for the soft spring night.

Somewhere less than an hour away, Treasure mused, Fortner was probably sitting before a campfire gambling and drinking with Bear-John and the Thorpes. Hank would be there, too. The thought came again that it seemed strange that the old peddler had taken part in collecting the ransom. At least Fortner had not handled the money.

She looked across at the clothing discarded earlier when she had taken advantage of the brass tub of lovely warm water someone had brought up for her. The memory of the luxury of warm water and scented soap on her skin brought a smile to her face, and she brought a wrist up to her nose to smell the lingering fragrance again. Something from the pile of clothing gleamed warmly in the candlelight. Was it a pearl handle? Hurrying to make sure and then sucking in a doubting breath, Treasure slipped the knife Blackie had made for her from her holster. She knew that no other in the world fit her hand as that perfectly balanced piece of steel did. With a forefinger she traced the ''T'' carved in the ivory handle by her father.

Where was the other knife, and how had her knife gotten here? she wondered while her mind whirled. Supposedly she had left hers back on the rock . . . in Amos Greeson's body. Her heartbeat sped up. Something was out of kilter.

Outside, insects were making strident calls. Treasure walked to the window and frowned out into the darkness. The mystery of the knife's reappearance plagued her considerably, but uppermost in her mind was the nagging thought that she had not told Fortner good-bye.

Treasure had not told him good-bye, Fortner thought for the fourth or fifth time since leaving her back at Lindwood before dark. He showed his cards and raked in the winning pot.

"That's it for me tonight," Fortner declared. "I'm ready to turn in."

"We'uns need to split our take," George Henry said. He emptied the contents of the bag Percy Lindsay had thrown to Hank. "When I checked it earlier, I saw it was jes' like we ordered—two fat eagles for each of us." He held up a gold coin in the light of the campfire for all to see.

"I don't want any," Fortner said, rising and watching the outlaw with open disgust. He saw then that Hank, sitting close by, appeared keenly interested in what was going on. "Maybe Hank has a claim to mine."

"What makes you say that, Fortner?" the old peddler asked, sending a hand to jerk at his wig.

"You did ride over to Lindwood and make the demands of Mr. Lindsay," Fortner replied matter-of-factly.

"I was just doing what the boys wanted me to do. An old man traveling the Trace has to get along with everybody," Hank explained, his pocked face reddening in the firelight while he rose to his feet. "I think it's time for me to check on my horses and then get some sleep."

"I know what's eatin' ole Fortner," George Henry said with a sneer as Hank headed into the darkness. "That wild woman got to you, didn't she? Take the money. You earned it havin' to put up with her all these weeks."

"I don't want it." This time Fortner's voice was deadly.

"Well, there'll jes' be more for us." George Henry cut a suspicious look up at Fortner. "Never seen a man think he's too good to take his cut when he up and done his part."

"I never said I was too good, just that I don't want it. The only reason I went along was to make sure Treasure and the boy were turned over to Mr. Lindsay."

"I don't want a share either," Bear-John said, rising to stand beside Fortner. "Doesn't hardly seem right to charge a man to have his grandkids brought to him when they didn't have any place else to go."

"Good God amighty!" George Henry exclaimed. "What'a you two think you are—angels?" He played with the ten gold coins in his hand, his eyes gleaming at their sheen in the firelight. "Awright, Juno, that leaves more for you an' me . . . and Whitey."

"Give my share to Whitey," Juno said, standing and stretching lazily. "I ain't much for takin' money to deliver folks to their family either."

"Damn you, little brother!" George Henry jumped to his feet then and grabbed Juno's shirtfront. "What makes you think you's any better'n me? You know what happened to Felsenthal and how we all agreed—"

"Whitey and you agreed," Juno pointed out, reaching up and slapping George Henry's hand away. "I never did agree. No amount of money is goin' to bring back our brother. Now take the money and cram it up your asshole, for all I care."

Juno walked to stand near where Fortner and Bear-John were already kneeling beside their saddles and bedrolls. The old friends exchanged startled looks at the surprising turn of events. Never before had Juno stood up to George Henry so forcefully.

"You always did think you were better than your family, Juno Thorpe," came Hank's tremulous voice from the darkness. "Who in hell do you think you are?"

All four men turned in surprise. Obviously angry, the old man was striding from the dark underbrush and glaring at the Thorpe brothers. A low limb of a locust tree caught his wig and lifted it from his head as he rushed underneath it. As all stared, shoulder-length gray hair tumbled about the old man's shoulders and face.

Whitey! Fortner mouthed to himself in disbelief. A hot bitterness filled his throat. Already squatting beside his saddle, he untied the thongs holding his whip. Quickly looping the coiled whip over one shoulder, he grabbed his loaded rifle. Before he moved off to one side of the campfire, he whispered to Bear-John, "Whitey!"

Nodding his understanding, Bear-John reached for his own rifle and joined Fortner just outside the circle of firelight.

Chapter Nineteen

George Henry and Juno appeared disinterested in the movements of Fortner and Bear-John. Their attention was riveted to the white-haired figure rushing toward them from the darkness.

"I never thought I'd see the day when a Thorpe turned against a Thorpe!" Hank yelled in a voice suddenly gone higher. His broad face was livid by the time he reached the campfire. He seemed unaware that his wig had stayed behind on the thorny tree branch or that Fortner and Bear-John had stepped off to one side with their weapons at the ready. "Your pa would have been ashamed of you, and your ma—"

"Hold it! Git a grab on yoursel'!" George Henry interrupted forcefully. "We'uns got too many curious ears about." He glanced around for Fortner and Bear-John, his small eyes narrowing when he saw them standing together out in the shadows. "What's them rifles all 'bout? Good God amighty! You ain't lettin' some ole peddler's ravin' get to you, are you?"

While George Henry was speaking, he kept sending sideways glances toward his saddle and rifle. The pistol stuck barrel down in the waistband of his breeches was the only weapon he had with him. Juno was staring fixedly at his brother, ignoring Hank who had halted between the Thorpes and, with arms akimbo, was sending accusing looks at first one and then the other.

Though he hadn't missed a word or an action among the three men by the campfire, Fortner sensed stealthy movement out in the dark forest. He wasn't too familiar with the predators of the area and their habits, but he figured that no wild animal would brave attacking such loud men with a campfire so near. No ordinary human being would have hung around after the startling actions of the past few moments, Fortner reasoned, not even for the ten ten-dollar gold pieces and whatever could be found in individual pockets. The moisture laden air quivered with tension and unanswered questions.

Fortner's every thought, then, honed in on the three-some before him, a part of that brutal gang terrorizing his family nearly three years ago before burning them in the family home. And they likely were the ones who had killed Blackie Ryan back in January. His blood boiled. Whitey had been disguised as the old peddler right before his eyes. No wonder he had been suspicious of Hank Marcellus ever since he first met him.

"Maybe you need to do some explaining, George Henry," Fortner replied after giving the ticklish matter some thought. He wasn't ready yet to let the outlaws know everything. His rifle rested in his right hand, the barrel cocked down slightly. A one-inch lift of his hand would aim it at any one of the three men bunched close beside the campfire. From the corner of his eye he saw that Bear-John's actions imitated his own.

" 'Bout what?" The outlaw sent a hand to smooth his beard as he squinted through the bright light of the flames to see Fortner's expression. His voice took on an unnatural oiliness. " 'Pears like we'uns don't owe you nothin'. I ain't got no quarrel with you or that half-breed frien' of your'n—that's why I ain't pulled my shootin' iron."

"What about Treasure Ryan, for starters?" Fortner asked. He had no idea what to expect of Juno, but he noted that Juno had not pulled his pistol from his waistband either. Likely the brothers knew well that for both Bear-John and him to have them covered with their rifles lessened their odds considerably at pulling, cocking, and firing their pistols before they or their leader, Whitey, received a blast. "What do you know about a black hat with a docked red feather—like Felsenthal wore—being found by the sheriff in the smithy's shed near her father's body last January?'' He watched George Henry's face grow tense and his eyes narrow considerably. Juno darted looks at Hank and then at George Henry. Fortner added with confidence, ''I saw your devil's claws in that shed when I stopped by to get a shoe replaced on my horse in April. Did all four of you jump Blackie and do him in?''

''No,'' Juno denied in a whining voice. ''Whitey wasn't there. It was jes' the three of us. And I didn't lay a hand on Blackie, so help me! I didn't have nothin' to do with killin' him.''

''You was too busy stealin' his horses and meddlin' through his cabin, big mouth.'' George Henry glared at Juno.

''Juno didn't have to tell me that Hank is actually Whitey, your leader,'' Fortner said. ''I figured it out.''

''What business is this of yours, Fortner?'' Hank asked. He scowled at the Thorpes standing on either side of him. His hand went up to straighten his red wig, as if from habit, and paused when it landed on the long white locks. His face showing his surprise that the wig was gone and his hand falling back to his side, he pulled his stout body up taller. ''Are you a lawman . . . or a bounty hunter?''

''Neither one,'' Fortner snapped, sickened anew that what Treasure and he had figured out about her father's attackers was true. All the hate and the burning need for revenge seething inside for so long seemed distilled now, as if the bubbling and boiling had created something new. He could not take time to ponder the change. Staring at the old peddler he asked, ''Are you the one who made Treasure believe she killed Amos Greeson and was an outlaw, and then told George Henry that lie?''

Hank relaxed his shoulders and made a cackling sound suggesting laughter. ''Her knife did kill old Greeson, but I'm the one who stuck it in his chest.''

''What were you doing down by the river?'' Fortner asked.

''I followed Amos and Treasure because the bastard saw

me take the devil's claws," Hank, or Whitey, replied.
"He threatened to tell Treasure and then the sheriff, and I
wanted to hear what he said to her. Too many folks knew
they belonged to George Henry. What difference does it
make? I always had a liking for both those Ryan kids, and
that's why I stepped in when Amos was about to choke
Treasure to death. That way, I took care of two problems at
once. I slipped the girl's knife back to her tonight before
she went to her grandpa. No lawman is going to chase her
clear from Tennessee."

"Amos Greeson is alive," Bear-John said, lifting the
barrel of his rifle an inch to point directly at Hank. He
could tell that Fortner was too choked up to make a reply
right away. "The soldiers back at Colbert's Stand told
Fortner that they had visited with him the week before we
got there. He was cut up but very much alive. Nobody's
looking for Treasure Ryan, but the sheriff will be mighty
interested in knowing about those claws and who killed her
pa."

"Good God amighty! Is that all there is to this?"
George Henry exclaimed with an exaggerated shrug of his
shoulders. "Seems like we got no more 'splaining to do.
The whole mess with the Ryans jes' turned out to be a
mix-up. We didn't go there lookin' for nothin' but some
horseshoein' an' a spell of gamblin' like we done with
Blackie in Nashville over the years. Blackie beat up
Felsenthal so bad when he thought he was cheatin' at dice
that he died within a week, so the score's even."

"You and Whitey made sure you evened it by trying to
punish Blackie's children, didn't you? Whitey was pretending
to be helping them get to Natchez. All the time, he was
covering his own bloody tracks and yours. You never
expected that I'd fight you to keep you from his daughter.
Did you and Whitey think you should have her?"

"No," Whitey answered heatedly. "I never agreed to
that."

George Henry glared at Whitey, then said, " 'At's right.
Whitey was dead set agin' my takin' the gal."

His tone grim, Fortner replied, "When you lost Treasure

to me, you made plans to avenge Felsenthal's death by making Mr. Lindsay pay money for his grandchildren's return. I should have shot you through the head that night you slapped Treasure.''

"But you didn't,'' George Henry pointed out with a gap-toothed sneer. "You kin see Whitey never meant no harm to them Ryans. He'd took a likin' to 'em way back when they was little an' he was a'callin' on their folks. Now put up them fool rifles and let's get some sleep.''

"Hold up there,'' Fortner warned in a deadly voice when George Henry turned as if to go to his nearby saddle where his rifle lay.

The wily outlaw spun around and kicked a burning log out of the fire toward where Fortner and Bear-John stood before diving for his rifle on the ground. Fortner fired into the campfire, splattering burning coals and splintered logs onto Hank and Juno before they could scramble for their own weapons beside their saddles on the ground. Fortner was already readying his rifle for another shot when Juno pulled his pistol and fired a wild blast into the woods behind Fortner and Bear-John, then rolled onto the ground out of the circle of light. Hank followed Juno, and both slapped noisily at their smoking clothing.

Realizing that George Henry had his pistol out now, Fortner threw his rifle to Bear-John and let his whip slide down his arm. His hand settled on the two-foot stock of the eight-foot braided lash. Instantly he took a step forward with the whip poised. Like the report of a pistol, it cracked deafeningly when it snaked out with lightning swiftness. The fringed buckskin popper on the end of the tapered lash bit flesh from George Henry's neck at almost the same moment.

The groaning, startled outlaw dropped his weapon and clutched wildly at the choking whip. Once he was free, George Henry struggled to his feet, his hands groping at the bloody gash on his neck. The second blow of Fortner's whip landed over the howling outlaw's shoulders and ripped his shirt and his back before swishing back quickly to its owner.

"What the hell's goin' on with you, Fortner?" George Henry snarled in a murderous tone after silence claimed the violent scene for an instant. He still rubbed at his bleeding neck, but he stood glaring at Fortner defiantly.

"I want all three of you to listen and listen good," Fortner replied. "Remember a few years back when a boy named Hiram Copeland joined your gang?" He watched George Henry nod slightly and scowl. Over in the darkness, he couldn't be sure what Juno and Hank were doing now that they had stopped their clothing from smoking, but he figured they had been scrambling for weapons before he demanded their attention. He was counting on Bear-John to cover them with the two rifles he held. "I'm a Copeland, and Hiram was my youngest brother. When your crow bait gang came for him that night, I watched from a ridge as you rode away. If I had come home sooner, Bear-John and I wouldn't have had to track down you and your leader, Whitey. I could have killed you right there at the scene."

"Your brother, Hiram, had the take. He was a hothead." George Henry's eyes had never before appeared round or big. His voice became wheedling and full of self-pity. "Fortner, I never knew you was a Copeland. Don't you see? We had no choice. The money weren't Hiram's to keep. He was a thief."

Maddened at the self-serving excuse for murdering and destroying everything he had cared about in the world, Fortner flipped his whip and rushed to keep up with it as it coiled around George Henry's upper torso. Somehow the wily outlaw managed to lift his right arm and keep it free. Only two feet away now—the length of the lash's handle—and ducking easily to escape the searching fist and kicking feet, Fortner said through clenched teeth, "We'll see what the sheriff in Natchez thinks about your tale."

"Whitey!" George Henry hollered over his shoulder while Fortner spoke. "Hand me my claws!"

From the shadows Hank appeared with the brass implements and slipped them over the tips of the outlaw's fingers stretched behind him. Not loosening his hold on the handle, Fortner ducked the vicious blow aimed at his face and kneed George Henry in the groin. Juno, his pistol aimed at Bear-John, walked to crouch behind both Hank and the struggling George Henry.

Bear-John's aim was effectively blocked by Fortner, and he yelled, "Hit the dirt, Fortner! Whitey has a pistol."

At that instant Fortner dropped to a knee and yanked on the whip stock, bending George Henry's body over. Bear-John fired his rifle at the exposed Whitey—or Hank, as he had been known before losing his wig to the locust tree. Fortner heard a groan followed by the sound of a body crumpling to the dirt.

Bear-John saw the cursing, enraged George Henry lean to slash anew with the devil's's claws at Fortner, who was still kneeling on the ground to keep the whip in place around the outlaw.

"Let go of the whip!" Bear-John called. "I'll shoot him."

"No!" Fortner yelled back. "I want him alive when I turn him over to the law."

Bear-John might have given in to his friend's wish if at that moment George Henry had not howled and appeared to go crazy and slash at Fortner's bent head with the claws. With deadly accuracy, Bear-John fired Fortner's rifle with his left hand at George Henry. He glimpsed a flash of something silver streak from the darkness and land in George Henry's shoulder right before the bearded man gasped horribly and fell to the ground. He knew that the gaping gunshot wound he had put in his throat would bring a quick death to the writhing outlaw.

"Drop your gun, Juno!" came a husky voice from the edge of the woods. "If Bear-John misses, I won't."

"Treasure!" called Fortner from where he crouched upon the ground beside the dying George Henry. He sat up and saw her as she moved cautiously toward the bug-eyed Juno with her rifle aimed steadily. Her eyes were tawny and threatening in the light of the dying campfire.

"Treasure!" Bear-John echoed, walking toward the spot where Hank and George Henry lay motionless upon the ground near Fortner. Bear-John had pulled his pistol from the waistband of his breeches to cover the only standing outlaw, but Juno seemed disinterested in moving from his spot. He had dropped his pistol to the ground upon seeing Treasure come into view with her rifle barrel pointed at him. "What in thunder are you doing here?"

Treasure looked at Fortner, who was rising to his feet, and blinked hard before answering. Her prayers had been answered: he was unharmed. "I had some unfinished business."

Fortner asked, "How long have you been out in the woods? You could have been hit by Juno's stray shot."

"I came when Hank—Whitey—lost his wig," she replied, her eyes big and full of pain.

"Then you know all about—"

A great crashing through the woods interrupted Fortner's words, and before he could do more than stand protectively in front of Treasure, seven men on horseback galloped up. They all had guns in their hands.

"Sheriff Horace Coates, boys," the man in front boomed as he pointed his gun at the three men and lone woman beside the campfire. His eyes raked over the two dead bodies lying on the ground. After his six armed companions guided their horses into a rough semicircle around him, he asked, "Anybody want to tell me what's going on here?"

"My name is David Fortner Copeland," Fortner replied. "The young lady was just passing by and needs somebody to escort her back to her home." He gestured toward Bear-John, who was easing his pistol back inside the waistband of his breeches, and then toward Juno. "We got some old business settled here this evening."

Big and looking every inch a man of the law, Sheriff Coates dismounted and walked over to where Treasure stood beside Fortner. "Would you be having a name, miss?"

"Treasure Ryan," she answered quietly.

"Then you're Percy Lindsay's granddaughter," the sheriff said with open surprise. "Mr. Lindsay sent me a message after dark saying that the Thorpe Brothers' gang had held you and your brother against your will and then demanded money for your release.'' He looked around the small clearing. ''What are you doing here alone at this time of night? Have you been harmed in any way? Did they come back to Lindwood and take—''

''No, I haven't been harmed. I slipped off and rode my horse here on my own,'' Treasure broke in to say. ''What my grandfather reported is only a partial truth, sheriff. I want to explain—''

''Tomorrow will be soon enough for that, young lady,'' Sheriff Coates assured her, turning his attention then to his deputies who, with guns cocked and aimed, had swarmed around Bear-John, Juno, and the still bodies of Hank and George Henry. ''Abner,'' he said to the young man standing closest to him, ''I'm asking you as my chief deputy to ride with Miss Ryan back to her grandpa's house. The rest of you get these three outlaws tied up and let's get on back to Natchez.'' A hand rubbing thoughtfully against his chin while he walked over to kneel beside the two dead men, he added, ''We might as well throw these bodies across their horses and take them into town to the burial parlor. Old Dub can use the business, and he does love stretching out notorious outlaws. He don't get many with their heads still on.''

''Sheriff Coates,'' Treasure said. ''Please listen—''

Fortner, putting his hands behind him for a deputy to tie together with a rope, interrupted her this time. ''Treasure, go on back to Lindwood with the man. This is no place for you.''

Treasure shook her head vehemently, tears already pooling in her eyes at the sight of her beloved being arrested. She leaned over close, her hair falling forward and framing her face and shoulders. ''No, I can't leave you like this. They don't know what kind of man you are.''

Summoning forth more steel in his voice than he had thought possible, Fortner tore his gaze from her beautiful face and snapped for her ears alone, ''And neither do you.

Go away. You acted like a hotheaded fool coming here. I don't want to lay eyes on you again."

Treasure winced at Fortner's scorching condemnation, her head jerking as if someone had pulled it. Without another word, but with her slender body held tall and her old black skirt billowing out around her legs, she stalked off into the woods where she had left Vagabond. Abner, the deputy assigned to escort her back to Lindwood, grabbed the reins of his horse. He had to run to keep up with her.

Later Treasure might recall that the day she convinced her grandfather to allow Danny and her to appear before the sheriff in Natchez was warm and sunny and the first of June. On that afternoon when Uncle Robert accompanied them to make the call, though, neither weather nor calendar had anything to do with Treasure's ruminations. The small tempest breaking inside Percy Lindsay's study right after breakfast had quite worn out everyone involved in the family confrontation.

Little conversation took place among the three people on their way into the small town of Natchez. Uncle Robert seemed to favor private thoughts. Just as intent upon her own, Treasure barely noticed the frame houses perched on the hills overlooking the Mississippi River. The stormy-eyed young woman's thoughts centered on Fortner and on what Aunt Rebekah and Grandpa Lindsay had insisted she endure to be granted her wish.

"Treasure, are you still mad about having to wear Aunt Rebekah's dress and ride in a buggy?" Danny asked, leaning from his saddle to look into her face. With the adults riding in Percy's best buggy and the boy on horseback, the three traveling from Lindwood were pulling up before the rambling building serving as the jail for Natchez and Washington. "I think you're lucky that you two are about the same size and that her things look so pretty on you."

"What makes you think I'm mad about anything?" Treasure hedged, her face flushing at Uncle Robert's suddenly keen examination of her. Just as quickly, he returned his attention to guiding the horse pulling the two-seater buggy down the narrow dirt street of Natchez.

"I can tell you have on your 'mad mouth,'" Danny replied in a teasing manner. "After you raised so much Cain with Grandpa for us to get down here to help Fortner and Bear-John, I'm surprised that you aren't looking happy now that we're here."

"I'll look happy when this business is over." Treasure sighed and shook her head in annoyance, the little action reminding her of the small straw hat perched atop her head and held on by green satin ribbons meeting in a saucy bow tied beneath her left jaw.

With distaste Treasure glanced at the white lace mitts on her hands, folded demurely in her lap as the soft-voiced slave, Bitsy, had told her was expected. Her gaze swept down to the low round neck and the brief sleeves of the bright green gown of watered silk, then on to the white, lace encrusted petticoat revealed by the draped skirt. The tip of a matching green satin slipper showed down on the leather-covered floor of the trim black buggy.

Not only did she look like a stranger, Treasure mused, but she felt like one—a hot, sticky stranger at that. Now that they had left the deep shade of the Trace at the edge of town and were in bright afternoon sunshine, mosquitoes and gnats seemed less inclined to hover about the occupants of the buggy. Uncle Robert had explained about the stifling hot air and how the Mississippi added its moisture to that floating up from the Gulf of Mexico to the south, but Treasure still found it difficult to breathe normally. She guessed it might be a curse from having been born and reared in the hills of Tennessee where the air was crisp and seemed made for breathing.

What had caused her to soften and allow Grandpa and Aunt Rebekah to win such a giant battle during her first twenty-four hours at Lindwood? Treasure wondered. She sighed at the troubling answer: Fortner. David Fortner Copeland was in trouble, and only Danny and she could save him and his half Chickasaw friend, Bear-John, from facing a judge. The two of them being locked up with Juno Thorpe was a mistake.

Treasure had chosen to ignore Fortner's final words of last night. He had merely been pretending not to want her around, she had assured herself by the time the deputy had escorted her back to Lindwood. Before daylight, she had convinced herself that he would be so glad to see her if she showed up at the jail that he would likely put aside his notions of living the bachelor life of an adventurer. He would be filled with gratitude and confess that he couldn't live without her.

"As your lawyer as well as your uncle," Robert Lindsay said to Treasure and Danny, "I'm warning you that you must leave most of the talking to me. You could do more harm than good for your friends if you repeat what you've told Father and me."

Treasure and Danny nodded their agreement, both of them eyeing the low, unpainted building before them. While waiting for Danny to hitch Buck and for Uncle Robert to come around and help her down from the high, thin-wheeled buggy—as he had requested her to do—Treasure studied the small barred windows of the jail. She shuddered, annoyed that her pulse was speeding up. The thought of Fortner in jail had kept her awake most of the night.

Keyed up as she was, Treasure welcomed the chance to laugh at the mess she made of handling the voluminous skirt and petticoat when it came time for her foot to find the small ledge and step down to the ground. When the tall blond man trying to assist her added his own quiet chuckle at their mutual awkwardness, Treasure felt a rush of warm feeling for her mother's brother. So this was what it was like to have family, she mused with new gratitude, taking Robert's proffered arm and smiling at Danny as he approached. She felt better already.

Sheriff Horace Coates welcomed the well-known lawyer and his niece and nephew. He pulled up three chairs and leaned on his desk when the callers were seated. Though he took part in Robert's small talk, his round face showed that he had no inkling as to why they had appeared in the front room of his jail.

Soon after beginning his well-planned dialogue in his unhurried, cultured manner, Robert Lindsay captured the sheriff's undivided attention.

"Well, now that you've brought all this up about Fortner and Bear-John," Sheriff Coates said, "I'll admit that I already figured them two was of a different cut of cloth from that Juno Thorpe. Still and all, though, they was right there with the gang last night, and they ain't denying they'd been coming down the Trace with 'em, or that they killed them two out there beside Locust Creek."

Robert spouted some legal talk that impressed Treasure and Danny almost as much as the sheriff, ending up with a thought provoking remark. "My father will see fit to supply the sheriff's office with a horse, gear, and ammunition for a year if you can consider taking a deposition—a sworn statement—from his grandchildren who traveled with the gang from Tennessee. He says your prompt action last night made him think about how he needed to pay more attention to civic duties."

The sheriff scratched his jowls and walked behind his desk, his boots loud upon the rough plank floor. "By the way," he said while opening a drawer and taking out a small leather bag, "Fortner and his 'breed friend told me these ten gold eagles belong to Mr. Lindsay." After handing them over to Robert, he returned to the earlier subject. "That's mighty commendable of your pa to offer a horse and all. What would this deposition say?"

"We want to tell that Fortner and Bear-John saved our lives at the risk of their own and never did bodily harm to anyone while we were with them," Treasure said, no longer able to refrain from speaking. "Fortner protected me on the Trace when Danny and I were forcibly separated. My brother was left to travel with the outlaw, Whitey, the man that we knew as Hank, a peddler."

Sheriff Coates sat down in the chair behind his desk then, shaking his head as if puzzled. "There's been a right strange development about the one you just called Whitey,

Miss Lindsay.'' He directed his next remark to Robert. ''You know how I always carry my corpses over to old Dub Campbell's parlor? Well, Dub come rushing over here about noon all het up. Seems this Whitey weren't a man a'tall. He turned out to be a woman.''

''Whitey was a woman?'' Robert asked, his smooth face a study in disbelief as he leaned forward in his chair. ''How could that be?'' He looked over to see the shocked expressions of Treasure and Danny.

The sheriff went on. ''I asked my three new prisoners that very thing. Only one, Juno Thorpe, had an answer. It seems that this Whitey, or Hank, was really his mama, the mama of the Thorpe brothers.''

Treasure and Danny gasped and asked all kinds of questions, in spite of their uncle's disapproving looks. Hank—a woman?

''The way Juno tells it,'' Sheriff Coates replied in a wondering voice, ''when J. Y. Thorpe, his pa, got caught and strung up, his ma—who J.Y. always called Whitey— took over running the gang. She wanted to get even with the world for killing her old man and nailing his head to a tree beside the Trace in Tennessee. They had a kind of system worked out. As Hank, the peddler, this Whitey kept the Thorpes posted about who was traveling the Trace with valuables and who might be easy pickings. Don't that beat all?''

The news about Hank being the Thorpes' mother stunned Treasure and Danny. By the time Sheriff Coates had left to fetch a deputy to serve as the second witness to the statements they would make, they had accepted the startling revelation. In a short time Treasure and Danny were answering Uncle Robert's questions truthfully. Afterward they signed the deposition he had composed in the sheriff's office.

''May we see Fortner and Bear-John before we leave?'' Danny asked, not surprised when Treasure sent him an especially loving look. He watched her face turn pink and almost asked her what she was blushing for. Maybe it was the fancy clothes, he mused, but his sister didn't seem at all like her usual self.

"You can see them unless your uncle says different," Sheriff Coates replied, glancing at the lawyer where he still sat behind the desk. The thought of a year's free use of a fine-blooded horse from the stables of Lindwood, or of something equally pleasant, brought a nice twinkle to his eyes.

"I see no harm in a brief visit," Robert said after a moment of thought.

Leaving Danny and Robert in quiet conversation, Treasure rose and paced around the small office while the sheriff and his deputy disappeared behind a large door that obviously led to cells in the back. When she heard the unfamiliar rustle of her silk dress, she looked down at its elegance and sighed. Only her mother's locket resting above the swell of her breasts seemed right. What would Fortner think about her in such finery?

Aunt Rebekah had angered Treasure that morning when she had refused to approve her wearing the blue cotton dress that Fortner had bought her at Colbert's Stand. She had wanted him to see her in it and remember the night of the dance—and afterward in their room. Would he figure out that someone had told her that the simple blue dress was not fitting for a young lady from Lindwood to wear on an outing? Shakily her white gloved hand went up to touch the little hat, then to finger the long curls trailing down her back. Bitsy had tamed her hair with a curling iron into what the young slave had called a fashionable cluster.

Inside, Treasure was even more trembly. What would Fortner say when the sheriff told him that Bear-John and he were free because of what Danny and she had sworn to? Not that any of it was untrue, but still, they would have had to wait for a trial had she not pleaded so passionately with her grandfather. Would Fortner rush and take her in his arms and . . .

To Treasure's surprise and disappointment, Fortner and Bear-John returned with Sheriff Coates and all but ignored Danny and her after the first formal greeting. The released prisoners seemed far more interested in meeting Uncle Robert and then talking with the sheriff and his deputy about Whitey and how shocking it was to learn that a woman had pulled off such a trick for several years.

"Whitey—or Hank—was a big person, so I guess size and an unusually deep voice for a woman had a lot to do with her getting by with passing as a man," Fortner said after the talk died down a bit. "None of us suspected that the red wig hid long gray hair instead of a bald pate." He was achingly aware that Treasure had watched him constantly from where she sat near the desk, sometimes openly and sometimes from behind partially lowered eyelashes.

Unable to hear from his cell what went on in the sheriff's office, Fortner had been surprised when Sheriff Coates told Bear-John and him that they were free to go. Not until they came out into the office did he know that three visitors were there. Seeing Treasure looking so elegant and beautiful in her green dress and sassy hat melted his initial resolve to demand what she was doing there. Her presence and her blond loveliness threatened to devastate his tenuous composure.

How quickly Treasure had taken to the life awaiting her in Natchez, Fortner thought without any of the pleasure he was supposed to feel for her good fortune. Wasn't that what he had wanted for her? He was grateful that so many men were around to dominate the conversation, for he wasn't sure that he could do more than greet Treasure politely until his racing pulse slowed.

"Fortner, these two young people gave a mighty good statement about you and your friend, Bear-John," Sheriff Coates said, indicating Treasure and Danny, then returning his piercing gaze to Fortner. "If you're planning on hanging around Natchez, I can promise you I'll be expecting the best behavior, the kind they told about. You and your friend can wind up back in a cell with Juno Thorpe mighty easy."

"Our behavior won't create any problems," Fortner replied.

"None at all," Bear-John added.

"We appreciate what Danny and you did for us, Treasure," Fortner said, forcing himself to walk over to where Danny and she sat side by side. He felt as if he had been running at full speed up a mountain and hadn't yet recovered his wind.

Danny stood and took Fortner's proffered hand. "Will you come to see us at Lindwood?"

"That won't be possible, Danny," Fortner answered briskly. "You heard what your grandfather said last evening." When he heard Robert Lindsay clearing his throat behind him, Fortner went on. "He was right to be looking after you two that well. You don't need to be hanging around adventurers like me. You both need to put all that happened this year behind you and get on with your new lives here."

Disappointed that Fortner was not even trying to put up a fight to see her again, Treasure rose and met Fortner's heart-stopping gaze directly. One condition that Percy Lindsay had tacked onto his agreeing to let Robert escort Danny and her to the jail was that Fortner and Bear-John were never to make any effort to see his grandchildren again. In order to free her beloved, she had bowed to the inevitable. One word or look from Fortner would change her world. Would he do as she was praying? "Will you be going West right away?"

"Probably, thanks to Danny and you." Fortner wondered if she knew how beautiful she looked in the green dress. He saw the white lace gloves on her hands then and hungered to bring them up to his lips, remembering in an instant how her skin would feel and smell if he dared. "You did a mighty decent and kind thing to come to the jail this way with your uncle, but then I spotted you from the first as being no ordinary woman." *You're the woman I'll always love, but you belong here with your family.*

"You treated us with even more kindness." Treasure wished she could make everyone but the two of them disappear. How could she bear never to see the handsome blue-eyed Fortner again? His casual manner indicated that he truly did not care for her at all. How foolish she had been to hope and expect..."We're grateful. I'll never forget." *I love you. Don't leave me! I don't belong here.*

Robert Lindsay walked over to stand beside the young couple with their eyes locked on each other's faces. He cleared his throat when neither seemed aware of his immediate presence. "Treasure, I believe it's time for us to return home now." He held out his hand toward Fortner, not surprised that the returned handshake was firm and courteous. "Mr. Copeland, my family and I will ever be thankful for the way you stepped in and prevented the Thorpes from harming Treasure and Danny. I wish you the best of luck in your future ventures, whatever they may be."

Before Treasure could intervene and wangle a moment alone with Fortner, the little drama jumped into its final scene. Bear-John was adding his thanks to Fortner's and everyone seemed to be talking at once, and then Uncle Robert was holding her arm and leading her out to the buggy.

Treasure was still looking back and trying to get a glimpse of Fortner through the open door of the office when Uncle Robert turned the horse and buggy back up the dirt street that had brought them from Lindwood. Not much had gone the way that she had hoped—except that Fortner was no longer held behind bars. She had freed him, and now he was walking out of her life as casually as he had entered it that April morning in Tennessee.

Chapter Twenty

Life at Lindwood over the next week allowed Treasure little time for giving in to her wish to crawl off alone and lick her heart's wounds. She sometimes felt as if she might be on a runaway horse, for the little everyday dramas rushed by so rapidly that she seemed no more than a bedazzled spectator on a madcap dash to the unknown. During the humid nights, her dreams splayed golden images of Fortner smiling and beckoning for her to come to him on some distant mountain soaring upward to a startlingly blue sky. Try as she might, Treasure never found the right path to reach him before awakening with a start.

On the morning after the trip to the jail in Natchez, Aunt Rebekah brought Mamie, the coffee colored seamstress for the Lindsays over the years, and several bolts of rich fabric to Treasure's bedroom.

"Why do I need so many changes of clothing, Aunt Rebekah?" Treasure asked. "The green silk you gave me seems enough for right now." So accustomed was she to owning no more than two skirts and a few waists that the thought of needing multiple choices of pretty gowns to wear had never occurred to her. The blue cotton dress that Fortner had bought her back at Colbert's Stand had seemed the ultimate luxury until now.

"For one thing, we dress for supper here every night," Rebekah explained with a fond smile for her husband's beautiful niece. "And there will be countless parties for you to attend and social calls to make upon old friends of your mother's. With your cousin Caroline already here from Mobile and attracting the attention of our handsome bachelors, we at Lindwood will have the gayest summer ever. I'll be surprised if you aren't getting married before this time next year." Longing to put an arm around the obviously depressed younger woman, Rebekah settled for a pat on her shoulder. "You're too lovely not to have a swarm of suitors around you as soon as they learn you're here."

Treasure sighed. Aunt Rebekah was both pretty and kind. The pleasant slave, Mamie, continued to flip lengths from the many colored bolts of fabric laid out on Treasure's bed. "I never rated any notice up in Tennessee."

"I'm sure that's because none of the handsome young

bachelors knew you were there." Robert had told Rebekah what he had surmised from Treasure's accounts to his father and him as to the straitened circumstances of the Ryan household. Rebekah smoothed at her silky dark chignon and then gave in to her earlier urge to hug Treasure tenderly. Last night Robert had confided to his wife about the quiet but emotion-charged farewell between his niece and Fortner Copeland. Her compassion laced her soft drawl as Rebekah said, "Don't worry, dear. Everything is going to work out fine, and some handsome young man will sweep you off your feet. You'll see. You'll soon forget about all the ugliness you've had to endure."

Despite the wan-faced blonde's lack of enthusiasm, Rebekah and Mamie eagerly made plans to create new garments to supplement the ones brought from Rebekah's wardrobe. Mamie made the occasion enjoyable by recalling little anecdotes about Treasure's mother, Marie, during her early years at Lindwood when she had been the one being measured for pretty new clothing.

Treasure welcomed new knowledge about her mother, and she made no protest about the grand plans being made. She had already decided that since Fortner obviously had no wish to take her with him to the West, she would have to make her life there in the Mississippi Territory. Hadn't it been her dream to reach her mother's relatives? What choice did she have but to bend with the combined forces of family and society? she wondered with a new meekness that had permeated her being since Fortner had permitted her to walk away with Uncle Robert. A young woman had only one chance for happiness, according to her dead mother and the happily chattering Aunt Rebekah. She must marry a good man who could provide security for herself and their children.

Rebekah's sons Nathan, eleven, and Stuart, nine, hung around Danny as though he were a long-lost royal cousin. By the morning of his second day at Lindwood, Danny had joined the boys in the room set aside for lessons from the tutor, Cyril Wood. Wanting to check on her young brother, Treasure sought him out and stood at the doorway watching and listening. She beamed. Danny was reading Shakespearean sonnets aloud for the tutor—and doing a commendable job of it, judging from the rapt smile on the sensitive face of the frail looking Cyril Wood.

"Please reconsider and go riding with me," Caroline Lindsay begged Treasure on the third afternoon after the arrival of the Ryans. "You've done little since you came but stand for Mamie's tedious fittings and listen to Bitsy and her gossip. It might be nice to learn more about your mother's youth from old Mamie, but I vow, I believe I'd be running over with tales from the past by now."

With the practiced grace of an eighteen-year-old co-quette, Caroline brushed prettily at the dark curls framing her lovely face. She had found her taller, slightly younger cousin in the large living room with a book open on her lap. "When Papa insisted I leave Mobile and come visit Uncle Percy and his family for the summer, I thought I'd plain die from having nobody around near my own age. The past two weeks have been hopelessly dull, but now that you're here, Treasure, I just know I'm going to enjoy my visit a lot more. Won't you come riding?"

Laying aside her unread book on the sofa, Treasure smiled up at her cousin. "I would if Aunt Rebekah hadn't insisted that I must learn to ride sidesaddle. I was riding bareback before I was six, and Papa bought me my saddle for my fourteenth birthday. The whole notion of sidesaddles seems absurd."

"Fiddle! You can't let that stop you from getting out and having fun," Caroline scolded affectionately. Glancing over her shoulder, she confided softly, "You can't fight all the rules that grown-ups make up; I learned that back home in Mobile."

Treasure met her cousin's earnest dark eyes. Only the night before Caroline had slipped into her bedroom and sat on her bed and told how her father had shipped her off to spend the summer at Lindwood in order to thwart a romance with a young man not to his liking.

Caroline coaxed, "Go up and put on that riding outfit

Mamie altered for you, the dark blue one. I'll send word for August to saddle your horse.'' When Treasure hesitated, she added slyly in her thick drawl, ''Unless you're afraid you might not be able to manage a sidesaddle.'' Her brown eyes sparkled with mischief.

Treasure laughed. She had taken to her friendly, dark-haired cousin on that first night at Lindwood. Never before had Treasure been around a young woman near her own age, and their intimate conversation of last night had been a new experience. Caught up in the mood of confession, she had told a lot about herself, but nothing at all about Fortner. ''All right, Caroline. I recognize a dare when I hear one. I guess it's inevitable that I'm going to have to conquer the sidesaddle.'' She rose and hurried up to her room.

Masculine laughter floated from the living room when Treasure returned downstairs shortly. With the trailing skirt of the dark blue riding habit draped over her arm, in the way that her personal servant, Bitsy, had shown her, she crossed the spacious hallway and entered the room.

''Treasure,'' Caroline called, turning from the sandy-haired young man sitting beside her on the sofa. ''I want you to meet our neighbor who says he's going to accompany us on our ride this afternoon. I already know from his visits last week that he's marvelous company!''

Treasure watched as the young man rose and turned toward her. He looked to be almost as tall as Fortner, she thought. Something about his trim, well-formed body seemed different though, and she decided it had something to do with a thicker chest and shorter neck. Was she destined to compare and contrast every man she met with Fortner? she agonized.

''Treasure Ryan, this is Thornton Crabtree from Merrivale, the plantation next to Lindwood,'' Caroline said. She gave the young man an admiring gaze as he made the proper remarks to her cousin in a careless, drawling bass.

Once close to him, Treasure almost let out a little gasp of surprise. Thornton Crabtree did indeed have pale blue eyes! She choked back her impulse to blurt out something about this unbelievable discovery. No heavy brown eyebrows arched above them, though, and no thick black lashes accentuated their paleness. The young man's sandy eyebrows and lashes matched the pale eyes with his hair and coloring in a compatible way, as if no other color of eyes could have existed in such a face. Her cheeks grew warm from recalling how she had wished more than once that Aunt Olivia's son might have eyes like Fortner's.

Putting away the disturbing thought, Treasure saw that Thornton had a dimple in one handsome cheek when he smiled in a lazy way while acknowledging their introduction. A small, neat mustache, the same sandy blond as his hair, seemed to set off his full lips and beautiful teeth.

"My mother saves every letter from you. She'll have to send for her smelling salts when I tell her that you're actually here at Lindwood," Thornton said, releasing Treasure's proffered hand after holding it overly long. "She's in New Orleans this week, but she'll visit you as soon as she returns. I can't believe that at last we've had the chance to meet, Treasure Ryan."

"I had no idea that you two had so much to talk about," Caroline said, moving to stand closer to Thornton and to peer up into his face with a pout on her pretty lips.

Thornton's easy charm put Treasure at ease before she could become edgy over meeting the man that Fortner had teased her about coming to Natchez to marry. The horrible thought came to mind, while the visitor made small talk with Caroline and her, that she might forget and call him Thurston. Damn that Fortner! He had always known how to get her riled. Not any more though, an inner voice reminded her. The adventurer was gone, and the sooner Treasure forgot him, the better.

"That's a damned pretty sight to these old eyes," Percy Lindsay said musingly to Robert one afternoon as they talked business in the library. Treasure and Danny had been at Lindwood over a week.

A younger version of his long-limbed father, Robert rose from his chair and joined the gray-haired man at the window facing out on the front yard. He watched Treasure, Caroline, and Thornton Crabtree riding their horses abreast down the drive, talking and laughing with apparent happiness. "So Thornton is still coming here to ride with the girls in the afternoons," he remarked with a smile that revealed pleasure as much as the one creasing his father's face. "I've been wondering how Caroline is taking to competition right under her nose—or if she's still pining after the young man back in Mobile that Uncle Harold was so dead set against."

"I don't know, but from what Harold wrote when he asked me to invite his flighty young daughter here for the summer, she needs to sort out her feelings about what kind of man to marry." He squinted through the afternoon sunshine. "Thornton seems like a decent man, now that he's growing up and paying a little attention to the way Merrivale is run. I hear he still spends too much time fencing, though."

"Fencing is a fine way to keep trim, Father. Every time Cyril has a day off from tutoring the boys, he goes over to Merrivale and practices with Thornton. It's common knowledge that Olivia has spoiled him dreadfully, what with him being an only child and having lost his father so long ago." Robert took in a deep breath. "I can't help but think that Marie would have been pleased to see her daughter taking horseback rides with her childhood friend's son. Thornton couldn't have been much more than four or five when Marie wrote Olivia about Treasure's birth."

Caught up in his own thoughts and only half listening to his son, Percy watched the young people ride out of sight. "What about the young man that Treasure was so all-fired determined to get released from jail last week? I couldn't help but be reminded of the way Marie defended Blackie just before he stole her from me. Did you suspect there was something going on between Treasure and this Fortner Copeland? And did you make sure he went on and left Natchez?" When Robert seemed to be taking his time in answering, he added, "I don't want the same thing happening to Treasure that happened to Marie. Young ladies shouldn't be exposed to such riffraff as gamblers and such. Proper marriages are too damned important.''

"Father, forgive me for being blunt, but had you not lost so much gambling at that dive in Natchez-Under-the-Hill and forced Blackie Ryan to come here to collect what you owed him, Marie never would have met the man. As for Treasure and Fortner Copeland, I'm not sure what I saw pass between them the other day at the jail. The man seemed quite personable. They likely became close friends during their weeks of riding down the Trace.''

That Robert had told his wife, Rebekah, a different version of what he suspected he saw in the exchanged looks between Treasure and Fortner troubled the younger man not at all. He was still madly in love with Rebekah after twelve years of marriage, and he had never sympathized with his father's unwillingness to believe in love as a leveler of a person's ideals and reason enough for marriage. Neither did Robert go along with what seemed to be the general attitude among planters toward their wives as pretty possessions, serving only as breeders of heirs and grand hostesses of their mansions.

In a way, Robert was relieved that he barely remembered his dead mother; he had a suspicion that his parents' marriage had not been dictated solely by mutual love. From digging into official records in his work as a lawyer, he had learned as fact what he had always heard: Lindwood's three thousand acres had been only eighteen hundred acres before Percy Lindsay married the daughter of the owner of the now defunct plantation called Three Oaks.

Harrumphing his disapproval of Robert daring to bring up the way Blackie Ryan had met the young Marie and stolen her away within a few short weeks, Percy broke the silence. "Cyril reports that Danny is one of the brightest pupils he has ever tutored, even counting your own two smart boys. He said that when he visited discreetly with Treasure as I asked him to, he found that she was well-read and conversant in most subjects. I suppose Marie made sure that her children got the proper foundations as best she could.''

"Not through any efforts on our parts, I'm ashamed to confess. I shouldn't have allowed your protests to prevent me from answering Marie's letter begging your forgiveness after she left. She truly loved that handsome Irishman, you know. Maybe people have no control over such things, Father." Robert sighed. Percy's face still wore that long-suffering look. "There's no use looking back, though. What we can do for Treasure and Danny now will be all the more rewarding since we neglected their mother's needs. I'm inclined to assure Treasure and Danny that they have our love even when we might not approve of their actions."

Percy shifted his slightly stooped shoulders as if to dismiss unseen burdens weighing on him. "Didn't I hear Rebekah say that Olivia called yesterday to meet Treasure and mentioned something about a party at Merrivale?"

"That's right," Robert said, a bit disappointed that his father still could not loosen up and talk about his obvious feelings of guilt over the way he had turned his back on his only daughter after she eloped with the gambler and went to live in the Tennessee hills. "This coming Saturday night, to be exact, we're invited to Merrivale for supper and dancing."

"My, yes, I think Merrivale is even more beautiful tonight than when I first saw it in the daylight the other day," Treasure replied to Thornton's eager question on the night of the big party. The two of them were standing alone in the huge hallway running through the center of the mansion. Most of the guests had assembled in the living room off to one side to sip glasses of champagne before crossing the hallway to the ballroom. A comfortable buzz of light conversation and laughter floated out to the fashionably dressed young couple.

"You're looking more beautiful than I've ever seen you," Thornton said in an intimate voice. "Whoever chose to put you in that gown of rosy silk was inspired." His eyes feasted lazily on the expanse of fashionably exposed breasts and shoulders. He admired the way an off-the-shoulder flounce edged in fluted satin ribbon curved temptingly across the tops of her bosom and upper arms. The simple gold locket she wore gave him an excuse to let his gaze drift to the tight cleavage between her full breasts. As his pulse and breathing suddenly grew more rapid, he whispered, "I never seem to get a private word with you."

"Thank you for the compliment, but I don't see that what we have to say is so private. I'll tell Aunt Rebekah that you approve her choice of gowns that Mamie sewed for me." Treasure stepped back, smiling and taking in her admirer's clothing and appearance. Thornton had been so nice to call on Caroline and her all week and tell about who was coming to the party that she wanted to let him know how much she appreciated his neighborliness. "You might not know that your blue coat and embroidered vest make you look especially handsome tonight." She cocked her head to one side as if making a solemn judgment, in the way that she often did when teasing Danny. "Mayhap I should tell you." When the dimple appeared in his cheek, she shook her head hard enough to send dangling curls switching from one side of her bare shoulders to another and cut off her smile. Half serious and half teasing, she said, "No, on the other hand, mayhap I shouldn't. It might do what Caroline says such things do—make you more conceited."

"Did Caroline say that about me?" A much sought after bachelor throughout the Mississippi Territory and New Orleans as well, Thornton liked the idea that the two beautiful young women had been talking about him.

"She said it about all handsome men." Treasure looked around for the dark-haired Caroline, surprised that she had not come to join them already. She didn't like listening to Thornton's compliments. They reminded her too much of those a young man she had believed to be an outlaw had paid her back at Colbert's Stand when she had worn a simple blue cotton dress. "Where is my pretty cousin?"

"I suspect that Damon Deveny of Deveny Dell has cornered her somewhere to put his name on her dance card." He made no effort to join Treasure's obvious search among the crowd in the living room to locate her cousin. Gazing at the tall, slender blonde seemed to fill all his needs at the moment. He could hardly wait for the dancing to begin so that he would have an excuse to touch her and get his arms around her.

"Damon does seem like a nice young man," Treasure countered. What was wrong with Caroline to be missing out on a chance to be with Thornton Crabtree? It seemed clear to Treasure that her cousin was more than casually interested in their handsome neighbor—from Merrivale, she added, trying to follow the local custom of identifying each person with his or her residence. When her mother had done that Treasure had thought it was just Marie's way of calling up memories more clearly. She was learning, however, that one's residence was apparently a vital part of a person's identity in this society made up chiefly of planters. Was she, perhaps, Treasure of Duck River Farm?

Treasure chided herself for her foolish woolgathering and returned her attention to the pale blue eyes gazing down at her—eyes without startlingly black lashes framing them like the ones that she kept finding in her dreams. Actually, she had decided, after having been around Thornton for the past several days and giving the matter some thought, that his eyes were a deeper shade of blue than Fortner's. And they never appeared silvery and mysterious. "Maybe Caroline and Damon will be along soon."

"I love watching your eyes turn all golden like that when you're thinking about something," Thornton said. "What were you thinking about?"

A bit flustered at his question, Treasure glimpsed Caroline and the dark-haired Damon Deveny coming toward them. "Here they come now, Thornton."

"Good. Now we can go on into the ballroom. The orchestra should be all tuned up by now." Thornton slipped Treasure's hand to rest in the crook of his elbow and turned to greet the young couple approaching them.

There had been a few times in the past ten days since she had last seen Fortner at the jail in Natchez that Treasure could go for almost an hour and not think of him.

To her dismay, she had found that too many things reminded her of the pale-eyed man who had ridden up to the Ryan cabin that April morning. She was far from working him out of her heart. And then tonight came the awful business of the dance at Merrivale.

Treasure looked down at the tiny, decorated dance card dangling from a ribbon tied around her left wrist. She recalled how Aunt Rebekah had explained that it was cause for gossip and speculation if any but engaged or married couples danced together more than once. Penned in neat handwriting, Thornton Crabtree's name filled two spaces.

None of her troubling thoughts showed on Treasure's face when the fiddles—no, violins, Thornton had called them—started the stately music for the first dance. Already she had seen that among the group by the ornate fireplace there was no whiskey jug, no Jew's harp . . . and, mercifully, no banjo.

No moon or crisp mountain air or grassy front yard, either, Treasure noted when the memory of that night at Colbert's Stand hovered about in the same insidious way as the heavy, humid air. Tonight's fashionably dressed dancers would step and glide—never heel and toe—on gleaming hardwood floors beneath the soft lights of a myriad of candles in a giant crystal and silver chandelier. Four huge windows, reaching from the tall ceiling to the floor in the ballroom, were open to let in the gentle, moisture laden breezes of the June night.

"You seem to love dancing, and you do it so well," Thornton said. Treasure looked up at him, her eyes luminous and her face solemn. The sweet scent of three miniature pink roses caught up in the gleaming mass of golden curls atop her head had become her personal fragrance somehow, and he breathed it in with longing. "Did I say something wrong?"

"No."

"Do you like the music?" Her lips looked as soft and pink as the tiny roses in her hair.

"Yes." The music was dreamy and pleasant, she reflected,

but not at all exciting. Not once had she felt that it sang to her in a private way.

Drawn inexplicably by the woebegone expression on his dancing partner's beautifully sculpted face, Thornton hushed and held her closer than his dancing instructor in New Orleans would have advised. The joy of holding Treasure and having the long fall of her honey colored hair brush across his arm at times pleased him in ways that he had not expected. But what was flitting about in her mind and bringing a vulnerable look akin to pain to her mysterious, golden eyes?

Thornton had connived with his good friend Damon Deveny to pay court to Caroline tonight so that he himself might spend some time alone with Treasure. How he had hoped to have her laugh and talk as she had done during the past week when he visited with her and her cousin at Lindwood. As soon as the next interlude came, Thornton decided, he would suggest a stroll outside and see if he could find out what troubled her. It had occurred to Thornton more than once recently that he might be falling in love with Treasure Ryan . . . of Lindwood.

After the next dance, Thornton was waiting to claim Treasure before her dashing partner, Peter Hurst of Winterhurst, had time to do more than murmur his thanks for the dance.

"I shall look forward to seeing you again later," the good looking Peter Hurst said to Treasure as he bowed over her hand and kissed it with continental flair.

"And I also," Treasure rejoined politely. Peter's kiss upon her hand had surprised her. During their dance, he had entertained her with fascinating accounts of the horse races held on the sandy shores of Natchez-Under-the-Hill. Her heart had ached when she recalled Fortner telling her about the small settlement below Natchez proper—and a place called the Silver Slipper where Bear-John and he had stayed last year.

After Peter Hurst strode away, Thornton murmured, "You might not find Peter the finest of Southern gentlemen."

"He did seem a bit different from anyone else I've met, but he was every bit a gentleman while we danced."

Choosing not to pursue the subject of another man, Thornton said, "There's to be an interlude now. I thought we'd take some champagne and stroll through Mother's rose gardens out front."

Treasure put a hand to her damp forehead and summoned a faint smile. "I've only heard of champagne, but I'll try it. Can you tell that I'm getting a mite warm?"

Soon the couple had glasses in hand and were on their way across the veranda, along with several other couples who seemed interested in more private pleasures than could be found in the crowded house. Thornton slowed enough to introduce Treasure to his friends and relatives whom she had not met earlier. All evening she had pleased him with her natural ability to show the right amount of interest and friendliness to all, though she had confessed before the party began that she never had been to many social affairs and none so grand as tonight's promised to be. There was a candor about Treasure that charmed Thornton along with her unique beauty. He knew for certain that he never before had met such a fascinating young woman.

"The fresh air is wonderful, Thornton. Aunt Olivia's roses are the prettiest I've ever seen," Treasure said as Thornton walked beside her down the path separating the beds furthest from the house. Torches stuck in the ground at intervals around the spacious grounds gave adequate light, even where they strolled close to the public road out front. She had heard a horse nicker a few minutes earlier, but when she peered through the trees toward the road, she saw no passerby. How ridiculous for her to think that it sounded like Brutus! The cigar smoke that she was smelling, she mused, likely was coming from a smoker walking closer to the house. "I glimpsed the roses the other afternoon when Caroline and I rode over to visit Aunt Olivia. Up close they're even more breathtaking. I love to smell their wonderful fragrance."

"Did your mother raise roses?"

"No." Her mother had not raised anything, Treasure recalled, unless one counted a vegetable garden during those early years before she became ill. Aunt Rebekah had assured Treasure that for her to dwell on the disappointments and hurts of her former life in Tennessee would only distress her more and might sadden her new friends, so she held back what might have come out spontaneously. Would there ever be another with whom she could be as natural and frank as she had been with Fortner?

Treasure felt that she might be two people wrapped up as one package—one standing there dressed up in pink silk finery sipping champagne and receiving warm appreciative looks from a handsome blond man, the other trapped inside and pining for the familiar, resonant voice of a pale-eyed adventurer. Never with Fortner did she have cause to be anything except herself . . . well, something demanding honesty pointed out, not after that glorious night at Colbert's Stand, at least. She chided herself for her thoughts. Why couldn't she stop thinking of Fortner? He was miles away by now, on his way West.

"Are you happy that you and your brother have come to live at Lindwood?" Thornton asked, wounded a little that the earlier look of pain seemed to have claimed her face again. Never before had a young woman borne such aloofness when walking alone with him in semidarkness. Was Treasure, perhaps, overly shy without the presence of the talkative Caroline?

"Yes, everyone has been very nice and loving to us. Danny is doing very well. Cyril Wood, the tutor, says that he's sure Danny will be a member of the first graduating class at Washington Academy in a few years."

"That's wonderful news. When I was visiting with him the other day Danny told me he wants to become a lawyer like his Uncle Robert." So Treasure liked to talk about her little brother, Thornton reflected. That was fine. He truly liked the boy. Her eyes were sparkling in that way he had dreamed about as she smiled up at him over her glass of champagne. "Would you object if I taught him how to fence? I've a practice room down at the stables."

"I don't mind, if Danny and Grandpa think it's a good idea. I don't know much about fencing. Is it as dangerous as it sounds?"

"Not at all. You don't see any scars on me, do you?" Now that Treasure seemed to be relaxing her guard, Thornton's mood soared. He clowned and assumed a partial on-guard position, angling his face this way and that toward the distant torch, laughing down at her. Her lovely face was animated, and her eyes danced with an obvious love of the ridiculous. "Except for this blasted dimple—no doubt put there by my first meeting with a foil when I was too young to recall."

The champagne combined with Thornton's surprising high spirits and deep laughter soothed away some of Treasure's ache. Giving in to impulse, she tossed back her hair and joined in his laughter as he took her empty glass and set it down on the walkway with his own.

Thornton pulled Treasure into his arms then and kissed her protesting lips with tender reverence. Her sweetness and nearness tripped up his heartbeat, and he chose to ignore her attempts to step back from his embrace.

Treasure felt a new kind of sorrow when the handsome Thornton's lips did no more than feel pleasant and masculine against her own. His arms hinted at a sense of security and warmth, but at nothing that excited her. The night air seemed strangely permeated with a touch of urgency and sadness. Long-held tears welled up from the bottom of her heart and pushed at her closed eyelids.

Thornton Crabtree was handsome and clever and fun; he was everything she should be looking for in a good husband, Treasure agonized. He even had a plantation mansion that lacked a young mistress. Would there never be another set of arms to hold her closely against a tall, lean frame and set her very blood on fire—never be another pair of lips to charm her own into total surrender? Suddenly she felt bereft.

"Please," Treasure murmured when Thornton reluctantly freed her and stood looking down at her with an expression she was unwilling to decipher. Her lips trembled, and her eyes were wet golden orbs. "I must be alone for a few minutes."

Thornton turned in bewilderment as the honey haired Treasure, her pink silk skirt whispering in sensuous rhythm with the light steps of her satin slippers, ran from him along the dimly lighted walkways between the rose beds. Were those unshed tears that had turned her normally husky voice even throatier? Could it be that he was the first to kiss the blond beauty and she hadn't known how to react to a surge of passion?

His long legs serving him well, Thornton hurried after Treasure, determined to catch her before she reached the veranda and assure her that he would never rush her that way again. Tantalizing, encouraging thoughts were sending his heartbeat into a frenzy.

"I was delighted to see Thornton and you coming up on the veranda," Percy Lindsay said to his granddaughter after the next dance began and she came into his arms. "I was afraid you had forgotten my name was on your program."

"Thornton and I stepped outside for a breath of fresh air, Grandpa." Still a bit breathless from her flight through the rose garden, Treasure found it easy to smile at her gray-haired dancing partner. He cut a handsome figure in his white coat and red satin vest, she reflected with fondness. "How could I forget this dance was yours?"

"Thornton is a fine young man, and good looking, too, don't you think?"

"Yes, sir, I do." Treasure thought she could detect a calculating look in Percy's dark blue eyes. No doubt he, as well as the rest of the family—with perhaps the exception of Caroline—would be thrilled at the idea of a match between her and the heir to Merrivale. In her letters over the years, Aunt Olivia had always expressed her dream for a marriage between her only son and Marie's daughter. Now that Treasure was living next door to Merrivale, her mother's childhood friend had all but smothered the young woman with affection and attention since her return from

New Orleans. It was likely that Aunt Olivia was already choosing the material for the dress she would wear to the wedding, Treasure mused with no appreciation for the absurdity of the thought. "I suspect that Caroline agrees with us about Thornton's attributes."

Percy looked thoughtful for a moment. "Caroline seems not ready yet to settle down. She's a bit flighty, like most young women."

"Are you saying that I'm flighty?"

"No. You seem to be remarkably sensible. And I believe you're even more beautiful than your mother was."

"Are you eager to marry me off?" Treasure thought of the petite, blue-eyed Marie and shrugged off the compliment as no more than sweet words designed to soothe. She knew that her hair was not nearly as blond as Marie's had been and that she was too tall and big-boned to compare with her mother. Only Fortner had ever made her feel beautiful, she thought with such sadness that she almost missed a beat of the music.

"Not at all, my dear," Percy assured Treasure. "If you become engaged by the time you're eighteen in October, that will be soon enough. Everybody around here loves June weddings."

Treasure dropped her gaze. There seemed little doubt that she was expected to be married by this time next year. Grandpa Lindsay's ideas dovetailed exactly with Aunt Rebekah's. She glimpsed the tiny dance card dangling from her wrist. Her future seemed to be as well thought out as the progression of dance partners at the formal dance, she agonized. It was almost as if such personal matters could not be entrusted to the people directly concerned, and certainly never left to chance or fate.

Without looking again, Treasure knew that two lines on her dance program held the name of Thornton Crab-tree . . . and that his signature had graced those spaces when Aunt Olivia presented her with the card upon her arrival. Others wishing to claim her for a dance had come up to her and asked permission to enter their names on her card. Not Thornton. He had presumed special priority.

Sensing that someone watched her covertly, Treasure searched among the whirling couples. Was it the hard-eyed Peter Hurst or one of her earlier dance partners? She saw Peter dancing with Caroline and apparently intent upon the pretty brunette. It wasn't Thornton, for he was dancing with his mother and not paying any attention to Treasure and her grandfather dancing by one of the large, opened windows. Shivering suddenly, she decided that she must have imagined she was the focus of someone's scrutiny. Other than those she had met and danced with, who might be interested in what she was doing?

During intermission, Thornton escorted Treasure across the hallway to the dining room where a long table held numerous platters and bowls of savory food, the likes of which she had never seen or smelled. Some of it she could not have labeled before her arrival at Lindwood.

Some of the other guests were already in the dining room, laughing and talking jovially. When they filled their plates, they wandered from the dining room to find standing or sitting room so as to partake of the sumptuous midnight supper.

With a gold-edged plate of hand-painted porcelain in her hand, Treasure allowed her eager host to fill it with small portions from some of the many foods offered.

There was a reddish, cured ham, with sliced servings resting in little pools of redeye gravy. Treasure saw crusty fried chicken forming golden mounds on two enormous silver platters and nodded her approval when Thornton chose a small piece of white meat for her plate. Small side dishes offered crisp pickles made from cucumbers, miniature spears of okra, and burgundy colored peaches. Green peppers and radishes, their red skins curled back, decorated a round platter of deviled eggs nestling on beds of watercress. Tiny pink potatoes, only half peeled, swam in a sauce of butter specked with sprigs of parsley. There were green beans no longer than Treasure's little finger.

Kept warm inside a domed silver server, and causing

Treasure to sniff at the heavenly fragrance when the cover was pushed back, were little yeast rolls with golden tops and the shape of a three-leaf clover. Three rounds of cheese, each a different shade of yellow, rested upon a slab of marble. Small ears of sweet corn lay stacked high, generous pats of butter already melting across the golden kernels.

"Treasure, are you sure you have all you want to eat?" Thornton asked.

"I'm sure." She turned to Caroline and Damon Deveny who had arrived at the laden table soon after Thornton and she had. "Caroline, have you ever seen so much food?"

Partially aware of her cousin's simple upbringing, Caroline smiled. "I'm not sure that I have. Are you having as much fun as I am tonight?" She slid a provocative look up at the attentive Damon, then let it drift over to Thornton.

"Yes. I must not have believed my mother's accounts of this part of the world. Everything seems so unreal that I wonder if I belong here. I feel that I might wake up any minute and find myself back in the hills of Tennessee." When all three turned to the musing Treasure with polite but uncomprehending expressions. she added, "Everything here seems almost larger than life."

"Hear! Hear!" Thornton replied with a dimpled smile. "Perhaps that's a compliment and a vote of confidence for our little world." For her ears alone, he added, "And you fit into it perfectly."

Treasure lowered her eyes and pretended interest in the array of food upon her plate. It would not do for Thornton or anyone else to guess her thoughts.

Chapter Twenty-one

David Fortner Copeland and Bear-John McHenry didn't tarry at the jail in Natchez after being freed that June afternoon.

Treasure, Danny, and their lawyer-uncle, Robert, had not had time to reach Lindwood before the two friends were riding their horses down the steep, angling road to the area called Natchez-Under-the-Hill. The Silver Slipper, the large two-story building providing them with food and lodging upon their stays in Natchez the past summer, appeared unchanged.

"Well, hoss," Bear-John said with obvious relief, "one good thing about our trip down to the Silver Slipper this summer is that we don't have to act like outlaws so as to be taken in by the Thorpe brothers."

"Right. And I don't think I ever want to hear the name Thorpe again."

"Neither do I." Companionable silence ruled for a brief distance. "Are you going to light out across the Mississippi tomorrow and head West?"

Fortner deliberated. He couldn't leave until he knew for sure that Treasure was fitting into her new world. "Not for a while yet." He turned to study the big half Chickasaw riding beside him. "Have you made up your mind to go along?"

"I won't be going. I got an itch to go back to Colbert's Stand before I make up my mind where I'll end up."

"His pretty daughter Celeste wouldn't have anything to do with that, would she?" Fortner smiled to see the faint flush rising beneath the dark skin of his friend's face.

"She might at that," Bear-John conceded after a while. "After all that happened last night, I decided there's a heap of living I want to do without a gun being a part of my right hand."

"Good point. We can both be thankful for your deadeye shooting last night."

Fortner deliberately closed his mind on the violence of the preceding night and focused on what lay around them. There would be time later, maybe too much of it, for pondering on that . . . and the woman he had come to love and told good-bye for the last time. In spite of the breeze blowing from the river with its pungent odors of fish and waterlogged wood, he found himself remembering the sweet fragrance lingering behind Treasure back at the jail.

Fortner stowed the memory and looked around. Silver Street remained as he recalled—a series of hard, pinkish clay and sand ruts promising rough passage for wagons and carriages. He had noted last year how the frequent rains played havoc with attempts by road crews to keep the road smooth. Rising sharply behind him were the sandstone hills that held the town of Natchez aloft in isolated splendor. From his first sight of them the strangely smooth edges of the hills had baffled him and made him think of a giant cake of some-hundred feet in thickness with half of it sliced away by a sharp blade.

Pausing to look at the motley assortment of buildings and wharves alongside the eastern bank of the Mississippi, Fortner and Bear-John wondered aloud if new buildings had joined the numerous ones lining the single thoroughfare. Last summer they had learned that the extremely damp climate turned any unpainted lumber gray before it was a year old.

Not many of the restaurants, saloons, gambling houses, whorehouses, and stores had ever seen a coat of paint, Fortner mused. They squatted on the wide stretch of sand that had been deposited by the giant river once during a flood and had been left there high and dry for years. He wondered if the mighty river might not rise some day and return to reclaim the discarded sand and dirt.

Fortner reasoned that what he had heard about how the rowdy settlement got started was probably true—that Under-the-Hill first came into being to prevent the undesirable sailors and transients loading and unloading the ships' cargo from climbing the steep hill to satisfy their wants in the little town of Natchez. It was obvious that the good citizens of Natchez and Washington had played a big part in keeping the place thriving and growing during the past several years. Under cover of darkness, many sneaked down from the soaring cliffs housing respectability and joined the raucous, brawling assemblage. Once there, Fortner had learned last year, they raised considerable hell on their own.

Looking out across the wide sandy shore of the roiling Mississippi before them, Fortner saw the many ships anchored nearby. They creaked and bobbed as they fought against the swift, muddy current. He noted that downriver a way, a few horses and their low leaning riders seemed intent on making one more practice lap around the simplistic but popular racing course before darkness set in. Later, he reflected, he might be tempted to enter Brutus and vie for what he had heard were good purses. He would need extra money, for he wanted to buy a packhorse and supplies for the trek West. After yanking his hat brim lower, he slapped at the mosquitoes buzzing around his face.

Inside the whitewashed Silver Slipper, the two old friends from the Cumberland River saw again the large gambling hall opening off one side of the spacious foyer. They exchanged quick grins, recalling without saying so that a huge bar curved against one wall of the gambling hall. Soon they could step up to it and order fine whiskey. Sounds of a tinkling piano—the only one in Natchez-Under-the-Hill—and men's amiable voices floated out. Within the hour the sun would set across the Mississippi, behind the newly acquired portion of the United States called the Louisiana Purchase.

A fair-sized dining room lay on the other side of the foyer. Mouth watering smells of freshly brewed coffee, fried catfish, and corn fritters tempted the two so recently released from the jail up the hill. A few quick words with the innkeeper, busy in the small cubicle behind the receiving desk until the newcomers rapped their knuckles on the polished wood, resulted in Fortner and Bear-John holding two brass keys to rooms set far back on the second floor.

Later that night, after baths and whopping servings of catfish and corn fritters, Fortner and Bear-John joined the boisterous group in the Silver Slipper's gambling hall. They found empty chairs at a table where a game of poker was already in progress and plunked themselves down for a night of gambling.

"Gentlemen," Fortner said to the solemn trio still at the table a couple of hours later, "I'm betting my pile on this hand, 'cause it's my last of the evening." He brought his cigar up to his mouth and puffed while squinting through its smoke at the five cards in his hand—a full house headed by three aces and rounded out by a pair of tens. Now that the fifth poker player had departed, he mused, maybe his run of bad luck had walked off with the man.

"I don't believe you've suddenly run into good luck," drawled the black-haired man with eyes to match. He eyed the considerable pot on the table, then reexamined his three jacks. "You say you're quitting after this hand," he said as he shoved out a stack of coins to match Fortner's. "You must be hitting the saddle early in the morning. I saw you and your friend ride up this afternoon on some fine horseflesh. That long-legged gray looked like a racer."

"If I roll out early," Fortner replied casually, "it'll be to hunt a job." He ignored the remark about Brutus. When Bear-John and he had wandered over to the table earlier and asked if there might be room for two more, the man now bragging on Brutus had introduced himself as Peter Hurst. His manner and speech plainly revealed that he was from the area. His shiny black broadcloth coat and snowy cravat suggested that he might be fairly well off, as did his smooth hands and unblemished teeth. Though there was something about Peter not quite to his liking, Fortner found him far more congenial than the other man at the table, a surly drummer from New Orleans named Levi Stater. "My friend and I are planning on hanging around Natchez a while."

Bear-John studied the pot, then his cards. "By me, hoss," he said with a bemused smile, tossing his cards facedown on the table. "Count me out." He picked up his whiskey glass and finished off its amber contents.

The drummer, Levi, had tapped his fingers on the table during the light talk. All evening he had been the most frequent loser. Sliding out a stack of coins to cover the bet, then adding five more after a slight hesitation, he said, "I'll call and raise you five."

Fortner grinned. He didn't have to look at his cards again. "Fine. It's your funeral." He tossed out five more dollars, liking the way they sounded when they clinked against the others.

"Will you be looking for a job even if you win the pot?" Peter Hurst inquired as he carelessly added five coins to the growing pile.

"Yep," Fortner answered, not bothering to remove the stub of a cigar from his mouth. Sending a satisfied look around the table, he fanned his cards faceup and laid them on the table with a nice little rippling sound. "Full house, gentlemen. Aces and tens."

"Beats me," Peter grated, his mouth tightening into a grim line. He slapped his cards down without showing them.

"And me and my full house," Levi said sullenly. He showed his losing hand, the three nines and two fours winking in the candlelight of the overhead chandeliers in the large room. The drummer gathered up his depleted stack of coins and stalked from the hall.

Though Peter Hurst had appeared angry at having lost to Fortner, he hung around, even after the three had cleared the table of their winnings and risen. "Why don't you two join me for a nightcap? If you know anything about riding horses, I might know of a job hereabouts."

And so it was that within the next hour Fortner and Bear-John were agreeing to report to Peter's plantation, Winterhurst, the next day and show their horsemanship on some of his racing stock. The pay sounded good, especially when it included rooms over the stables, keep for their horses, and food in the main kitchen of the mansion. They had no doubt that they would qualify to exercise and help prepare the man's horses for an upcoming race at the track near the Silver Slipper.

"You'll not have any trouble finding Winterhurst," Peter told them before they went to their rooms. "It's right off the Natchez Trace up near Washington, next to a place called Merrivale."

One of the alternate runs for exercising his racehorses was on the Trace at twilight, Peter Hurst explained to his new employees the next afternoon. At that time of day travelers on the Trace were unlikely to be present in large numbers. The return course made use of a side road looping in front of neighboring Merrivale and in front of its other neighbor, Lindwood. After giving his instructions, Peter left Fortner and Bear-John in the care of Cato, his slave serving as hostler.

That first afternoon as Fortner and Bear-John rode the Hurst horses around the prescribed path, Fortner glanced up the narrow road winding to Lindwood. He hoped to glimpse Treasure or Danny somewhere around the white mansion with its sprawling side wings and numerous chimneys. He leaned over to tell Bear-John that this was the spot where he had left Treasure and Danny with their grandfather that evening.

Their view of the Lindsay home was limited, what with

the house being set back several hundred feet and the road leading to it curving through a thick stand of moss-draped trees. They saw no one on the veranda or around the house. It was too early for candles to show through the huge windows from such a distance.

After thirty minutes of giving the horses their heads, Fortner and Bear-John slowed them to a walk. Up ahead they saw another plantation home set among towering oaks.

"That must be Merrivale," Fortner said. When Bear-John looked at him questioningly, he explained, "Treasure told me it was next to Lindwood and that Thornton Crabtree lives there with his widowed mother. Winterhurst lies on the other side of it, according to what Peter told us."

"Whooee!" Bear-John exclaimed as they neared the imposing two-story house with massive white columns across its front. A straight drive led down to the public road, offering any passerby a full view of the red-washed brick mansion with verandas across its front, both on the ground and upper levels. "That place looks even grander than Winterhurst or Lindwood. Look at those flower gardens. Have you ever seen the like?"

"Not often, though there are some as grand in Nashville." Fortner eyed the carefully tended rosebushes and the neat brick paths setting off rectangular groups of plantings. On one side of the tree-lined driveway walkways and plantings reached down close to the public road. In his mind's eye Fortner could see the golden haired Treasure—as Mrs. Thornton Crabtree—moving about the gardens, the green silk skirt of yesterday swaying against the blossoms as she leaned to smell them or perhaps snip some for decorating her plantation home. A tight knot settled in the back of his throat.

"Wait up, hoss!" Bear-John called when Fortner suddenly kneed his mount and galloped off toward Winterhurst.

That night in the small room above the stables at Winterhurst, Fortner lay upon his bed and reviewed some

of the happenings of the trip down the Trace. The recent
stay with the wounded Treasure in the Choctaw village
seemed almost unreal. He confessed that he had truly liked
tending to her needs while she was ill. If they had not had
that private time together he might not have found out
about the Thorpes' connection to her father's death and
been able to get the story straight for her peace of mind.
She had been breathtakingly beautiful wearing the skimpy
buckskin covering across her full breasts. In deference to a
flare of heat in his groin, he switched the direction of his
ruminations.

By the saints! Treasure was a demon with a rifle and a
knife, as good or better than most men he knew. He had at
first thought to scold her after her arm healed. She was
always too quick to interfere in what he considered men's
affairs—something she seemed to feel was her privilege,
no matter that she was a woman. Common sense stepped
in and changed his mind. Had Treasure not distracted the
Kentuckian and taken his poorly aimed shot in her arm, it
was likely that Fortner would have been shot in the back
and killed.

Who would ever know how much Treasure's appearance the other night with her rifle aimed at Juno had to
do with the last outlaw's instant surrender of his weapon? True, Bear-John was readying his pistol, but . . . Fortner
was yet amazed that Treasure had sunk her knife into
George Henry's shoulder without Fortner's knowledge
of her presence. Of course, he reminded himself, he had
been busy trying to steer clear of those devil's claws
and keep the culprit imprisoned within the coils of his
whip.

Strange, Fortner thought, how his original plan to kill
the Thorpes and Whitey had turned into no more than a
burning need to turn them over to the sheriff for judgment
from the law. He guessed that justice had been served
when Bear-John had been forced to shoot Whitey and
George Henry to keep Fortner from serious harm. He
remembered how surprised he had been to see Treasure's
knife handle protruding from George Henry's shoulder

when the deputies had draped the dead outlaw's body over his horse.

Sheriff Coates had handed the pearl-handled knife, along with their own weapons, to Fortner and Bear-John when he released them from jail. Bear-John had made no comment when Fortner claimed it; no one around Natchez should learn that Percy Lindsay's granddaughter was extremely talented with a knife. Ashamed of having inflicted additional pain on the already shocked young woman that night, Fortner recalled spouting ugly words to Treasure in order to trigger her temper and get her to return to Lindwood without further ado. How else could he have gotten her to leave? he agonized.

Not to be overlooked, Fortner mused, was the admirable way Treasure had testified about Bear-John and him to the sheriff and secured their freedom. She had brought along Danny, too. What other young woman would have dared admit to spending so many days and nights with a man who was not her husband? Most would have feared gossip and scorn from family and society. Not Treasure, he reflected with a slight smile at her uncommon spunk and talents. What other woman could shoe a horse as well as she could bake a syrup pie or cook up a pot of squirrel stew with dumplings? What other woman would have pulled a pistol on the man to whom she had just surrendered her virginity? His smile widened at the memory of the way she had stood up to him back in the cave.

Yes, Treasure was always herself. A strange thought came to Fortner's mind: She seemed not to view herself as a woman but rather as a person called Treasure. No doubt her hands-off upbringing had much to do with her unique sense of self. Whatever the source, Fortner knew that he loved her because of it . . . or maybe in spite of it. A thought trying to surface for quite some time popped into his mind in full form: Treasure Ryan would be an able companion to a man heading West. She would not be a hindrance, as an ordinary young woman might be.

Fortner tossed on the bed and scolded himself for the wayward thought. What was wrong with him to be hungering still after the beautiful blonde with the golden eyes? He could never ask her to marry him and follow him into the wilderness. To dwell upon the possibility was nothing but selfishness, a fanciful dream springing forth from being so madly in love with her. He had seen no choice when it came to Treasure's welfare. What could he offer her but an uncertain future as the wife of an adventurer set on finding his place in the undefined West? Adding to his misery was another bothersome question: Why did he think that she would consent to marry him even if he asked her?

Seeing Merrivale late that afternoon had jolted Fortner. He had tried to reassure himself that, as he had decided back at Colbert's Stand upon recognizing his love for her, Treasure belonged there as mistress . . . or at some similar grand plantation mansion. Why then had he urged the horse forward with uncharacteristic ferociousness? Why was he now aching all over and mooning over her? He had done the right thing to remain silent about his feelings for Treasure. Besides, she likely was already finding that a drifter from Tennessee could not hold a candle to the rich planters around Natchez—if she ever thought of him at all.

The first week at Winterhurst gave Fortner time to examine his real reason for wanting to hang around Natchez for a while before heading across the Mississippi toward whatever lay West. He had not lied when he told both Bear-John and Peter Hurst that he wanted to build a nest egg before leaving, for there was the need to buy a packhorse and more equipment and supplies than he normally carried on the trail. His nightly sessions of thinking about Treasure reminded him that he was still in Natchez because he wanted to make sure that she was happy and getting settled.

"What if the planters and their families treat Treasure as an outsider because she wasn't reared amidst the finery and luxury that they probably take for granted?'' Fortner asked Bear-John one night as they rode back to Winterhurst from a session of gambling at the Silver Slipper. ''And what if they learned she's ridden down the Trace with a bunch of outlaws? Can you imagine how they might scorn her if they were to learn she's the Avenging Angel along the Trace in that ridiculous new song we heard tonight at the Silver Slipper?''

''You're hunting up things to worry about. Nobody's going to connect Treasure with that crazy song,'' Bear-John replied. ''It's not likely it'll be sung anywhere but Under-the-Hill. When we saw her riding sidesaddle again this afternoon with the dark-haired woman and the big, strapping blond man, they seemed to be treating her like a real lady . . . and she sure as hell looked like one, too, didn't she?''

Fortner shifted in his saddle. He didn't like recalling the way Treasure had looked riding sidesaddle in a blue riding outfit with a little hat atop her golden curls. He had felt he might be looking at a stranger. ''We weren't close enough to see their expressions or hear their talk, though. They might have been ignoring her.''

Bear-John had attempted a time or two to talk to Fortner about his obvious love for Treasure, but the subject was one neither seemed able to handle for more than a moment or two. He had tried once to tell Fortner that it seemed plain to him that she was as crazy about Fortner as he was about her, but he might as well have been talking to one of the rail fences edging the pastures in the area. His friend had seemed not to hear. ''I still don't see why you don't just ride up to Lindwood and call on her and ask her to marry you.''

''I can't do that. Her grandfather forbade me to come around Lindwood, and I gave him my word I wouldn't. Anyway, what if I did and she said yes?''

''Then you could take her with you to the West.''

''That wouldn't be much life for a woman.''

''Hoss, we both know that Treasure Ryan is not like other women. Why not let her decide for herself?''

"What if she said no?"

Bear-John let out a sigh of exasperation. He confessed silently that he was glad not to have fallen in love with a woman yet, especially if it might lead to him becoming as addled as the usually levelheaded Fortner had become. Thoughts of pretty Celeste Colbert often flitted to mind, but he knew that what he felt for her was no more than infatuation. He was still finding pleasure romping in red-haired Lilli's bed at the Silver Slipper, whereas Fortner wouldn't even respond to a wink from Lilli or any of the other harlots.

As Fortner and Bear-John had both learned to do, they let the subject of Treasure Ryan drop. Later, when Fortner had his usual difficulty in falling asleep in the room above the stables, he sneaked down and saddled Brutus. Somehow he felt better once he was on his way toward Lindwood. He did not expect to get a glimpse of Treasure that late at night, but just being near where she lived would make him feel better.

The first spying trip at night pleased Fortner, and he began making it an almost nightly occurrence. The ride seemed a good way to tire him enough for sounder sleep, he reassured himself after the third trip.

Since he followed the exercise route of the racehorses, Fortner told himself that the frequent rides were good for Brutus as well. Who knew when he might wish to enter the gray in a race down on the hard-packed sand beside the Mississippi and pick up a fat purse? Brutus had won more than once back in Nashville. If there was one thing Fortner could count on the temperamental horse to do, it was to run like the wind when given the reins. Games Brutus did not care for, Fortner thought wryly. Treasure and an entire Choctaw village had learned that, too. Recalling his aborted attempt to show off like a school-boy for the beautiful blonde brought a half smile to Fortner's lean face.

After the first time Bear-John and Fortner had glimpsed Treasure riding with the woman and man, they began seeing the trio nearly every afternoon while they were exercising Peter Hurst's racers.

Sometimes the elegantly dressed riders rode in a grove of trees beside a large pasture near the road, and sometimes they rode down the public road that the Winterhurst horses followed on their daily exercise runs. Fortner wondered what he would do if Bear-John and he failed to spot the little group soon enough to rein off into the woods. He had no wish to face Treasure or for her to know that he had not already left the area. All he wanted was to make sure that she was where she belonged . . . and that others felt that she did as well.

Fortner accidentally learned of the party being held at Merrivale from Cato, the hostler at Winterhurst.

"Yassuh," Cato said when Fortner showed rare interest in one of his tidbits of gossip from the big house. "Mr. Peter got his best shirt all boiled and white for the dancin' tonight over at Merrivale. You kin see lots'a buggies passin' out front already. They carries the ladies, an' the gent'mens rides they horses alongside. Some from a fur piece done passed, 'cause they'll be a'spendin' the night. Most all the planters and they ladies be goin'. I hear tell they's got a orch'stra comin' out from Natchez, and two shoats been a'hangin' in the smoke house all this week."

"Sounds like a big affair," Fortner commented, hoping Cato knew more to tell.

"It is. Mr. Thornton been callin' purty reg'lar over to Lindwood on some young lady livin' there now." Cato scratched his gray head. "Some says he's callin' on Miss Marie's gal what come back there from Tennessee to live. But some says he's callin' on her cousin, Miss Caroline from Mobile, what's stayin' for the summer wit' the Lindsays."

Fortner pursed his lips and repositioned his hat on his head. So the dark-haired young woman he had seen riding with Treasure late in the afternoons was a cousin, and the tall blond man was no other than Thornton Crabtree. He almost smiled when he recalled how his deliberate references to the man as Thurston had riled Treasure. The next thought killed off any possibility of a smile: Her mother's old dream for her daughter must be close to coming true. "Do you suppose Mrs. Crabtree is giving the party to announce her son's engagement?"

"I 'spect not, or we would'a already heered somethin' 'bout it. Mos' likely the party's jes' to let folks meet the two young ladies from Lindwood." Cato left then to check on the horses already shut into their stalls for the coming night.

While Fortner was returning to the stables after having eaten supper in the kitchen of the main house, he saw Peter Hurst ride off on his horse and turn in the direction of Merrivale. That the owner of Winterhurst had seldom come around the stables since hiring Bear-John and him to get his racers in condition pleased Fortner for some reason. The man had an air about him that was unsettling. A big race was coming up soon. Both Bear-John and he had decided they would leave Winterhurst the night before the race; their jobs would be completed.

Fortner could hardly wait for the long line of buggies and horses to pass on the road out front in the gathering darkness. Earlier he had urged Bear-John to ride to the Silver Slipper without him, offering the excuse that he had some mending to do on his gear. He had in mind that he might be able to get close enough to Merrivale to spot Treasure and set his mind at ease about how she was fitting into the society of the planters. If she seemed happy and contented, then he would take the ferry across the Mississippi and ride West.

Lighted up as it was with torches on the grounds and with each room inside ablaze with candles, Merrivale presented a pretty picture when Fortner rode near on Brutus. He tied the reins to a curving branch of a young tulip tree off to the side of the front grounds and moved through the shadows of the huge oaks, careful to remain out of the spots made bright by the torches. Soulful music drifted from a large room with tall windows looking out onto the lower veranda. Through the open windows, Fortner glimpsed couples dancing.

Fortner's throat became too full when the memory of the evening at Colbert's Stand surfaced. What fun it had been to teach Treasure how to dance and then to hold her as she laughed and twirled to the rollicking melodies from the mountain band. Was she, perhaps, recalling her introduction to dancing?

Ducking his head behind a thick tree trunk, Fortner took out his flint and steel and scraped sparks to light a dry twig. Within minutes he was puffing at his cigar and leaning against the tree. He had already decided that if he chose to wander nearer the house, he would keep in the shadows on the other side of the drive. Trees grew much thicker there, likely because the rose garden was on this side, he reasoned. If someone saw him and questioned him, he could always pretend he was a traveler who had lost his way from the nearby Trace.

Fortner was still smoking his cigar and contemplating his next move when he heard voices in the rose garden. He peered around the tree. Several couples were strolling among the rose beds. How could he be so lucky! The couple wandering far down the little path in the rose garden were none other than Treasure and the blond rider, Thornton Crabtree. They seemed to be coming toward the farthest group of rosebushes that lay about thirty feet from the tree concealing him in its shadows.

The way Treasure's full skirt floated prettily about her feet reminded Fortner of the beruffled blue dress he had bought her at Colbert's Stand. He hated noticing the low cut of her bodice, for it made him recall the way he had teased her about the possibility of her breasts falling out of her dress that night. Everything about that night had been too close to magic for him to examine it in great detail.

When Treasure and her escort came near enough for Fortner to recognize her husky voice and hear her call the man Thornton, he stubbed out his cigar in the dirt. Did she ever remember how he had always referred to him as

Thurston? Feeling like all kinds of a fool for eavesdropping and spying, he sat still and craned his neck for a new view. He was grateful that low hanging falls of gray moss from overhead limbs provided additional coverage. What in hell was Thornton doing plying Treasure with wine? She was sipping from the fancy glass as if she had already had plenty of practice and smiling up at Thornton as if she found him damned good company. She looked like a princess might, Fortner agonized upon getting a closer view of her pale gown and hair in the half light.

Fortner's heart was near bursting at seeing his beloved from such a short distance. What was the man saying that caused her to laugh that throaty laugh he had been starving to hear again? His heart threatened to explode when he realized that the blond man was pulling Treasure into his arms . . . and kissing her! Blood and tobacco! How could he stand such torture? He stood up, ramming his hands in his pockets to keep from running out and choking Thornton Crabtree. Another peek showed him that Treasure's arms had not crept up around Thornton's neck, that they seemed to be pushing at the man and seeking freedom. His breathing was erratic. Was he going to have to reveal himself and knock thunder out of—

At that moment Treasure stepped back from Thornton. Fortner strained to hear what she said—something about wanting to be alone. Why didn't she slap him or kick him? It wasn't like the Treasure he knew to submit to anything she didn't choose to accept. What had happened to that spirit of hers? Or had she actually enjoyed the kiss?

His heart lurching painfully, Fortner watched her tall slender figure rush up the path toward the brightly lit house. When Treasure passed near one of the torches, he saw that her swaying gown was pink and that the curls dancing upon her back were the same rich gold he remembered. Thornton started up the path after her then and blocked Fortner's view of the young woman.

Shaken, Fortner crossed over into the thicker stand of

trees soon after Treasure had disappeared onto the shadowed veranda. One look through the opened windows at
the dancers, he told himself, and he was heading back to
his room above the stables at Winterhurst. He should not
have come and spied on her. He should have known that
she would fit in anywhere she chose to fit in.

Treasure's golden curls caught Fortner's eye soon after
he reached a vantage point some hundred feet out on the
grounds. The room was poorly lighted, but he thought he
recognized her white-coated dancing partner as Percy Lindsay.
The music sounded so precise and uninspired that he had
no trouble figuring out why the dancers appeared stiff and
unreal. He thought back to the kind of music that he had
grown up listening to and loving, the mountain variety that
Treasure and he had danced to so happily beside the
Tennessee River.

From his hidden place, Fortner watched the beautiful
blonde turn sedately with her grandfather. She seemed to
be looking around the large room and then out the open
window. Who would have believed that only a few weeks
ago she had danced her first step . . . with him, a man she
had believed then to be an outlaw? She obviously belonged
at Merrivale, he admitted with a sigh. She was safe now.

His heart heavy, Fortner made his way back to Brutus.
Not until he was halfway back to Winterhurst did it occur
to him that he should not be feeling glum. Had he not
wanted to learn that Treasure was fitting into her new world?

Chapter Twenty-two

"Treasure, I never thought living at Lindwood would be
so much fun." Danny smiled at his sister. They were

walking among the fruit trees in the plantation orchard and enjoying some rare time alone. "Now that we've been here three weeks, I feel like I might have been living here all along."

Treasure returned her brother's smile. How could she not? The boy was obviously brimming over with contentment. "I'm tickled that you consider this your home now. Don't you sometimes miss the hills?"

"Heck, no!" His dark gaze washed over her face. "Do you miss them? We had so little there, and here we have so much."

"I wonder if mayhap there isn't too much of everything here."

"I like it this way. I wish we had come sooner. Here we've got everything anybody could hope for. It's nice that you don't have to work anymore." Danny appraised Treasure's pink morning gown with its demure neckline and white ruffled apron. A shiny pink riband held her long blond curls at the base of her neck and completed the pleasing picture of a young woman of means passing a leisurely morning on her grandfather's plantation. "You don't have to do anything now but look pretty and have a good time, and I'm glad."

Danny made life seem so simple, Treasure mused. Scolding herself for not taking to their new lives as readily as the twelve-year-old, she changed the subject. "How did we manage to sneak off for a minute without Nathan and Stuart tagging along?" She looked over her shoulder toward the big white house, fully expecting to see their young cousins charging after them.

"They both have to copy their spelling words over for Mr. Wood," Danny replied.

"Do you still like studying with the tutor? Are you still doing well for him?"

"I like it fine. He has so many books for me to read that I wonder if I'll ever get them read in time to enter Washington Academy in a few years." Looking not at all worried about what lay ahead, Danny stretched to reach a purple plum peeping from a cluster of green leaves. He offered it to his sister. When she shook her head in refusal, he bit into the succulent yellow meat and chewed vigorously. "After talking with Uncle Robert, I've decided for sure that I'll be a lawyer like him. Nathan and Stuart are lucky to have such a smart papa. I want to be like him when I grow up."

"That's the best news I've heard in ages." Treasure hugged him before he could guess her intentions and step away as he had come to do ever since their reunion. She still had difficulty accepting that Danny was no longer a little boy dependent upon his older sister. He hardly ever sought her out anymore, apparently finding it more to his liking to spend time with their uncle or grandfather. She sighed, thinking that Danny would soon be thirteen. She hadn't realized how much the boy had needed a father. Blackie had paid him almost no attention since their mother's death. Thank God she had gotten him to Lindwood. She had far more to be grateful for than to be sad about, she reminded herself. "You'll make a fine lawyer. I'll be so proud of you—Sean Daniel Ryan, attorney at law. By jingo! Wouldn't Mama have been happy for you?"

"What about you?" Danny asked. "She'd be happy for you, too, now that you're at Lindwood being courted by Aunt Olivia's son." He noted the closed look upon her face, the one he had so often seen there ever since their arrival at the plantation. "Has Thornton asked you to marry him yet?"

Treasure flushed. Ever since Thornton had kissed her that night in the rose garden, he had treated her with remarkable tenderness and showered her with effusive compliments. She was grateful that his apparent courtship had progressed no farther. "No, of course not. We hardly know each other. Danny, you're not supposed to ask such questions of grown-ups."

"Why not?" he countered with a big grin. "Ever since the party at Merrivale Thornton has been visiting at least once a day. I'm not a little boy anymore, and I can tell he's calling on you, not Cousin Caroline.''

"Do you like Thornton?"

Danny took the last bite of the plum. "Yes. He's been nice to teach me fencing. He says I'm going to be pretty good at it some day." He flipped away the pit, his gaze lingering on it when it landed on the grass. "But he doesn't make me laugh like Fortner did." The only sound for a moment was the drone of some honeybees circling an overripe plum lying nearby on the ground. "I don't hear you laughing with Thornton like you did with Fortner."

Her face flushing even deeper than before, Treasure retorted, "I do laugh with Thornton. You're not around much when he calls. You can ask Caroline; she's nearly always with us. He calls on her as much as on me." When Danny still looked doubtful and wasn't put off at all by her don't-get-smart-with-me look, she added, "Anyway, people can't go through life laughing at everything."

"It sure as heck beats frowning," Danny countered with a mischievous grin. A serious look crossed his fine features then. "I sometimes think about how Hank hardly ever smiled all those weeks we were traveling down the Trace. I reckon because he was really a woman without a husband and a house he couldn't be very happy. Plus Hank must have felt bad about thinking he had killed Amos and let you take the blame. Uncle Robert suspects Hank may have had some kind of sickness of the brain to have done the things he did. The whole thing was sad, wasn't it?''

Treasure had fretted at first that the revelation about Hank's identity and his connection with the Thorpes might upset the boy. After all, like her he had had no prior inkling that the Thorpe brothers might be the men who killed Blackie and ransacked their cabin. She had hurried to her brother's room that night after they learned of Hank's final deception to offer him comfort.

To Treasure's surprise, Uncle Robert had been with Danny. The two had been calmly discussing the peddler and her outlaw sons while they drank milk and ate sugar cookies. There seemed little for Treasure to do but chat with the pair a few moments and return to her room. She was not needed.

"Yes," Treasure answered, putting away her private thoughts. "The entire business with the outlaws was sad."

"Did Uncle Robert tell you the news? He heard this morning that Juno escaped from jail."

"No, I've not seen him since breakfast. I hope Juno doesn't stay around here." Treasure glanced around the orchard, then toward the house and the outbuildings in the distance. A quick memory of that night of violence three weeks ago brought a shudder of repulsion. Though at times Juno had seemed less evil than his brother, she could not forget that it had been Juno who had plundered the Ryan cabin and stolen her mother's locket and shawls. Her hand went up to touch the small locket. If Fortner hadn't won it in a poker game with the Thorpes, she might never have seen the treasured necklace again. "I've seen all of the Thorpes that I care to."

"The deputy told Uncle Robert that he believes Juno ferried across the river to Concord and kept on traveling West. Nobody can figure out how he and the only other prisoner got out of jail." Danny pondered a moment. "I hope Fortner doesn't run into Juno out there somewhere. No telling what would happen."

"I'm sure Fortner must be miles and miles away from here by now." Her voice sounded huskier than normal, and she cleared her throat.

"You ought to sound happier. Didn't you tell me that going West was what Fortner wanted to do all along?"

"Yes, and I am happy for him."

"Wonder why he didn't ask you to go with him?" When he saw her blush and fidget with her hair, Danny added, "Or maybe he did, and you turned him down."

"What a ridiculous idea," Treasure retorted, her voice tight. "I need to stay here and look after you . . . and find a husband and have a family."

"I love you, Treasure, but I don't need you looking after me the way you had to before we came to Lindwood. I like learning, and I can see how much there is for me to do to get ready for college. You keep thinking I'm a little boy, but I'll be thirteen in September." He postured, his fists clenched and his forearms tightened. "Look how my muscles are filling out. The other day my voice sounded like it tripped and fell down for a minute. When I asked Uncle Robert about it, he said that was a sign that I'll soon be talking deeper all the time."

Treasure ruffled his black hair, loving him with her eyes as well as her hand. She was unprepared for losing the little boy for whom she had cared for so long. It was too soon. She mustered a smile. "I apologize for not seeing how grown-up you're becoming."

Hails from their boisterous young cousins, Nathan and Stuart, came from behind them then, and they turned to welcome the gangling boys running toward them from the house.

Soon the three boys were scattering the hovering honeybees as they noisily robbed the plum tree. Treasure accepted the plum that Danny offered her that time. Nibbling at the juicy yellow meat, she listened to the three boys joking around while gorging on the purple fruit.

When, with thumbs and forefingers, the boys began squirting the slick pits at each other like missiles, Treasure had to duck to get out of their firing range. One pit landed on her sleeve with a splat, and she twisted around in time to spot the culprit darting around the tree. In no time at all she was eating plums furiously. Then, aiming her own pits from between thumb and forefinger and cavorting about in the orchard, Treasure joined the little war. She laughed along with the high-spirited boys.

Late that afternoon, Treasure hurried down the stairs to the living room. While helping her mistress don one of the new riding outfits that Mamie had made, Bitsy had told her that Thornton had arrived to go riding with her. Damon Deveny had also come to join the party.

The group in the living room seemed less talkative than she would have imagined, Treasure mused as she crossed the wide hallway. Not until she walked through the large double doors did she understand why.

"Good afternoon, Miss Ryan," Peter Hurst said, rising and standing tall in his black coat and yellow riding breeches. "I came by to invite everyone at Lindwood to come watch the races tomorrow afternoon at Natchez-Under-the-Hill. I'm riding my favorite horse, Diamondhurst, and I plan to win. I hope you'll find the idea intriguing and come."

Treasure sensed that neither Thornton nor Damon approved of the older man's presence, in spite of the fact that both now were speaking in favor of her accepting his seemingly gracious invitation. Rebekah, busy with her embroidery as she sat by the window, offered no protests when Caroline said that she would like to attend the races.

"I suppose watching the horses race would be fun," Treasure said when everyone became quiet and awaited her answer. She could never deny her intense love of horses. A break in the rather humdrum routine at Lindwood might lift her sagging spirits. "I've never seen a race run on a track such as you described. Back in Tennessee, they raced on a straight section of a road or pasture to a marked point, then turned around and returned."

"You ladies can watch comfortably from buggies parked on a little ridge overlooking the finish line," Thornton said as he sat beside Treasure on a sofa. "Almost everyone from around here will be there. It'll be quite a gala occasion, what with baskets of refreshments in the buggies and visiting back and forth among the spectators on the ridge. The riffraff from Under-the-Hill always stand down near the track."

"Since I play the role of chaperon for you young ladies," Rebekah said, "I'd like you to know that Robert and I hardly ever miss a race. We'll be going whether you choose to attend or not.''

"May we wager on the outcome?" Caroline asked, cutting her dark eyes up at Damon Deveny and then across at Peter Hurst. "Last year in Mobile I bet on a handsome bay and doubled my money. It was quite the most exciting thing I've ever done.''

Damon smiled approvingly at the petite brunette. "Yes, we'll place bets for any of you ladies wishing to gamble.''

"If you like winning, you'd best bet on Diamondhurst and me," Peter remarked. "I hired two remarkable horsemen who have spent the past few weeks getting the horse in finest form." He seemed to be replying to Caroline, but his black eyes rested on Treasure. "I intend to win, as I always do.''

Thornton and Damon exchanged knowing looks, but made no comment. Rebekah returned her attention to her needlework.

Before Peter left to return to Winterhurst, all had agreed that they would be at Natchez-Under-the-Hill on the morrow.

The next afternoon was typical of June in the Mississippi territory of 1805—hot and bright with sunshine and with white clouds lining the southern horizon. When Percy Lindsay had announced on the preceding afternoon that he would be staying behind to go fishing with his grandsons, Thornton had insisted on driving Treasure and Caroline to the race in his buggy. In their small two-seater, Robert and Rebekah followed closely behind the young people.

As soon as Thornton's buggy left the town proper and started down the steep incline to Natchez-Under-the-Hill, Treasure's eyes widened. The view of the Mississippi across the flat expanse of shore was awesome. She had not realized that the river was so broad that one could barely identify anything on the other shore. Unbidden, her first thought was that Fortner had crossed over those muddy waters. She bit her bottom lip in vexation at her stupidity in allowing it to surface.

Never before had Treasure seen so many people gathered together. She guessed there must be hundreds. She found it impossible to take in everything at once.

A dozen or more buggies were already positioned on a dirt ridge back some hundred yards from what was obviously the finish line of the racetrack. Near the course of hard-packed sand, a rope strung between waist-high stakes marked what Treasure assumed was the boundary for holding back spectators. Their faces and shapes no more than moving blurs in the distance, a milling crowd continued to grow behind the rope. She watched hurrying figures stream from the unattractive buildings lining a street and get lost in the noisy, shoving crowd. On the far side of the elongated track the wide Mississippi flowed along sluggishly.

Treasure saw an array of pretty pastel skirts blossoming from the buggies parked on the treeless ridge. When Thornton drove closer, she recognized many faces from the party at Merrivale and from the smaller ones held at other plantations since. Caroline and she returned the friendly calls and waves.

Some of the women had stepped from the buggies and were shielding their faces from the sun underneath gaily colored parasols. Treasure glanced down at her own parasol, noting how its yellow silk was the exact hue of the tiny flowers sprigging her white dress. With her cartwheel hat of loosely woven straw held on by yellow ribbons tied beneath her chin, she couldn't imagine needing further protection from the sun. Not for the first time since arriving at Lindwood she agonized that it was not so much the sunshine that plagued her and left her feeling drained as it was the heavy moisture riding the air.

A couple of small men wearing orange wigs and grotesque white paint on their faces capered for the spectators watching from the ridge. Treasure clasped her hands and smiled upon seeing the motley coats and baggy breeches worn by the clowns, the likes of which she had never seen. Laughing and wishing that Danny had not stayed behind to go fishing with their grandfather and their cousins, she joined in the applause when the clowns ended their act of juggling balls and bottles while pretending to be clumsy and in danger of losing their balance any second.

When the entertainers bowed and tossed their hats up to a group of young planters standing near the edge of the rise, Treasure watched with amazement as Damon Deveny emerged from the group and took it upon himself to walk among the well-dressed group and ask for coins to reward the performers. What a strange way to earn a living, she mused. She dug into her reticule for a coin to add to those being placed in the hats.

"Are you going to place a bet, Treasure?" Caroline asked as she leaned forward from the half sized back seat of the buggy toward where Treasure sat up front. She was still preening from the handsome Damon's remark that he would return to be with her as soon as he gave the hats back to the clowns.

"I have a few coins," Treasure confided, "but I'd have to see the horses and riders before I'd consider betting." She did not add that, as the daughter of an inveterate gambler who seldom came out a winner, gambling in any form held little appeal for her. She was trying hard to mold herself into the young woman everyone expected her to be. It was even harder not to look back. Without wanting to, she was recalling how she had earned the coins in her reticule. Fortner. Her heart seemed to turn over. Fortner had given her the money for his room and board that day back on the farm beside the Duck River. The ragged breath she sucked in made a small, woebegone sound.

"Are you all right, Treasure?" Thornton turned from where he was standing outside the buggy with some other young planters. When she blinked her tawny eyes and nodded so hard that the wide-brimmed straw hat threatened to slide off her blond curls, he asked, "Would you like me to get some lemonade from the crock I brought along?''

"Yes, thank you. That might be what I need," Treasure replied. She knew that she lied, but what good was it for her to continue pining for one so long gone as Fortner? She noted that in the bright sunshine, Thornton's blond hair and trim mustache took on a golden sheen. Seeming to borrow deeper color from the brilliant sky, his eyes sparkled at her in that warm way of late. He smiled before turning to fetch the lemonade, and she saw the dimple dance in his cheek. Could she ever come to care for the handsome heir to Merrivale?

Aunt Rebekah arrived then and climbed into the little rear seat with the assistance of her courteous husband. The older woman's explanations of what was going on below and what would happen took Treasure's mind off her private misery.

"The horses start when a gun is fired. They circle the track twice—I think it's about a half mile around. Robert says that there are seven in the race today, and that each man put up twenty dollars," Rebekah explained. "The winner gets one hundred dollars, with the rest going to the man who comes in second and to the judges. Bigger purses can be won by those who bet on the winner through the numerous brokers standing beside the judges' stand. I understand that the riders often bet huge sums on themselves."

By the time Thornton had served each of the three women in the buggy with cups of lemonade from a stoneware crock in the rear of his buggy, Treasure was nodding her understanding about how the race would be conducted. It occurred to her that if Peter Hurst was as certain his Diamondhurst would win as he had bragged, he likely had laid quite a large bet on his horse. She had not missed the several references to Peter's questionable tactics in racing. Was it something about the way Peter treated horses that seemed to set him apart?

"Where are the horses and riders?" Treasure asked, fanning herself idly with the lacy fan Bitsy had found for her. The pitch of the many voices had been rising over the past hour as everyone awaited the race. She could see the clowns entertaining the crowd standing down near the ropes. Over to one side, vendors were selling what Aunt Rebekah said were boiled peanuts.

"They wait over there by the wharves until just before the race," Thornton told her. "Those who haven't already decided which horse to root for go and size them up."

Treasure looked across the way and saw several horses surrounded by a knot of men. They were too far away for a definitive look, but her pulse jerked. She took a big sip of the tart lemonade, aggravated from thinking for an instant that the gray horse could be Brutus. There she went again, she scolded herself, letting the least matter remind her of Fortner. She was torn between wanting to curse him for turning her life upside down and haunting her dreams nightly and wanting to thank him for saving her life and teaching her all about love. As miserable as she was at the moment, she voted for the curse: *Damn you, Fortner!*

At least the absurd thought that the handsome adventurer was among that group of men down there had snatched her for a moment from her lethargy, Treasure mused with a wry smile. But what about those strange feelings over the past week when she had taken a solitary turn around the pastures at Lindwood after everyone else had ended the afternoon's ride? Had she not at those times felt that Fortner was close by? She had been wrong then. She was wrong now. There were any number of gray horses in the world. Still, she couldn't deny that her attraction to the gray must mean something. She felt strangely exhilarated.

"I'm not going to wait until the horses make their appearance to place my bet," Thornton said. "Everything gets quite hectic then." He was standing with a group of men near his buggy, both Robert Lindsay and Damon Deveny among them. Conversation moved easily from the men to the women sitting inside the shaded buggy.

"I may not care for his methods, but Peter never loses." He turned to Treasure sitting alone on the front seat and spoke privately. "I'm going to send down a bet by a runner. Would you like to bet on Peter and his Diamondhurst?"

"No, but I do want to place a bet," Treasure surprised herself by saying. She scooped up the coins in her reticule and held them out toward him. "I want to bet on the gray."

Thornton frowned. "That would be foolish. I strongly advise against it, Treasure. Peter Hurst never loses. The man is a demon on a horse . . . quite literally, I'm afraid." When she merely lifted one eyebrow and made no comment, he cleared his throat and took the money. He never before had seen her eyes flash with golden fire. "Are you sure you know what you're doing?"

"No, I'm not sure." She returned his level gaze. "But since it's my money, I'll bet as I choose." Treasure was not surprised to see the handsome face so near her own take on a brooding look. She doubted if any woman had ever before crossed Thornton Crabtree, even in something as piddling as a small bet on a horse race. Well, she reflected, if he intended to court her with marriage in mind, it was time she started acting a bit more like her real self. She had no idea where the old spunk was coming from, but she welcomed it in some strange way. She had not felt so alive since her arrival at Lindwood.

Thornton leaned even closer, making sure that no one but Treasure could hear. "I'm trying to advise you on a matter that young ladies know nothing about. Aren't you being a bit stubborn about this?"

"Yes," she murmured with certainty. Her eyes met his boldly. "I get that way sometimes."

Thornton jerked back, his face flushing and his full lips thinning beneath his mustache. He turned to the rear of the buggy where Caroline and Rebekah were discussing the gowns of the women in a nearby buggy.

Treasure chose not to pay close attention to what was

being said behind her. It was obvious, though, that the two women were following Thornton's advice and handing over their money to be placed on Peter Hurst. Caroline's pleased giggle rose above the increasing noise of the conversation among the men standing close by. Treasure was tempted to turn and tell Caroline that she could have all of Thornton Crabtree's attentions from that moment on. Caroline was far closer to being a capable mistress of Merrivale than she was—and, Treasure reflected, such a berth in life was all that her cousin dreamed of. Whereas she, herself . . .

Within a short time those congregating around the Crabtree buggy had placed their bets. They handed over their money and instructions to one of the planters' young teenaged sons. Excitement grew as they watched the boy make his way down the rise and through the crowd to where a trio of men wearing tall black hats and striped coats stood on a small elevated stand.

"I can't believe you didn't bet on Peter's Diamondhurst," Caroline said to Treasure. "I did, and Damon said he did, too. Thornton told Rebekah and me that Peter always wins and that you're going to lose your money." She narrowed her eyes and watched the horses move toward the track. "How could you tell from this distance that the gray might be worth a bet?"

"I guess I played what my father used to call a hunch," Treasure answered with a shrug of her shoulders.

"You made Thornton very angry," Caroline pointed out, her pretty face showing her disapproval. "You really shouldn't give in to your feelings like that. It isn't ladylike."

"I know, but I don't care."

Rebekah intervened then. "My stars, Caroline, don't try to make Treasure feel guilty for doing what she feels like doing. Who says that she can't make up her own mind about her bet?" She smiled and winked at her niece. "Maybe it'll be good for Thornton to learn that some of us women other than his mother do have a smattering of brains."

Caroline's expected defense of the handsome Thornton never came, for the horses and their riders filed onto the track then. All eyes riveted upon the seven prancing animals. A noticeable murmur rose from the spectators. Treasure had already learned that the race would start within ten minutes of the appearance of the horses. She angled her head for a clearer view of the gray, but it was moving in the center of the others. Her head felt light and her pulse was acting up again. The rider sat the animal exactly like Fortner. She wondered if she might be losing her mind as well as her breath.

When the horses turned to make a final walk before the judges' platform, they moved in single file. Treasure felt that she might be going to faint. There was no doubt now that she was looking at Fortner Copeland astride his horse, Brutus. What was he doing at Natchez-Under-the-Hill?

A wave of anger at Fortner's obvious deception swept over Treasure. Damn him! Why had he led her to believe that he was leaving the day after he was freed from jail? The reprobate! Why had he left her without a private word—and after all they had become to each other? There was much they had not had time to discuss. How could he not know that, he who had always been so quick to pick up on her thoughts? Another searching look at the tall lean figure on the gray, however, and her relief upon seeing him again was overriding her anger. Even from the distance of over one hundred yards he appeared handsome and dashing. She felt alive all over.

Afraid that Uncle Robert might recognize Fortner, Treasure darted a glance his way. He seemed too engrossed in conversation to notice her frantic look. From where she sat she could not see any change in Robert's features as he gazed down at the riders on the track. He had never made derogatory remarks about the man she loved, but still, he was not likely to cross his father and stand up for Fortner, either.

Treasure racked her brain for an excuse to get away from Thornton and her family and rush down to the edge of the track. She craned her neck, searching for a glimpse of Bear-John in the crowd. There were too many people around for her to pick out the tall half Chickasaw, but it was likely that he was down there to cheer on his friend. She felt that she might be trapped in an ant bed, and she squirmed in her misery.

"Would you like to get down and stand outside during the race?" Thornton asked, coming to stand beside Treasure. His marginal smile told her that he had not forgotten her little show of spirit.

"Yes, thank you." Treasure put her hand in Thornton's. Finding the narrow foot ledge was much easier than it had been that first time in front of the jail with Uncle Robert, she mused, and she made a fairly graceful descent from the buggy. If only she didn't feel so hemmed in!

"You look beautiful enough to pose for a portrait," Thornton whispered as he slipped her hand inside the crook of his elbow. Truly, he thought, he never before had seen Treasure looking quite so radiant and alive. Maybe for her to have shown a flash of temper was not so bad—this one time.

Treasure was too intent upon watching the riders line up their horses to hear Thornton's compliment, much less respond. Fortner had obviously drawn a middle position, while Peter had no doubt won the favored inside slot.

"Is the rope to be the starting line?" Treasure asked, indicating the hand-held rope across the track.

"Yes." Thornton peered down at her intense face. "You're getting all het up about this race. I've not seen you this interested in anything since I've met you. You must really love horse racing."

Treasure turned to her escort and smiled. He really was a gentleman of the finest sort. Already she was visualizing Caroline standing beside him one day as hostess of Merrivale. Her pretty cousin had never completely hidden her attraction for Thornton, even after he had made it clear that Treasure was the one he preferred. "I truly do love horses, Thornton. And I'm quite sure I'm going to enjoy this race. Why don't you ask Caroline to come stand with us?''

The crowd hushed. A gunshot boomed, and the restraining rope across the track fell. The horses took off amidst sprays of sand and roars from the spectators. By the time the horses reached the first turn, Peter's bay was leading by a nose. Treasure pressed her fist against her mouth as she saw that Brutus was behind by half a length when the horses thundered around the second curve on their way to passing directly in front of the judges. One animal faltered and fell behind when they reached the curve again. Brutus pulled up then to run nose to nose with Diamondhurst on the river side of the track, the other horses close upon their tails but posing little threat. Treasure recalled the temperamental gray's action that afternoon back at the Choctaw village and pressed her fist harder against her mouth. What if Brutus turned traitor again? What if he decided to quit on Fortner?

Peter Hurst seemed to be leaning toward Fortner and slapping with his short whip. Was he beating on the rider or the horse? Treasure wondered in horror. She saw Fortner duck and then reach out and grab the whip. For a second or two the men seemed to be wrestling each other even as their horses strained to keep abreast. Unpleasant roars from the crowd echoed Treasure's misery. One or both of the men could fall from the racing animals and be killed or maimed beneath the horses charging along behind. There could be a pileup of all seven! The struggle between the two men continued while their horses galloped around the final curve as if driven by the furies.

Treasure breathed easier when she realized that Fortner had managed to wrest the whip from Peter. With Fortner leaning low once more over Brutus' neck, the handsome gray seemed to stretch its hammering black legs even farther on the hard-packed sand. The black mane and tail danced in the bright sunshine. The sounds of the horses' hooves became louder as the animals headed down the final stretch. First a nose ahead of Diamondhurst, then leading by a head, Brutus was thundering toward the finish line with victory written all over his powerful body. Treasure jumped up and down and screamed her joy.

"I don't know how you knew to bet on the gray," Thornton said when she calmed down a little. "Judging from the movement and cheers down there, you weren't alone. The gray was obviously the favorite of those from Under-the-Hill." He squinted at the rider of the winning horse. "I don't know who the man is who dared fight with Peter out there on the track, but I'll bet there'll be another worse fight now that the race is over."

"Peter has been inviting trouble for the past year," Robert said. "I've tried to warn him that one day somebody would stand up and challenge his dirty tricks. Never before have the judges been able to see what Peter does on the far side of the track because never before has anyone had the guts to try to make him stop while riding at breakneck speed. I'd like to shake the hand of the man riding the gray." He paused and squinted through the bright sunshine. "There's something familiar about him. Does anyone know who he is?"

Treasure heard the conversation between Uncle Robert and Thornton, but her heart was too full for her to reply. Fortner had won the race. Maybe he had stayed on in Natchez with the idea of accumulating enough money to take her with him to the West. Did he know that she was watching? She waved her arm wildly, just in case. Would he, perhaps, come to Lindwood that night and ask for her hand?

To Treasure's utter delight, the judges soon had a big sign hoisted. Brutus, first. Diamondhurst, second. The riders had slowed their horses a short distance down the track and turned them around to canter back to the finish line. The noisy crowd surged and pressed forward against the rope boundary when Fortner and Peter rode back to where the judges waited to award the prizes. Treasure craned her neck desperately, but she could no longer find her beloved in the mob surrounding him and Brutus.

Even before the boy acting as runner delivered Treasure's considerable winnings to her, a large group of the spectators down beside the track had formed a giant party. Those watching the race from the rise rapidly turned their mounts and buggies toward the climb to Natchez proper when the race ended. Almost all had bet on Peter's Diamondhurst, and they had no reason to linger for any kind of celebration.

As Thornton's buggy followed the others up the steep hill, Treasure kept looking back, hoping to catch one more glimpse of Fortner. She never did.

Chapter Twenty-three

Treasure tried to show enthusiasm for her grandfather's outing the next morning, but she had slept poorly and had little taste for pretending all was well.

When Fortner did not call at Lindwood on the preceding evening, Treasure had despaired that he ever would. The fact that he had not gone West had nothing at all to do with her, she had decided by the time she went to bed. If he had any feelings for her, he would not have paid heed to Percy Lindsay or anyone else who sought to keep him from a woman about whom he cared a great deal. Had she not seen for herself that he was not lacking in bravery? As she had feared secretly all along, she was nothing to David Fortner Copeland—not even a friend worth a private farewell.

Tossing and fretting, she had alternately cursed him for not calling and wept with longing to see him. Sleep did not end her misery. The torturous dream assailed her, the recurring one where a smiling Fortner beckoned to her through a golden mist from a hillside against a blue sky.

"I thought riding our horses into Natchez so that I could show you and Danny my new cargo ship would make you happy, my dear," Percy Lindsay said when the three of them started down the hill to where the ships lay anchored on the far side of Silver Street. "From what everyone told me, you won quite a sum yesterday at the race. What are you planning to buy?"

Letting Vagabond find his own path down the rutted incline, Treasure switched her attention from the deserted racetrack up ahead to Danny riding beside her. Her look dared him to tell anything about the gray horse and its owner. He had been delighted yesterday afternoon when she had whispered about seeing Fortner, but, as she was fast learning, he had a mind of his own. During supper last night, she had suspected Uncle Robert of fixing her with knowing looks, and she wondered if he might have recognized Fortner as the rider of the gray horse. She would not put it past Danny to have confided in their uncle.

"I have nothing special in mind to buy, Grandpa," Treasure answered. "What could I need when you've given me so much?" It had occurred to her that when they reached Natchez-Under-the-Hill she might see the place that Fortner had mentioned, the Silver Slipper. Was it possible that he was staying there? Again she would have the insurmountable problem of slipping off from family to speak with him, she agonized. Besides, what would she say to him? That she wanted to thank him one last time and give him a farewell kiss for good luck? He obviously had put her out of his mind as well as out of his life.

"Wow!" Danny said when Percy led the way on his horse to a loading dock with a large ship tied up alongside. "Is that your new ship, Grandpa? I'll bet it can carry lots of cotton down to New Orleans."

"It will, my boy, and other cargo as well during the off season." Percy smiled at his grandchildren. "I'm thinking of calling it *Lindsay's Treasure*." His gaze centered on Treasure, he asked, "What do you think about that?"

"I'm flattered," Treasure replied, leaning forward to pat Vagabond's damp withers. Not wanting to get the horses overheated, they had taken a full two hours on the journey from Lindwood. Even so, the horses had drunk deeply from the first public drinking trough on a street in Natchez.

Percy insisted then that they all dismount and let the captain of his ship show them around. The stout captain was friendly enough, but after Treasure learned the answers to her key questions about the first ship that she had ever seen, she pursued something of keener interest.

While the excited Danny kept asking questions of their grandfather and the captain, Treasure wandered about the vessel until she gained a clearer view up the single street. At last she spotted a white two-story building down the way with a sign out front: The Silver Slipper. She turned away and feigned interest in the activities on the wharves as her mind whirled. Probably Fortner had left that morning on the very ferry that she was now watching float up to a huge dock nearby. She noticed that it appeared three times as large as Colbert's Ferry up on the Tennessee River. But the Mississippi was several times wider and appeared to be more treacherous than the Tennessee, she reflected. With its sturdy handrails, the ferry also looked far safer.

Danny finally ran out of questions. Percy escorted his grandchildren from the ship to the dockside warehouse where he stored Lindwood's crops for shipping.

From an open door on the street side of the large building Danny yelled, "Fortner! Bear-John!" Before either of the adults could speak, the boy was running across the hard, jagged ruts in Silver Street toward the two men. A red-haired woman dressed in purple walked between them on the boardwalk. "Wait up! I thought I might not ever get to see you two again."

Awed at her good luck in seeing in person the one man who filled her thoughts and dreams, Treasure watched Fortner and Bear-John welcome the boy, then introduce him to their buxom friend.

Harrumphing and shaking his shoulders in disapproval at the unexpected turn of events, Percy escorted Treasure across the street. Danny had ignored Percy's command to return at once; he had, in fact, acted as though he had not heard it.

"Miss Ryan, Mr. Lindsay," Fortner said when all stood too close on the boardwalk to pretend the others were not there. With little enthusiasm he introduced Treasure and her grandfather. "This is Lilli," he finished lamely.

Treasure had thought she wanted nothing more than to see Fortner face to face again. Now she wished that she were anywhere but there in front of him and his . . . new woman. She found it difficult to carry on a sensible conversation, even with the congenial Bear-John. Not that she needed to talk, what with Danny's loose tongue. She was burning up. Her supposedly cool riding outfit of pale blue cotton was sticking to her everywhere. Perspiration was forming a private little stream between her breasts. She was glad that she had worn the large straw cartwheel hat, for she could feel the color rising in her cheeks. The sun must be unusually hot beside the river, she assured herself. Seeing Fortner with another woman was *not* what was setting her afire.

"I thought you were leaving Natchez and going West, Mr. Copeland," Percy said to Fortner when Danny and Bear-John paused in their animated conversation. He fixed the young man with an accusing look.

"Grandpa, you don't need to worry about Fortner or Bear-John," Danny said. "They're adventurers. Daniel Boone once visited the Cumberland River where they grew up. He taught Fortner how to shoot, like Uncle Robert is going to teach me."

"Humph!" was the white-haired man's reply. "And likely you two have been down here doing nothing but gambling ever since my grandchildren and my son got you freed from jail.''

"No, sir,'' Bear-John replied before Fortner could manage an answer. He was concerned that his friend might be having some kind of spell, for his eyes looked strangely fixed and the color had faded from his usually tan face. Was running into Treasure affecting him like that? "We hired out to exercise the racehorses at Winterhurst until the past couple of days.''

"Actually, I'm leaving on the first ferry in the morning,'' Fortner said, not liking the way his voice sounded. He cleared his throat. "I hung around Natchez to put together a nest egg before heading West. After winning the race yesterday, I'm all set to leave tomorrow.''

"That's good to hear,'' Percy said. "I heard about the race and how Peter acted a fool and striped up somebody.'' He studied Fortner's face and neck. "Did he put that slash on your neck?''

"Yes, sir.''

"You ought to see Peter Hurst today,'' Bear-John said with a devilish grin. "I'll bet he can't open either eye after Fortner 'thanked' him for being such a good sport. They almost tore up the edge of the racetrack out there before Peter apologized. He looked like a cyclone had picked him up and mixed him into dog meat.''

Percy pursed his lips. Giving in to impulse, he smiled at the mental picture. "Maybe you should have come down this way before now, Mr. Copeland. Peter Hurst has been needing his ears trimmed for a number of years. I knew he was infamous for mistreating his racers, but I never knew him to strike a rider before.''

"Maybe he thought he had the right since Bear-John and I had worked out his horses for two weeks,'' Fortner said. "Maybe he thought I was being a bit disloyal, but he found that I'm not one of his slaves. I earned my pay and then I left.''

Percy let out a sound of disgust. "The man's a poor loser, that's all. It was time for him to learn a lesson. Maybe it'll make a better man out of him.''

Danny spoke up. "Fortner, Treasure bet on Brutus and won a pile of money."

Fortner looked at Treasure directly then while Danny rambled on about what she had told him about the race. He wished he hadn't. Her eyes drew him into their golden depths as quickly as eddies out in the treacherous Mississippi were swallowing up floating logs. Never had he seen her look so beautiful or so vulnerable. What was going on behind her still face? Oh, he was going to have to be cagey to hide what her presence was doing to him! She must not know that every part of him was screaming to touch her. The forefinger and thumb on his left hand met and rubbed together lightly. He tried for a casual tone. "I thought I saw you up on the rise yesterday after the race. I'm glad you bet on us and won."

"Brutus seemed to be in fine fettle. I gather he has given up being a traitor." Treasure wondered how she could talk about something so insignificant when she wanted to yell at him for having cast her aside. She had seen the red welts on his neck when she had first walked closer to him and had hungered to tend them. The crazy thought came that his eyes were even more mysterious than she had remembered. Her pulse was running wild.

"It's time for us to get on back home," Percy said to Treasure and Danny, not approving of the way his granddaughter was staring at the handsome young man. He touched her on the arm to signify it was time to leave, then turned back for a moment. "I wish you good luck on your adventures West, Mr. Copeland, and you also, Mr. McHenry."

"Thanks," Bear-John said, "but I'm going to hang around on this side of the Mississippi awhile." He put an arm around the pouting Lilli and winked at her. "Fortner's going to tackle that territory all by himself while I stay behind at the Silver Slipper a day or two before going back to Tennessee."

Treasure did not miss Bear-John's casual announcement or his telling actions. Her grandfather insisted on leaving then, and she succumbed to his insistent grip on her arm without sending a final look at Fortner over her shoulder. She sensed that he watched her every step and felt goosebumps trailing down her spine. Outwardly she conversed with Percy and Danny as if she had no more on her mind than where Percy might take them to find a noon meal in Natchez.

All the way back to their horses near the waterfront, the news that the red-haired woman was with Bear-John instead of Fortner hammered in Treasure's brain and heart. Fortner did not have another woman! He was not leaving until dawn tomorrow.

It was nearly ten before a cloaked figure on a high-stepping horse rode down the alley beside the Silver Slipper and eased through the back door. Once inside the shadowy hallway, the armed, draped figure met up with a young woman carrying a tray with a bottle and a glass upon it. Within minutes a whispered conversation had taken place, and two silver dollars rested inside the serving woman's apron pocket.

As the newcomer disappeared up the back stairway with the tray in one hand and a rifle in the other, the servant retraced her steps down the hall to attend to other duties. What did she care if the standoffish young mister in the back room was likely still in the tub of warm water she had helped carry up to his room only minutes earlier? Maybe the person covered up in the black cloak and hood was the one he had been saving his gorgeous self for all along. And if it wasn't, then it would serve him right for ignoring all of her carefully laid ploys to get into his bed.

Come to think of it, the serving woman mused, there was no telling for certain from the husky voice if the person creeping upstairs was a man or a woman. Well, she reassured herself, she never before had received such a generous tip for doing absolutely nothing, and she wasn't going to give the matter another thought. Mayhap the big tipper would return often.

* * *

"Come in," Fortner responded to the knock on his door. The serving maids at the Silver Slipper were not usually so prompt, he thought with annoyance at the interruption, but he would be out of the tub soon and ready to enjoy his bottle of wine. After having run into Treasure that morning, he had had little appetite and even less luck at the gambling tables. It had seemed the sensible thing to bid Bear-John farewell and return to his room and prepare for his departure at dawn. Everything was ready except for his personal belongings.

Fortner heard the opening and closing of the door but no further footsteps upon the wooden floor. There was little doubt that someone was in his room, for the back of his neck was feeling itchy. He finished rinsing his hair after saying, "Set the tray on the table over by the chair, please." He heard movement then, like footsteps followed by rustling of clothing. It must be that silly serving girl who had been trying to sneak into his bed ever since Bear-John and he had returned to the hotel from Winterhurst two days ago. "Leave the corkscrew, and I'll open the wine later."

A clattering sound followed by a definite pop met Fortner's ears when he lifted his head from the water. "You can go now. I said I'll open the wine later."

"Why wait?" a husky voice asked from very near the wooden tub where Fortner sat.

"Treasure!" No other voice touched a secret spot as hers did. Slapping at the rivulets of water streaming from his hair onto his face, Fortner whipped his head around. She was a watery vision of golden hair and laughing eyes. He spluttered and groped blindly on the floor for his towel. "What in hell are you doing here?"

Treasure let out a low laugh and picked up the towel. "Is this what you're looking for?" She had not believed her good luck in finding Fortner in such a vulnerable position. The obvious flush of embarrassment on his face tickled her beyond reason. The first sight of his wet chest and muscles had sent little shivers down her spine. The raised red whelps on his neck and back from Peter Hurst's crop did not seem as serious as she had feared. She was close enough to see that the black eyelashes framed his pale eyes in wet, spiky clusters. The look he was sending her was the one she had hoped for—warm and intimate and smoky with memories. Her decision to surprise him had been the right one, she exulted. She realized then that she had been holding her breath as she looked down at him and that her heart was jumping around like crazy.

"Give me that towel."

Treasure let out the captured breath. "Please?" Her unbound hair spilled across her shoulder as she cocked her head and smiled teasingly.

"Please," he growled. Could she see the way his pulse was drumming wildly? Something reminded him that she could see anything she bloody well chose to see. He felt like a fool for having left his door unlocked for the wine to be brought up.

When Treasure handed him the towel, Fortner plopped it over his head and patted his sopping hair before raking it back from his face. He had a clearer view of Treasure then in the candlelight. She was wearing her old black skirt and her father's oversized shirt—and he took back his thought of that morning that she had looked more beautiful then than at any other time. Now was the high point of her beauty. She seemed to glow from within, and he knew that of all the stored images of the young woman that he loved, this was one he would never forget. His determined grip on the damp towel was all that kept his hands from reaching out to touch her.

A degree of sanity returned, and he asked again, "What in hell are you doing here?"

"My, aren't we testy this evening? The devil in you must be in charge. It's a good thing I asked for an extra glass and opened the wine." Treasure fetched two glasses of wine and settled on the floor beside the bathtub. She held a glass toward him. "Drink up. This may be the last time I ever offer to serve you in a bathtub."

The madness of the ludicrous situation set Fortner on

edge. Any minute he expected some of her family—or perhaps Thornton Crabtree—to burst through the door and string him up without the courtesy of a single question. And there he sat, naked in a tub of water. He snatched the glass of wine and took a big swallow.

"Get out of this room, Treasure Ryan," he ordered. She merely lifted a delicate eyebrow and smiled coquettishly. Where in thunder had she learned to flirt like that? A flame licked in his groin, and he shifted in the tub. "You could at least have the decency to go over in the corner so I can dry off and get dressed."

"Who said I was decent? You, of all people, should know I'm a woman of fallen virtue." Her voice plumped with amusement, she said, "Don't tell me that there have been so many women beyond Number Thirty-eight that you've forgotten me."

Grimacing at the reminder of his teasing remark made that night in the cave, Fortner said, "There hasn't been anyone since you." Instantly he wished he had not been so honest. What if she read the truth in that statement—that since falling in love with Treasure, no other woman held any interest for him. He sensed he needed to plunge ahead before her quick mind delved into his statement. "Are you pregnant?" The thought had nagged at him more than he cared to admit, had even crept into the form of prayer that it not be so.

"Not yet."

"What in hell does that mean?"

"Figure it out, Fortner. We've got all night."

"The hell we do! This is no place for you to be."

"Your language has gone downhill since we've been apart."

"I'm going to get out of here and take you back to Lindwood where you belong."

"I might have something to say about that."

"You have your trusty rifle, I gather." Fortner glanced over by the door and saw it propped there.

"Yes, and I intend to get my knife from you."

"How do you know I have it?"

"Because the sheriff told Uncle Robert that he gave it to you. You could have returned it, you know."

"Your grandfather made it clear that I was not welcome at Lindwood. Take your knife and go. It's over by my saddlebags."

Treasure removed her shoes and stockings, then tucked her legs underneath her skirt. "It was not gentlemanly to plan on leaving without telling Number Thirty-eight goodbye. I think I deserve at least a kiss." After taking a long sip of wine, she leaned her head within inches of his, widening her eyes in mock accusation and pouting in the way she had seen Caroline do. "Don't you?"

"I never claimed to be a gentleman." He ignored her question, for her nearness was intoxicating. Her wine-dampened lips fascinated him. He drained his glass and set it on the floor. "Turn around. I'm getting out of this tub and taking you home." His head was spinning, and his mouth felt as if it might be stuffed with cotton.

Laughing low in her throat, Treasure set down her own glass. Fortner's crippled gaze was failing to match up with his words; it seemed to be inviting a look into his soul. Her arms shot out and embraced the startled man. She pressed her lips to his, gently at first, then with trembling urgency. A soft moan trilled deep in her throat as his wet arms grabbed her around the shoulders and pulled her close to the edge of the tub.

Along with Fortner's indrawn breath, Treasure heard the water swish from his sudden movement and felt the wooden side of the tub press painfully against her rib cage. His mouth tasted like warm wine and honey and the wonderfully masculine Fortner she had dreamed about. A marvelous, golden haze enveloped her mind. Her body became a warm feminine mass without delineated edges. Her every sense quivered with delicious expectancy. She felt that her entire being might go up in flames, and she had the insane wish that it would—together with his.

One of Fortner's hands moved up into Treasure's hair and worked magic at the base of her skull while his tongue reclaimed former territories inside her mouth with devastating mastery. Her heartbeat jigged and danced a fiery rhythm. If only for this one last time, she thought, she was fully alive and where she belonged—in Fortner's arms.

"I must dress and take you home," Fortner said when at last they ended the breath stealing kiss. Shakily he rose to his knees in the tub. His pale eyes worshipped the golden ones so near. "You don't belong here."

"I'm not leaving until you make love to me one more time, Fortner." When he sucked in a harsh breath and cocked his head at her in question, she added, "I'm not sure how a woman goes about seducing a man." Watching the stunned, disbelieving Fortner the entire time, she stood and unbuttoned her shirt and let it settle onto the floor with a soft plop. She wore nothing underneath it. His silvery gaze turned her bare skin into a million tiny points of prickling sensation. "Is this a good start?"

"Don't do this to me…to us…please." Fortner reached for a towel and stood, drying himself off while drinking in the sight of her lovely breasts with their erect nipples. He swallowed at the rush of fullness back in his throat. The flame in his groin was flaring rapidly, and the ache to touch her was consuming his self-control. When he stepped from the tub, he fastened the towel around his middle to hide his growing desire.

Her eyes moving over Fortner's nakedness and swelling manhood with appreciation and raw hunger, Treasure removed her skirt and underdrawers and edged them out of the way with a bare foot. Flinging her long hair over her shoulders, she took the four steps required to reach him where he stood as if transfixed. "How am I doing?" she whispered in her throaty way.

"Why are you torturing me this way?" As so often when they had traveled the Trace together, Fortner felt that her low-pitched voice affected more than his ears. All over he was feeling stimulated, newly vibrant. The fragrance of her hair was working its old magic on him. He knew then that logic had slipped out of reach.

Treasure smiled up at Fortner and sent her hands sliding up through the damp black curls on his chest. The only sounds were those of their labored breathing and an occasional sputter from the low burning candle on a table. Her fingers spread out and slowly savored each masculine swell of hard muscle, not stopping until they had traced the shape of his biceps and wandered on up to caress his neck. She loved the way Fortner, his arms akimbo, stood watching her through half closed silvery eyes with a waiting look about his mouth, as if he might be going to spring some devilish trick on her any minute.

The cruel welt on Fortner's neck and back received especially tender ministrations before Treasure outlined his lips with a forefinger. When her fingers playfully tipped up the corners of his mouth before moving on to the planes of his cheeks, a secretive smile remained on his handsome face, as if answering her own enigmatic smile. For an indeterminate spell, they stood that way, drinking in each other's features while her hands rested upon his face. Their bodies were so close to touching that the tiny space between them seemed to pulsate.

Though Fortner deliberately kept his arms away from her, Treasure brought her hands back down the same exciting paths. They paused at the towel draped over his flat belly only long enough to undo the loose knot. By the time the towel fell on their bare feet with a little plopping sound, her soft hands were continuing their exploration of his lean body, lower and lower. She felt him tremble beneath her loving touches.

"Did you call this torture?" Treasure asked, leaning forward enough to reach behind him and cup her hands to his firm buttocks. Without meaning to, she brought him closer. The feel of his pulsing tumescence against her lower belly brought a gush of hot dew to the gateway to her womanhood, and she almost gasped at the torrent of desire washing over her. Her breasts pushed against his furred chest, and she felt her throbbing nipples perk up into tight pebbles. "When you did this to me, I thought it was divine." Her eyes read a kind of pain in his when she took his swollen manhood in her hand. "Now tell me to go away, that I don't belong here."

"Oh, God!" Fortner cried hoarsely. "You're driving me crazy, Treasure." His arms went around her then, and he scooped her up and held her loveliness close against him. His heart was beating so hard that he could hardly speak. "How can I tell you anything now but that I want to love you?" He could not add what was threatening to destroy him: *for one last time.*

Treasure hugged Fortner around the neck and welcomed his brazen kiss with one equally as bold. She burned and trembled all over as his mouth plundered hers. Her response was wild and wanton and she yearned to scream for joy, for something within had found life again upon seeing him yesterday at the races. Now that she was in his arms, she wanted to experience a rebirth of her former self. Only within Fortner's arms could such a transformation take place, she had realized when she had seen him that morning on the boardwalk. A vital part of her that she had feared dead had been merely asleep. Tonight was her last chance to keep it alive. If only she could show him that he could not leave her behind, that he needed her as much as she needed him.

"Fortner, I—"

"Hush, Treasure," he whispered as he walked with her to his bed. "Now it's time for loving." He looked down at the golden cloud of hair framing her beautifully sculpted face and realized that the silken strands draped over his arm bound him to her as firmly as iron chains could have done. How could he live without her in his life?

Fortner wanted no exchange of thoughts there in the dimly lighted room, did not even want to listen to his own. His senses reeled from holding his beloved in his arms when he had expected never to see her again. Her bold flirting must mean that she had found as much pleasure in their previous lovemaking as he and that she wanted one more night in his arms before settling into her life at Natchez . . . as the wife of some wealthy planter.

Desire for Treasure controlled Fortner totally as he laid her on his bed and cradled her naked body next to his. He wanted nothing to put his brain in control again as it had been since that night at Colbert's Stand when he had first realized that he loved the beautiful blonde and was the worst possible choice for her to marry. Treasure had offered herself in farewell, had all but begged him to put aside rational thought. He wanted to revel in one final night of making glorious love with the passionate young woman in his arms.

First, Fortner wanted to caress her warm breasts and suck their sweetness into the marrow of his bones for safekeeping. He gave in to that need there in the shadowed room. His mouth left reverent kisses on the satin mounds— she sighed with open contentment. Then his mouth and tongue teased—she moaned her pleasure and lifted her swollen breasts with her hands for his gratification. And when his mouth and teeth became more insistent with pentup hunger, she arched her body and cried out for him to take her at that moment.

Treasure whispered in a voice rich with love, "You make me feel all woman." *How I love you!*

"That's because you *are* all woman." *You're my woman, and I'll love you forever.*

When Fortner laughed softly in denial of her pleas for him to take her that instant, Treasure frantically pulled his mouth back to hers. She wanted to feel the firm length of him against her flaming, restless body. Inside, she burned with a roaring need for him to enter her and touch her molten center. She wanted to soar with him again to that once visited star out in infinity and maybe get lost there with her beloved forever. There would be no need for dreams then; she would be living the finest of them all.

Even as Fortner's trail-roughened hands made sizzling claims along the outer and inner sections of her soft, yielding feminine flesh, Treasure's capable hands stroked his broad back and his lean hips and buttocks with equal tenderness. Every speck of him had become so dear and so essential to her that she longed to absorb his essence into her skin and keep that part of him as her own long after he rode away. Already she had breathed in the remembered, heady fragrance of her handsome lover fresh from his bath and added it to the hoarded smells of his skin and his musky manliness. How could he not know that she belonged with him forever?

"Darling," he whispered when he paused to look into her lovely face. He was unaware that she had been awaiting the word, but he loved the way she smiled up at him upon hearing it.

"Lover," she whispered back, almost drowning in his silver eyes edged with black. Her fingers lingered upon a wave drooping over his forehead.

A new fierceness in their lovemaking took over Treasure and Fortner as they resumed their impassioned kissing and caressing in the wavering candlelight. Long suppressed appetites led them to marvelous new discoveries of the delights of willing flesh—hers so soft and yielding, his so firm and demanding. The tremulous moment came when neither could restrain any longer from becoming one. They had been uncaring about time and tomorrows during those other two passionate couplings, content to savor the moment. Now both realized that an end lay ahead. Tonight was the end.

Neither could reveal what lay behind the white hot passion that drove Fortner to rise above Treasure and enter her with a movement akin to violence. It was the identical force that led her to cry out from the ecstatic pain of his hot length suddenly sliding into her burning core. Delirious and wondering if she truly might be close to bursting into flame, she wrapped her legs around his hips to pull him closer. They moved in frantic rhythm . . . throbbing . . . burning . . . seeking . . . soaring ever higher. The star miraculously awaited on that unseen horizon and once more took in the desperate lovers sailing as one.

Treasure wept. Fortner lost his breath for a moment. Their love for each other careened around the small space of their embrace and cried out to be voiced, but was denied. They clasped each other in gloriously spent arms and recognized in secret that the shared ecstasy was already another perfect memory to be treasured after their parting.

"How will you explain it if someone has missed you or, worse, sees you returning at this ungodly hour?" Fortner asked Treasure when they glimpsed the lighted lantern that always hung between the large house and the stables at Lindwood. Moonlight had made the ride from Natchez-Under-the-Hill easy.

"I told you that I had been helping tend to one of Grandpa's prize mares this week," Treasure replied. They had ridden the hour-and-a-half journey with little talk other than discussing Hank and the surprising truth about the old peddler's identity. Both had seemed intent on private musings, all of them sad if expressions counted as signs. "I'll just say that I've been sitting up with the mare. She's going to foal within the next week and has terrible colic at times."

"I really should go on up with you. It's unfair to—"

"Fiddle! I'm the one who planned what happened tonight." She smiled at him in the moonlight. Though Fortner had not told her that he loved her as she had hoped, Treasure was glad that she had given in to impulse and spent this final evening with him. "You did try to make me leave, remember?"

They were at the end of the drive where he had turned Danny and her over to Percy Lindsay a little over three weeks ago. "I should have been man enough to bring you home when I got out of that tub. Your impetuous nature always gets you in trouble."

"Not always."

"What about the night you left a dance and strayed far from the others and found yourself fighting off the amorous Thurston Crabtree?"

"How would you know about that?" Treasure's mind raced, skipping over Fortner's annoying habit of mispronouncing Thornton's name. That night in the rose garden at Merrivale when she had been assailed with thoughts of Fortner, had suspected she heard Brutus' whicker, had believed she smelled cigar smoke—could it be . . .

"Never mind," he retorted, angered to have revealed so much. "Has the great Thurston proposed to you yet?"

"No, and his name is not Thurston." She watched him in a shaft of moonlight. The thumb and forefinger on his left hand were making that tiny rubbing motion that she had noticed several times when they were traveling on the Trace. Had she not seen the same telltale movement that morning when they had met on the sidewalk at Natchez-Under-the-Hill? What had him deep in thought—then and now? Did it have anything to do with her and leaving her behind? Her heartbeat went wild.

"He will, and you'll fit right in as mistress of Merrivale. Your mother's dream will come true." When she kept watching him with her golden and mysterious eyes, Fortner put away the thought that moonlight became her and forced himself to say what he must. "I'll stay and watch until you reach the stables. Good-bye, Treasure."

"Fortner," she said, leaning from her saddle and reaching out her hand to him. She took in a deep breath. "You're wrong about my belonging here. Maybe I belong out West . . . like you." She had done everything but ask him to take her along, she agonized.

"You're out of your mind! You're exactly where you belong—with your family and Thornton Crabtree." Ignoring her outstretched hand, Fortner grated, "Besides, I have no wish for a woman to be looking out for any longer. Go on now. We've said our farewells."

Treasure recoiled from his cold tone and her face flushed from anger at his rebuff. How could she have been so foolish as to think he might love her . . . a little? She had misread every look from him. "Take care, Fortner. I'll think of you every time I see a rattlesnake."

Kneeing Vagabond lightly, Treasure rode up to Lindwood

without a backward glance. She didn't dare look back. She had no wish for Fortner to see her tears.

Chapter Twenty-four

After Treasure reached the stables at Lindwood, everything worked as she had hoped. She heard August's steady snore coming from his room beside the tack room as she led Vagabond to his stall. When she checked the ailing mare, she found the horse was sleeping peacefully.

Grateful that no one seemed to be awake, Treasure hurried to her room without incident. Moonlight filtered through her window and lent a ghostly loveliness to the bedroom that had once belonged to her mother. Her thoughts whirled as she lay upon her bed. Something about the night's happenings did not fit.

Had Fortner's actions echoed his words? During their tempestuous lovemaking, he had seemed as enthralled by their mutual passion as she. She shivered when she remembered the way his adoring eyes had caressed her even while his lips were forming words designed to send her away before they made love. It made no sense at all.

What had possessed him to be spying on her that night at Merrivale? It seemed likely that at other times he had ridden over from nearby Winterhurst and watched her. She recalled her eerie feelings of having sensed his presence at times when she rode Vagabond alone late in the afternoons. Would a man who did not love a woman care so much about what she was doing? Her pulse became lively.

Treasure flopped from her back to her stomach on the

verbena-scented sheets and noticed how unblemished the bedroom looked in the moonlight. She knew that the room was beautiful, but she also knew that it had signs of wear and was not as perfect as it now appeared. Had she allowed her love for Fortner to shadow her ability to think logically—perhaps in the way that the moonlight was glossing over the bedroom's imperfections? Her mind moved into a new realm.

Fortner was obviously a man of heart and conscience. Had she not heard him make comfortable reference to the Bible, and had she not seen with her own eyes the worn Bible traveling in his saddlebags? She thought of the way he had looked after his widowed sister-in-law, Hannah, and her children. Had he not placed their welfare and happiness above his own?

The memory of Fortner's quick defense of her that night when George Henry had slapped her and tried to claim her rose and lingered. And there were others. When Fortner had stayed behind to tend to her gunshot wound in the Choctaw village, he knowingly had lost out on a chance to meet up with Whitey. She remembered the way he had attracted the wild boar in the canebreak to seek him out for attack rather than her. It seemed clear that Fortner was the kind of man who placed the desires and needs of those he cared about higher than his own. Treasure's heart raced. She sat up. She knew what she must do.

Fortner did not look back when he rode away from the Silver Slipper at the first sign of dawn. His grieving heart weighted his spirit to an all-time low. Never had he loved Treasure more than when she had reached her hand out to him a few hours earlier and told him that she did not belong in her new world. It never before had occurred to him that she actually might consider leaving all that she had recently found and follow him to the West. Had he been a fool to watch her ride away from him to Lindwood?

Brutus and the recently acquired packhorse, Sunshine,

were calmed by Fortner's quiet reassurances and they allowed him to coax them onto the rough boards of the ferry. Two other horses stood tied to the sturdy railing where he secured his animals. Behind him he heard the steps of another horse and passenger approaching, but he did not turn with his usual curiosity.

Fortner was still too wrapped up in reverie and misery to care that anyone other than the ferry captain was awake at such an ungodly hour. Stretching and allowing himself a giant yawn, he leaned against the railing and stared out into the mists rising from the dark Mississippi. Somewhere on that western side lay his future. Why wasn't his heart rejoicing?

"Do you know anybody who needs a horse shod, mister?" came a low-pitched voice from right beside him.

Fortner stiffened. He was hallucinating because he hadn't slept all night. He must be more in love with Treasure than he had thought, and his mind was playing cruel tricks on him. He dared a sideways glance. His heartbeat skipped.

"Treasure!" He saw her eyes lifted to his, sparkling and full of trust in the predawn light. He struggled for breath and held out his arms. No longer could he deny his love for her. When she rushed into his embrace, he murmured against her hair, "How I love you, Treasure! Am I dreaming?"

"If you are, then I want to be a part of that dream, David Fortner Copeland." Treasure lifted her head and smiled up at him. To hear him declare his love for her gave her new strength. "It seems to match my own." When he would have kissed her she laid gently restraining fingers against his lips. "Listen to me before you try to be gallant and send me away again. I've realized that the dream for Danny and me to come to Natchez and for me to become mistress of a plantation was never my dream, Fortner. It belonged to my mother . . . and then you kept draping it back over me every time I was about to let my own surface. I do have a dream of my own, and it's golden with promise for a lifetime of loving . . . with you. I can never love anyone but you."

"Can you leave Danny behind to pursue your mother's dream for him?" He felt the lurch of the ferry as its mooring lines were freed and it began drifting with the current.

"Yes, because it's what he wants, too. I spent the last hour at Lindwood talking with him. I left letters behind for Grandpa and the others, begging them to understand that I love you and must pursue my own dream. I asked Danny to come along, but he said he was where he belonged. Though it has hurt to see him outgrow his dependency on me, I agree with him. He did say he wanted us both to return for his graduation from college, and I promised we would. Can we manage that?"

"I love you, and you say you love me. Together we can manage anything." Fortner kissed her then, his mouth savoring the taste and fragrance of hers. He groaned and ended the kiss, trying for a stern tone. "I thought I had convinced you that you belong in Natchez."

Treasure smiled and shook her head so vigorously that stray curls from her unbound hair fell forward over her shoulders and formed a lovely frame of gold for her shining face. "Nope, but it was a fair try."

Bending to sample her saucy lips again, Fortner whispered against them, "How did you know that what I really wanted to say was that I love you more than anything in the world and that I want you to be my wife?"

"Because," Treasure replied in her husky voice as she sent him a flirty look from behind thick lashes, "I'm not an ordinary woman, as you've often told me. I'm not dumb enough to love a man who doesn't love me back." She jabbed at his chest playfully with a forefinger. "You might have passed as a pretty good highwayman, but you don't impress me as a good liar."

They hugged and kissed with fiery passion while their eyes carried on an exciting exchange—about love and forever and what each was going to do to the other as soon as they reached Concord on the Louisiana side of the

Mississippi River and found a preacher and then a hotel room. When they ended the kiss, Treasure nestled against Fortner for a moment of private thanksgiving. She felt his heartbeat dancing in rhythm with her own, almost in rhythm with the mighty current of the river beneath the wooden deck of the ferry. So alive! With Fortner she always felt fully alive.

"I guess you realize that there's not going to be a number thirty-nine in your life, don't you?" Her eyes flashed with mischievous, golden fire as she looked up at his handsome face with unmasked adoration.

Fortner winked roguishly and tapped her sassy nose lovingly with a forefinger. "I can't even count that high."

With deep sighs of contentment, the couple turned as one and watched the first fingers of dawn point out the nearing Louisiana shore. Not once did they look back. They breathed in the sweet western breeze dipping and tickling their noses with the fecund smells of the river at dawn and the green forests looming closer through the morning mists. With their arms around each other, they exchanged huge smiles that turned into peals of delicious laughter.

Treasure and Fortner saw that the ferry captain was looking over at them as if they might be mad, and they laughed even harder. Ahead lay the West and a lifetime together. Who wouldn't laugh to have such a promising future?

Dear Readers,

If my story pleased you, then you can imagine how much your letter telling me so will please me. I welcome comments other than good ones, too, for I write for your pleasure and need to know when and how I might have missed the mark.

You may write me in care of Warner Books, 666 Fifth Avenue, New York, New York 10103.

Myra Rowe
Monroe, Louisiana